SHERLOCK HOLMES AND THE OCCULT DETECTIVES

VOLUME ONE

SHERLOCK HOLMES AND THE OCCULT DETECTIVES

VOLUME ONE

Edited by
John Linwood Grant

Belanger Books

2020

Sherlock Holmes and the Occult Detectives
© 2020 by Belanger Books, LLC

ISBN: 9798649552813

Print and Digital Edition © 2020 by Belanger Books, LLC

All Rights Reserved. No part of this book may be used or reproduced in any manner whatsoever without written permission except in case of brief quotations embodied in critical articles or reviews.

This book is a work of fiction. Names, characters, businesses, organizations, places, events, and incidents either are the products of the author's imagination or are used fictitiously. Any resemblance to actual persons, living or dead, events, or locales is entirely coincidental.

For information contact:

Belanger Books, LLC

61 Theresa Ct.

Manchester, NH 03103

derrick@belangerbooks.com

www.belangerbooks.com

Cover and Back design by Brian Belanger

www.belangerbooks.com and www.redbubble.com/people/zhahadun

Volume One
Table of Contents

Ghosts Need Apply! *by Derrick Belanger*	9
Editor's Note *by John Linwood Grant*	11
The Adventure of the Faerie Coffin *by Rebecca Buchanan*	14
The Adventure of the Russian Mystic *by Stewart Sternberg*	54
The Case of the Manchester Mummies *by Davide Mana*	77
Sherlock Holmes and the Ghostly Reunion *by Christopher Degni*	110
The Adventure of Marylebone Manor *by Naching T. Kassa*	138
The Village on the Cliff *by David Marcum*	169
The Tale of the Tantric Detective *by Geoff Dibb*	202
The Adventure of the Three Rippers *by Edward M Erdelac*	234
The Case of the High Pavement Ghosts *by Teika Marija Smits*	270
The Adventure of the Abominable Adder *by Will Murray*	303
Special Thanks to Our Kickstarter Backers	338

COPYRIGHT INFORMATION

All of the contributions in this collection are copyrighted by the authors listed below, except as noted. Grateful acknowledgement is given to the authors and/or their agents for the kind permission to use their work.

"Ghosts Need Apply!" ©2020 by Derrick Belanger. All Rights Reserved. First publication, original to this collection. Printed by permission of the author.

"Editor's Note" ©2020 by John Linwood Grant. All Rights Reserved. First publication, original to this collection. Printed by permission of the author.

"The Adventure of the Faerie Coffin" ©2020 by Rebecca Buchanan. All Rights Reserved. First publication, original to this collection. Printed by permission of the author.

"The Adventure of the Russian Mystic" ©2020 by Stewart Sternberg. All Rights Reserved. First publication, original to this collection. Printed by permission of the author.

"The Case of the Manchester Mummies" ©2020 by Davide Mana. All Rights Reserved. First publication, original to this collection. Printed by permission of the author.

"Sherlock Holmes and the Ghostly Reunion" ©2020 by Christopher Degni. All Rights Reserved. First publication, original to this collection. Printed by permission of the author.

"The Adventure of Marylebone Manor" ©2020 by Naching T. Kassa. All Rights Reserved. First publication, original to this collection. Printed by permission of the author.

"The Village on the Cliff" ©2020 by David Marcum. All Rights Reserved. First publication, original to this collection. Printed by permission of the author.

"The Tale of the Tantric Detective" ©2020 by Geoff Dibb. All Rights Reserved. First publication, original to this collection. Printed by permission of the author.

"The Adventure of the Three Rippers" ©2020 by Edward M. Erdelac. All Rights Reserved. First publication, original to this collection. Printed by permission of the author.

"The Case of the High Pavement Ghosts" ©2020 by Teika Marija Smits. All Rights Reserved. First publication, original to this collection. Printed by permission of the author.

"The Adventure of the Abominable Adder" ©2020 by Will Murray. All Rights Reserved. First publication, original to this collection. Printed by permission of the author.

Ghosts Need Apply!
An Introduction by Derrick Belanger

Sherlock Holmes always dismissed otherworldly explanations in his adventures, most famously in 'The Adventure of the Sussex Vampire', "This Agency stands flat-footed upon the ground and there it must remain. The world is big enough for us. No ghosts need apply." But, did Holmes really believe this? Did he perhaps direct his Boswell to add this quote to SUSS to cover-up occult connections? What if he felt the world was not ready for such knowledge?

After all, there are hints of the occult in some unwritten tales. As Watson writes in 'The Problem of Thor Bridge', his tin dispatch box is "...crammed with papers, nearly all of which are records of cases to illustrate the curious problems which Mr. Sherlock Holmes had at various times to examine... Among these unfinished tales is that of Mr. James Phillimore, who, stepping back into his own house to get his umbrella, was never more seen in this world. No less remarkable is that of the cutter Alicia, which sailed one spring morning into a small patch of mist from where she never again emerged, nor was anything further ever heard of herself and her crew. A third case worthy of note is that of Isadora Persano, the well-known journalist and duellist, who was found stark staring mad with a match box in front of him which contained a remarkable worm said to be unknown to science."

Were these cases kept out of the public's eye because they were unsolved or because the solutions would have changed our understanding of the universe? Were they kept under lock and key to spare the public from news that would shake our beliefs to the core? Even the most famous untold case, that of the Giant Rat of Sumatra, we are told cannot be written. Holmes explains it is "a story for which the world is not yet prepared." Could the world be unprepared because the giant rat is not the name of a ship or person, but an actual oversized rodent?

These questions are not necessarily answered in this collection of adventures. What is answered is what might happen if Holmes collaborated with other detectives, detectives with connections to the occult? These stories, the first in the Great Detective series, imagines Holmes collaborating with other detectives from the Victorian and Edwardian time period, even into the 1920s. Here you will find Holmes solving cases alongside Auguste Dupin, Dr John Silence, and Professor Van Helsing, as well as other 'new' occult detective characters from the era.

While these adventures have Holmes working with occult partners, the stories remain grounded in tradition, with the occult often having its own 'logic' and basis in the rational. I hope you enjoy Holmes's foray into the unknown working alongside his great and magical colleagues. For these adventures, dear reader, ghosts may apply!

Derrick Belanger
December 2019

Editor's Note

I was gratified to be offered such an inventive range of stories to choose from for this anthology project, and only sad that I still had to leave out some interesting ideas, mostly due to lack of space in these already bulging two volumes. In making the final selection, I wanted to showcase both occult detectives invented by contemporary authors and also some older, more established figures, either as co-protagonists with Holmes, or as characters within the mysteries.

There should, I hope, be something within for both the canonical reader of Holmesian conundrums and the occult detective enthusiast. The tales selected contain many different takes on Holmes's (and Watson's) attitudes to the supernatural, including "Balderdash" and "Poppycock", a degree of grudging acceptance under murky circumstances, and even deliberate employment of others' less mundane abilities to achieve a solution where logic alone just would not answer. One additional pleasure worth mentioning was (given the relative scarcity of women detectives in the literature of Holmes's time) being able to include some fascinating female investigators, including one Mary Morstan – who later married Dr John Watson, of course – in a most unusual role.

For those wondering which characters herein have other literary or real life connections, a few source notes on some of the relevant names are given below, purely for amusement.

Editor's Note by John Linwood Grant

There are no spoilers, but if you prefer to spot or hunt out such links yourself, you might wish to skip this part...

C Auguste Dupin made his first appearance in Edgar Allan Poe's 'The Murders in the Rue Morgue' (1841), often considered the first fictional detective short story. **Luna Bartendale** was created by Jessie Douglas Kerruish and appeared in 'The Undying Monster' (1936). **Professor Abraham Van Helsing** comes from the 1897 Gothic horror novel 'Dracula', by Bram Stoker. **Dr John Silence** comes from the pen of Algernon Blackwood, appearing in 1908. And although we do not have a story of William Hope Hodgson's **Carnacki the Ghostfinder**, it is worth noting that Joshua M Reynolds' character Charles St Cyprian comes from the long-running series of Reynolds's Royal Occultist tales, St Cyprian having been Carnacki's apprentice.

Rose Mackenberg (1892–1968) was a genuine American investigator specializing in fraudulent psychic mediums, known for her association with Harry Houdini, and joins us in 'Five Burnt Portions of Bread'. **Eusapia Palladino** (1854–1918), mentioned in 'Sherlock Holmes and the Ghostly Reunion', was a noted psychic who was exposed as a fraud by Houdini and others. **Charles Peace** (1832–1879), referred to here in 'The Case of the High Pavement Ghosts', was a real life felon who operated for a while in the same Nottingham setting, and **Major General Henry Ponsonby** (1825–1895), of 'The Case of The Talking Board', was genuinely Queen Victoria's Private Secretary. Heháka Sápa, widely known as **Black Elk** (1863–1950), who features in 'The Adventure of The Three Rippers', was a Lakota medicine man who toured with Buffalo Bill's Wild West show.

Editor's Note by John Linwood Grant

Conan Doyle and his characters are well represented. Not only does he have a pivotal role in one tale himself, his creation **Irene Adler,** featured in the Conan Doyle short story 'A Scandal in Bohemia' (1891), is known to have married Godfrey Norton – hence the appeal from one Clara Norton, her daughter, in 'The Ghostly Reunion' here. **Mary Morstan** made her first appearance in the novel 'The Sign of the Four' (1890); the boy **Wiggins**, popping up in 'The Adventure of Marylebone Manor', was one of the canonical Baker Street Irregulars mentioned in the first Holmes tale ever, the novel 'A Study in Scarlet' (1887). The German agent **Von Bork**, who plays a surprising role in 'The Aerodynamics of Bees', is originally from 'His Last Bow. The War Service of Sherlock Holmes's, published in 1917. Also in 'Marylebone Manor', we find another old adversary of Holmes, but naming that particular person would be spoiling the twist. Finally for Conan Doyle, **Dr Hardacre**, seen here in 'The Monkstree Horror', appeared in Doyle's 'The Story of the Brown Hand', an explicitly supernatural, non-Holmesian, short story first published in The Strand Magazine in May 1899.

And as many of our tales are set later in Holmes's career, we should close by mentioning the importance of bees and beekeeping. It's an aspect of the Great Detective's life which has long caught the public imagination, and in recognition, it seemed fitting that the bees themselves should have a starring role, as they do in 'The Direction of Sunbeams'.

My thanks, of course, to all the writers for meeting the challenge. I do hope you enjoy this cavalcade of mysteries featuring characters new and old.

John Linwood Grant, January 2020

The Adventure of the Faerie Coffin
Being the First Morstan and Holmes Occult Detection Case

by Rebecca Buchanan

"Miss Morstan. May I join you?"

I closed my eyes, shutting out the chaos of the rail station. The sounds of whistles, shouts, and carollers were only slightly dulled by the window.

Of course he was here.

I inhaled slowly, feeling the breath fill my chest, spread through my arms and down my legs; an old habit, learned long ago at the feet of one far more skilled than me.

Calmer now, I turned and offered him a smile. "Of course, Mr. Holmes. Please, have a seat."

He was not dressed in his usual attire. His clothes were not neat; rather, they were stained and wrinkled and slightly too large for his frame. His shoes were scuffed. The glasses perched on his nose — pink from the cold — subtly changed its length and shape. The threadbare hat did much the same for his head, hiding his thinning hair.

Of course he had altered his appearance. No doubt he had been following me from the moment I left my rooms at Mrs. Forrester's home. I should never have declined his dinner invitation the previous evening. There had been something in my note — a curious curve to an *s*, an odd slant to a *t*, a wrinkle, a stain — that had piqued his curiosity.

And so here he was, right where and when I least wanted him.

How John tolerated it, I failed to understand.

He settled easily into the seat opposite, legs crossed, hands folded in his lap. Silent. Still. Waiting.

We stared at one another as the whistle blew loud and piercing, and continued to stare as the train lurched forward, down the track, north, away from London. Only when we reached the outskirts of that great city did he finally speak.

"You are not breaking your engagement with Watson." A statement, not a question.

"No."

"You have only ever served as a governess in London, therefore you are not paying a sentimental visit to previous charges."

"Correct."

"This train is bound for Edinburgh. Your mother's family hails from that country originally, Deòireach being her surname. You were born and lived with your family in India until you were eight. After your mother's death, your father sent you to the same boarding school that she had attended. The Frazier Academy. You remained there until you were seventeen, at which point you travelled south to seek respectable employment. You made no return trips north until today. A curious change to your usual habits, Miss Morstan."

Another calming breath. "I will not be able to persuade you to leave this be, will I?"

"No."

Recognizing the finality of his statement, I relented. Slipping my hand inside my travel jacket, I pulled out the letter which had arrived only the previous afternoon.

He took it solemnly from my hand, carefully studied the envelope, and then slid out the letter.

The paper showed the wrinkles where I had gripped it too hard and then tried to smooth it out, where I had folded and reopened it a dozen times.

I knew that letter by heart now.

12 December 1888
My dearest Mary,

It is with no little reluctance, and with shame, that I find myself writing to you in need of your assistance. Though I strictly forbade you to make use of your unusual abilities while you attended my school, I fear that I now have need of them. I hope that you will set aside the harsh words of the past, and consider my plea sincerely.

Just a fortnight ago, I and the rest of the staff were awakened in the middle of the night by a terrible weeping and wailing. The sounds seemed to emanate from the central courtyard, but, upon investigating, we found no one there. When the strange sounds awoke us again the next night, we considered that perhaps this was a prank being perpetrated by the students. All swore their innocence, however. After we were awakened a third night, we moved all of the students into the dining hall to sleep, along with the staff.

Again, the awful weeping and wailing awakened us for a fourth night.

And so it has been every night for two weeks.

In addition, we have been plagued by increasingly dangerous accidents. Or, were it not for the nightly haunting — yes, I have dared to call it a haunting! — I would consider them to be accidents. But they cannot be. A door was violently opened, striking a student and leaving her badly bruised. A gargoyle was knocked from the top of the courtyard wall, landing just inches from my feet. An entire bookcase was tipped over in the library, nearly crushing another student.

And, just this morning, a hearth — in which no fire was burning! — filled with smoke, almost suffocating a student, who could not flee the room as the door would not open. On each occasion, there was no one about who could have perpetrated these incidents.

I am begging you, Mary. Please help. I fear that, if this continues much longer, someone will be killed.

Respectfully,
Edith Fearghasdan
Headmistress

He read the letter twice, then carefully folded it back into its envelope, and returned it to me.

And then he sat silent, staring out the window.

I pulled needlework from my travel bag, careful to leave Mrs. Forrester's tissue-wrapped package stowed away at the bottom. Needlework. An innocuous, proper activity for a woman.

It is not only Mr. Holmes who has mastered the skill of hiding in plain sight.

*****

Miles upon miles of countryside passed, the trees bare and the skies grey. I left him to his silence, and enjoyed a fine meal of hearty soup and bread in the dining car. When I returned, he was still staring out the window. I pulled out my needlework again. When it grew too dark to see the stitches clearly, despite the low light outside the cabin — there can be no mistakes in my Work — I returned the cloth and thread to my bag, leaned my head back against the seat, and closed my eyes.

"What is the complement of the Frazier Academy?"

Sighing, I lifted my head and opened my eyes. "The Frazier Academy closes for the Christmas holiday. Those among the faculty and students who are able to do so, leave. As such, if the current student body is typical of previous years, I would expect there to be perhaps half-a-dozen students still on the premises. Similarly, I would expect no more than three or four staff, in addition to Mrs. Fearghasdan."

"And did you remain at the school during the holiday?"

I paused, catching the faintest hint of a thoughtful frown cross his face. Tilting my chin, I answered, "I did not, as a matter of fact. I travelled to my mother's ancestral home just outside Dùn Dè."

"Alone?"

"No. With my own governess, Mrs. Webster. She was my mother's governess first, but stayed on until I was grown."

"Even accompanying you to school?"

It was too dark in the cabin now to see his expression, but there was a curious note of challenge to his tone. "Yes. She was as much family as my father. Perhaps more so, as I never saw him again after I left India." My hand twitched, fingers beginning to reach for the necklace hidden beneath my blouse. I stifled the impulse and instead smoothed the collar of my jacket.

"And where is Mrs. Webster now?"

"Living in that same home outside Dùn Dè." I paused, then found myself defending that statement with, "It only made sense to allow her to live out her remaining years there, while I sought employment in the south."

"Indeed."

And that was the last word he spoke all night.

*****

The Adventure of the Faerie Coffin by Rebecca Buchanan

Dawn found us both in the dining car, this time for a filling breakfast of sausages, eggs, fried bread, and tea. We spoke of inanities — the weather, the food, John's trip to Wales — and so I knew his conversation to be false. Sherlock Holmes does not engage in inanities. Only as we sat drinking our tea did he again raise the subject of the letter.

"To what abilities was Headmistress Fearghasdan referring?"

I took another long sip of tea. Then I raised my head, looked him directly in the eyes, and answered, "You are not the only person who assists others in solving unusual problems. My methods, however, are... different... from yours."

The server came by our table at that moment to collect our plates. When he left, Holmes tilted his head, studying me. The corner of his mouth twitched. "I look forward to studying these different methods."

*****

We arrived in Edinburgh late in the afternoon of 18 December. A cold wind blew in from the North Sea, pushing thick grey clouds, and snow dusted Arthur's Seat. I could just see that hill through the high windows of the station and across the rooftops of the city, tree branches dancing wildly.

In all the years that we had lived in Edinburgh, how many times had Mrs. Webster and I climbed the Seat? I could not possibly count them all, but a few stood out in my memory. Sewing through the night and lighting tapers on Candlemas. Washing our faces with dew on Beltane's Day. Toasting nuts and weaving oat stalks on Hallowe'en.

A voice called out across the station and I caught sight of a woman garbed in a heavy green and blue dress, her cheeks and nose bright from the cold, a scarf loose around her throat. She raised a tentative hand, an equally uncertain smile touching her lips.

I raised a hand in return as Holmes came up beside me, my luggage in his hands. His hat was pulled down low around his ears and his back and shoulders were hunched, disguising his true height.

"For the time being, Miss Morstan, I think it best for you to refer to me as Sigerson."

"As you wish," I murmured, hiking my smaller travel bag onto my shoulder, and setting off across the station.

Moments later, I found myself standing in front of Mrs. Fearghasdan. I clasped her hand, feeling the thrum of her heart even through the thick gloves. "Headmistress, it is good to see you again."

"Mary, thank you. I was so grateful to receive your telegram. I... I am so sorry to have called you away from your... uh, duties in London, especially this close to Christmas." Her eyes flicked over my shoulder. "I... did not anticipate that anyone would be accompanying you."

"No apologies are necessary, Headmistress. This is an urgent matter." I waved my free hand at Holmes. "This is Sigerson. He is also in the employ of Mrs. Forrester, who suggested that he accompany me. I hope he will prove useful."

Holmes pulled off his hat and pressed it to his chest, muttering an almost unintelligible "Pleas'd ta meet ya, Mum."

"Yes. Quite. Well, then, there is a cab waiting. This way, please."

The wind bit into us as soon as we exited the station. I pulled up the collar of my jacket and reached into my travel bag to pull out a knitted scarf. It was my own creation, a solid dark green, but with three different alternating stitches. The result was a subtle, but powerful, pattern. I wrapped the scarf around my face and, within only a few breaths, my skin was warm again.

The Adventure of the Faerie Coffin by Rebecca Buchanan

Mrs. Fearghasdan clutched her own scarf tightly, and Holmes tucked down his chin, turning his face away from the wind. When we reached the carriage, he passed my luggage to the driver (who seemed unconcerned by the cold; the scotch bottle sticking out of his pocket gave me a good idea as to why), and we hastily climbed inside. The interior of the cab was frigid, but at least we were out of the wind.

Mrs. Fearghasdan tugged her scarf down. Even in the dull light, I could see the lines of worry and stress that bracketed her eyes and mouth. "I fear there has been another incident since I posted my letter to you." She paused, her gaze flicking to Holmes.

And so I found myself faced with a difficult decision, one of the most difficult of my life. I had no doubt that Holmes would eventually uncover the truth about me. The longer I kept my distance, the longer it would take. But learn the truth he would. And he was here, now, not three feet away, watching, observing, fitting the pieces together and solving the puzzle that was me. Mary Morstan.

Breathe. Feel that breath filling your body.

I offered the Headmistress a tight smile. "It's fine, Mrs. Fearghasdan. You may speak freely in front of Sigerson."

"Very well. There has been a further accident. Miss MacPherson, the chemistry teacher, was in her classroom when... well... she said a figure came out of the wall. It was making that same awful wailing sound. Miss MacPherson was so frightened that she ran from the classroom. She tripped and fell down the stairs and—" Mrs. Fearghasdan blinked rapidly, fighting tears. "Both of her legs are broken. I fear that she will never completely recover."

"I am so sorry," I murmured, pressing a hand to her clenched fingers.

She grasped my hand, apparently unaware of how her grip tightened with every word she spoke. "This thing, whatever it may be, must be dealt with before the students and faculty return after the New Year. I will not risk anyone's life. I will shut down the Frazier Academy if I must."

"No. I will not allow that to happen. The Academy is too important. Where else can deserving young ladies, regardless of their social status or economic circumstances, receive such a thorough education? It is not only governesses that you are turning out, but linguists and scientists and philosophers. The Academy will not close. You have my word."

At that, her hold on my hands loosened. She sank back against the seat with a sigh of relief and closed her eyes.

All the while, Holmes sat silent, watching.

*****

The carriage pulled through the archway and into the central courtyard of the school. The walls all around us — four stories, most of the narrow windows dark and shuttered — blocked the wind. Three figures, young enough to be students, huddled on the far end. Mrs. Fearghasdan paid the driver and then excused herself, explaining that she had administrative tasks to attend.

"You might have need of these," she added, handing me a ring with a dozen keys, all old and heavy. "These will open every door in the school. Go where you must. I had a bed made up for you in the dining hall, alongside everyone else." She coughed. "I am afraid, Mr. Sigerson, that you will have to sleep elsewhere. Perhaps in the groundskeeper's room?"

He pulled off his hat and shuffled his feet. "'Es, Mum. Very gud, Mum."

"Dinner is at seven sharp. Do please join us."

I nodded my agreement. She cast a frown towards the group of students, then left via a dark wooden door.

"This place has the look of a barracks." His voice was low, not meant to be heard by anyone else.

"Originally. The building was purchased by Lady Grizel Frazier in 1670. She had sat in on several lectures by Newton, and thought it ridiculously unfair that women were only being schooled in sewing and cooking when men were learning mathematics and philosophy. So she founded the Frazier Academy, even opening it to the daughters of merchants and tradesmen. That tradition has continued for two hundred years — and I am not going to allow some spirit—"

"Mary Morstan? Is that you?"

I turned on my heel and spied two figures emerging from a door on the far side of the courtyard. Based on their attire and age, I took them to be teachers.

The woman on the left offered me a curiously stiff smile, her breath clouding. "Surely it has not been so long that you don't recognize an old friend?"

I studied her for a long moment, my mouth dropping open in surprise when I finally recognized her. "Evelyn Baxter. You are an instructor here? Now?"

"I am. Botany. And this is my colleague, Susanna Couper, who oversees the history and archaeology departments. Miss Couper, may I introduce an old friend and former sister student, Mary Morstan."

Miss Couper thrust out her hand, shaking mine vigorously. "Pleasure to make your acquaintance. Are you joining us then? Which field? Need a new chemistry teacher, unfortunately. Bad thing, that. Liked MacPherson. You don't look the chemistry type, though. Theology, then? Not going to try to convert us, I hope. Got no use for it myself. I've read enough to see all the problems religion's caused. Why, the witch trials alone—"

"Yes! No!" I extracted my hand as gracefully as possible. "I am not joining the faculty. I am visiting friends for Christmas and thought that I would stop on my way to see Mrs. Fearghasdan. It has been far too long."

Evelyn Baxter's eyes narrowed, but Susanna Couper nodded emphatically. "Aye. Can see that. Well, hope to see you at dinner tonight." With that, she turned and made her way towards the huddle of students. "Right, you three! Inside afore you catch cold! Go on!"

"Well, then." Another stiff smile from Miss Baxter. "Enjoy your visit." And she slipped away after Miss Couper.

He came up to my side, my luggage in his hands. "She was not your friend."

"No. She was not my friend."

*****

After stowing my luggage next to a cot in the dining hall — one wooden table and its benches had been moved out of the way to make room for a dozen of the small beds — Holmes announced that he wanted to see the scene of each accident. As I knew the location of the chemistry laboratory, and thus of Miss MacPherson's tragic fall, we began there.

The lab was housed on the third floor of the north wing. Holmes stopped at the ground floor landing (where Miss MacPherson had come to a painful halt), dropping to his knees to study it and each step carefully.

There was no blood, but there were deep gouges and scratches, fresh, pale wood against the older, dark stain. They were visible down all three flights of stairs and across all three landings.

She must have been grabbing frantically at anything, everything, to save herself.

What force could be powerful enough to throw a grown woman down three flights of stairs?

I shuddered, and lifted a hand to trace the pearls beneath my blouse. My gaze lifted towards the chemistry laboratory. Electric sconces protruded from the walls, jarring and out of place against the centuries-old stone, but even with all the light they cast, pools of shadow clung to corners and sharp angles.

As I lowered my gaze, I noticed Holmes turning his head away.

Hastily dropping my hand, jaw tight, I made my up the stairs. Let Holmes poke and sniff and lick at every odd stain and scratch on every step. I had my own methods of detection.

The creaks and groans of the wood beneath my feet were familiar, almost comforting. Despite the disapproval of Mrs. Fearghasdan, my years at this school had been happy ones: I had Mrs. Webster at my side, ready access to books on every imaginable subject, and I was surrounded by students as eager to learn as I.

The chance for other girls to know such happiness was now being threatened.

My grip firm on the banister, I topped the third floor landing and turned towards the chemistry laboratory. Second door on the left. Locked. After some juggling, I found the correct key and pushed the door open.

The room was dark and reeked of sulphur, chlorine, sodium, and a dozen other chemicals. Beneath that, the very faint scent of withered grass and rain.

Flipping on the electric lights, I moved further into the room. The long rows of tables looked the same, as did the cabinets filled with liquid and powdered chemicals. Shutters covered the windows along the far wall. Portraits of noted chemists hung high near the ceiling, most of then drawings or sketches, but a few actual photographs; Pasteur hung prominently towards the front.

Every piece of glass in the room was shattered, chemicals in powder and liquid form splashed across the tables and floor.

If I moved the shutters aside, I wondered if I would find the windows cracked, as well —

No. Not every piece of glass.

Moving carefully around the rows of tables and pieces of glass and pools of liquid, I made my way towards the far end of the room and the tall cabinets. One stood untouched, the wood black with age, the metal which criss-crossed the glass-fronted doors nearly as dark.

I traced the iron with one finger, feeling its dullness even through my glove.

"Oh, dear," I whispered.

I hastily pulled the pearl necklace from beneath my blouse, allowing it to settle atop my clothing. I caught a quick reflection in the glass, the pearls soft and shimmering.

They were all I had left of my father. He could not have understood what he was doing, what he was bringing into my life. But they were mine now, my power and my curse.

"Miss Morstan?"

"Yes, Mr. H — Sigerson?" I knelt even as I turned slightly. He stood in the doorway, tall and frowning, looking more like himself and less like his alter ego. I pulled my little travel bag around, reaching inside to find what I needed: a square white cloth; a charcoal disk from juniper wood, pressed inside a bronze container not much bigger than a pocket watch; a small flint; and a copper needle.

I spread the cloth over the floor. Mrs. Webster had woven complex patterns through it, and I had added more patterns with multicoloured thread: black along one side, red another, green, and blue. The four colours came together as a stylized thistle in the centre of the cloth.

That was where I set the charcoal, still in its container, and then reached for the flint.

"A moment, please, Miss Morstan." Holmes firmly closed the door, then moved across the room to the shutters. He shoved the wooden panels to either side, revealing the cracked window, and then opened that, too.

The temperature in the room quickly dropped, and the reek of sulphur and other chemicals dissipated. The scent of rain and withered grass remained.

"Ah, yes, thank you. I would ask you to be quiet for a few moments." My tone was brisk, a pathetic attempt to hide the nervousness which made my heart thump and my hands quiver.

I was about to perform a Working in front of Sherlock Holmes.

Even my beloved John had seen this only once, and never spoken of it again.

Shaking that memory away, I struck the flint, lighting the charcoal. The fire filled the little bronze container. I settled back on my knees, the needle between two of my fingers, and whispered the Gaelic words that had been taught to me so long ago, weaving them round and round. I traced the pattern of the words in the air with the needle, my heart calming with the soothing, familiar movements. Looping, endless, thread of word and sound and movement and will.

And then I dropped the needle.

It fell flat, directly into the flame. It stopped a few inches above the burning charcoal, hovering, bright and hot. And then it began to spin, slowly at first, then faster and faster.

Then, with a metallic flash, it shot across the room and buried itself sharp-end first in the door.

For a long moment, neither of us spoke, simply staring at the needle.

I opened my mouth, but he quickly held up a hand. His eyes narrowed, he pressed a finger to his lips. I nodded in understanding.

He moved around the tables and splashes of chemicals with surprising speed and silence. When he reached the door, he clasped the handle and flung it open.

There was a squeak of surprise and a thud as someone fell to the floor.

Hastily whispering my thanks, I flicked the lid of the container shut, smothering the fire. Keeping my body between my sacred tools and whoever had been spying on us, I moved as quickly as possible towards the door.

There, I found Holmes towering over a young girl. She was perhaps thirteen years of age, her dark blonde hair a tangle down her back, her eyes wide and threatening tears, her dress old but serviceable.

"I recognize you." I crouched, offering her a tentative smile. "You were in the courtyard when we arrived."

Her chin quivered.

"I'm Mary. And this is Sigerson. What's your name?"

She inhaled sharply, but her breath became a rough cough.

Holmes caught the girl up in his arms and carried her quickly across the room towards the open window. Within a few moments, her coughing fit had abated and she was breathing more easily. While Holmes settled her on one of the chairs, I flipped the window shut and closed the shutters.

"Ailis," she finally answered. "Ailis Arasgain."

"It's a pleasure to meet you, Ailis." I crouched down in front of her, offering another reassuring smile. I kept my tone gentle and inviting. "You must be quite good at finding your way around the Academy, if you got all the way up here without Sigerson noticing you."

The girl swallowed hard, flicked a quick glance up at Holmes, and then focused on me. She nodded unsteadily.

"Were you here when Miss MacPherson was hurt? Did you see?"

Ailis shook her head hard. "No, ma'am, but I heard it. We all did. Judith and Beatrice and me — I. We were in the kitchen, making up biscuits and jam. And we heard her, we heard her

The Adventure of the Faerie Coffin by Rebecca Buchanan

fall, and we heard her scream…" Ailis panted, her face pale with fear.

"Did you hear what frightened her, what drove Miss MacPherson down the stairs?"

Another quick glance up at Holmes and then back down at me. A nod. "Yes, ma'am. It was the same. The same that's been waking us up every night." She pressed her hands to her ears, hunching low in the chair. "It was the faerie! The faerie! And it's all my fault!"

Hysterical, Ailis collapsed back in the chair. Her breath caught again, her sobs turning to racking coughs that shook her whole body. I lifted her up, slipped into the chair, and pulled her onto my lap. While I rubbed her back and whispered soothing nonsense, Holmes moved to open the shutters and window again.

When he returned to my side, I saw his eyebrows were raised in disbelief. He tilted his head at me in a silent question, and I could only nod.

After long moments, Ailis's coughing eased and she was able to sit upright. Arms shaking, she pushed herself to her feet and stood before us, tangled hair obscuring her face. I gently pushed it aside and tilted her face up. "How could this possibly be your fault?"

The girl sniffled. "It is. Mine and Judith and Beatrice. We went up to the Seat. Everyone else had already gone for Christmas, and it was just us, and we were so bored and tired of just sitting in the library reading and so we snuck out."

"And you went hiking on Arthur's Seat."

Ailis twisted her hands together. "Aye. We weren't looking for it, but was just there, tucked into this little cave. Like it had been hidden behind some rocks, but they had fallen down, and we just had to reach in and take it."

Holmes was utterly still beside me.

I covered Ailis' hands with my own. "What was it, Ailis? What did you find?"

She stuttered. "A — a — c-coffin. Tiny. Tiny little coffin. It was so beautiful. Flowers and everything. And we opened it, and — and — it was so beautiful, and we couldn't just leave it there, and no one would believe us if we left it there and so we brought it home back to the school but then we thought to keep it secret to keep it ours and then then then the wailing started and Judith got hit by that door and Beatrice almost got crushed in the library and I — I—"

Holmes's voice was low as he finally spoke. "You were trapped in a smoke-filled room, despite there being no fire in the hearth."

Silent, her eyes huge, Ailis only stared at him.

I tightened my fingers around her hands, drawing her attention back to me. "Where is the coffin now, Ailis?"

Her chin quivered again, tears spilling down her cheeks. "I don't know! I don't know! We wanted to take it back, after that first night — we did! But we went — we went to where we had hidden it — and it was gone! It was gone!"

*****

Down three flights of stairs, through the kitchen, through another door, and down another flight of stairs, Ailis holding my hand the whole way. My tools safely back in my bag, I clutched my copper needle in my other hand. Holmes followed along behind, shuffling his feet, playing at the role of Sigerson again.

The stairs to the basement were much steeper and narrower than those above ground, the stone walls crowding in on either side. There were no electric lights down here, only gas lights that flickered intermittently.

At the bottom of the stairs, Ailis led us around piles of boxes, trunks, old cabinets, mouldering stacks of books, and jumbles of animal and human skeletons. She stopped far along the right wall, lifting one shaking hand to point at a huge old iron stove.

It was difficult to make out at first, its true girth lost to the shadows of the basement. Then there was a flick and a flash of light, and Holmes held a lantern aloft. I couldn't even recall seeing him pick one up. A golden glow fell across the stove, and I saw that it was massive, at least a century old, and covered in dust.

Except for the grated door, which hung open, revealing the dark and empty interior.

Holmes slipped around us and crouched in front of the stove.

"Ailis, you and your friends hid the coffin in there?"

"Yes, ma'am. No one ever comes down here. We're not supposed to. Headmistress says it's dangerous."

Holmes grunted.

I clasped Ailis by her shoulders and turned her towards me. "Thank you very much, Ailis. I need you go back upstairs now. Don't tell anyone what you told us, or what we have done. I'll see you at dinner."

The girl hesitated. She licked her lips, cast a glance at Holmes, then looked back at me and nodded. She turned, then stopped. "Miss MacPherson is my favorite. Always encouraging me. I never — we—" She shook her head and was quickly lost to the darkness and debris. I was only certain that she was gone when I heard the faint thump of the door at the top of the stairs.

Holmes was bent over the stove, poking and frowning. "What is the Gaelic term? As proud as you are of your Scottish heritage, I assume that you object to the English *witch*."

"...Is that what I am?"

"I am not mad. I am in full possession of my faculties. Therefore, I trust the evidence of my own senses — and the evidence, at this time, supports no other conclusion. I might argue that some lesser known or otherwise forgotten branch of the sciences is behind your activities, but this is not the time."

"And what evidence does the stove provide?"

He turned on the balls of his feet, quirking an eyebrow in my direction. "*Quid pro quo*, Miss Morstan. What did you learn in the laboratory?"

I hesitated, squaring my shoulders. "It seems likely that another is looking for this... coffin, though I am not certain that is what the object is. Let us call this searcher a faerie, for convenience, as the girl did."

He frowned, but nodded.

"It cannot go near iron," I continued, "and so only the glass which was bound in iron was left untouched in the lab. I wove a like-to-like Working, hoping to trace the faerie." I lifted my hand, revealing the copper needle. "Instead, it led us to Ailis, indicating that she has been touched by it, retained some of its essence."

"Contamination?"

"Of a sort. Rather like the perfume left behind after flowers have been removed from a room. The Working could not find the faerie, either because it was gone or well-hidden, but it did find traces of the faerie in Ailis." I stepped closer. "*Quid pro quo.*"

He bowed slightly, a hand pressed to his heart. "Footprints in the dust, and finger smudges on the grate. Three of the pairs of footprints are small."

"The students."

"Correct. The fourth is larger, and also female. There is a clear impression of the heel, there, and the swirl in the dust just to the left was made by a trailing hem."

"Well, that certainly does narrow the list of suspects. It must be Miss Baxter or Miss Couper."

He quirked an eyebrow again. The expression was beginning to annoy me. "Not Mrs. Fearghasdan? Or even someone from outside the school?"

"Mrs. Fearghasdan would never place the Academy in such danger. And I highly doubt that anyone could make their way onto the grounds, through the hallways, and down here without being seen — assuming they even knew to look for the coffin inside an iron stove in a corner of the basement."

"Mrs. Fearghasdan has made her opinion of magic well-known. If she took the coffin, it was under the assumption that it was a trifle. Only it proved not to be a trifle, and you are the only person of her acquaintance who possesses the wherewithal to deal with the matter. She could not confess what she had done without bringing blame upon herself, and the ire and derision of her staff and her students' families." He swung the lantern around, focusing again on the stove. "As for an outsider, are you the only person in Edinburgh with such abilities? Surely there are others who can cast Workings and who would be interested in a 'faerie' coffin."

My mouth fell open. For long minutes, I could only watch him in stunned silence as he examined the stove, the walls around it, the floor, and various piles of crates, trunks, bones, and books.

He broke the silence with a "Ha!" of satisfaction and pressed his hand to a brick in the wall roughly level with his shoulder. There was a low grinding sound and a section of the wall sank in, swinging just wide enough for him to slip inside.

"Come along, Miss Morstan!" he called back, his voice echoing.

My stunned confusion gave way to exasperation. Rolling my eyes, I squeezed after him, my skirts catching and tearing on the brick.

The light from his lantern filtered down from above, revealing a spiralling stone stairwell even more narrow than the one we had originally descended to the basement. There were no windows here, but plenty of cobwebs and evidence of rats and mice.

There was no way to avoid all of the cobwebs as I climbed after Holmes — I could feel them trailing over my shoulders and in my hair — but I lifted my skirts high and did my best to step around the piles of excrement and the occasional rodent corpse.

Some of the webs were already broken, and not by Holmes. And there was a second set of footprints in the dust. I set my foot down beside one. Roughly the same size, and with a heel.

"As students, we all liked to tease one another with stories about the hidden passageways inside the walls." My voice echoed oddly, cold, mixing with our footsteps as I continued to climb after him. "Stories of students who became lost in them, never to be found again. Of malicious teachers who used them to sneak into students' rooms to punish them in their sleep. Girls who had secreted paramours inside. Even that Grizel Frazier herself still roamed the passageways, keeping an eye on the Academy she founded."

"Is there any truth to the tales?"

"Some, probably." I wrinkled my nose as I stepped over a particularly large rat carcass, the bones showing through the hide. "I imagine that the Commandants of the barracks found the passageways useful, as did the soldiers, for smuggling and... other activities. Once it became a school, they would have served a similar purpose for both the staff and the students. Ailis and her friends obviously know of at least one passage, that which leads from the library to the outside of the western wall."

"Do you know of others?"

"Just the passageway from the kitchen to the great dining hall, but everyone knows about it. The serving staff use it as a shortcut. And there's the secret room behind the Headmistress's office."

He paused, swinging the lantern around to look down at me.

"Grizel Frazier used it to hide books of which church and government authorities alike would not have approved. And, yes, we can check it for the coffin, but we will not find it there."

"Mm."

He turned away and, after another dozen steps, we came to a heavy wooden door banded and bolted in iron. There was no lock, but there was a latch. Handing the lantern to me, he leaned sideways, pressing his ear to the wood. Satisfied, he lifted the latch and pushed the door open. He paused on the threshold, expression a curious combination of grim and satisfied.

I pressed forward, trying to see over his shoulder.

After a moment, he spun to the side and out of the secret door, holding it open far enough for me to squeeze out of the passageway, through the side of a cabinet — and into the chemistry laboratory.

*****

Dinner was not silent. While we sat in the kitchen, sipping soup and munching on bread and mutton, Miss Couper maintained an animated lecture on the tumuli and barrows of the British Isles and the Continent.

"...Wayland's Smithy being a prime Neolithic example. And then there's Maeshowe up on Orkney. Chambered cairn. Unique to the Orkneys. Don't see that anywhere else. Well, that we know of. Could change at any moment. Always making new discoveries. Even the Americans are doing good work, digging up Indian mounds —"

"Miss Couper, could you pass the salt, please?" I held out my hand, smile stiff.

"Eh? Oh, aye."

Miss Baxter hid a smirk behind a bite of mutton.

Ailis and the other two students, whom I now knew to be Judith Fleming and Beatrice Gordon, sat across the table from me. They remained alarmingly quiet, their gazes fixed on their plates. Like Ailis, Judith and Beatrice also wore older dresses; charity students, then, without the funds to travel home for the holiday.

Mrs. Fearghasdan sat at the head of the table, frowning with concern.

Holmes hovered around the edges of the room, watchful.

I cleared my throat, shaking some salt into my soup. "How will all of you be celebrating the holiday? Cider and carols after church? Will you be bringing a tree in?"

Miss Couper raised her spoon. "Interesting history to that—"

"No tree, I'm afraid," Mrs. Fearghasdan interrupted. "But we plan for a yule log in the main hearth in the great dining hall. Dawn services at St. Giles, of course."

"And you, Miss Morstan?" Miss Baxter smiled at me, her eyes gleaming. "Will you be burning a yule log?"

I set aside the salt, folding my hands in my lap. From across the table, Ailis watched me through her hair.

"I do recall that you and... oh, what was her name? Weaver? Walker?"

"Mrs. Webster."

Miss Baxter clapped her hands. "Yes, that's right! Webster! The two of you would slip away at the oddest times of the year." She turned to Miss Couper and continued in a loud whisper, "Did you know that Miss Morstan here was the only student at the Academy who had her own nanny? The rest of us, of course, had long out-grown our nannies, leaving them behind in the nursery. But, well, I suppose when one is born in a distant heathen land, one needs some sort of comfort when one rejoins civilization."

Miss Couper shifted uncomfortably, her expression uncertain.

"You are quite right, Evelyn." I smiled thinly, holding my back and shoulders so stiff that they began to ache. *Breathe. In, out.* "It was a shock to leave the beauty and warmth of India for Scotland. It took me some time to come to appreciate the lochs and moors and heaths — beautiful, but a spare and striking beauty in comparison to India. And, of course, I had just lost my mother, and my father, loyal down to his marrow, would not abandon his duty to the Queen. And so Mrs. Webster kindly agreed to accompany me back to my homeland, to love and care for me as if I were her own daughter. And I came to care for her as a second mother — but more, as a role model, an example of compassion and honour and courage. The sort of woman I could only hope to become myself, caring for the children in my charge as she cared for me. As Mrs. Fearghasdan does. As I am sure all of the teachers here do."

Mrs. Fearghasdan cleared her throat. "You are very kind, Mary."

Her face flushed, Miss Baxter glared at me. "And is that how you acquired that pearl necklace? I do not believe that I have ever seen its like. A gift from a grateful student? Or perhaps a grateful *parent*. I am sure —"

"Evelyn! That is quite enough!" The headmistress slapped her hand down on the table, hard.

Beatrice jumped, Judith appeared to be near tears, and Ailis's frantic gaze darted back and forth between the adults around her.

Mrs. Fearghasdan stood. "Girls, prepare for bed. You may read for a short time, but I expect you to be under the covers with your eyes closed by nine sharp."

The three girls stood, bobbing their heads and murmuring "Yes, Headmistress."

Miss Baxter patted at the corner of her mouth and tossed aside her napkin. "Well, if you will excuse me, I have some work to attend to in the botany room. Miss Couper, I believe that it is your turn to clean up." With that, she stood and quickly left the kitchen.

Miss Couper huffed a sigh.

"There's no need. I'm sure that Sigerson would be more than happy to take over any cleaning duties this evening." I turned on the bench and smiled at Holmes. "Wouldn't you, Sigerson?"

He answered with a barely audible "Yes'm."

"Excellent. And the three of us can retire to the dining hall, as well. Perhaps with a pot of calming tea?"

Mrs. Fearghasdan frowned. "Well... I suppose..."

Miss Couper offered me a grateful smile. Minutes later, we were settled into deep leather chairs in front of the flickering hearth. While Judith and Beatrice read in their cots, small lanterns set beside them on makeshift nightstands, and Ailis snored under her blankets, we spent a delightful hour discussing the works of Sir Walter Scott and Robert Louis Stevenson.

When Miss Baxter appeared some time later, already dressed in her sleeping gown, she ignored us. She climbed into her cot, and showed us her back.

Only as the clock struck ten did our conversation draw to a close. Miss Couper bid us good-evening and left to change into her own sleeping gown.

Slipping forward in my chair, I whispered to Mrs. Fearghasdan, "At what time may we expect to be awakened?"

She flinched, pulling in her shoulders. "Sometime between two and three in the morning. It does not last long, however. Ten minutes. Perhaps fifteen."

"In that case, we had both better get some rest." I gathered up the tea pot and cups. "I will return these to the kitchen."

She stayed me with a hand on my wrist. "And... what precisely will you do?"

I offered her a reassuring smile, not unlike the one I had offered Ailis earlier in the evening. "Whatever I must."

With that, I bid her good-night and made my way down the dark corridors to the kitchen, only a few electric sconces lighting my way.

As I suspected, Holmes was nowhere to be seen. I could smell him, however. A faint whiff of tobacco leaked under the back door which led to the central courtyard. There, I found him leaning against a column, feet crossed, an old briar pipe between his lips.

Pulling the door shut, I crossed my arms against the cold and waited.

"As you said, there was no faerie coffin. The room behind the Headmistress' office does not appear to have been used for many years."

"Proof that we live in more enlightened times?"

"Mm."

"And Miss Baxter?"

His teeth gleamed in a quick smile. "After she was finished pollinating, transplanting, and pruning, I thoroughly examined the botany laboratory. The few pieces of iron there proved to be of no consequence and I could see nowhere that she might hide the coffin."

"Miss Couper, then."

He did not answer.

"Or, as you argued, someone from outside the school." I shivered. My lungs were beginning to hurt from the cold. "We can expect to be awakened between the second and third hours of the morning. I have preparations to make. What will you be doing?"

He turned, a halo of bluish smoke circling his head. "Continuing my education in occult detection."

*****

Using the keys that Mrs. Fearghasdan had entrusted to me, I locked the dining hall doors, both those that opened onto the main corridor and those that led through the secret passage to the kitchen. Across both thresholds I laid a mixture of sea salt, thistles, and powdered briar and blackthorn. I laid a semi-circle out from one edge of the door to the other, giving Holmes and I room to sit or stand as needed. At the top of the semi-circle, I drew a stylized thistle with the mixture: three spokes poking up, two poking down.

"Mr. Holmes, if you would, please? A nail. There should be plenty of iron ones in the door." My voice shook just a little as I made my request. A combination of exhaustion, uncertainty, and giddiness. I could feel my face flush as he hesitated, then dipped his head without comment and turned to the dining hall door.

He pulled a knife from his boot and, within a few moments, had pried loose a single, straight nail, clean of rust.

"Thank you." My voice shook slightly less.

I carefully laid the nail in the centre of the thistle, in line with the arch of the semi-circle. An effective bar against any faerie. Energy could still flow into the safe space as I needed it, but nothing malign could enter.

Sitting down, I found as comfortable a position as possible on the stone floor, and drew additional supplies from my travel bag: the same threaded cloth I had used in the chemistry laboratory, the bronze canister with a fresh disk of juniper charcoal, my flint, my copper needle, and Mrs. Forrester's package: a loose net, dark green in colour, painstakingly woven from crushed and threaded nettles.

It had taken Mrs. Forrester years to create the net. I'm not sure that I would ever be able to repay her for giving it to me.

Holmes settled down beside me. "Salt for purification and protection, I gather."

I hesitated and cleared my throat. I had been taught the importance of secrecy from the cradle. Speaking openly now of my Work was... disconcerting. Even with my beloved John I had been able to say only so much.

I cleared my throat again. "I will have your word that you will not speak of what I am about to tell you with anyone else. Not without my permission."

He pulled his briar pipe from his pocket, but did not light it. "Not even Watson?"

"If you are implying that I did n—"

A fierce wail echoed down the corridor, high-pitched and jarring. I lurched onto my knees while Holmes scrambled to his feet. The air above the salt line shivered, and I could only wonder at how much worse it would have been without that protective barrier.

Another wail followed, then weeping, sobs of grief that made my own eyes tear up in sympathy.

At the far end of the corridor, a figure came into view. Female, and taller than most men, long-limbed and thin. White-green hair trailed down her back and along the floor, like grass touched by frost. Her dress was not cloth, but the withered stalks of flowers, bare twigs, bundles of birds' nests, clumps of feathers, bits of fox and rabbit fur. The dress rasped and rubbed against the stone floor. Blue markings (paint? ink?) swirled and arced across her forehead, down the sides of her face, and across her cheekbones. And her eyes, they were the icy blue-grey of a Highland lake in winter, so cold with anger and grief that I felt it down to my bones.

The wailing continued as she moved towards us, her inarticulate cries giving way to words, than sliding back again into moans of pain. Not Scots Gaelic. Not even Old Irish. But Pictish, understood by only a few who maintained the old ways.

My breath caught as the meaning of her words became clear.

The faerie stopped, brought up short by the line of salt and herbs. The air rippled again. This close, I could see the shape of her bones through her too-tight skin, and how strands of her hair moved in a wind that only she would feel.

She stared at us, the dead and dried flowers in her dress twitching with every breath.

The faerie opened her mouth and screamed. The ripples above the salt line became chaotic, frantic miniature explosions, like a hail of pebbles falling into a lake, and the iron nail bounced.

"Miss Morstan?" Holmes shouted, and I realized that he had a pistol in one hand and his knife in the other.

I dropped back to the ground, hastily lit the charcoal, and scooped up the net. Whipping it through the smoke created by the charcoal, I speared the trailing line of the net with my needle, then wrapped it around my hand to get a good grip. Stepping closer to the faerie, I whispered my Working, weaving Pictish words round and round.

The faerie went abruptly silent. She tilted her head, blue-grey eyes wide.

I took another step forward, toes just inches from the iron nail.

The faerie sneered, her lips pulling back in a predatory grin.

I kicked the nail aside. The air snapped. I threw the net, casting it over and around the faerie. She howled, lunged to the side. The net caught her shoulder and arm, tangling, tearing at the dry stalks and bulbs of her dress. Bits of it ripped free, floating through the air.

The faerie heaved backwards, yanking me with her. The salt line smeared and broke. Another hard yank, my shoulders straining as I stumbled forward.

An arm wrapped around my waist, catching me close. Holmes's other arm descended passed my head, his knife quick and bright as he flung it through the air. The blade sank deep into the faerie's shoulder, slicing through several strands of the net.

The faerie shrieked, shimmering blood staining her flesh and gown. With a snarl, she yanked the knife from her body. It clattered to the floor. She spun, twisted, pulled, and we toppled forward as the net strained.

With a final heave, she pulled free, the net ripping away. She fled back down the corridor, dripping blood and wailing.

And then, just as suddenly, the sound was gone, the corridor silent.

I dropped my head onto my arms, panting hard. The trailing line of the net was wrapped so tightly around my hand that I could no longer feel my fingers, and my shoulders were on fire.

"Are you injured, Miss Morstan?" Holmes tugged his arm loose from around my waist and pushed himself to his knees.

"Her child-self." I rolled my head so that I could look up at him. "The coffin. We have to find that coffin."

*****

The following morning, after a hasty breakfast of eggs and biscuits, Mrs. Fearghasdan and I took a cab to the northern quarter of Edinburgh. Holmes — as Sigerson again — rode up top with the driver, hunched and muttering about the cold, a stack of books in his lap. Miss Baxter and Miss Couper and the three girls, agitated and terrified by what they had heard during the night, remained in the dining hall. When I laid a new salt line across the door, handed them each an iron fireplace poker, and told them not to leave the room, even Miss Baxter could only nod.

"I still can't believe... I don't understand..." Mrs. Fearghasdan shook her head, hands clenched in her lap.

I studied the Christmas decorations which lined the streets, catching occasional glimpses of Arthur's Seat around the buildings and hills. "The faerie is clearly targeting those who have had contact with the coffin: Ailis, Beatrice, Judith. The fact that she attacked Miss MacPherson can only mean one thing."

"But..." The headmistress pressed her lips together. "What about me? The stone gargoyle that nearly crushed me in the courtyard — oh." She sank back in the seat. "I was speaking with Ailis."

We were silent for the rest of the journey.

The cab eventually rolled to a stop in front of an elegant brick house, the narrow yard bright with heather, pansies, and even an acer tree.

Holmes clambered down to help us out of the cab, then followed us up the steps, books in his arms.

Mrs. Fearghasdan knocked and, a few moments later, the door was opened to reveal an older woman, a heavy shawl over her shoulders.

The headmistress smiled. "Mrs. MacPherson, I do hope that we are not intruding?"

"Certainly not." The woman stepped aside and waved us into the house. "My daughter has not received many visitors. I am sure that she will be only too happy to see you."

As we entered, I could see directly down the hallway to the solarium at the rear of the house. At this distance, I could not be sure, but I thought that I recognized several of the plants.

Introductions were quickly made and the books ("Gifts from a grateful faculty.") were handed over to a maid. Sigerson was invited to warm himself in the kitchen, while Mrs. MacPherson escorted the headmistress and myself upstairs.

Trailing behind the others, I motioned Holmes towards the solarium, pointing and mouthing instructions. He just blinked at me, but I was not sure if he did not understand or if he was staying in character.

We found Miss MacPherson propped up in her bed, her face lined with pain. A medicinal bottle sat on the nightstand beside her, but I suspected that it contained something other than laudanum. Blankets covered her from chin to knees. Below that, heavy casts wrapped her legs.

Fortunately, the elder Mrs. MacPherson stayed only a few moments. As soon as she was gone, I turned to the young teacher and asked, "Where is the faerie coffin?"

Miss MacPherson gaped at me. "I don't — I have no idea."

"Yes, you do. You took it from the stove where Ailis, Beatrice, and Judith had hidden it. The faerie is hunting it. You have placed everyone in danger. We must return the coffin to her immediately. Where is it?"

Miss MacPherson's expression turned mulish, the lines in her face deepening. For long minutes, she was silent, staring at me, at Mrs. Fearghasdan, at the walls, the ceiling. Her fingers twitched nervously.

"Whatever you were planning, it will not work. As soon as you remove the coffin from its hiding place, the faerie will descend upon you. You are not strong enough to defeat her—"

Miss MacPherson snorted.

"— not in your current condition. Even assuming you regain enough of your strength to face her, that time is months

The Adventure of the Faerie Coffin by Rebecca Buchanan

away. If not longer. She will have torn the school apart by then, injuring and possibly killing the students and other teachers in the process. Is that what you want?"

Miss MacPherson licked her lips, studying me from the corner of her eye. Her gaze dipped towards the pearl necklace, then lifted slowly.

"Please, Maighread." Mrs. Fearghasdan leaned forward in her chair. "The girls are terrified. The Academy will have to close down. *End this.*"

The young teacher exhaled, heavy and low. She closed her eyes, then turned to us. "It's under the hearthstone in the great dining hall, inside an iron box."

I pushed to my feet, Mrs. Fearghasdan quickly following.

"And just so we are clear..." Miss MacPherson paused, tilting her chin up at me, her expression proud. "I was most definitely strong enough. And I will be again."

My own fingers twitched, longing for my copper needle.

Mrs. Fearghasdan gently touched my wrist, and I left the room without saying another word.

*****

"Mandrake, wormwood, garlic, rosemary, rue, asafoetida, mugwort, St. John's wort. Taxidermy, as well." Holmes walked quickly at my side, our steps echoing on the stone. Mrs. Fearghasdan panted behind us, struggling to keep pace.

"Which animals?"

"Weasel, rat, fox, dog."

"Mmm. That means they have the bones. Not just the daughter, but likely the mother, too."

We rounded the corner and came within sight of the dining hall, the doors still shut.

Holmes looked down at me. "Should we be concerned about them interfering?"

"They won't have time." I hastened my steps, kicking my skirts out of the way. Stepping over the salt line, I shoved the door open. I ignored the squeal of surprise from Judith and the way Miss Couper lurched to her feet, iron poker held high.

Instead, I made straight for the hearth. Pushing a chair out of the way, I knelt in front of the fireplace. Holmes dropped down next to me, feeling along the edges of every stone.

"Here. Scratches as from a lever of some sort." Pulling the knife from his boot, he wedged the blade into the seam. With only a little effort, the stone tilted up, far enough that we were able to squeeze our fingers beneath it and tip it out of the way.

There, in a narrow space beneath, sat an iron box. It was not even two feet in length and a foot wide.

Holmes bent down and lifted it out. "Miss Morstan?"

I looked up to see that the others had surrounded us, their eyes wide and wary.

"Over there." I gestured to a space between the large table and the dozen cots. "I need room to work. Mrs. Fearghasdan, I suggest you take everyone into the kitchen. Hopefully, this will all be over soon."

Ailis voice shook. "W-what are you going to do?"

I offered her a small smile. "Set things to rights."

With a firm nod, the headmistress took Ailis's hand and led her towards the secret passageway to the kitchen. Judith and Beatrice trailed after. Miss Baxter pursed her lips, appearing on the verge of another cutting remark. Before she could open her mouth, however, Miss Couper grabbed her arm and gave her a not-so-gentle push towards the kitchen. She saluted me with her fireplace poker, and then Holmes and I were alone with the coffin and its tiny occupant.

"Her *child-self*, you said?"

I strode across the room and cut the salt line in front of the door. "There are many kinds of faerie. Some change as the land changes, their younger and elder selves sleeping and waking with the seasons." I returned and laid down a salt circle around us, the box on the floor at our feet. "If she does not retrieve her child-self, she will die with the Spring." I slipped the pearl necklace over my head. I broke the clasp, pulled off one pearl, and tucked the rest in my travel bag. Whispering words, I looped and cut my needle through the air, and, with a final flourish, impaled the pearl on the needle.

"Keep your knife at the ready, Mr. Holmes."

He did not answer, instead pulling his pistol from a hidden pocket and cocking the hammer. In his other hand, he held his knife low at his side.

I opened the box, pulled out the coffin, and set it on the ground.

It *was* beautiful, just as Ailis had said. Oak, the wood vibrant and alive. Flowers sprouted from the surface, growing, fluttering open, shrinking down, and growing again. Delicate vines wrapped around it, thrumming softly with sap.

A wailing shriek, rising and falling. It quickly drew closer. Closer.

And then she was there, teetering at the threshold of the dining hall. Her dress rasped and rustled, her hair curled madly, and the blue markings on her face almost glowed. With a sweep of her hand, the broken salt line was blown away, but the circle around us held.

As she advanced across the room, her blue-grey eyes cold with anger, I pushed to my feet. I clutched the needle between my fingers. "Stay close to me."

"And you to me, Miss Morstan."

I backed up a step, then two, Holmes following, putting space between us and the coffin.

The faerie stopped, seething, when she reached the barrier of salt, thistle, briar, and blackthorn. The wound in her shoulder looked ragged, but no longer bled.

"Beautiful lady!" I called out in Pictish.

She hissed at me.

I continued in that ancient tongue. "Those who took your child-self are children themselves. They did not understand the offense they caused. Take your child-self and return to your great hall under the earth. Go in peace."

I scraped my foot backwards, breaking the barrier.

The faerie surged forward. She scooped up the coffin, hugging it tight to her chest. For a moment, the dead flowers of her dress brightened with life and colour. The faerie moaned, rocking back and forth, her eyes closed. Then they withered again.

She hissed low. The beds, table, and benches lifted off the floor. The glass of the electric sconces shattered. Then, between one blink and the next, she lunged for us, one hand extended, fingernails like curved rose thorns.

A gun barked, a knife flashed.

The faerie spun, twisted around, and lunged again.

I lifted the needle, chanting, the pearl shining. Not Gaelic or Pictish, this time, but classical Sanskrit, the language by which the pearl was created. It recognized its mother tongue, opalescence spinning across its surface.

The faerie skipped around us, so fast. The beds, table, and benches spun in the air, crashing into one another, into the walls, splinters flying.

A blackness crept across the pearl. It sizzled, a thin tendril of smoke rising.

The faerie hissed again, louder, but fell back a step. And another.

More black covered the pearl, the opalescence nearly gone.

My knees shook. Sweat ran down the sides of my face. I forced myself a step forward, Holmes at my side, and the faerie fell back. Another step.

The pearl turned ashen, beginning to collapse in on itself. Flakes of it floated up through the air.

There was a *whoomp*, a puff, as the pearl imploded. The concussive wave rushed through the air, growing stronger as it travelled. When it reached the faerie, the wave threw her backwards, tearing loose pieces of her dress.

Shrieking, she tumbled, righted herself—

— and was gone.

The furniture crashed to the floor, the racket pounding in my ears.

I tasted rock and realized that I had collapsed. My whole body was shaking, my fingers spasming around my needle.

Holmes gently rolled me onto my back and tossed his coat across me. "Miss Morstan? Mary?"

I tried to smile, slurred a reassurance, and then knew only darkness.

*****

I slept through the afternoon and all through the night, tucked into a mattress that had been placed near the fireplace. I woke infrequently, and each time found that I was not alone. Mrs. Fearghasdan sat with me, and Miss Couper; even Miss Baxter. Of Holmes, however, there was no sign. At one point, I opened my eyes to find Ailis at my side, staring blindly towards the hearth.

She started when she saw that I was awake, then licked her lips. "It's gone, then?"

"For the most part." My voice was scratchy. I cleared my throat. "The faerie was banished, but she is still... quite angry. She may return. I will leave protective measures in place. You must promise that you will contact me immediately if anything happens."

She looked towards the hearth again. "Will you teach me?"

"Ailis, I do n—"

"Please! I have to know! I have to — you have power! You can do anything!"

"Ailis!" I reached out, managing to snag her wrist. "It's not that simple. And I certainly cannot do anything. There are limits —"

She yanked her hand away and jumped to her feet. Her expression became hard and stubborn. "If you will not teach me, I will find someone who will."

I called after her, but she ignored me. With a last look of anger and disappointment, she stormed away.

*****

Early on the afternoon of 20 December, Holmes and I took a cab across Edinburgh to the train station. Mrs. Fearghasdan had bid me a heart-felt farewell in the Academy's central courtyard, her thanks so sincere that I felt tears threaten.

Miss Couper was more brusque. She shook my hand firmly and declared that I had "opened her eyes to new possibilities."

Miss Baxter was silent for a long moment, her gaze narrowed. "I always knew there was something odd about you."

Judith hugged me, Beatrice offered me a shy thank you, and Ailis ignored me.

As we waited on the crowded platform, many people clutching brightly wrapped packages, Holmes moved closer to me. "I apologize for not remaining at your side as you recovered, Miss Morstan."

I shifted my travel bag, the ticket to Dùn Dè crinkling in my hand. "No apology necessary, sir. I only needed rest. And I assume you had an important task to attend."

"I did. After the... incident in the dining hall, I left you in the care of Mrs. Fearghasdan. I thought it prudent to check the grounds of the school. I encountered the elder Mrs. MacPherson in the courtyard."

My fingers tightened.

"She was quite vexed when I explained that the faerie and coffin were both gone. She had some harsh words to say about you. I followed her home and remained on watch until this morning. She spent quite some time in the solarium, and in her daughter's room, though I cannot attest as to the exact nature of her activities."

"Likely nothing good." There was a blast of steam and a surge of noise as one of the trains moved out of the station. "I must offer my own apology, as well, sir." He quirked an eyebrow — again. I swallowed and forged ahead. "I did not initially welcome your company. I thought this a matter that I should deal with on my own, in my own way. And... I was uncertain how you would react when you learned certain things about me."

"You thought I would denounce you to Watson."

"Among others."

He smiled, a rare expression that brought unexpected warmth to his face. "I trust Watson's judgement. He did not break off your engagement after you revealed your deepest secret to him. Quite the opposite."

"...Oh?"

"Mmm. The evening of 1 October. Watson returned from his dinner with you, proclaiming that you were even more extraordinary than he had realized. When I pressed him for details, he would only say that you were wonderful, and that he had given his word." He shrugged. "When the opportunity arose to learn what was so extraordinary about you — the woman who is to wed my closest friend — I seized it. For that, I make no apology."

I smiled up at Holmes. "I am glad that you are his friend."

A station agent moved through the crowd, down the line of track, announcing the last boarding call for the Dùn Dè train. I handed my luggage to him, keeping my travel bag. "John should return to London tomorrow evening, and I will follow in a few days. I shall see you both Christmas morning?"

He tipped forward in a slight bow. "Give my regards to Mrs. Webster, and please let her know that I would like to pay her a visit myself, if and when she is amenable."

"I will." I turned towards the train.

"Miss Morstan?"

I paused and turned back to him.

"How much of this incident should I relate to Watson?"

"All of it. I trust him. And now I trust you. Oh — and the correct term is not *witch*, but *buidseach*."

Another slight bow and he held out a hand to help me up the steps. The whistle blew loud and shrill as I made my way down the narrow corridor and found my cabin. As I settled into the seat, I looked out across the platform.

He was still there. He waved, tipped his hat, and turned for home.

The Adventure of the Russian Mystic

by Stewart Sternberg

I would have refused answering the pounding at my door had I thought he would go away, but I knew better; Sherlock Holmes would not leave without some level of satisfaction. The world's only consulting detective, as he generously referred to himself, strode in, reeking of rancid tobacco and bitter coffee. His deep-set eyes suggested too much time had passed since last he slept.

"Why didn't you respond to my message?" he demanded.

"I received it only a few hours ago," I snapped back. "If you wanted immediate response, you should have said so, and maybe supplied some details in the process."

"The mention of murder wasn't enough to spark some degree of curiosity? Nor the scene of the crime? The Diogenes Club?"

"Not everyone drops their social life at a snap of your fingers, Mr. Holmes. I was saying goodnight to a charming woman, and there are some things you do not rush."

"You had no intention of coming tonight, otherwise you wouldn't be in your night attire, dressed like a peacock."

"A marvellous example of deductive reasoning. I'm sorry you don't approve of my kimono."

"Typical childishness."

"Typical arrogance," I retorted. "Speaking of unfortunate personalities, where is your dear friend and chronicler?"

"I wished to spare poor Watson the torment of your company."

Dr. John Watson and I had recently had a falling out over a debt from a game of chance where he all but accused me of cheating. Precognition doesn't control the way the cards fall; it just occasionally nudges awareness of when to fold and when to raise.

Holmes adopted a serious expression. "Please get dressed, Styles; the constabulary is waiting on us, and the Foreign Service is growing anxious. I need your assistance."

Trepidation tickled the back of my neck; something wasn't quite right in the ether, something apart from the natural world. At one point in the evening Sherlock Holmes had met with magical energy. How could people walk through the world without awareness of the powers swirling around them? Perhaps ignorance was a means of protection. I confess I envied them.

I dispensed with my usual harassment of the poor detective and hurried into my closet for the proper attire. I shrugged on a light jacket with Holmes's assistance, and paused before a mirror, setting a bowler on my crown, and then instead selecting a blue wool cap with a small brim. Holmes watched my toilet with an aggrieved expression, and when I nodded at him that I was ready, he scowled and grabbed my arm, guiding me out the door.

The cool spring night air tasted of a recent rain, and I savoured the moment, listening to the muted sounds of the neighbourhood, noting the slight acidity that touched the back of the tongue, a remnant of the now dissipated fog, and the presence of a sour breeze wafting off the nearby river. Holmes no doubt took in the same detail but analysed and catalogued it without seeing its beauty or understanding the perfection of the moment.

Spring always moved me; always reminded me of the delight in life. I lived ambitiously. As my friend Oscar Wilde once said, "I can resist everything, except temptation."

Holmes ushered me into a waiting hansom, rapped on the roof, and settled back as our conveyance rattled into the night. I resisted the urge to prompt him for further information; I could see he wasn't in the mood. He was deep in his own mind, a labyrinth I avoided.

Holmes and I met some time back, not long after he invited Watson to share rooms with him. We enjoyed many common interests, although we parted at the supernatural. Holmes grudgingly admitted that I had abilities he couldn't yet explain. Sometimes, he found me useful. I found him at once annoying and exhilarating.

"I refuse ascribing supernatural qualities to events just because we are unable to explain them at this time," he told me once. "You have abilities? I accept that. I believe you can tap into some source of power that we are yet unable to quantify. But the time will come when we can understand all the energies surrounding us. Magic is science yet explained."

"Science! True daughter of Old Time thou art! / Who alterest all things with thy peering eyes," I retorted. "Why preyest thou thus upon the poet's heart, / Vulture, whose wings are dull realities?"

His dark eyes showed distaste. "I don't have much use for poetry, or excessive sentiment."

"What is a body without a soul?" I asked.

"You know, someday, we must discuss the truth behind your affectations," he said.

"My affectations? Ha!"

"Your disregard for convention, your difficulty with authority, and of course, your struggle with reality. You know why you study the dark arts? It isn't to conquer them; you study them because they frighten you. You study them because you must."

I bowed at that last statement. Holmes was correct. He was always correct.

Only a small circle of people knew of my studies of magic; I learned long the dangers of revealing my abilities or my knowledge of the arcane. Instead, I wrote a few boring texts on ancient cultures and flirted at the fringe of academia. I also enjoyed freely spending my inheritance while barely putting a dent in it, all the while working hard at my reputation as a self-destructive womanizer and a non-productive sloth. It allowed people to feel sorry for me, or superior, at least on a moral level, if not a financial one.

Behaving badly was my avocation.

*****

We were soon approaching the exterior of The Diogenes Club, a tall, old building on Pall Mall; unremarkable, even drab, which belied its importance. Holmes's brother Mycroft, one of the founding members, and allegedly most of London's diplomatic core, spent much time inside its walls, finding sanctuary from the pressures and political evils of government life. It amused me that politicians could abide the club's stringent rules; inside, no member could talk or take the least notice of another, except in The Strangers' Room.

Holmes studied me, his forehead creasing with apparent worry.

"Before we go in, I had best give you some background. Not much though, I want you to have no bias. As I said, we're here because of a murder. A member, a man of some importance, was found dead earlier in a private chamber on the second floor. He had been strangled. I won't give you the details, other than to tell you the door to the chamber had been locked from the inside. There is a window, but it was closed, and locked, as well."

"It sounds like something C. Auguste Dupin might face," I remarked. At mention of Poe's fictional character, Holmes's lip curled with an expression of disdain.

"I came to you," he said, casting aside my statement, "because once you have eliminated all that is impossible, then whatever remains, no matter how improbable, must be the truth. And when the improbable is impossible, then one must assume it falls into the purview of your unusual talents."

"When the improbable is impossible, it must then be magical," I said.

The hansom stopped and Holmes lithely jumped down, hastily checking both sides of the street, an act I suspect borne of habit. He gestured me out, and I'm sure had he a blanket, it would have been draped over my head. I suppressed a brilliant witticism as we approached the front door, where we were met not by a porter, but by a large individual with a massive brow and steely gaze. Although his stature was greater, and his hair lighter than Holmes, the resemblance was unmistakable. This was his older brother, Mycroft.

"Peter Styles?" he asked. "My God, Sherlock, why didn't you just fetch along that Scot who claims to float in and out windows?"

"I told you I would be trying something unorthodox," Holmes said. His tone ended debate on the subject, and Mycroft showed surrender by offering me his hand. I accepted it and a wash of impressions roiled into my consciousness. Like Sherlock, he had met the same unusual energy, but he knew nothing apart from a sense of urgency over the matter; the dead man had been important, someone working in the government. Mycroft's thick brows lowered into a deep frown, and he pulled out of my grip.

"Very well." Mycroft pinched the bridge of his nose and spoke with a tone of authority and importance. "I will escort you to the scene, and then after Mr. Styles performs whatever mystic act he does, we will head for The Strangers' Room. I have to ask that you refrain from any conversation outside that designated area."

"Imposed silence. The horror," I said.

Holmes almost managed to suppress a smile.

"You deserve one another," muttered Mycroft.

Entering the club, I was assaulted by an enormous domed atrium, the floor Italian marble. A dark red carpet ran up a flight of stairs where a bust of Diogenes gazed down upon us, his sculpted features possibly reflecting ironic amusement of being in the presence of the wealthy and powerful.

We passed along a hall, and I paused beside an enormous library, books on all walls, shelves from floor to ceiling. A few men sat at tables with green baize surfaces, while others reclined in comfortable chairs, most of them with books on their laps. Some were even reading. I recognized a few of the gentlemen here, and noted Merrick Cain, a man as unpopular as I was. However, his unpopularity stemmed not from bad behaviour, but bad politics, and perhaps that was worse.

Cain and I had exchanged insults when last we encountered one another. My verbal attacks were quite pithy, but since I had been drunk and slurred my words, the best of my banter was lost on him.

As one of the club rules was to avoid taking note of anyone, I turned away, quick to catch up with the Holmes brothers, who stood waiting for me. We continued, without a sound, down a hall of more busts and ornately framed paintings. We passed a billiards room, and then a room where gentlemen sat in leather chairs, many drinking tea and reading early editions of the morning newspapers.

We advanced up a back stair. Mycroft stopped outside a thick wood door and pushed it open. He gave us a knowing look and gestured for us to enter, leaving me with the feeling that I now had permission to perform, like a trained hound.

I approached, stuck my head across the threshold, glanced at a wall painted sensible tan, turned on my heel, and left, to proceed down the stairs, out of the front door and into the waiting cab. The Holmes brothers followed, Mycroft with an expression of indignation and Holmes looking amused.

"Definitely magic," I said.

"You didn't even enter," Mycroft sputtered.

"Technically he put his toe across the threshold," Holmes said.

"Ridiculous," Mycroft argued. "He's mocking us."

"As you will," I said. "I'm going home."

Mycroft addressed his brother: "I don't dispute the possibility of the paranormal, but be reasonable, Sherlock."

The Great Detective ignored him and asked for my observations.

I collected my thoughts. "If you go to the far wall of the room, you will find minute stress cracks in the plaster. About three feet from the floor."

"I noted them," Holmes agreed.

"The presence of magic created those stress marks," I said. "More specifically, they are the result of a portal manifesting. The stress is caused by the intersection of two realities. The presence I felt was masculine, and the magic brutish, forceful, not at all the sort of action taken by an educated practitioner who respects the arcane. He is not an intellectual, but he knows enough to manipulate raw power."

"You have that ability," Holmes said.

"I do."

"Then you should be a match for one another."

The Adventure of the Russian Mystic by Stewart Sternberg

I peered up at the Diogenes Club and sensed the uneasiness the building projected, the collective weight of knowledge and responsibility. What dreariness, within and without.

"This is only prelude, isn't it?" I asked. "You've both been actors, but what is the play?"

Holmes looked at Mycroft, with a satisfied grin. "You see? He's a valuable resource despite himself."

"My blushes, Holmes." I said.

My friend placed a hand on his brother's arm. "Now, tell him."

"Are you sure?"

"He needs to hear it all. It is what we agreed upon."

Mycroft cast a glance at the Diogenes Club, then back at me. I had the distinct impression his hesitation was feigned. At last he spoke: "The information I'm about to impart is secret, and I trust you'll keep it in confidence. This is a very grave situation."

He lowered his voice and stepped closer. A hint of brandy lingered on his breath. "The dead man was a Russian diplomat, here to lay the groundwork for an agreement with Britain to end our Great Game."

"Asia," I remarked. I wasn't keen on politics, but I knew that tensions over the competing spheres of influence between Russia and Britain had again made the newspapers.

"We must stop escalation," Mycroft said. "We don't have the stomach or the resources for continued struggle in the Orient, although our interests there are precious. No, we need instead to give Europe our attention."

"So, someone is interested in preventing further accords with Russia," I said.

"Our two countries have an opportunity to forge an agreement, and if we can do that, it is our hope it will become the foundation for further treaties. War is costly for the Empire, and our colonial interests are strained these days—"

Holmes interrupted. "The dead man's name was Boris Lvov. He was attacked from behind, strangled by a knotted handkerchief left at the scene of the crime. When I examined the area, I also saw those fractures you noted. They were rather localized, and not the result of a concussion, which might have given us evidence of a struggle. Extreme temperature changes might affect paint like that, or perhaps some sort of electrical discharge. However, there was no evidence of charring. I noted, too, grime on the rug. Footprints made by someone in mid-stride, but they could only have been made by someone emerging from the next room."

"Neat trick without a door," I noted. My flippancy was a cover for my growing worry about what they were going to ask me to do. They didn't understand magic, the danger it posed, and the sacrifice it required.

"We believe it was the work of Dmitri Pressoff," Holmes said. "That knotted handkerchief is his trademark. He left it to mock us. This is the second murder. The first was another member of the political class."

I pressed my hand to my chest. "Why would anyone harbour malice against a politician?"

"Don't be droll," Mycroft said.

The power necessary for a creating a portal like the one Pressoff must have used was frightening. I didn't know Dmitri Pressoff — not that I knew everyone claiming membership in metaphysical society, but someone with this ability might have made an impression.

Creating a portal so exactly that it opened within feet of a target, that was more than impressive, and it meant the presence of a locator, an object acting as a magical beacon. I explained this, watching Mycroft's shoulders sag while his facial muscles tightened.

"The handkerchief wasn't just the murder weapon," I said. "I believe it was also the locator. I'm sure of it. Someone either left it in the room ahead of time or planted it on him earlier."

"Good God," Mycroft said. "I can just see how such a revelation will read in a report to the Prime Minister. 'The Russian Diplomat, Boris Lvov, was strangled by an enchanted handkerchief.' Oh, yes, that will be received nicely."

Holmes lowered his head and spoke with great gravity, "You know this means we have a traitor among us. Someone who is either able to enchant the item himself, or someone who obtained it from our killer."

Holmes's statement stabbed his brother, who winced and gave curt nod. "We suspected as much," he said. "A member of the club."

"Perhaps not," I said. "Couldn't the handkerchief have been planted on the victim elsewhere?"

"Perhaps without his knowing?" Holmes produced his own handkerchief, twirled it about his finger, and palmed it with the skill of an expert prestidigitator.

"What a superb criminal you would make," Mycroft quipped. He frowned at the night sky, and then spoke in a tired voice. "We must remain open to all possibilities. Supposition is worthless in court."

"The Diogenes is an establishment unmistakably linked with members of the government." Holmes frowned. "A stain on The Diogenes is a stain on Britain."

"Lvov wouldn't have been a member of the club," I said. "Who invited him as a guest?"

"Merrick Cain," Mycroft said after a moment's thought.

Indeed. My ego suffered a moment's irritation. "You deliberately led me past him earlier," I said. "How disingenuous of you. There's no doubt that the two of you came from the same seed."

"Don't be petulant."

"I don't like being led," I said. "I wager when the murder occurred Cain was nowhere nearby."

"You would win that wager," said Mycroft.

"But since Cain invited Lvov, doesn't that throw suspicion on him?" I asked.

"Cain is an esteemed member."

Merrick Cain. He was handsome, with thick black hair and a strong, expressive brow. He entered a room and took control. What a pompous, conceited, selfish, acerbic, self-absorbed, grandiose fraud.

"Why not just pick up this Russian mystic? Pressoff?" I asked. "Question him. Give him to the Yard."

Holmes and Mycroft exchanged an annoying expression of superiority with one another. "Because Mr. Pressoff is in Pentonville Prison," Mycroft said.

Hearing of that place again deflated my spirit; Oscar Wilde's soul died in that vile hole.

"We would be hard-pressed accusing Pressoff of the murders, then," Sherlock said.

"Or Cain."

Holmes agreed, but added: "Cain has been in financial straits for some time, but apparently he recently had a streak of good fortune. All his debts are paid off. I understand his purse has grown heavy."

I sat back and folded my arms across my chest, looking first at Mycroft, then at Holmes. I understood then the path plotted out. I reviewed all that had preceded this moment in their little well-choreographed melodrama.

I hated the Holmes brothers.

"Well, I'm sure you have a plan," I said.

"Now you that you mention it," Mycroft said. "We do indeed."

*****

I stood in the lobby of a well-known hotel and sought the courage necessary for what was to come.

I spied Dr. John Watson sitting in a chair, reading a copy of The Strand. He was nervous, his thoughts touching upon a female toward whom he was developing fond feelings. I envied him.

"You there!" I called out. I pulled a revolver from my coat, and I pointed it at Watson.

He stood, raising his arms in a supplicant manner. I wasn't sure what to say next, but when in doubt, fall back on Shakespeare. "You peasant swain! You whoreson malt horse drudge! How loathsome and foul is thy image!"

Holmes glared at me from across the room; apparently, not a devotee of the theatre. I fired three times. Several people screamed; many began making their way for the doors. Watson grabbed his chest and dropped; his shirt now stained red from previously placed packets of paint. I knew he was having trouble keeping a smile from his lips.

Inspector Gregory of Scotland Yard, who just happened to be in the lobby, leaning against a wall, aimed a finger in my direction. "Grab that man!"

Holmes charged, threw his arms around my chest and drove me to the floor. He used unnecessary force, in my opinion, and seemed to enjoy his role far too much.

That is how I ended up within the walls of Pentonville, a relatively modern prison created to be humane but succeeding only in more effectively crushing the spirit. The cold establishment was designed with five arms radiating from a central area from which security could be efficiently maintained. Prisoners were isolated from one another, and like the Diogenes Club, communication was forbidden.

Although better lit than a dungeon, the prison still managed a gloominess that stamped down hope and other emotions that made survival tolerable. Some of its brick walls were painted, and some not, and the odour of human waste and lye permeated the atmosphere.

Even knowing my stay here would be brief, and that if I truly wished to leave, I could, I nonetheless entered confinement with growing dread. It went against everything in my nature. I passed several prisoners, and all of them carried the same anger and humiliation, the same crushing sense of loss. Even the guards seemed infected; at best they were indifferent, and at worst, they drew some satisfaction from their station.

I was given a uniform of loose-fitting hemp, dyed in black and white stripes; it not only itched, but the material resonated with the personality of its former owner, a recently executed Irishman who killed his mother, and well she deserved it. He also buggered and killed a handful of young boys, but their murders remained uninvestigated. The pious turned a blind eye in their attempt to remain aloof from the undercurrents that tainted the lie of civilized society.

"You can do this," Holmes had said. He gripped my shoulder and gave me the sort of sincere encouragement one has when sending someone to his death.

"We will make sure that information is spread that a new agent has been secured for negotiations with the Russians. It will sound as though our relationship with Russia is strained to breaking, and that this is a last desperate attempt for us. Word will be put out that our man will be off for an unspecified location in a day. It will force the traitor to act within that short window of time. Once he places his locator with the intended victim, we'll have proof of complicity. And when Pressoff makes his appearance, and you shut the portal behind him, then we'll have the two snared in our trap."

Holmes and Mycroft would owe me for this, never mind my patriotism for Queen and Country.

The Adventure of the Russian Mystic by Stewart Sternberg

"And you will be able to close the portal behind him. Correct?" Mycroft asked.

"I can disrupt it."

Holmes waved a hand. "But you can do that once he passes through the portal?"

Theoretically, that was correct. I nodded.

"We will have him red-handed then."

"I don't like it though," I said. I kept the growing anxiousness from my voice, but they were astute enough to read it in my posture and subtle movements.

"We'll have guards watching you," Holmes said. His tone was compassionate. "Mycroft won't let you come to any harm."

"That's not it," I said. "It's the magic of it. Reaching through realities, reaching through space and time, and then tampering with something someone else has constructed. Magic is personal. It's an extension of one's own will."

"Well, if you can't do it..." Holmes said.

"You've done it before," snapped Mycroft.

"Not like this," I said. "I'll be tapping into energies, manipulating them, finessing power. Pressoff doesn't need to do that. He just exerts himself."

"Then all the more reason we need to stop him."

Mycroft dismissed the tension in the air. "You'll enter prison under the blanket of a charade; we don't want any suspicion. I've already set things in motion, so the trap for Cain should reach fruition that very night!"

"And if not that night?"

"Then the night after."

"And... if not?"

Mycroft showed signs of irritation. "Why not just consult your precognition?"

"Yes, I suppose that would be more reliable than your deductive reasoning and illusory manipulations."

"Ass."

The Adventure of the Russian Mystic by Stewart Sternberg

I flashed a winning smile, but it was a shallow display of fortitude. Holmes brought both his brother and myself back to business. "I have faith in you, Peter."

"Once we have Pressoff, then what about Cain?" I asked.

"Leave that to me. Cain will fall with Pressoff."

"There is much at stake here, Mr. Styles," Mycroft intoned. "I pray you are up to this. Sherlock feels you are."

"I shan't disappoint," I said, and managed not to laugh.

Perhaps after this affair ended, I could go abroad for a time. Offend new people in a new land. America came to mind.

*****

Time passed, and I shielded myself from Pentonville's depressing atmosphere. Meditation helped, but as night approached, my uneasiness heightened. The desperation of those around me increased, and their torment pierced my guard. My abilities sometimes made me too vulnerable to the many emotions of those we encounter through the course of a day. How did Pressoff tolerate this environment?

He could leave at any time but chose incarceration; I sensed not just as alibi, but as a statement, that he didn't suffer the same as the rest of us, and that prison bars were of no consequence. Or could it be he didn't stay here night after night or day after day, but instead created an empty doppelganger as a ruse while leaving the prison? I had seen a Hindu holy man achieve such a feat.

No, that would be a complex spell, and I had already established he didn't practice the magic arts as such. What if he could pull it off by just force of will? I dismissed that. If he had such power, why hadn't he just used magic as a weapon? Because a physical threat would be one the Russians would understand and accept; one they would see as a possible betrayal, or a complexity that made a political agreement difficult, especially in the tense political atmosphere currently gripping Europe.

I lit a small candle left me by Mycroft.

With reluctance, I set to preparations. First, I drew a pentagram by the wall shared with Pressoff's cell, and then sprinkled salt at protection points. I took a deep breath, feeling the old excitement, and then the trepidation of channelling such dangerous forces. I opened my mind and directed power into the pentagram and circle surrounding me, infusing them with my will, and then as an extra precaution, one I had not taken since abandoning my necromantic practices, I scraped my arm against a jagged spot of the stone wall until I bled. I let blood trickle into the centre of the defensive circle.

Blood committed life energies to magic, magnifying its properties.

I paused, drawing the courage to continue. I had been cautious with magic these last few years, afraid of what waited in the shadows, in the impossible corners of night. Recent past explorations had left a negative mark on me and left to my own devices; I might have continued exploring the theories of magic rather than the practice.

I thought of Pressoff and his fearlessness in powering through the ether.

When arriving at the prison I tried communicating with him as they marched us along for exercise, but the guards discouraged contact, and Pressoff himself ignored my attempts. He was a huge man, a monster with broad shoulders, and a face that looked as if it had been formed by haphazardly chipping away at rock until semi-human features formed. He had coarse hair, close-cropped, and a wild black beard. His teeth appeared rotten. Perhaps his dental situation was at the root of his unfavourable disposition, though I doubted it.

The other prisoners seemed afraid of Pressoff. I was afraid of Pressoff.

Closing my eyes, I saw him as he sat in his cell now, legs folded lotus style, palms against palm, breathing slow and steady. The calmness of his meditation was contagious, and several minutes passed before I broke contact.

My guard slipped for a minute and the prison's darkness touched me. The sorrow, the anger, the bitterness that accompanied hopelessness. The horror of monotony, without let up until the mind could no longer bear it. I had always looked at my abilities through a glass coloured by potential, but now my vision seemed corrupted by limits.

The first hint of change came with the bitterness of an ozone smell, and this was followed by the hairs along my arms raising. Pressoff was working his spell. I shivered, and then I placed my forehead against the brick and cleared my mind, my ritual before attempting magic. "*Vide telam. Tange in virtute,*" I whispered. "*Aperi ante portas.*"

The words let me reach within myself. I touched the threads of power spinning around me and saw Pressoff's magic, a sloppy club pounding the energies into submission.

A crackling ripped through the ceiling, and I fought back my anxiety. Magic demanded complete commitment, not the hesitation of someone unsure of himself. I gritted my teeth and pressed against the brick separating me from the Russian.

Disrupting his spell would be easier than creating one of my own, but it would all be in the timing. I listened to the energies around me like a cracksman listening to the tumblers of a safe.

The portal opened.

Pressoff stepped through.

I started working my web, weaving energies until they touched the magic energies conjured by Pressoff.

"Won't you be shocked when you look up and see Mycroft and members from the Yard waiting for you?" I said. And wouldn't it be a stunner when he turned to flee and found his portal gone? A neat plan.

An inner voice whispered for me to act. With a shudder I closed my fist and twisted the stream.

"There you go," I said.

The portal didn't behave as expected, and the surprise made me laugh, but not with joy. I had been too eager or waited too long before gathering magic to counter him. Of course, I had. Thank God I added my blood to the protective circle. No matter what transpired now, I needed to anchor myself.

As if pulling the reins of a runaway horse, I dug my heels into the floor and resisted the pull. I didn't want to let the Holmes brothers down, nor did I want this brute who had no appreciation for his gift to abuse it. I drew upon whatever ability I could claim and clutched the stream, twisting it, trying to shut it down at this end.

A flash of white and...

"Oh, blazes," I said. "Damn! Damn, damn, damn."

Instead of closing the portal, I had passed through it. Stupid luck, that. I should have anticipated it.

"I swear I left the handkerchief with the target," someone said. I was in a room, standing against a wall as I had been standing in the prison. A candle burned on a nearby table, and I saw it was a study, with a writing desk and several bookshelves. The wall in front of me was adorned by an old painting of an aristocratic family and my handprints, singed into the wallpaper.

"Something is wrong," another person said, and I recognized Pressoff's deep growl.

"Look, it is here in my pocket, but I don't know how it got there! I swear I placed it."

"You don't play trick."

"No, Dimitri. I don't know what happened. I must have somehow placed the wrong handkerchief and kept one of the ones you gave me by mistake."

Silence. I knew Pressoff had gestured for an end to conversation, that he had sensed something else was wrong. He would turn and see his portal closed, and if he reached out, he would feel me in the other room, and sense my growing anxiousness.

What could I do to protect myself from a magical attack, presuming the Russian still had enough energy to pose a threat? I traced a symbol in the air, concentrating on defence, drawing on my own reserves. I didn't have much time.

Cain stepped into the study, the large Russian behind him. I didn't need those defensive spells; they would do no good against the Belgian Bulldog revolver in Cain's hand.

"He was in the prison," Pressoff said.

"Peter Styles," Cain said. His arrogant manner bordered the preternatural. He had a reputation for charm that I had never seen.

"Who is he?"

"A fop and a card cheat," Cain said.

"Not always," I protested.

Pressoff rubbed his chin and grinned, his face uglier for it. "You are magic?" the Russian asked. "You followed me here to challenge me, yes? You are magic man?"

"Not in the least. I didn't follow you here, it was a mistake. An accident."

The situation obviously struck Dimitri as one of hilarity, for he threw back his head and bellowed. "You are boy!"

Cain didn't share his compatriot's mirth. "This has all gone to hell, Dimitri. But we can get still get away."

The Bulldog aimed at my heart, and I prepared for the discharge and final blackness. The Russian had other ideas; he pushed Cain aside.

"Not like that," he said. "Magic Man, stand your ground."

He held out a hand and sent a wave of power in my direction, a thickness that would enter my lungs and drown me. Only it didn't. Instead, it dissipated. While I might be standing here physically, magically, I was still linked to the blood infused pentagram in the cell at Pentonville and would remain so for as long as I didn't sever myself from its protection. And I had no intention of doing so.

Pressoff crept closer, eyes brightening at the challenge.

You had to like him.

I learned something in that moment that the Russian didn't realize — he was dying. Magic sought balance. Without manipulating the energies with care, artfully directing them, one subjected oneself to the consequences. He exerted his will with natural ability, but without the knowledge that would protect him.

Pressoff again sent magic my way, and this time the air crackled as the thrust interacted with the pentagram. His face darkened with the strain of battling through my defences and I closed my eyes, seeking calm, finding the concentration necessary for strengthening my protections. The strands disturbed by Pressoff's magic whipped about like snakes seeking a target, but I guided them back into balance.

"Good," Pressoff said. His face had a greyish shade, and his voice lacked the vigour of a few minutes ago. He was spent. I wasn't sure how I had withstood the attack but thanked those long hours of study that I had before rued as avoiding the practice of the arcane. Balance.

"Once more?" he asked. But it was an empty statement, he had no strength left. I shook my head, and he returned my gesture with a nod of respect and acquiescence.

"Enough!"

Cain came forward, arm raised, and fired his Bulldog. The slug struck my chest and I stumbled back, leaving the area of protection. Another shot went off, but this one was wide. Pressoff had his arm around Cain's neck and was choking him.

Dark spots danced about my field of vision, and I sought something to lean against, but instead knocked over a chair, and joined it on the floor. Breathing was difficult, and I knew I was seconds from passing out. From the other room came the sound of wood splintering and voices raised in alarm. More shouting, and I recognized Holmes's voice, calling for Watson.

"Come on, Styles, don't close your eyes."

I couldn't resist the velvety blackness and surrendered to it.

*****

When I awoke, I recognized that I was in a hospital room, and felt a sense of sadness as well as a loss. I shut my eyes, and slept again, but when I once more came to my senses, Holmes and Dr. Watson stood by my bed, engaged in a quiet discussion about people whose names I didn't recognize. They both fell silent when the realized I was sentient.

"My dear Styles," Holmes began. He put out a hand and squeezed my shoulder. "We were worried about you."

"The bullet should have done more damage," Watson said. "You were fortunate."

"My heart?" I asked.

"It entered your chest here and nicked a lung. We'll keep you until we're sure you're free of infection. We live in a marvellous time. Ten years ago, maybe even five, and you might have died."

He sounded cheerful.

"What I'd like to know, is why you followed Pressoff into the portal?" Holmes asked. He sounded piqued, and his tone irritated me.

"Not now," Watson interjected.

The Adventure of the Russian Mystic by Stewart Sternberg

"And I'd like to know why you put that handkerchief in Cain's pocket," I said. I had no intention of letting Holmes know my following Pressoff had been unintentional.

"By trapping both rats in the same room, we had them cold. As long as you closed the portal behind him."

"I closed the portal," I said.

"But you were on the wrong side."

We fell silent, the rhythm of our discussion serving its purpose, putting us back in comfortable footing. I almost smiled.

"What of Cain?" I asked.

"Dead. Pressoff strangled him."

"And Pressoff?"

"He died as well," Holmes said. "Although Dr. Watson was unable to fathom any medical reason for his demise. I was hoping you would fill in the blanks for us. What happened? Why did you pursue Pressoff? Why did Pressoff kill Cain? We heard two gunshots. That's when we charged in. I assume Pressoff ruined Cain's second shot. A good thing, considering the damage of the first. It is remarkable you are still alive."

I shut my eyes and nodded.

"Well? What can you tell us? What happened in that room?"

Poor Pressoff. He was a brute and a killer, and he had never appreciated what power he had at his hands. Or maybe he did.

"A dreamer is one who can find his way by moonlight," I said.

Holmes waited, but impatience showed in his posture and the set of his jaw.

"Do you know his punishment?" I asked. "He sees the dawn before the rest of the world."

"Why isn't that his reward?" Watson asked, and his question made Holmes grit his teeth. My laughter came out as a wheeze.

Holmes stepped away from the bed and grabbed a cane and hat resting on a nearby chair. He put the hat upon his head and tapped the cane upon the floor.

"Are you leaving?" Watson sounded astonished.

"I know Styles. He's not giving us anything else. We'll have to be satisfied that scandal has been averted and the criminals are no longer a threat. We know Cain's reasons were financial, although Pressoff is still a mystery to me. But his motivations are no longer pertinent."

Holmes strode to the door and stopped. "Heal quickly, Styles. Remember though, dreams are nothing but the children of an idle brain, begot of nothing but vain fantasy."

And having quoted Shakespeare, he was gone.

The Case of the Manchester Mummies

by Davide Mana

"If you don't mind, Watson," Holmes said, walking briskly in my study, "I need to borrow a book."

The maid helplessly followed him, carrying his hat and trying to get hold of his coat. She gave me a desperate look.

Dismissing poor Evelyn, I stood and turned to stare at my old friend, who was already browsing the shelves of my medical library, as if it were a second hand books stall in Cecil Court, and not my rooms in Queen Anne Street. He caressed the backs of the volumes with his first and second finger.

"Do you have a specific title in mind," I asked, not without a certain amusement, "or at least a subject?"

While we no longer shared the apartment in Baker Street, we still cherished the opportunity of spending some time together, for a dinner or a theatre, and Holmes still treated my house and my study as an extension of his apartment.

He turned to me. "I am looking for your copy of Davidson's Hygiene & Diseases of Warm Climates."

"Third shelf from the bottom," I said.

Holmes gave a satisfied exclamation as he slipped the massive volume from its place. "I hope you don't mind," he said, opening the book and running his finger along the index.

"Of course not," I said in turn. My friend was in his habitual state of over-excitement, a sure sign his brain had latched on some gratifying problem. "But would you care to tell me what you are seeking — there are more up to date books than Davidson's, you see." He did not appear to be listening to me. I squinted at him. "Is this for a case?" I feel no shame to admit I had been missing my involvement in my friend's investigations.

"What? Yes, a case, of course. Unusual, confusing at first, but now — ah! You mentioned some better reference work? I only have Johnson's book, in my collection—" he waved a hand in the air, frowning. "The Influence of Tropical Climates on European Constitutions. Fascinating work, but not exactly current, if you know what I mean." He stared at me like it was the first time he saw me. "Which of course you do, you being a doctor."

I laughed. "Same shelf," I pointed. "Manson's Tropical Diseases. Is there any way I could help you? Being, as you so kindly remembered, a doctor?"

Holmes unceremoniously dropped Davidson's book on the floor and picked up Manson's, and again checked the index.

"I see you last used this book six months ago, in the case of a young boy suffering from what appeared to be Mediterranean Fever," he said, his eyes still on the page. "In Belgravia. Only it was not, wasn't it—? Mediterranean Fever, I mean."

"No, it was—" I stopped and stared at him. "By Jove, Holmes," I ejaculated in exasperation, "what is this all about?"

He smiled at me. "It's really a trifle," he said.

The clock on the mantelpiece chimed in that moment.

"What about you telling me over dinner?" I said.

*****

The Case of the Manchester Mummies by Davide Mana

"Two months ago," Holmes said, "I received a visit from a woman."

He let Evelyn remove his plate, and then he intertwined his hands, his elbows over the table.

"Miss Angela Eakersley is in her early forties, unmarried. Strong features, straight nose, a decisive deportment that masks a rather romantic temperament. She is the sole heir of Eakersley & Burns, the renowned cotton works in Manchester."

I admitted I was not familiar with the company, but Holmes waved the thought away. "Her family's business," he went on, "owns a vast stretch of land in the Delta, where cotton is grown. Because of this, ever since a young age Miss Eakersley had the opportunity to visit Egypt, and is still in the habit of spending at least part of the year there. She usually travels with a younger companion, a Miss Brock. She owns a villa outside of Cairo, as well as a mansion in the outskirts of Manchester, and an apartment in London. Recently returned from her last trip in the land of the Pharaohs, Miss Eakersley came to see me hoping I would be interested in looking into the emancipation of her luggage."

"Emancipation?"

"A minor matter. I found little to attract me in what was presented as a simple case of a Continental bravo, trying to steal from a steamer trunk in Marseilles. The French have a police force for dealing with such accidents, and I said so to the lady, even providing her with the name and address of some colleagues of mine in southern France."

"So you refused the case."

Holmes's expression hardened. "So I did, and I can assure you I was as courteous and kind to the poor woman as the circumstances dictated."

"Of this I had no doubt," I said. I knew my friend could be harsh at times, but never on purpose, and I prided myself with having instilled in him a modicum of patience for the failings of the common people during the years we spent in Baker Street.

"In the following weeks," Holmes went on, "I heard twice again from Miss Eakersley — once in person and once by way of a long letter. It seems the matter with the luggage was just the first of a series of disturbances whose gravity increased over time, gravely spoiling the lady's piece of mind. On our second encounter she appeared perturbed and nervous.

"She had an encounter with a gentleman of the Egyptian persuasion, she told me, that much perturbed her. Of course I did look into that, post-haste. I called on Wiggins — I think you remember him. He's a grown man now, and working for one of the evening rags. He traced a Mahoud Hakimi to a small hotel by Marylebone, but when we got there he had left already."

"What did this ruffian want with Miss Eakersley?" I asked.

"Ah!" Holmes clicked his tongue. "But we are not talking 'ruffian' at all. A Doctor Mahoud Hakimi is a lecturer at the University of Cairo, and appears to be the same man that confronted Miss Eakersley."

We moved to the fireplace, where I poured a measure of brandy for the both of us.

"As for the reason why Doctor Hakimi approached Miss Eakersley," Holmes said accepting a glass, "it is easy to say."

He sipped the liquor.

"A romantic young woman, Miss Eakersley was captivated by the mysteries of the ancient Egyptian empire through her frequent stays in the land." Holmes explained. "After she inherited her family's business, she helped funding various excavation campaigns, in some of which she was invited to participate. She knows Professor Flinders Petrie personally."

I went back and sat on the other leather chair.

"In her passion for all things Egyptian," Holmes said, "Miss Eakersley turned her house into a veritable museum. She has collected through the years a wealth of ancient artefacts, including pottery and jewellery, and also the odd mummy or two. And for a while, she hosted unwrapping parties for the dubious delight and modest edification of the Mancunian elites."

I had a certain familiarity with the bizarre practice of exposing the dead body of some poor Egyptian scribe or priest thousands of years dead, and if, as a medical professional, I could admit to a certain curiosity, the idea of the mummified body being poked and examined by amateurs as they sipped claret and ate sandwiches made me cringe.

"Many of these things, I am sure, she imported by—" my friend snorted in amusement, "let us say by sidestepping the official regulations."

"You mean contraband?" I asked.

"That's probably too rough a word. The Egyptian authorities are after all somewhat absent-minded in their duty to protect the past of their country, and it would not be difficult, considering the large volume of cotton bales and other goods travelling between the port of Alexandria and the Manchester seat of Eakersley & Burns, to slip a few crates of antiques through the customs."

"You think that it was because of this that her luggage was interfered with?" I asked. "Someone was looking for the loot?"

Holmes arched his eyebrows. "It is not impossible," he conceded. "For certain, Doctor Hakimi went to see Miss Eakersley about some artefacts, and demanded their restitution, claiming the papyri and the jewellery belong in a museum."

"It is quite understandable."

"It is indeed. And yet it seems that our zealous doctor exceeded on the side of—" he waved a hand, "shall we say folklore?"

I stared at Holmes, uncomprehending. He took a letter from the inside pocket of his coat. "Miss Eakersley mentions the sensation of being spied upon. Strange noises. The suspicion that someone broke into her London apartment, and later in Eakersley Hall. Even vaguer things, again not the sort of events that would grant an investigation, but ones which caused in her a growing sense of doom, as she wrote to me one week after leaving the Capital."

He handed me the letter.

Miss Eakersley's hand was nervous and angular. She had highlighted certain words, and one in particular was always underscored with two lines. That word was 'curse'.

I looked at my friend, his sharp features outlined in the dancing light of the fireplace. "But you are certainly not going to investigate, what, some supernatural occurrence? Some Curse of the Pharaohs?"

Holmes smiled without mirth. "You know my methods, Watson. I do not care for the supernatural. And indeed, it is not this letter that piqued my interest, for all the obvious human misery it conveys, but something that happened five days ago, and that has been tugging at the strings of my mind, so to speak, ever since. It was another letter, this time from Miss Eakersley's attorney, a man by the name of Jarvis Trent. He explained that, such is the distress she has been suffering, she is often in a state of physical exhaustion. He therefore asked me to refrain from writing to her, or further upset her, and requested that all further communications be directed to him."

"And that finally explains your need for the book about tropical diseases," I exclaimed, as I suddenly saw the case perfectly outlined in front of me.

"You think the visions and—" I huffed, "disturbances the woman mentions might be caused by some exotic ailment, a brain fever from the mosquito-infested banks of the Nile. Some sort of malaria, that now has her confounded. Miss Eakersley often travels to the Delta, you said. And the timing — two months would fit with the incubation time of a Nile fever of some kind. What we are dealing with might not be a criminal case at all, but just an unusual medical occurrence."

"Excellent, my dear Watson," Holmes said.

"It would not be unheard of."

"But what of the emancipation of the luggage?" he asked. "What of Doctor Hakimi?"

I shrugged. "As you said, some Gallic bravo, the event totally unrelated with the Egyptian professor. Certainly the encounter with this man Hakimi, and his babbling of ghosts or whatever might have contributed to colouring the perceptions of the poor woman, already befuddled by illness."

"A brilliant reconstruction," Holmes admitted.

"I had a very good teacher," I said, not with a certain pride.

"And yet your explanations leaves one problem unsolved," he said, raising a finger. "To wit, who it was that broke into Eakersley Hall last night, leaving poor Miss Brock —the companion, you'll remember — in such a state of shock that she has been unable to answer any question for the police?"

I stared at him, my mouth open. "What?"

"As reported in this morning edition of the Manchester Herald," he added. "As you see, coming to a conclusion based on partial information is never a good practice, my friend."

We were silent for a long moment.

"I imagine this means we are going to Manchester," I finally said.

"There's a train at midnight from St Pancras," he nodded.

*****

The early light of a cold October morning dawned as a lugubrious butler let us into the cave-like entrance hall of the Eakersley estate. I looked around, making sure my mouth was not hanging open in surprise. The building, on the outside rather anonymously Palladian, was on the inside a true monument to ancient Egypt. The columns that flanked the wide staircase to the upper floors were shaped like the pillars of the temples found along the course on the Nile, and painted in the bright colours of those ancient monuments. On our right, a tall statue of a woman with a lion's head looked down upon us, her arms crossed over her chest holding two crooked sceptres. In front of her on the other side of the hall, another sculpture, of a man with a long-beaked bird's head stood impassively, one foot forward, leaning on a long staff.

We were expected, and the butler led us to the parlour.

Angela Eakersley looked older than her forty-two years, silver strands already evident in her chestnut hair. Her face was pale and drawn, dark circles under her eyes. She was sitting on a couch, wringing her hands in her lap, tormenting a lace kerchief. At the sight of Holmes she gasped, and stood, and came towards us.

"Mister Holmes!"

He bowed to her. "Miss Eakersley, allow me to introduce my colleague, doctor John Watson."

Her eyes were the same pale chestnut as her hair. "Doctor Watson, yes, of course," she said.

Holmes helped her back to her couch, and we sat with her.

"It's been terrible," she said, "terrible. That man—"

"What man?" asked Holmes softly, glancing at me. I had my notebook ready.

"That horrible Egyptian, the man in a fez—"

"The one you met in London?" Holmes asked, frowning.

"Yes!" she hissed. "He was here, two days ago."

"You mean the day before the breaking in?" Holmes said. "Are you sure of this?"

"Of course I am sure!" she snapped. It was easy to see that underneath the fatigue and the fear was a woman that was in the habit of wielding a certain authority.

"You saw him? Here in Eakersley Hall?"

"Jarvis — Mister Trent talked to him. It was a short unpleasant visit. He will be able to tell you—"

"Can you relate the events as they happened?" Holmes asked.

"I don't know—"

"We actually have a fair idea of what happened," said a voice from by the parlour door. Three men stood there. One was in his sixties; he carried a doctor's bag and had that mournful countenance that are a trademark of the old family practitioner. The one that had spoken was younger, with a shock of red hair and thick handlebar moustache.

"Mister Holmes, eh?" he said, coming forward, and offering his hand. "Jobson. Inspector. Manchester Police. Never would have imagined meeting you. An honour and all that."

The third man remained silent, and moved to the side of Miss Eakersley. He was in his thirties, with black hair and black piercing eyes. He placed a hand over Miss Eakersley's shoulder, and kept staring at us.

"Been upstairs with Doctor Napier," Jobson went on, nodding at his aged companion. "See how the Brock woman's doing, maybe find a way to ask a few questions."

"Henrietta—?" Miss Eakersley gasped.

"How is Miss Brock?" I asked in turn. Doctor Napier pressed his lips close, and sighed. "I cannot find anything wrong with her physically, but her mind seems to be still in a state of — of flux."

"But now finally the famous Sherlock Holmes is here," the black-haired man said, with a cruel twist of his lips. "And everything will be solved, isn't it so?"

Jobson looked at him, clearly embarrassed.

Miss Eakersley placed her hand over the man's. "Jarvis, please—"

So, as I had suspected, this was the attorney. Holmes ignored his impertinence and turned to Doctor Napier. "Would you mind," he asked affably, "if my friend Doctor Watson sees the lady and offer a second opinion?"

"I don't mean to overstep my position—" I was quick to say, casting a wary glance at Trent, but Napier was more than amenable to the proposal. With the mistress of the house's permission, we went upstairs, leaving Holmes and Jobson with Miss Eakersley.

*****

A maid let us into the patient's room.

Henrietta Brock was a thin woman in her mid-thirties, face framed by dark hair spread on the white pillow. She laid supine on her bed, whispering. A continuous flow of gibberish poured forth from her parched lips, meaningless syllables that momentarily reminded me the mellifluous sounds of some Indian dialect. I looked at Doctor Napier, who shook his head.

"She was found in this state," he said.

I leaned closer.

The room was suffocatingly hot. In the glow of a lone lamp, it felt more like a sepulchre than a bedroom. And yet despite the heat, the sing-song voice of the woman on the bed gave me a shiver.

"Can we air this place?" I asked, approaching the bed.

The maid stood there and looked to Trent, who reassured her I was "a specialist from London".

"Fresh air," I repeated. "And light, please."

The maid pulled the curtains and opened the window a few inches. The cold morning air poured in, and I set out to check the conditions of the patient.

Miss Brock's eyes were open, staring fixedly at the ceiling, the pupils reduced to pinpoints. And the strange words kept coming, like a litany or a prayer.

I placed my hand over her brow, and found her temperature to be normal. Her eyes did not react when I lit a match, the tremulous flame's reflection floating over her glazed stare.

Feeling both the doctor and the maid's eyes on me, I proceeded to take routine observations. The pulse was steady, if a bit slow, her temperature was normal, her breathing regular. There was no visible inflammation of the glands, no breathing difficulties. Nothing about her seemed to indicate anything but a deep slumber, and yet she did not react to any stimuli.

"She's been like this since yesterday night," Doctor Napier said. He glanced at the maid, and said no more.

And still the woman on the bed whispered ceaselessly the same string of unknown words, in a continuous cycle, like some unholy litany.

The maid pulled the curtains closed again as we left the room.

*****

I rejoined Holmes downstairs, and as Doctor Napier sat down with Miss Eakersley, we followed Inspector Jobson to the library.

"As I was saying," the inspector said, "we have a defined idea of the events."

"Indeed," said Holmes.

"But really, it will be a privilege to be able to see you at work, and then compare notes," the policeman said with a wry smile. Holmes did not reply.

Like the rest of Eakersley Hall, the library had been designed like a wing in some museum of Egyptian antiquities. A tall black sarcophagus stood in front of the double-door, its painted eyes fixed on anyone entering the room. By the sides of the double door were two glass cabinets. The one on the right held the sere body of an Egyptian mummy, partially unwrapped, its gaunt features stretched in a mirthless grin, its eyes closed, the arms crossed over its chest. The cabinet on the left had been smashed, shards of glass still hanging to the broken wooden frame.

It was not the only sign of destruction in the room. Books had been pulled off the shelves and strewn on the floor. A table by the couch had been upturned, dislodging the phonograph that had sat on it. The expensive Edison machine rested on its side, the trumpet pointing at the ceiling. One display box on a side table had been broken into and left empty. And one of the French windows leading to the terrace had been broken through. As I walked into the room, the light from the windows caught the glass fragments embedded in the carpet.

"Is everything as it was when you first arrived on the scene?" Holmes asked.

He crouched on the floor and ran his fingers over the carpet. He held a narrow sliver of glass between thumb and forefinger.

"Aye, sir," Jobson replied.

One stuffed chair had been upturned.

"The girl was hiding behind there," Jobson said.

A wooden box, obviously of great antiquity, sat on a table, open. Scrolls were piled by the side. Four clay vases, their tops shaped like animal heads, were aligned on a shelf. More glass cases contained ancient relics, statuettes and painted scrolls had been left undisturbed, except one.

"What are your conclusions?" Holmes asked.

He stood straight and rubbed his fingers against his thumb.

"Well, the thing is pretty straightforward," Jobson said. He pointed at the French door. "The thieves came in from there," he said. "They had a go at the room, looking for valuables. The noise attracted Miss Brock, who came in and caught them in the act. There was a confrontation, and such was the shock poor Miss Brock lost her mind."

Holmes nodded. He stood at the centre of the room, his hands on his hips, and slowly turned around, his keen eyes catching, I was certain, every detail of the scene. "They must have made a lot of noise."

"Quite a racket, I'm sure," Jobson nodded, pulling a notebook from his pocket. "Miss Eakersley confirmed she heard the noises from her room. And the servants, too."

"Any idea of what was stolen?"

"A gold and silver pendant," the inspector went on. He nodded at a damaged display cabinet. "It was kept in there. Quite valuable, I am told."

"Priceless," Mister Trent said. "An ancient necklace, from Tell Nebesheh. It was a personal gift to Miss Eakersley from Professor Petrie."

"And a bunch of papyruses," said Jobson.

"Papyri," Trent corrected him.

"Aye, that," Jobson nodded, paying the attorney little attention. "And then of course, a mummy." He pointed at the smashed cabinet by the door. "Bandages and all."

"Quite a bizarre object to steal, don't you think?" Holmes asked.

Jobson shrugged. "Mister Holmes, sir, we both know some blokes would steal anything. I guess they figured it must be valuable."

Holmes stared at the policeman for a moment. "They had some kind of vehicle waiting for them, obviously."

"Beg your pardon?"

"We are a few miles out of town. Do you imagine these mysterious individuals prancing across the countryside, carrying an Egyptian mummy?"

Jobson laughed. "I did not think about that. I'll have the boys ask around—excellent suggestion, Mister Holmes, sir."

Holmes waved dismissively, and approached the smashed mummy case.

"But we will get the miscreants," Jobson added. "It's not as if he can hide for long in a town like Manchester. We have a description and all."

Holmes turned sharply. "Description?"

"Aye, sir." Jobson looked at Trent. "The thin man in a fez—"

"You mean Doctor Hakimi?" Holmes said. "The one that confronted Miss Eakersley in London?"

"And that you failed to track down, yes," Trent said.

Holmes arched his eyebrows.

"He came here," the attorney went on. "He had some ridiculous story about a curse, and some stolen book or other. He wanted Miss Eakersley to hand back what she had—" he sneered "in his words, stolen from Egypt. He blathered about a curse. Tried to scare me. The cheek of the man!"

"When was this?" Holmes asked.

"Two days ago. I caught him as he was creeping in the garden by the obelisk. He wanted to see Miss Eakersley. I was sure it would not be a good idea, considering how much she had been distressed by their meeting in London. So I talked to him. Right here in this library. I am sure he took mental note of everything."

"But we've got his description," Jobson said, tapping his notebook, "and there's no way an Egyptian in a red fez can disappear up here. We're keeping an eye on the stations and everything. He won't get away."

After we took our leave from Miss Eakersley as she retired to her rooms, I followed Holmes in the gardens. He was in a pensive mood, his eyes on the horizon and head set to a side, the chin slightly up, like a hound smelling his quarry. We walked and soon came by a folly, a pale obelisk that rose like a bony finger towards the leaden sky. Obviously another token of Miss Eakersley's Egyptomania. Holmes stopped there and leaned on the white marble monument for the time required to smoke a cigarette. I knew him too well to try and talk to him when he was in this state of deep concentration, and waited by the side, hands in my pockets, looking at the bleak countryside.

A fine drizzle started falling, and we returned to Manchester, seeking comfort against the cold in a pub.

"What do you make of this whole affair?" I finally asked. We had taken places at a side table.

"Quite a straightforward affair," Holmes said. "Extremely unpleasant, but ultimately commonplace. The facts are plain to see for anyone with a spark of wit. We have a motive, a method, a villain. If only—"

"Inspector Jobson seems convinced he will soon apprehend this mysterious Egyptian, Hakimi," I said.

"A nice young man," Holmes said after a pause. "He has no idea of what he is doing, but hopefully the Mancunian criminal underworld is not beyond his modest detection skills. Sadly there is for him no Egyptian to apprehend."

This took me aback. "You think there is more to the whole matter than it meets the eye?" I asked.

"Did you observe any sign of violence on Miss Eakersley's companion?" he asked.

"Nothing visible, nor did Doctor Napier mention anything. Whatever the problem with the woman may be, it's of a purely mental, and possibly hysterical nature."

"Just as I imagined. Not the reaction one has when meeting some burglars."

"Miss Brock might be a very sensitive and delicate person," I said.

"She might, and yet—"

Again he remained silent for a long moment, his food apparently forgotten.

"There is a single fact in this whole sordid story that still baffles me," he said finally. "And no matter how I try to fit it into the picture, it is out of place. It is disquieting, really, because everything seems to carry me in a direction that is — ah!"

He snorted, irritably.

The rest of our frugal lunch we spent in silence, Holmes's gaze lost in the distance, his fingers turning and twisting a strip of yellowed fabric while his wondrous brain turned the pieces of the puzzle around and around.

"There is no other way!" Holmes exclaimed suddenly, slapping his hand on top of the table, and that did turn a few heads.

We paid for our food and drinks, and went in search of a post office, Holmes needing to send two telegrams.

*****

Later in the afternoon a telegram came in reply, apparently to my friend's satisfaction, and as a consequence we found ourselves waiting on the platform of Manchester Station for the five fifteen train from London, just as the sun set and a chill wind started blowing. Holmes paced the platform nervously, keeping away the biting cold. He had refused to reveal anything to me, as was his wont. After so many years, I said to myself, I should have become used to my friend's mood swings and secretive ways, and yet I could not but feel a pang of irritation.

Then, with much sound and fury, the train came to a stop, and the carriages disgorged their noisy multitude of passengers.

"Ah, fine!" Holmes exclaimed, as he recognised a figure approaching. I stopped and stared, feeling a strange awe.

Through the steam billows that obscured the platform, a woman walked towards us, wrapped from head to toe in a long cloak of a deep maroon. A pale face seemed to float in the shadowed recess of the hood, and she lifted a pale hand, holding a folded telegram.

"You have come," Holmes said.

Her fingers crumpled the paper gently, making a sound like dry leaves. "You are a hard man to deny, Mister Holmes," she replied. There was a hint of amusement in her husky voice. "But you are a more courteous man than your brother."

Then she turned to me. "Doctor Watson, I suppose," she said.

"I am, indeed, Doctor John Watson," I said.

"Please meet Miss Valerie Trelawney," Holmes said. She inclined her head on the side, acknowledging him. "Miss Trelawney is a colleague of sort," Holmes explained, glancing at her, "and she will help us clear the more obscure details of this case."

"Hypothetically," she said. I caught the glint in her eyes, and guessed more than saw an ironic bend of her lips. There was an air of etherealness about her, and surrounded by steam she seemed to glide a few inches above the ground. She offered me a carpet bag, and I blinked and nodded before I took it from her. Its weight brought me back to reality. My friend and the mysterious woman had already started towards the gates of the station.

I helped her climb in the cab, then I joined her and Holmes. He rapped on the top and the we moved, the wheels creaked, the horse's iron-shod hooves resounding on the flagstones as we headed for the suburbs, and the ugly Palladian nightmare that was Eakersley House.

While Holmes briefly brought her up to date on the details of the case, I sat back and discreetly observed our new companion. My idea was to apply Holmes's method, in order to divine her character, and guess why my old friend had requested her presence.

A well-cultured member of the upper class by her voice and manners, I placed Miss Trelawney in her early thirties. The lack of a wedding ring pointed at her spinsterhood. She was obviously in good physical condition, based on the ease with which she had carried her luggage. Her family name did not give away any special information, and as far as I knew, there were twenty thousand Trelawneys in Cornwall.

As for her looks, a high brow denoted a sharp intelligence and the mouth, with small lines at the corners, signified a cheerful attitude that the lady had so far refrained from showing to me. A mole on her chin gave her a piquant expression. Lustrous black hair, combed in a soft pompadour, left her well-proportioned ears exposed. She wore long silver earrings, of a barbaric design, that together with a large ring on her right hand seemed to be her only jewels. Her sharp cheekbones and her hawk-like nose gave her a Levantine air. I imagined some oriental blood in her family, maybe a Greek or a Persian mother or grandmother.

For a moment she turned and looked at me, her green-grey eyes shaded by long lashes. She was, I decided, of an artistic disposition. Her distinctive lack of a corset pointed at an affinity with the so-called bohemians that lingered in art galleries and bistros.

She was holding her hands in her lap. Long fingered, the nails short and polished. I thought I spotted a callus often associated with writing. The locket ring on her right hand carried a large brown-red stone. An intaglio showed what at first I took for the Greek letter Omega, but upon closer scrutiny it turned out to be a circle resting on a horizontal bar.

Her acquaintance with Mycroft Holmes suggested a clerical job, possibly in some government office. And yet, Holmes had called Miss Trelawney a colleague. I wondered what I was missing.

"You might simply ask me, doctor," she said suddenly, in a dispassionate voice.

I think I jumped on my seat. "Pardon?"

But we were crossing the gates of Eakersley Hall, and she turned to squint at the dark skeletal poplars that lined the lane.

*****

Shadows were deep in Eakersley Hall as the butler let us in. There was something about the house that had a quality of empty, abandoned places, as if the inhabitants were a mere accident, a passing disturbance that would soon be gone.

Striding purposefully, Miss Trelawney walked in. She placed a hand on the butler's chest and gently but firmly pushed him out of her way. He looked at her in amazement but did not dare to speak, such was the authority she emanated. She stopped at the centre of the floor and did a slow turn. She gazed for a long minute at the lion-headed statue, and then gently ran her fingers over the folded skirt of the ancient goddess.

"You were not exaggerating," she said, glancing at Holmes.

"I rarely do," he replied.

Miss Eakersley came down the staircase, her attorney following her suit.

Miss Trelawney stood in front of the mistress of the house. "Do you have the slightest idea of what you are doing?" she asked, without any preamble.

Miss Eakersley stared at her for a moment, and then turned questioningly at Holmes.

"Please meet Miss Valerie Trelawney," Holmes said. "She is—"

Miss Eakersley's eyes widened. "Trelawney? Are you by any chance related to the noted Egyptologist, Abel Trelawny—?"

"He is my father," Valerie replied. "Or so I have been told."

Miss Eakersley rushed to embrace Miss Trelawney, just like she had met a long lost relative. "What a pleasure—" she said.

"Miss Trelawney will help with the case," Holmes said, "given her deep knowledge of all matters Egyptian."

"Yes, of course!" Angela Eakersley enthused. "I met your sister," she said to Valerie, "two years ago, at the dig in the Valley of Kings. Margaret, is it?"

"My half-sister," Miss Trelawney replied rather stiffly. In the ensuing silence, she turned to Holmes. "You mentioned another woman—?"

Holmes pointed at the stairs. "Miss Brock. She is upstairs."

Without another word, Valerie Trelawney walked up the stairs, a black-cloaked form we all followed.

*****

The situation of Miss Brock had not changed. She lay on her bed, her hair spread on the pillow, and still stared fixedly at the ceiling, her parched lips barely moving as she whispered hoarsely her continuous litany. As we filed in, the room became crowded, oppressive. There was a dusty smell in the air I had not noticed that morning, and the air was unpleasantly warm.

From a carafe on a side table, I poured a glass of water and approached the bed. Valerie took the glass from me. "Let me do it," she said in a low voice.

She sat on the mattress and gently poured a little water in Miss Brock's mouth. Much dribbled along the patient's cheek. Miss Trelawney ran a handkerchief along the wet cheek, and then over Miss Brock's forehead.

"How long as she been like this?"

"It is almost forty-eight hours, now," Trent said.

Whispering something that I imagined quite unladylike, Miss Trelawney handed the glass back to me and bent forward, her head so close to Miss Brock's that her long earring brushed the comatose woman's chin. It was like Miss Brock was whispering in her ear.

"Do you understand her?" Miss Eakersley asked.

Miss Trelawney did not reply. She just remained like that, eyes closed and her face close to the delirious woman, for what seemed an impossibly long time. Then she straightened up, a displeased frown darkening her fine features. She pulled her ring off her hand, and pushed it on Miss Brock's finger. Taking a deep breath, she started speaking in syllables I could not understand. The comatose woman's own speech slowed down, and Miss Trelawney's words fit into the pauses, falling into the rhythms of a conversation. This went on for no less than three minutes, and all along Miss Trelawney held the patient's fingers in her right hand, and used her left to caress cheek and forehead.

Miss Brock fell. With a deep sigh, she closed her eyes, and appeared to ease into a quiet, deep slumber.

Miss Trelawney stood briskly. "We need to talk," she said to Holmes.

*****

Miss Trelawney strode into the library like she owned the room, the house and the land around it for five miles in every direction; Holmes closed the doors after we had came in, locking Miss Eakersley and her attorney out.

"If you would excuse us," he said, but it was not like they had much choice.

The room had been cleaned during the day. The books were back on their shelves, the carpets had been cleaned and the upturned furniture put back in its original position. Only the wreck of the glass cabinet remained as a witness of the violent intrusion, and the French door, that had been momentarily repaired with some planks.

The young woman gave a look of open distaste at the body in its cabinet by the side of the door, and moved towards the couch, but did not sit down. She shrugged off her black cloak, revealing a rational dress, black and almost Puritan in its simplicity. Her burning eyes took in every detail of the room, and then she crossed her arms and stared at Holmes in defiance. I could have sworn there were electric charges flying between them.

"What is going on here, Holmes?"

My companion's lips twisted into something that was not a smile. "I need your help to find out," he said.

"This house is an abomination," Miss Trelawney said. She started pacing the room, like a tigress on the prowl. "There is so much we don't understand, and should be wary of, randomly amassed between these walls that—" she snorted. "It's surprising nothing worse happened, and sooner."

"There is, indeed, evil afoot," Holmes said.

Miss Trelawney scoffed. "Nice of you to notice."

"Would somebody care to explain?" I asked, trying not to sound too peevish. "I understand, Miss Trelawney, that you are an expert on matters Egyptian, and I am quite impressed by whatever it is you did upstairs, yet—"

"Miss Trelawney is more than a simple expert in matters Egyptian, Watson. And by the way, I was under the impression you spelled your family name with an e."

"I do," she said, straightening her back. "A single letter to distance myself from Abel Trelawny." She turned her limpid gaze on me. "And as for what I did upstairs, it was a commonplace ritual to put the extraneous *ba* at rest. It is a temporary solution."

"The extraneous *ba*?" I echoed her.

Miss Trelawney approached the shelves, and started browsing them. Her posture and movements reminded me of Holmes, barely twenty-four hours before, as he looked through my library.

"I can give you a preliminary assessment of what happened here, Mr Holmes," she said without turning. "But many of the details still need to be brought into focus."

Holmes sat on a stuffed chair. "Please do, Miss Trelawney," he said, curtly, "and rest assured: I too am still trying to fit some of the pieces together."

Out of habit, I took out my notebook.

"Someone tried to bring one of the mummies back to life, and things got out of hand," she said, in a deadpan tone.

Pencil poised on paper, it took me a moment to shut my mouth and turn to Holmes. "This is preposterous!" I blurted.

"You know me, doctor," Holmes said. "And yet there is no denying that the glass cabinet over there was smashed from the inside."

I was speechless. "What?" I finally managed to say.

"The pattern of the glass shards on the carpet left little doubt about that. And indeed, the window over there was also broken from the inside out. I am sure you noticed the fragments of glass when we walked outside this morning. Where I found this."

He handed me the strip of ancient cloth he had been toying with. It smelled of dust and brine and tar.

I looked at Holmes and then at Miss Trelawney, who was staring at us, her arms crossed. "But certainly," I said, feeling like one drowning, "the burglars, upon being discovered, made a hasty retreat and crashed through the window!"

"The window that reasonably they had opened to get in?"

"They could have closed it behind them to avoid detection—" I tried.

"—by anyone casually walking in the garden late at night?" Holes asked. "Believe me my friend, I don't like what the evidence tells me any more than you do, and yet the logic of it all is inescapable." He turned to Miss Trelawney. "How is what you describe achieved?" he asked.

The woman finally sat down with us.

"There are rituals," she said. "The most obvious is the one in the Scroll of Thoth, a minor sacred text from the Third Dynasty, more or less the time of Pharaoh Dzoser. The book is somewhat notorious for its sacrilegious teachings, pertaining to the re-conjunction of the soul with the body, and the rising of the dead." She glanced at me. "Among other things."

"And you believe such a ritual was performed in this house?" I asked.

She nodded. "It was performed in this room, and it went wrong."

"How do you know?" I asked.

"Have you seen the woman upstairs, doctor?"

"I did not mean that. How do you know it was performed in this room?" If Holmes was ready to humour this woman, I still felt offended by her unscientific attitude.

She pointed at the smashed cabinet. "Isn't that obvious? But I see what you mean, so let me explain. To perform the ritual you need a complete body. Indeed, the Scroll recommends using the body of someone that was buried whole, and not subjected to the canonical preparation. When working with a prepared body, not simply the mummy, then, is needed, but also the internal organs that were removed upon mummification, and placed into the four canopic jars." She pointed at the four vases on the shelf.

She approached the shelf and picked up one of the vases.

"Exquisite," she said. "Probably from Flinders Petrie's excavations at Faiyum, that the Greeks called Crocodile City—" She stopped and frowned. "What do we have here?" she asked.

She turned the vase in her hand, the one carrying a human head, and then shook it. It made a distinctively metallic sound. Holmes sprang to her side, and she opened the vase.

Using two fingers, she pulled out and untangled a thing of gold and enamel, its colour shining brightly in the light of the lamps. The stolen necklace.

"That is another puzzle solved," Holmes said.

"Two," Valerie said. "Now we know why the ritual failed: the vase was supposed to contain the liver, but whoever placed the necklace in, got rid of the content."

She walked to the fireplace and prodded the ashes with the poker, without any result. She put back the iron poker and rubbed her hands. "So what happened was, the ritual was executed, but when the incomplete body was re-animated, the *ba* refused to take residence into it. Seeking some kind of sanctuary, it moved to the closest whole body. That your Miss Brock fainted when the mummy came alive made the invasion easier. The missing *ba* on the other hand deprived the mummy of its reasoning power, reducing it to an animated corpse possessed of animal passion and hunger, but not of thought."

She nodded towards the boards that replaced the damaged window. "And it acted accordingly."

"Are you seriously claiming there is an undead body roaming the grounds?" I asked.

Holmes ignored me. "How do we stop it?" he asked.

*****

The maid served us a late-night tea and Mister Trent tried to take advantage of her arrival to come join us; Miss Trelawney was dismissive, and the man retreated to his rooms with a bruised pride. I went upstairs with the servant to check on Miss Brock's status, and found her sound asleep, and apparently at ease.

I returned to the library, walking alone the dark corridors of the house like I was trapped in an ancient pyramid. Not a suggestive person myself, I did welcome the amber light in the library, the haze of tobacco and the heartening comfort of a cup of tea.

Holmes and Trelawney were still deep in conversation.

"Bringing a five-thousand years old mummy back to life just to scare a woman is simply too much," Miss Trelawney said. I noticed she was smoking one of Holmes's cigarettes. "Effective? Undoubtedly. But—this?" She blew a plume of smoke towards the ceiling. "Out of proportions. And why sabotage the ritual by tampering with the jar?"

"The person who performed the ritual clearly did not know what they were doing," Holmes said.

Miss Trelawney snorted in a most unladylike fashion. "Then why perform the ritual in the first place?"

Holmes shook his head. "We are still missing something."

"Whoever did it was a fool," Miss Trelawney sentenced.

I poured myself another cup of tea, and shuddered. There was an unpleasant draft coming in from the damaged window, but it was not only that. I caught myself watching the curtain as it moved in the breeze.

"This house is most ominous after sundown," I observed, to break the silence.

"As the sun sets," Miss Trelawney replied, "Ra becomes Atun, and then joins with Osiris as he enters the underworld. This is the time in which Apepi, the spirit of evil, is free to roam, but stands to be defeated by Set, the god of destruction. It is a bad time to be surrounded by so many tokens of a dead past we do not really understand, doctor."

"Do you really believe all this?" I asked her.

She gave a shrug. "Belief is something that should be handled with extreme caution, doctor."

She squashed her cigarette.

"We should play some music," I said, pointing at the phonograph, "to cheer ourselves up. But then the noise would awaken—"

"Watson," Holmes exclaimed, standing up, "you are absolutely brilliant!"

"Really?"

Miss Trelawney's eyes widened. "A record."

Holmes was already rummaging in the box of cylinders by the music machine.

"No need to know the ritual if you have it recorded," Miss Trelawney said, joining him.

"And if all you need is some strange gibberish to seep through the floor and scare the person sleeping above," Holmes said in turn, "that would suffice."

Miss Trelawney was looking at the floor. Then she went on all fours, and dug under the couch. "Found it!" she called.

She stood, holding in her hand a wax cylinder. "Doctor Watson," she said with a bright smile, "all I heard about you is true."

I took that as a compliment.

*****

"So, Holmes, have you finished playing your little games?" Trent asked, as we all sat down in the library, enjoying the weak heat of the fireplace, and waiting for the revelations to come. Miss Eakersley placed her hand on his, and whispered something. Behind the couch where he was standing, Inspector Jobson gave me a look, like he shared my poor opinion of the lawyer.

"This is no game," Miss Trelawney said, drily. "Defying the laws of men and of nature is never a game."

"I am sure Mister Holmes will explain everything," Miss Eakersley said. "Please go on, Mister Holmes."

My friend cast a glance in the direction of Miss Trelawney.

"You first," she said.

Holmes nodded, and Miss Trelawney started prowling the room as was clearly her habit.

"What we have here," Holmes said, "is a rather plain, if extremely unsavoury, petty little crime. A vulgar attempt at taking advantage of a good-hearted, highly suggestible woman, for the purpose of appropriating of her wealth."

Miss Eakersley stiffened, and blushed.

"We will not tolerate—" Trent said.

"Yes, you will," Miss Trelawney said. "Go on, Mister Holmes."

Holmes smiled at her. "Miss Eakersley," he said, "you are the sole inheritor of your family's impressive fortune. You have also shown yourself to be, if you will pardon me for saying so, somewhat impressionable. It is my opinion, which of course has little import on the solution of the case, that a continuous acquaintance with the relics and mysteries of ancient Egypt is somewhat conducive of a superstitious mindset."

"A fascinating hypothesis," Miss Trelawney observed, piqued. Holmes bowed slightly at her.

"The meeting with Hakimi and its effects on Miss Eakersley," Holmes continued, addressing the whole company, "was what convinced Mister Trent that there was an opportunity for him to improve his condition. Dramatically so."

Trent gasped and stood. "What—?"

Jobson placed a hand on his shoulder. "Sit down, Trent," the inspector said genially. "Let Mister Holmes finish."

"Miss Eakersley, am I right," Holmes asked, with a nod of thanks to the policeman, "in surmising that should for any reason you be unable to mind your family business, Mister Trent would take your place with powers of attorney?" He paused, and arched his eyebrows. "Being, as he is, your attorney?"

"Well, yes," the woman said. "But this is—"

"This is ridiculous!" Trent snarled.

"All that Trent needed," Holmes went on ignoring him, "was to support and promote his employer's increasing paranoia. Which was not particularly difficult to achieve, as he could avail himself of the help of Miss Brock."

Now it was Miss Eakersley's turn to be outraged. "Henrietta would never—"

"Cause minor disturbances? Move some of your things around, so that it looked like someone — or something, indeed, had interfered with your belongings? Claim to have witnessed certain occurrences in order to increase your state of apprehension — a strange noise, some ghostly movement — things she could later deny should she be interrogated about them? Things that you yourself would in the end doubt actually happened, thus increasing your sense of panic and confusion?"

"I do not intend to suffer any more—" Trent ejaculated. Once again, Jobson pushed him back in the couch.

"But what of Hakimi—?" Miss Eakersley was on the verge of tears. "He came to me in London. He menaced me. He mentioned the curse—"

"And then, realizing there was nothing else he could legally do," Holmes said, "with a typical Oriental fatalism, he went back to Egypt."

"But Mister Trent saw him no more that three days ago!"

Angela Eakersley cried, turning to look at her attorney.

"And nobody else did," Holmes replied. "I interrogated the servants." He pulled a telegram out of his pocket. "And Doctor Hakimi is currently in Cairo, as he himself confirmed yesterday night a little before I came here, by answering a telegram from me. So either this is a case in which the esteemed doctor projected his astral body, his *ka* as the Egyptians called it—"

"Please," Miss Trelawney whispered.

"—or Trent lied. And I tend to be sceptical about astral projections."

Miss Eakersley was staring in horror at Trent, whose features had gone pale and hard, his face a horrid smirk.

"What was exactly that Hakimi wanted of you?" Miss Trelawney asked, stepping in. "He knew about the recording, didn't he? That was what he had come to London to warn you about."

Miss Eakersley let out a strangled cry.

"A recording," Holmes went on, "that Miss Brock was to play on the phonograph the other night, another small piece of the illusion the two villains were building. Meaningless sounds, strange voices chanting in an unknown language, in the darkened corridors of a big house, to provoke fear and anguish and push Miss Angela Eakersley towards a mental collapse—"

Miss Trelawney started the Edison, and the distant, eerie voice of a man chanting rose through the air. The library was perfectly still in the early light of the rainy morning.

"You set yourself in position to control all incoming communications, Trent," Holmes said, ignoring the chant. "And it is strangely ironic that it was the story with which you tried to divert me, pursuing an investigation I was not exceedingly interested in pursuing, that ultimately brought me here."

Jobson shook his head and pulled a pair of manacles from his pocket. He started walking around the couch. "Well, Trent, I guess we'll have to continue this conversation back in town—"

Trent sprang to his feet, dragging Angela Eakersley with him. She cried, but he shook her, and placed a blunt revolver against her head. "Nice job, Mister Holmes—" he said, grinning evilly.

"Don't do anything stupid," Jobson growled.

"I am afraid he already did," Miss Trelawney said.

And just then the boarded up window exploded, and in staggered a thing of absolute horror.

The mummy was not exceedingly tall, and strips of dirty linen hung from its skeletal, desiccated frame. It had spent time outside, in the cold and the rain, and its dried-up tissues were showing signs of increased damage. Bones pushed white through the corrupted flesh the ages had blackened, and the thing moved in jerks and spasms, like a broken puppet.

My hand went to the gun in the pocket of my jacket, and my heartbeat roared in my ears. Here was Miss Trelawney's animated mummy, to prove with its obscene materiality, its foul smell and its grimace, all that I had doubted so far. Madness was erupting around me, as Jobson tried to grab Trent, and Miss Eakersley let out a long, high wail and fainted. Holmes stood in the monstrosity's path, and the thing pushed him off like he was a rag doll.

"Watson!" he shouted.

I fired, six bullets slamming in the thing's chest, one after the other. It staggered. Air pushed through a paper-like trachea modulated a sinister moan. A piece of its ribcage detached from the body, hung briefly by the ripped bandages, and fell on the floor.

Trent tried to shoulder his way past me and to the library's door. The monster moved with sudden swiftness. It closed its gnarled hands on the attorney's head, and twisted. A spine-chilling crack, and the man slumped on the floor, dead of a broken neck.

Then the monster was upon me. I felt more than saw Inspector Jobson at my side.

The thing stopped, suddenly. It wavered, and then a long anguished wail came from its ragged lips.

"What in the name of God–?" Jobson breathed.

I looked past the abomination where it stood, gritting its broken teeth. Holmes was standing by the fireplace; Miss Trelawney was kneeling in front of the flame, which for a brief moment burned a heinous, noxious green.

As Miss Trelawney stood, smoothing the folds of her skirt, the mummy fell to its knees, its head reclined on its broken chest. Its body was dissolving into a snowfall of dry pale flakes. We watched in horror until only the twisted bones remained, and crumpled in a heap with what little was left of the bandages.

*****

"There is always someone who leaves," Miss Trelawney said, "at the end of a story such as this."

We had settled in a compartment of the three fifteen to London, and were waiting with a certain anticipation for the train to leave Manchester and its strange curses behind.

"You can't blame Miss Eakersley for wanting to abandon her mausoleum of a house behind," Holmes said.

"I find it unfair," I said, "that Henrietta Brock will not be punished for her part in this strange story."

"On the basis of what proof?" Holmes said.

We all agreed that a case could not stand in court, but would rather land all of us in Bedlam. "And yet it's unfair," I said.

Miss Trelawney smiled mirthlessly. "Her nightmares will be atonement enough."

The train shuddered. The station moved beyond the rain-splattered window, and we all drew a sigh of relief.

"I wonder where the ritual was recorded, and by whom," Holmes said musingly.

"That's a place where you do not want to go, Mister Holmes," Miss Trelawney said.

The wax cylinder had been melted in the fireplace, thus putting an end to the mockery of life that was the mummy.

"Have you it all down in your notebook, doctor?" A mocking smile played on Miss Trelawney's lips. "Quite a story."

"Not the story the world is ready to learn," Holmes said.

"A story I hope only to forget," I said.

And afterwards we sat in silence, as the train travelled south.

Sherlock Holmes and the Ghostly Reunion

by Christopher Degni

A lingering melancholy had settled into the chest of Sherlock Holmes. He could attribute it to many causes: the wintering of his hives; his imminent completion of the sixth — and final — volume of his magnum opus *The Whole Art of Detection;* the unseasonably grey and wet autumn, and... his fading relationship with John Watson. He'd only seen the good doctor a handful of times since they last worked together in the war effort, eight years prior, and Watson hadn't called in the last two years.

But none of those causes, or even all of them in concert, could account for the deepness of Holmes's gloom. He couldn't help but feel something else was behind it all, something he couldn't quite remember. It would come back to the great detective. It always had.

Fridays were Holmes's time to sift through the vast piles of letters sent to him, asking his help in all manner of affair, none interesting in the least. No matter that he hadn't given anyone, including the lads down at the Yard, any indication that he was available for consulting any longer. Watson's sensationalist accounts had granted him some measure of fame, and even after all these years, people were desirous to be associated with the great Sherlock Holmes.

Most of the letters went unopened — the stationery or the penmanship or the postal mark was enough to determine they were run-of-the-mill. These went into the fireplace. Occasionally, Holmes would go so far as to open an envelope and scan the contents when some detail aroused his curiosity. Even then the affairs tended to be mundane and uninteresting, and certainly nowhere near bringing the detective out of his comfortable retirement.

He ached for some stimulation now, more than he had in years. Perhaps an interesting case could snap him from his doldrums. But that depended on finding such an affair.

So Holmes paid special attention to each letter in the bundle brought to him by Mrs. Strathearn presently. He fought the urge to immediately burn those plain, cream letters with no return address, written in a common hand, even though he knew before opening them they contained nothing remarkable. He noted with interest one particular letter where the handwriting showed signs of a rare palsy, and his hopes were raised for a moment, but the letter hardly contained a case — it was an exultation of Holmes's career. He had no need of being told how great he was by people he'd never met. Into the fireplace.

The penultimate letter on the pile had post markings indicating an origin in the United States, with the sender named Norton. Holmes knew a Norton once, he was sure of it... but it was a common surname, certainly one of the top five hundred in Britain and nearly as common in America. Holmes turned the letter over in his hands, searching for other clues as to its provenance before he opened it.

The sender was left-handed, that much was certain. Well-off, but not obscenely rich, from the quality of the paper and the ink used to mark it; young from the style of penmanship; female from the faint whiff of perfume emanating from the envelope.

Dear Mr. Holmes,

You knew my mother once, and though you were on opposite sides of that affair, she always spoke highly of you. I hope that you will help her now. The details of the case look too silly to put into print, and I fear you would not come were I to divulge too much. Let me say that this case is more in my bailiwick than yours, but alas, I need the help. I would, of course, cover your expenses to travel to my Greenfield Estate in New Jersey, as well as pay you your customary fee. I look forward to your answer.

Faithfully yours,
Clara Norton

Holmes felt a pang of disappointment at not being able to bring Miss Norton's mother immediately to mind. He pulled out the old index file to fill the gaps his mind could not.

The index, unused in so many years, held a layer of dust that irritated Holmes's sinuses, but the joy of rummaging through the memorabilia of his old cases consumed him. He resolved to call on Watson. He forgot his surroundings for many a moment, and even forgot for a single moment why he'd unearthed the tome in the first place.

"Ah, Norton," he said to himself softly, navigating to the N section of the vast codex.

There he was reminded of the gentleman barrister Godfrey Norton, and his wife Irene. Irene Norton, née Adler. *The* woman had re-entered his life, and this time she needed his help.

He would take the case.

*****

Holmes's keen grey eyes took in Watson's form as the doctor entered the room. "Why, Watson, you've come from a funeral."

"Holmes, every time I think you've amazed me, you manage to outdo yourself. It borders on the otherworldly. How could you possibly know?"

Holmes smiled — a rarity even at this age — and said, "My dear doctor, while I may be out of practice, the art of detection never completely leaves a man. And surely you've seen me unravel more unwieldy tangles than this."

"I'm not sure I have," said Watson.

"The buttons on your waistcoat are in the distinctive style of those produced by Gieves & Hawkes, unlike your normal dress clothes which are of Wells of Mayfair make. You are wearing your best suit."

"But why a funeral?"

"Your skin's complexion is ashen, your eyes rimmed with red. You're a sight thinner than last we met, even though you're well into those years where a gentleman tends to put on weight. You've been ill, Watson. What event would occasion a man in recovery from what I take was a trying illness to wear his best suit, and attend despite his woe? Only two come to mind: a wedding or a funeral. A wedding is a beginning. You can send your regrets and have chance enough to call on the happily married couple in the future. But a funeral; well, that is the end."

"It is, Holmes." A fleeting shadow passed over Watson's face.

"Have I got the best of it?"

"You surely have."

"Watson, I cannot tell you how pleased I am that you answered my call. I have missed you. And in your current condition — you are not yet completely recovered."

"Have I ever been less than loyal?"

"No, my friend, you have not. And for your reward, I have a new case — a case that involves some old friends of ours." Holmes's eyes lit up with the familiar enthusiasm that accompanied a new case.

He pointed at the letter on the writing desk. "What do you make of it, Doctor?"

"I'm surprised you're even considering the case, Holmes," said Watson. "There's not much to go on."

"But that's it, Watson," cried Holmes. "If Irene Adler needs our help, it must be a singularly difficult case indeed."

Watson raised his eyebrows. "Holmes, you have heard of Miss Clara Norton, have you not?"

Holmes shook his head. "I've not kept as current as I'd like on events, especially those on the other side of the pond."

"She's rather a sensation at the moment. An occult detective. I assume that's what she meant by her 'bailiwick'." Watson clasped his hands. "She's pulling you into a case about the supernatural; I'm sure of it."

"Then we shall debunk her notions."

"She's met with some success."

"My dear doctor, you haven't gone to the side of the spiritualists in a mere few years of my leave, have you? A man of medicine would know better, I should think."

"You may find the world is larger than you think, Holmes."

"I daresay it's not that large. Come, Watson, we must be off to meet our young client. She may be convinced of the truth of ghosts and goblins, but we shall show the case is nothing more than ordinary. Are you up for a journey across the sea? I should appreciate your assistance one last time."

"One last time, Holmes. We can re-enact our younger days."

Holmes's severe features lit up into a smile more vibrant than he had worn for years.

*****

The ocean liner offered more comfort than Holmes was used to. Watson fell seasick and remained unavailable for most of the trip, though the two men stole some time to reminisce about the much rougher journeys they were able to handle in their youth. This trip was luxurious compared to working for passage on fishing vessels, or stowing away on scientific expeditions.

"Perhaps I underestimated our client's wealth," said Holmes. The two men shared a corner of Holmes's unexpectedly large quarters.

"Money was never a prime motivation for you, Holmes."

"Nor is it here, though it may play a part in the case. Every detail matters, for you never know which one will lead to the solving insight."

"On that note, I've done some research. You might be interested in what I've found. As I suspected, Miss Norton's case has some complexities to it. Her mother died a few years ago."

Holmes's face fell. "There was a time when I'd not have been caught unawares of the death of an acquaintance. But too much of life has gone by, and the list of those with whom I once tangled has grown far beyond even my ability to keep up with it."

"Yes, Holmes, neither one of us are in the shape we once were. There is no shame in it."

"I suppose you've seen it time and again in your line of work." Holmes proffered a wistful smile. "Back to your research: we must rule out all other possibilities before we are to accept the existence of spectres. I don't believe Irene Norton is trying to contact me from beyond the grave."

"It leaves the very fact of this case a mystery. Why has Miss Norton called for you, and in this manner? Does she believe in this ghost herself, or is it a ruse? What would such a ruse accomplish?"

"All questions I hope to answer in time. But we've yet to gather any data. I am loathe to hypothesize in such a state. We'll know more soon enough."

At the Chelsea Piers, Holmes picked out Miss Clara Norton in a small crowd from a hundred paces. Her face combined her mother's fierce beauty with her father's dark features and aquiline profile. Seeing the young woman transported Holmes to the day thirty-four years prior when he inadvertently became a witness at her parents' wedding.

"The papers here are buzzing with her most recent case, Holmes. You may not believe in those matters beyond human existence, but she's got the popular imagination captured."

"We may agree, Watson, that supernatural experiences are quite beyond anything we've ever seen — or are ever likely to see. That leaves several explanations, but all have the commonality that our Miss Clara Norton is, in fact, quite shrewd in how she deals with her affairs. To solve crimes, as you know, is no trivial matter; to do so while attributing the results to imaginary beings takes a special talent. I am eager to meet her."

Holmes and Watson approached Miss Norton.

"Mr. Holmes, I presume," she said. She gave Watson a peculiar look, but Holmes was used to his friend being viewed with suspicion. She continued, "I was expecting only you."

"Miss Norton, this is my dear friend Dr. John Watson. He is a consummate professional, and he has helped me close out many cases. We work as a team."

Miss Norton looked at Watson, frowned confusedly, and then looked back to Holmes.

Holmes continued, "I assure you, anything you tell me you can tell him. I must insist. He's come all this way with me. If the expense—"

"It's not the expense, Mr. Holmes," said Miss Norton. "Of course I will reimburse you. It's..."

Watson's eye twitched ever so slightly.

"No mind," said Miss Norton. "I'd be delighted if Dr. Watson were to join our investigation."

"I knew you would come around," said Holmes. "My dear doctor really is quite a capable companion."

"Holmes," said Watson.

"No, surely," said Holmes. "He takes far too little credit in his own re-tellings of our adventures. Sometimes I think he has no real conception of how much he allows me to test my own hypotheses."

"What he means, Miss Norton, is that my own clumsy deductions often point him from directions to avoid."

Holmes shrugged. "Now tell me about your mother. She has not joined you, I see."

Miss Norton squinted slightly. "I thought you knew, Mr. Holmes. My mother passed away three years ago."

"I knew," said Holmes, thankful for his partner's research. "I should not think you would have brought me all this way for a wild goose chase."

"And yet you came anyway," said Miss Norton.

"You claimed she required my help," said Holmes, an edge of testiness in his voice.

"She does," said Miss Norton. "Her spirit was asking for you."

*****

The Bentley pulled up to the front of a great estate, with expansive lawns and gardens wrapping around the sides of the house. An older, heavier woman and a thin man waited in front of the house. Miss Norton exited the Bentley first, followed by Holmes, then Watson. She greeted her servants, while Holmes fell back. Before approaching Miss Norton, he stopped, turned, and surveyed the lands, pausing to gaze in a certain direction before rejoining his hostess.

"Can you tell me about your household, Miss Norton? I assume this is your housekeeper and head butler."

Miss Norton nodded. "What else would you like to know?"

"You've recently hired a new gardener," he said. "The old one left abruptly."

"Remarkable," she replied. "How?"

"Your rose bushes," said Holmes. "They are all pruned, indeed as they should be at this time of year, but not all in the same manner. Those bushes at the front of the beds have been cut back using the modern method, flat and near the main branches. Those in the rear have been pruned in the style of the old country, using sharper cuts on smaller branches to minimize the disturbance to the plant. This estate is not large enough to have multiple gardeners, and the same man would not use both methods.

"The bed is small enough to be done in a single day. That two gardeners worked on it means one left, rather abruptly, but you found someone to complete the work."

Miss Norton raised an eyebrow at Watson.

"Show him a leaf blowing in the wind, and he'll tell you who planted the tree," said Watson.

Holmes hadn't finished.

"And which of the two was from Italy?"

"Well there you've gone wrong," said Miss Norton. "Our old gardener was American, a family stalwart who'd been with us for decades. He faced an emergency and had to leave us; the whole situation was rather sentimental. Luckily, he was able to recommend his own replacement, an Englishman named

Peterson. He moved into the servant quarters several weeks ago."

"And may I speak with Peterson?"

"I'm afraid not, Mr. Holmes. He's mute. Perhaps you can speak with his wife."

Holmes's eyes narrowed. "Shall we go inside, and you can tell me more about your case?"

"I'd be delighted," said Miss Norton. "Follow me, please."

As Miss Norton moved into the house, Watson leaned towards Holmes. "I know that look. You've found something already. What are you onto?"

"A minor inconsistency, Watson. Its significance, if any, remains to be seen. Let us hear what Miss Norton has to tell before we begin spinning hypotheses. We must collect more facts first."

Miss Norton led them into the lobby of the house. The thin man had disappeared, but the heavyset woman followed them as they wound through the hallways, past a stairwell, and into a rear room that served as a parlour. There, Miss Norton waved her hand at a pair of leather chairs. "Mr. Holmes, Dr. Watson, please sit."

The seat reminded Holmes of the very chair he had offered to countless guests at 221B Baker Street. He and Watson sat, and Miss Norton took her place on a small couch opposite the chairs.

"Tea?" she asked.

Holmes nodded; Watson demurred. Miss Norton motioned to the housekeeper and instructed the woman to bring service for two.

"Miss Norton, we must first lay out the facts of the situation. You've stated several times that your mother, who is no longer with us, needs my help. That she has asked for me. Please recount the experience, and leave every detail in, no matter how insignificant, for you never know which thread will unravel the knot. Start at the beginning."

"The sighting..."

"No, before that," said Holmes, his keen eyes flashing. "Tell me about becoming an occult detective."

Miss Norton blinked rapidly, and she looked back and forth between Holmes and Watson. "Surely it can have no bearing on the matter at hand?"

"I am sure of nothing," said Holmes, "for I have yet nothing to investigate. Even now I misspeak: I am sure of one thing only. Whatever you saw, it was not the ghost of Irene Adler. We will require all the information you can muster to figure out what exactly it was that you witnessed. So please, begin at the beginning."

"I have been investigating the occult for many years now," said Miss Norton. "One could say I started when I was a child. Mother had stories, oh the stories. She told me one of you, you know. In a strange way, you are responsible for what I have become. From a young age I wished to be a detective. Women, here as in your country, have little opportunity to help the police in any formal way. I had to find the occasion where I could.

"I also had other gifts as a child. From a very young age, I was sensitive to supernatural and otherworldly goings on, in particular, the movements of the spirit world. I came to realize I could see the dead where others could not. There was that Eusapia Palladino woman, for example, but she proved to be a charlatan. I am the real thing."

Holmes's eyes flashed at every mention of the supernatural. The young woman was either misguided, or more likely, putting on a show to gain notoriety. The showmanship had worked so far, if the popular vision of Miss Clara Norton was any indication.

"So you combined your two talents," he said.

"It was not that clean, Mr. Holmes," said Miss Norton. "After leaving England, my parents settled in France, where they raised me. I loved my mother, but my father and I had a special connection. He died when I was young, and it devastated me. Until I realized: I could still see him. Speak with him."

"Wishful thinking combined with an overactive imagination."

"I see my mother did not exaggerate your personality." Miss Norton smiled, a minuscule uplift at the corner of her mouth. "You know, you sound very much like her. Eventually I repeated back to her the stories my father's ghost related to me — stories I couldn't have known any other way — and it scared her. She told herself he must have recounted these stories to me before he passed, but she knew that was not the case.

"My constant talk of my father and the increasing evidence of the truth nearly drove her mad. She searched for a way out. We had money. Father did very well as an *avocat honoraire* in France, and he held a considerable insurance policy. Mother also had money in her family. She relocated us to her old family estate here in New Jersey, starting a new life and distancing us far from the ghost — and memories — of my father.

"My father's ghost did not travel with us, and I have not talked to him for two decades. I've talked with him my last, I'm afraid. Spirits do move on eventually, and I fear that I've lost my chance to say goodbye. I sank into a depression when we arrived here, and for a long time, I no longer saw the ghosts."

"Until recently."

"Until recently. When my mother passed several years ago, the ability returned. She'd never appeared to me, to my surprise, but I noticed other spirits. With nothing better to occupy my time, I decided to follow my youthful dreams and become a detective. Why would I ignore the gift of talking with the dead? And this led to my first big case."

"This is a remarkable narrative you've spun for yourself, Miss Norton. I almost believe you believe it."

"The truth does not depend on what you believe, Mr. Holmes."

Watson jumped in before Holmes could offer a rejoinder. "Maybe we should let her proceed."

"Yes, yes, get on with it." Holmes waved his hand.

"Crimes nearly solve themselves when one can speak with the victims after they've departed." Miss Norton rose from her couch and crossed the parlour to a small file cabinet. She withdrew a file folder and handed it to Holmes. "You can read for yourself about my first big case."

Holmes accepted the file. "Please give me an account of the high points." Confidence games were difficult to keep straight. Holmes planned to verify her spoken version against the details in the file. Any difference might provide a clue to the young woman's manner of thought.

"As you wish," said Miss Norton. In the moment, her irritation strengthened her resemblance to her mother. "You've heard of the Pinelli affair?"

Without his files of current events or his network of informational spies, Holmes was lost. "Watson?"

"Giacomo Pinelli, the leader of a minor Mafia family here in New Jersey. Miss Norton's work led to him being detained, awaiting arraignment."

Holmes said, "And you've provided evidence of Mr. Pinelli's guilt?"

Miss Norton glanced at the floor. "I've provided what I could. I've spoken to several victims of his."

"Murder victims, you mean."

Miss Norton nodded.

"Why not have them tell you their final resting places?"

"The Pinelli family has made sure those whom they murder are gone for good. Weighted and thrown into the ocean, or lost in the dense marshes, for instance. These spirits, confused and sorrowful, cannot be so precise as a police search would require."

Holmes smiled, his eyes narrowing. "You are a clever woman, Miss Norton. Perhaps I have underestimated you." He turned the file folder over in his hands. "I shall read these tonight. But perhaps we should now turn to the case at hand."

"My mother. She appeared two weeks prior, in this very house."

"Here?" said Holmes.

"Upstairs. I can show you after we take tea." The housekeeper had returned with tea service, which she laid on the table between Holmes and Miss Norton. "I know it sounds dreadfully cliché, but the night was stormy, and wind was rattling the house. The staff had retired to their quarters—"

"The buildings in the rear of the yard," said Holmes.

"Yes."

"Please continue."

"They'd retired for the night, and so I was the lone occupant of the main house. I heard the stairs creak — they only creak like that if someone walks upon them. I know this estate's sounds by heart. There were no signs of break-in, and the doors and windows were locked securely, as they always are. As you can imagine, I was curious who could be on the stairs.

"I rushed from this very parlour to the foot of the stairs, but saw nobody, even though a light shone upstairs. I climbed the steps, and from the landing at the top, looking into the sitting room in front of the balcony, there she was: my mother, as I remembered her from my childhood. She stood there for a moment, and I heard your name, 'Sherlock Holmes's. A gust of wind swept down the stairs, the light in the room was extinguished, and then she disappeared. I rushed through to the balcony, but there was no sign of her."

"Is this type of contact usual when dealing with spirits?" asked Watson.

"No," said Miss Norton. "It is quite unusual, in fact. For the spirit to disappear like that; and to think, my own mother." Miss Norton dabbed her eyes with her handkerchief.

Holmes was up out of his seat already, examining the room and the hallway that led to it. "Miss Norton, we ought not let belief in supernatural occurrences obstruct our view. There are many mundane explanations for the series of events that you have just described, and we simply have to weed out those not consistent with the facts to arrive at the truth. May we see the route to the balcony?"

"Of course," said Miss Norton, pulling herself together. "This way, Mr. Holmes."

Holmes and Watson followed Miss Norton from the parlour into the hallway, which immediately banked right into stairs upwards. Holmes followed slowly, stopping at points along the way and examining the sight lines both back into the parlour and up the stairs to the landing. He stepped forward and back, and stood and knelt, though no longer with the quickness of his younger days.

"And up the stairs, of course," said Holmes.

The upper landing of the stairs opened up straight ahead into a sitting room, then the balcony; on either side, hallways led to the bedrooms of the house. A pair of oversized French doors separated the sitting room from the landing, and a matching set separated the landing from the balcony. Holmes gave only a cursory inspection to the sitting room, but rushed out to the balcony itself, and looked out over the railing, down at the grounds of the estate. Holmes remained at the window for longer than seemed necessary.

"This is surely a singular set of events," he said. "Come, Watson. I have the seed of a theory, but I must put it aside to let it blossom." He consulted his pocket watch. "And it is time for dinner. Miss Norton, would you do the pleasure of joining us?"

Miss Norton called for the Bentley to take the three of them into town to the Essex Manor Restaurant. Holmes recalled the entire tale of the Bohemian king and Miss Norton's mother.

"Is this true?" she asked Watson, who nodded in assent.

"Your mother," said Holmes, "is the sole woman to best me." His eyes turned cold for a moment. "You must have known that, from the stories my dear biographer here has told. I admit, when taking this case, I believed it might have been a ruse to attempt to get the best of me once again — to what purpose, I did not know. But I see now that is not the case."

"Oh?" said Miss Norton.

"You believe what you saw," said Holmes. "While describing the occurrence to me, your pupils dilated, a response that cannot be trained by any amount of conscious effort. There was no hesitation in your story, yet it was not rehearsed."

"You acknowledge my mother's ghost haunts the estate?"

"Miss Norton, I said no such thing. I said only that you believed as much, which is the relevant detail here. We must discover what purpose making you believe such an outlandish theory would serve."

"But I do see ghosts."

"I do not think so."

"There we must disagree."

"You yourself said this spirit has not followed the pattern of other spirits you have communed with, correct?"

Miss Norton nodded.

"Then you admit it is at least possible that you are seeing something made by man. Certainly not supernatural."

"What would be the purpose?" she asked.

"Indeed," said Holmes. "Now we are asking the same question." He turned to Watson. "Doctor, I believe you haven't touched the soup I ordered for you."

"Lingering stomach upset from the journey, I'm afraid," said Watson.

Holmes and Miss Norton finished their dinner, and the three headed back to the estate. When they arrived, the housekeeper met them at the door.

"Ma'am, there's been a break-in."

"Perhaps this will shed additional light on the situation," said Holmes.

"How do you know that they are related?" asked Miss Norton.

"In my career, I've seen very few true coincidences." Holmes turned to the housekeeper. "Have you called the police? Have you touched anything?"

The housekeeper shook her head.

"Good," said Holmes. "Then there is hope that any link to our current affair may still be in place."

The housekeeper led Holmes, Watson, and Miss Norton to the rear door of the house, which had been pried open. Holmes walked through the doorway and examined the ground leading up to the house. When he re-entered the house, he seemed to have no new ideas. The floor held no footprints, and there were no obvious clues to where the thief had visited once inside the house.

"Where do you keep your valuables, Miss Norton?"

All of her jewellery was accounted for, and the house safes were untouched. Miss Norton took stock of the other valuable items in her chambers, but found nothing missing. Holmes pointed to a dark patch on the wall.

"That print had little value," said Miss Norton. "I do not understand."

Holmes scrunched his face, and a dissatisfied look crept into his eyes. "Are you sure nothing more of value was taken?"

Miss Norton shook her head.

"This barely qualifies as a case," said Holmes. "Something singular is going on. I cannot quite figure it, though. The pieces are so disparate, and there seems to be nothing to hold them together."

Evening had crept up. The house was darkening, the servants on the verge of retiring for the night.

"Perhaps we'll have better luck in the morning, Holmes."

"Perhaps," said Holmes.

"The butler will show you to your room." Miss Norton glanced at Watson. "Rooms."

The thin man appeared from nowhere and beckoned to Holmes. "This way, sir."

"I'm going to stay behind for a nightcap, Holmes, if you don't mind," said Watson. "I'll see you in the morning."

Holmes followed the butler to the upper level of the house. At the spot where Miss Norton claimed to have seen the ghost, he stopped for a moment and peered into the room which led to the balcony; he broke from the butler and entered the room, swinging the door open and closed, then let out a satisfied chuckle.

"Sir, please do not wander off. Follow me."

Holmes rejoined the butler, who showed him to a small but comfortable room containing a bed, a tidy reading desk, and a smoking chair. His valise had already been unpacked, his belongings laid out, and the folder of Miss Norton's prior exploits left on the desk for his perusal. The butler left Holmes as he began to dig into the dossier. There were no deviations in the file from Miss Norton's earlier oral account. She was telling the truth, at least as she saw it.

*****

"Mr. Holmes, you must really see this," said Miss Norton as Holmes descended the stairs into the dining room for breakfast. Watson, sitting at the table and examining a pair of photographs, looked up at Holmes's appearance and added, "They really are remarkable."

"They appeared overnight," said Miss Norton.

On closer examination, Holmes saw the photographs were of Irene Norton, though they were not any normal photographs. Irene's person seemed to emit a warm glow in the pictures, her body partially translucent. The young Irene of the photographs was the one Holmes remembered.

"Where?" said Holmes.

"On this very table," said Miss Norton.

"And how have they appeared? Has there been another break-in?"

Miss Norton shook her head. "Nothing else is out of place. It is more evidence. Even you cannot doubt the veracity of my story now, Mr. Holmes."

"It was not your veracity I doubted," said Holmes. "But I am still sceptical. Have you heard of Harry Price?"

Miss Norton shook her head.

"Harry Houdini, then?"

"Of course. What does an escape artist have to do with this?"

"Ah," said Holmes. "Houdini is not simply an escape artist. He is a student of illusion. And a champion of the rational over the occult. If you were familiar with Price's treatise, or Houdini's demonstrations, then you would know there's a relatively simple setup for producing spirit photographs. These bear the hallmarks of that method."

Miss Norton scowled.

Holmes continued, "As an occult detective, you might find their work illuminating. I recommend you look into it."

"What does it all mean, Holmes?" said Watson.

"The threads are coming together. Watson, I know we are not what we once were, but I am afraid I must ask you to put yourself in danger once again."

"I think I shall be none the worse for it, Holmes."

"My dear Watson! Ever the loyalist. You still trust me after all these years."

"I do."

"What are you proposing?" said Miss Norton.

"I must know your gardener's schedule. When will he be out of his quarters? And how does his wife come and go?"

"We do not need his permission. I can simply ask—"

"No!" said Holmes. "He must not know, for that may put you — and certainly us — in danger."

"He works the grounds from sun-up to sunset. I can arrange for his wife to leave the quarters, a small bungalow at the edge of the pond."

"Very good. Watson, I'll need you to stand watch."

"You'll be perfect for that, Doctor," said Miss Norton with a laugh.

"Watson's performed admirably in this role in the past," replied Holmes.

"Are you prepared to go now?" asked Miss Norton. "To reach the bungalow, leave by the main path out the rear door, down towards the pond, and bear right when the path splits. The quarters are on the edge of the forest. I shall engage Mrs. Peterson; it would be convenient if the two of you were perhaps taking a walk through the yard so you can see when we leave."

"We are ready now," said Holmes. "What is your plan?"

"Mrs. Peterson is lonely, and she will take any opportunity for a companion. We will take a stroll of our own. I expect fifteen minutes shall be enough?"

"It should suffice," said Holmes.

"Very well."

Miss Norton disappeared out of the room, and Holmes and Watson allowed several minutes head start before they, too, exited through the rear doors into the expansive back lawn of the estate. The yard sloped downward and looked out onto a great pond, and even from the cusp of the door, the bungalow was visible on the right side of the pond, the larger guest-house on the right. Holmes and Watson strolled leisurely down the path towards the water; Holmes examined the estate while ostensibly maintaining a conversation with Watson. The gardener was nowhere to be seen.

As Holmes and Watson approached the pond, they heard laughter from their right. Miss Norton and the gardener's wife were lost in conversation as they rapidly climbed the hill towards the house. The two could have been sisters. When they disappeared over the ridge of the hill, Holmes motioned to Watson and pointed out the proper position for the doctor to stand watch.

Holmes slipped into the cottage. The home was a single small room, kept in a much more disorganized condition than Holmes expected. He didn't know exactly what he was looking for, but any number of items could provide a verification of what he sought: more clarity on the gardener's history. He scanned the room: a pile of books here, a set of electronic components on a drawer top there — and then Watson's voice, yelling. Had fifteen minutes gone by so quickly?

"Holmes, get out!"

Watson's warning came a moment too late. When Holmes emerged from the house, the gardener stood waiting, a snub-nose S&W Model 10 in his hand.

"Peterson, if that's your name," said Holmes, "lower the weapon. You've committed only minor crimes. Do not compound your folly."

Peterson's attention was on Holmes, ignoring the doctor. Watson shot Holmes a look of helplessness. The gardener gestured with the gun towards the pond in the centre of the yard, and Holmes slowly moved in that direction.

"Watson."

The doctor backed away cautiously, as if waiting for an opportunity; Peterson scowled in confusion. Holmes's only hope was to keep the gardener preoccupied, allowing Miss Norton and Mrs. Peterson to return and provide a distraction. He held his hands forward, palms facing the gardener in a sign of surrender, but moving slowly backwards as the man stepped toward him.

A bead of sweat formed on the man's brow, and the hand holding the pistol exhibited a slight tremor. The man had never shot anyone before. Holmes breathed deeply.

"*Mi dispiace*," said Peterson.

"Not as sorry as you'll be if you fire that weapon," replied Holmes. He couldn't see where Watson had got to. He reached in his mind for a bit of Italian.

"Don't shoot. *Non sparare*," he said, with a slight shake of his head.

"Holmes!" came a cry from near the house, where Miss Norton crested the top of the hill, running towards the bungalow. In that moment, the gardener's attention lapsed, and Holmes, still quick enough in old age, pounced. He knocked the pistol from the gardener's hands and it flew across the lawn. The gardener's wife appeared over the hill, trailing Miss Norton by twenty yards. Watson had reappeared, but stayed out of the row. Holmes tackled the gardener, and Miss Norton reached the gun before anyone else.

"Pietro!" said the gardener's wife.

"*Siamo scoperti!*" said the gardener, as Holmes lifted himself off the man with a grimace.

Miss Norton pointed the gun at the gardener. "He's not mute!"

"No, my dear Miss Norton," said Holmes. "He's Italian."

*****

The police had arrived and taken Mr. and Mrs. Peterson — or Pietro Schiazone and accomplice — into custody.

"Holmes, I fear I was no help."

"It doesn't matter, dear fellow. You've not been well."

"I'm baffled by how you put the threads of this one together," said Watson. Miss Norton nodded her agreement.

"Clearly the apparition Miss Norton saw was not real," said Holmes. "Which led to several questions: what was the truth behind the sightings, why would someone go through such lengths, and why would they ask for me?"

"They might have mentioned you to make the illusion more convincing," said Miss Norton.

Holmes tilted his head. "Yes, they might have. But there were more effective ways to make the illusion convincing. They asked for me for a purpose. What purpose do I serve, have I served, in my career? I solve cases. That was my first clue: they asked for me because they wanted to be caught.

"Once I had in mind the illusion was false, and the perpetrators wanted me to unveil them — or more accurately, unveil the truth behind the illusion — I considered the reasons why they would go to such lengths. What benefit was there to uncovering a hoax that would require perpetrating it in the first place? It made little sense, so little sense that I began to doubt my initial deductions.

"Then I noticed the incongruity in the pruning of the rose bushes, which suggested that your new gardener was Italian. It is not unheard of for others to use the Italian method of pruning, however; so when you told me your gardener was English, I looked for corroborating evidence. Later on, though, looking out at the ground from the balcony, I noticed your parsley. It was planted in the shade, which is uncommon.

Unless, of course, it is not the usual species, but rather the Sicilian variety. Then I knew for sure your gardener was Italian.

"As you believed the gardener was English, well, that meant another deception was taking place. First the deception of the illusion, and second, an Italian in your household who concealed his true lineage from you. Often deceptions like this are related. And when you mentioned that you'd been short-handed and hired recent help, it made a lot of sense that the new household members could be related to the illusion in some way."

"These threads are tenuous at best, Holmes," said Watson.

"Indeed, Watson. There seemed to be much concealment of inessential facts. Perhaps the new houseboy simply wanted to conceal his heritage due to the anti-Italian sentiment so rampant across this country. Then I made the Pinelli connection.

"It was singular that your old gardener left under such abrupt circumstances, after a life of service to your family, and yet he had in hand an immediate recommendation for his replacement.

"This suggests he was forced out, probably under threat of harm, and his replacement dictated by the Pinelli family. When we explored the servant quarters—"

"Slow down, Mr. Holmes, please." Miss Norton herself was breathless even though it was Holmes who spoke at a rapid pace. "Where does the break-in fit into all this?"

"Pure misdirection. He needed the original photographs to produce the spirit versions."

"But he had access to the photographs and could have taken them at any time."

"Exactly! If they went missing, and you noticed, you would immediately suspect someone on the staff. But by staging a break-in, he took himself out of suspicion, while obtaining what he needed. And back to the quarters: there I found the evidence I needed. Watson, it was all due to you."

"Why Holmes, I didn't do anything in the servant's quarters."

"No," said Holmes, "you didn't. But you did write up our escapades in the past, and what did I see in the quarters, but a copy of one of your — overblown, may I say — journal accounts. I believe you titled it 'A Scandal in Bohemia.' Yes, Watson, the account of our meeting with Irene Adler. This was the link I was looking for.

"More snooping uncovered the beginnings of a rudimentary radio transmitter, which would account for the sound heard when the spirit asked for me. I've experimented with my own crystal set, though I see little value in radio outside of military applications. I would bet we'd find a similar set hidden somewhere in the upper room where the ghost was sighted."

"But how did they produce the ghost itself?"

"My dear Watson, that part is elementary! I thought you would have figured it out. The French doors, when opened partially, create an instance of Pepper's ghost: when the lights in the room were on, the ghost would appear corporeal, but once they went off, the ghost would disappear. Did you notice the resemblance between Peterson's accomplice and our dear Miss Norton, who herself looks like her mother? She hid in the corner of the room, her reflection illuminated like a ghost when the light was on, and safely concealed once it was extinguished. Miss Norton, a believer, would be in no mind to look for a physical presence. Combined with the sound of a woman's voice claiming to be Irene Norton and mentioning my name, the power of Miss Norton's mind filled in the rest."

"I... I think you are correct, Mr. Holmes."

"Of course I am, Miss Norton.

"As so often is the case, even though this only provided me proof of a link I'd suspected and no other information, that link freed my mind to discover the true motive behind the ruse. The gardener wasn't simply hiding his heritage because he was Italian; he hid it because he was a member of the Pinelli crime family. And then this peculiar set of circumstances all fell into place.

"Miss Norton gained fame providing evidence against the Pinelli boss. His hearing is coming up in a fortnight's time. Miss Norton is scheduled to appear and testify, and she is a public sensation. You are much too well-known and well-liked for them to try to remove you altogether. If anything untoward had happened to you, certainly it would have arisen in the hearing, leading to the very condemnation they were trying to avoid.

"No, it would have been much better for them to make you look like a fool. So they brought me in. What could be more damaging to her and her testimony than an expert witness declaring her methods are fraudulent. And who better an expert witness than Sherlock Holmes?

"You yourself mentioned Eusapia Palladino, another Italian — and a fraudulent medium. A perfect role model for the Pinellis when deciding on deliberate fakery. I would announce that your work was nonsense, and you would be discredited."

Holmes found himself on a roll and continued. "So you see, there was no supernatural event after all. Ghosts are manifestations of the desires of the mind. Their appearance can always be explained by logic and rational deduction."

Miss Norton glanced at Watson, then back at Holmes. "But Mr. Holmes—"

"I've discovered many strange explanations for many odd phenomena, Miss Norton, and not one of them has involved anything supernatural, contrary to initial impressions," said Holmes. "Including the case of your mother."

"Mr. Holmes, I concede this case being mundane, but I assure you, the supernatural is real." She turned to Watson. "Doctor, you haven't told him, have you?"

Holmes tilted his head as he observed the doctor. The melancholy in Holmes's core returned — or perhaps it had never left, the elation of solving a case having distracted him.

"Holmes," said Watson, a slight tremble in his voice, "I have observed you make deductions in far thornier and more abstruse situations than our current one. You are not incapable of figuring what is happening, but I do believe you may be unwilling. Look at me."

Holmes's grey eyes shone with a sadness and a fear he'd rarely shown in his life. He looked Watson up and down.

"Indeed. I think I must have known all along. There were many strange circumstances of our trip," he said, "but I believe it was the waistcoat that gave it away."

Miss Norton tilted her head. "Mr. Holmes, I know the destination, but you'll have to offer more details for me to follow your path."

"When Watson first appeared at my farm in Sussex, he looked sickly. The sallow complexion of his face was more consistent with one who is in the throes of an ongoing illness, rather than one who has recently recovered. Two weeks later, and nary a cough or sneeze or other subsidiary sign from you, Watson.

"That, of itself, is not enough. Add to it that you have not taken any sustenance in that time. Nor engaged in any physical contact, to my knowledge. These observations, too, add to the curiosity, but again, they are not enough. Outlandish claims require vast evidence.

"But combined with the waistcoat — a most elegant piece of clothing, my dear Watson, the finest you've ever worn, if I am not mistaken. You've not changed out of it since we met. I daresay you'll never change out of it again. You cannot change out of it. These are the clothes you'll wear for eternity.

"When I first saw you, I deduced that you had come from a funeral. You confirmed the truth of the matter, like a proper gentleman. But the piece you left unsaid — what you didn't tell me — was that the funeral you came from was your own."

Flashes of the past resurfaced in Holmes's mind, and he remembered the funeral, which he could not bring himself to attend, for to see Watson laid to rest would be to admit that his one true friend had left him alone on the mortal coil.

"My dear doctor, I am sorry," he said. Sorry for missing the funeral. Sorry for the end of a wonderful life. Sorry for forgetting it all.

"No need to apologize, my friend," said Watson. "It has been hard on us all."

Holmes turned to Miss Norton. "My dear lady, it seems I owe you too an apology."

"You must say good-bye to your friend, before he leaves."

Holmes turned back to Watson. Even now, the doctor's form shimmered and faded. Holmes's melancholy bloomed into full sadness as he remembered the many cases he'd solved with Watson. The good doctor's re-tellings weren't so bad after all.

"Farewell," said Holmes.

"Farewell." And Watson was gone.

A weight lifted from Holmes's soul. A whole new world of mysteries had opened up before him.

"What will you do now, Mr. Holmes?"

Holmes stared at the spot where Watson had been standing moments before. Then he snapped out of his reverie, and a twinkle came to his eye. "I have an additional volume of my magnum opus to write. Miss Norton, you must visit me in Sussex some time. I have a photograph you'd be rather curious to see, I think."

The Adventure of Marylebone Manor

by Naching T. Kassa

This case was discovered in the old tin dispatch box and is dated 25 March, 1909. It was to be opened only upon the death of John H. Watson M.D.

ONE

The events of 31st October, 1903, are seared into my memory. Even the passing of six years has not dulled recollection. And, though I have taken pen to paper scores of times to record them, the tremor in my hand has prevented my doing so. It was not until this very night, with the visit of a friend, that courage inspired me to set down an account of what occurred.

Those who know of the matter involving Lord Lightfoot will remember a more mundane explanation for his death on 29th October (the papers having carried the news far and wide). None, however, were aware of the more fantastic nature of the problem, nor of the role Mr. Sherlock Holmes played in it.

The morning of 30th October dawned chill and bleak. I had received an enigmatic telegram from my companion bidding me come to Baker Street and I braved the ominous blanket of fog which filled street and alleyway alike. When I arrived, Mrs. Hudson greeted me at the door and ushered me up to my old rooms.

The sitting room had not changed since the advent of my second marriage and departure from Baker Street. Holmes, as untidy as ever, had left the early editions of yesterday's papers on the floor and long strides were required to cross them. I stood before the blazing fire and observed the pipes which decorated the mantle and the jackknife which pinned Holmes's correspondence to it; there were more pipes in the coal scuttle, including the odious and oily black clay. The faint scent of chemical filled the air, bringing with it a sense of nostalgia and a call to those adventurous days I had once shared.

"Mr. Holmes should return soon," Mrs. Hudson said, taking my coat, hat, and walking stick.

"He is not here? His telegram bade me come right away."

"He's not been home since yesterday afternoon. Not since the lady came."

"Lady?"

Footsteps sounded upon the stairs at that moment, and the door flew open. Sherlock Holmes strode into the room.

His hands were thrust deep into his pockets and he bore a grim expression I had never seen before. Without removing his greatcoat, he collapsed into a chair before the fire and drew his knees up to his chest.

"Tea, Mrs. Hudson," said he, "and, a few slices of toast. Never mind the doctor. I doubt he is hungry for he's already consumed his share of toast and marmalade and washed it down with a hasty cup of coffee."

I glanced down at my person and seeing nothing which might tell him of my breakfast, uttered my surprise.

"However did you know?"

"Come now, Watson. You must be accustomed to my methods by now." He gestured toward me. "There is a dark stain upon your shirt where you have splashed the beverage in your haste. And, a blot of marmalade upon your right sleeve."

"Ah," I said, "you inferred the toast from the marmalade."

"No, I observed the crumbs in your moustache."

As I pulled my handkerchief from my pocket, some of the good humour returned to his face. He leapt up from the chair, and collecting his clay pipe from the coal scuttle, proceeded to pack it with the dottles he kept on the corner of the mantelpiece.

"It is a bad business," he said, before placing the stem between his teeth. "You've read this morning's papers? The account of Lord Lightfoot's murder?"

"I have. Lord Charles' body was found in a locked room. As of this morning, they've arrested the groom."

Holmes snorted. "As I thought. Inspector Harding is as dull as our London constabulary and just as foolish. He has chosen the only man with motive. There is no evidence to connect the groom. He will be released."

Having lit the pipe, Holmes returned to his seat.

"Her Ladyship, Catherine Rose Lightfoot, came to see me yesterday. She is a singular woman and quite formidable in her beliefs. Do you believe in spirits, Watson? You know my feelings on the matter."

"I have very little to say regarding them," I answered. "Though, my literary agent, Conan Doyle, could expound upon them. He is a believer and has taken part in many séances over the years."

Holmes frowned at the mention of Doyle's name. But, to my surprise, he did not begin his usual diatribe.

"He may be acquainted with my client," he said. "Séances are performed at Marylebone Manor every third Thursday of the month. She believes a spirit murdered her husband."

"Surely, she's not serious."

Holmes rose to his feet and paced before the fire.

"I have investigated every inch of the manor, Watson. And, do you know what I have found? Nothing. Not a fingerprint, not a footprint, nor a speck of mud. The murderer left no trace."

"But... how can that be?"

"There is no earthly explanation for it. You know the old axiom of mine. When you have eliminated the impossible, whatever remains, however improbable—"

"Must be the truth."

"Precisely." The grim cast overcame his face once more. "Can you get away, Watson? For a day or two at most? I am lost without my Boswell, and I feel this case may be of great interest to you."

"My wife has gone to visit relatives in Bedfordshire, and I have no appointments until Monday. I should be happy to come."

"Good. If you will meet me at Charing Cross Station within the next two hours, we shall travel to Crowborough."

Before I could say a word, Mrs. Hudson entered, tray in hand. She wore an expression of disgust, one which she reserved for a select few of our visitors.

Two boys trailed behind her, both around the age of thirteen. The first I recognized as Wiggins of the Baker Street Irregulars. The other, a rather shabby and pale looking fellow, was unknown to me.

"These boys—" Mrs. Hudson began.

"'Ave somethin' important to tell the guv'nor," Wiggins announced.

Holmes halted his pacing and paused before the window. "It's all right, Mrs. Hudson. Kindly set the tray upon the table."

"But, Mr. Holmes—"

"Thank you, Mrs. Hudson. You may take your leave."

The landlady muttered under her breath as she left the room. When the door closed behind her, Holmes turned to the table and poured a cup of tea. He took a sip.

"Well, Wiggins, what is it?"

"Jimmy'll tell you," the boy said. "It's about His Lordship

what died."

The pale boy had pulled the soft cap off his head, exposing a head full of dark curls. He stared at Holmes with bold, blue eyes.

"You're the one they call Jimmy Hampstead, are you not?"

The boy nodded.

"The same boy who found Countess Lorenzia's diamond ring? And who discovered the identity of the body in the Thames last week?"

"The same, sir."

"How did you come by this information?"

The boy glanced at Wiggins, who shuffled his feet and averted his eyes.

"You will not believe me, sir," Jimmy replied.

"Those who tell the truth may always count me as a friend."

"I am... a detective, sir. Like yourself."

Holmes flashed a quick grin.

"A competitor?"

"I prefer to be a collaborator."

"I do not think it prudent to collaborate with a runaway. Even one as well-spoken and educated as yourself. You should collect your wolfhound and return to Hampstead."

The pale boy did not blink, though a slight smile touched the corner of his mouth. Wiggins' eyes grew large.

"I can see by the face of your companion, I have hit my mark," Holmes said. He stepped forward and plucked a long, wiry hair from Jimmy's coat. "I have often considered writing a monograph on the attributes of certain breeds and how to identify them from a single hair. Few dogs possess fur of such colour and texture. The smaller breeds are eliminated by the muddy print upon your left shoulder. Only a large dog could possess such a print.

"And though you have been on the streets long enough to

adopt the mannerisms and dress of the other children, you have retained your manner of speech. Your accent and choice of surname inform me as to your place of origin. You were well-educated in Hampstead and have kept up on your studies. The callous on the middle finger of your right hand reveals your interest in writing, and you keep a small volume in your coat pocket — may I?"

Jimmy withdrew the book and handed it to Holmes. He studied it for several seconds, then returned it.

"Coleridge. An interesting choice."

The boy accepted the book and returned it to his pocket. "Everything you've said is true, Mr. Holmes, but I will never return to Hampstead. It isn't safe."

"If you fear for your safety—" I began.

"I do not fear for myself, Dr. Watson."

He fixed his bold stare on Holmes once more.

"You have demonstrated your powers of observation, sir. May I demonstrate the powers I have been given."

"By all means."

"Would you close the drapes, please? The light hurts my eyes."

Holmes complied and when he turned away, the boy reached into the inner pocket of his coat. He withdrew a small flask, opened the cap, and drank from it, shutting his eyes as he did so. When he opened them, I nearly gasped at the strange and unnatural sight.

The boy's gaze had transformed. His once blue eyes now glowed green-yellow, like those of some large jungle cat.

My blood ran cold, but before I could utter a word to Holmes, they had retained their familiar hue.

"You are no stranger to death," Jimmy said. "As a boy, you found yourself at the mercy of a clever poisoner, one who nearly succeeded in killing you and your brother."

In all the years I have known my companion, I can think

of only a few instances when he has shown astonishment. The boy's words caused his brow to raise and his cheeks to pale.

"Holmes?" I said, looking first at one and then, the other. "Is this true?"

Neither seemed to hear me. They gazed at one another while the boy continued. "I know death well and I am not afraid. Last night, an innocent was accused of this heinous crime. Tonight, the Lady may die. I mean to stop this and find the true killer." The boy's voice rose and cracked. His freckled face reddened as Holmes clasped his hands behind his back.

Jimmy cleared his throat and continued. "Your investigation yielded no clues, and yet, I know they are there. There are things I can see and you cannot. I believe you need my aid. And I am more than willing to give it. Would you take me to Sussex, sir?"

Holmes paused, and the air hung heavy with his silence.

At last, he dug into his pocket and tossed the boy a coin.

"You cannot travel as you are. Purchase clothing and meet us at Charing Cross Station within the next hour."

Jimmy caught the coin and nodded to Holmes.

"Do not be late. The train will not wait. Nor will I."

Without another word, the boys rushed from the room. The door slammed shut behind them and their footsteps thundered down the stairs.

The moment they had gone, Holmes hurried to the shelves which housed his commonplace books. He selected a volume under the letter *B* and began leafing through it.

"Holmes... what the boy said. Was it true?"

Holmes paused and gave a curt nod.

"How did he know?"

"I will have the answer for you in a moment," he replied, returning to the commonplace book.

"He's an odd boy," I said. "Did you see the flask he carries with him? And, his eyes... they are strange."

Holmes set the book before me on the table.

"Read here, Watson."

Several articles from the *Westminster Gazette* met my eye. I read the one Holmes had indicated aloud.

"23 September 1893—James King, son of the Honourable Jacob King of Number 22 Elm Row, Hampstead, was discovered wandering Hampstead Heath this evening after disappearing for several hours. The boy, aged three years, was reported missing by his nursemaid, one Ella Anders, and later found by Constable Robert Hope.

The boy said he had been approached by the 'bloofer lady', who asked if he would walk with her. He later awoke in the darkness on the heath.

James King is one of several children who have disappeared and upon being found, claimed to see this 'bloofer lady'. He, like the others, had small puncture wounds in his throat, with no memory of how they came to be there.

Parents are encouraged to watch their children and report any strange instances of wild dogs upon the heath."

I glanced up at Holmes. "I remember this case. Several children were attacked."

Holmes pointed at the photograph which accompanied the article. My eyes widened.

"Holmes, this boy... it's Jimmy Hampstead."

The room acquired a chill as I stared at the picture. Holmes motioned to the next article. "Read on," said he.

The next headline read, "GIPSIES SOUGHT IN DISAPPEARANCE OF BOY," and was dated 7th May, 1898.

"James King, son of Jacob King, has gone missing. The boy, age eight, was last seen playing on the Heath in the company of his dog during the mid to late morning hours.

A search was mounted for the boy without result.

A band of gipsies, who were observed camping on the heath, have also disappeared. It is feared they and their leader,

Danio Vano, have taken the boy."

"There you have it, Watson," Holmes said. "The Romany took the boy and raised him among them. No doubt he has learned their many confidence tricks and is using them to cover his own knowledge of the case."

"But, how could a street boy know of such things?"

"It is precisely why I employ them, Watson. They can go where others cannot and overhear what is useful. I know he is involved, but whether it is to help or hinder, I do not know. That is why I have consented to his presence on this case. It is best we keep him close to us."

TWO

A swift ride in a hansom cab, a short trip to my home, and a quick journey to Charing Cross brought us to the afternoon train. We found Jimmy Hampstead on the platform, wearing his new travelling clothes and tugging at the collar of his shirt. Within minutes, we had boarded the train and were on our way to Sussex.

Holmes remained quiet during the journey and, though I tried to engage him in conversation, Jimmy Hampstead also kept to himself. He settled against the window and soon fell asleep.

We were halfway through our journey when Holmes leaned forward and in a hushed voice said,

"Keep your voice low, Watson. I wish to detail what I have discovered without waking the boy."

I nodded my assent.

"Most details regarding Lord Charles' body were kept from the papers. None were allowed to see the body, save me. If not for her Ladyship's intervention, I would not have seen it at all. Inspector Harding was less than pleased with my presence on the case. He considers himself a professional whilst others are mere amateurs."

Holmes pulled out his pocketbook and consulted the notes within.

"His Lordship's throat showed considerable bruising but, according to the attending physician, strangulation was not the cause of death. Apparently, Lord Charles' heart failed him."

"Strange."

Holmes nodded. "There are all manner of odd things. The physician found the corpse's hands most baffling."

"How so?"

"What would you do if a man attacked you intending to throttle the very life from you?"

"I would raise my hands to deflect him. Or, pull his hands from my throat."

"There would be marks on your hands? Skin beneath your fingernails?"

"Yes."

"No such evidence was found on his Lordship. His hands and nails were pristine."

"He did not fight back?"

"The room bore signs of a struggle. Furniture had been overturned, and the rugs bunched up on the floor. A vase had been smashed against the wall and the pieces, along with several roses, lay on the floor at its base. It had missed the dressing mirror by a narrow margin."

"Was there anything in the vase?" a voice said.

Holmes and I turned to Jimmy Hampstead. His face remained placid and his eyes shut. For a moment, I wondered whether he had spoken at all.

"The housekeeper swears it was filled with water. But that is not what I found upon the pieces." Holmes replied.

"You found a foul-smelling and viscous substance?"

Holmes raised an eyebrow. "I did."

Hampstead opened one eye. "Ectoplasm."

A knock came upon the compartment door at that moment. I tore my attention from the boy and looked up through the glass.

A tall, distinguished man with a large moustache and the build of a champion rugby player stood outside. A cry of surprise fell from my lips and I quickly slid the door open.

"Conan Doyle!"

"Hello, John," my literary agent said. "I thought I saw you board the train. Are you on holiday?"

Conan Doyle peered inside. His eyes narrowed when he caught sight of Holmes and he gave my companion a curt nod. Holmes did not return it.

"I'm on a case," I confided. "I shall have a new story for *The Strand*—and you could be of great help."

"Me?"

I glanced at Holmes. Neither he nor Jimmy Hampstead looked up.

"You are an expert on the supernatural. Are you acquainted with Lady Lightfoot?"

"Yes. I attend her séances once a month. Does this concern the demise of His Lordship?"

"It does."

"I am headed there tonight. Lady Catherine plans to contact Lord Charles's spirit and discover the identity of his murderer. She has invited the great medium, Irina Herskovaya, to conduct the séance."

Holmes snorted. Conan Doyle seemed not to notice.

"Would you care to join us, John? There's always room at the table."

"I shall consider it."

"You will not be disappointed. Madame Herskovaya is a talented medium. I hope you'll come. Until then, good day."

"Good day."

Conan Doyle continued past, and I shut the door to our

compartment.

"Conan Doyle's hatred for me is legendary," Holmes chuckled when he had gone. "I believe he's disappointed I returned from Reichenbach unscathed."

"That is unfair of you, Holmes," I interjected. "He was quite saddened by your disappearance."

"Only because it kept money from his pocket. Those romances he commissioned you to write instead made very little."

THREE

We arrived at Crowborough an hour later and hired a dogcart to take us on to our destination. The October sky darkened from pink to crimson as we rode, and a dull chill filled the air. A twenty-minute journey from the station brought us to a long drive lined with tall oaks. Here our driver halted.

"You'll have to walk from 'ere," he said. "'Tis as far as I go since his Lordship died."

I tried to reason with him but to no avail. Our baggage, such as it was, was tossed to the ground and the driver went on his way.

"May I take your bag, Doctor?" Jimmy asked as the dogcart vanished in the distance.

The cold air had done little to assuage the pain from old wounds and so I agreed.

We walked in silence as darkness overcame us. I had seen no sign of Conan Doyle and wondered if his driver had left him as unceremoniously as ours or if he had reached Marylebone before us.

The air grew remarkably still as we approached the dark and foreboding manor. We were but steps from the door when Holmes froze, his eyes on the window directly above us.

"Look," he whispered. I followed his gaze.

A pale visage peered at us from behind the glass. Dark, cavernous eyes stared out. A preternatural glow shone from it and it scowled at us before vanishing.

"My God, Holmes," I whispered. "What was that?"

A woman's scream sounded then, a cry of fear and loathing. It filled the air, raising the hair at the nape of my neck.

Jimmy Hampstead dropped my bag upon the drive and rushed up the steps to the door. "Hurry!" he called over his shoulder.

Holmes and I quickened our pace. We joined him at the door, and I rapped on it with my cane. It opened a crack and the frightened face of a woman peered out.

"It is I, Mrs. Dornish," Holmes said.

"Oh, Mr. Holmes," the woman replied. "Thank the Lord you've come. Miss Catherine she—"

Another scream interrupted her, drowning out her words. Yet another followed, and then another.

"Come, Watson!" Holmes cried. He rushed past Mrs. Dornish and into the foyer. A staircase stood to the left of us and he bolted up it.

FOUR

In my younger days, I might have kept up with Holmes and the boy. Unfortunately, those days had long passed, and due to the work of the Jezail bullet, I could only manage a quick walk. It took far longer to mount the staircase than I would've liked.

When I arrived at the top, I found a hall lined with doors. Holmes and Hampstead had gone to the one at the end and already had their shoulders against it. I joined them just as the jamb splintered under their weight and they burst into the room.

My eyes swept over the large bed, the dressing table, the

standing mirror, and several overturned chairs before settling on the prone figure on the floor.

Her Ladyship lay near the window, her breathing shallow and raspy. Holmes and I hurried to her side.

Catherine Lightfoot had been a celebrated beauty before her marriage to his Lordship. And, though her red hair was streaked with grey, she had lost little of her charm.

An examination of her throat forced a gasp through my lips. Bruises dappled the delicate skin of her throat and neck. Thankfully, no permanent damage had been done. I glanced about, looking for something which might revive the stricken woman, and seeing nothing, charged Mrs. Dornish with fetching me a bottle of brandy. She hurried off.

With Holmes's help, I moved the woman to the bed and returned to my ministrations. It was then I noticed Jimmy Hampstead standing nearby. He had his flask in hand, having just removed it from his lips.

"Hand that to me," I said. "She needs it."

The boy shook his head. "No, Doctor," he said. "This is the last thing she needs."

I frowned at him. "In my opinion, it is the last thing you need. You should not be drinking at your age."

He looked up at me, regarding me not with his blue eyes, but with his cat-like stare.

"It is a strange thing, Doctor. A boy of my age is too young to drink, yet not too young to work in a mine or be placed in an asylum."

I fell silent as he tucked the flask into his inner pocket and approached the head of the bed.

Lady Catherine's eyelids fluttered open, and she stared at me with wide, frightened eyes. Holmes came forward to take her hand and she clutched at him, opening her mouth as though trying to speak. No words spilled forth.

"There now," I said, holding up a cautionary hand. "You

must rest. Your voice will return within a day or two."

"Watson has my complete trust," Holmes said. "He is a doctor."

The Lady's eyes turned to Jimmy, and he gazed back into them.

Holmes whispered to me in a low voice, "I shall look the room over as quickly as possible. No doubt the staff will wish to call Inspector Harding in before the night is through."

"You won't find much evidence," Jimmy spoke up.

"I have already found some," Holmes contradicted. "The Lady faced her attacker. He struggled with her and would've killed her if we had not broken in as we did. I am confident we shall discover his means of escape."

"You should check the looking glass then," the boy replied.

"What of it?"

"It is the only mirror within the house which remains uncovered."

Holmes crossed the room and stood before the full-length mirror in its gilt frame. He touched the glass with his forefinger, then pinched it against his thumb. Pulling his glass from his pocket, he went over the frame before turning his attention to the fireplace. Two pokers and a piece of twisted metal lay beside the blaze. An odd smile played over his lips as he bent to lift the piece.

Jimmy Hampstead continued to stare at her Ladyship. She gazed back and several times, I saw her nod.

Holmes continued his investigation of the room. He finished at the window by wiping the sash with his handkerchief. Then, he returned to my side.

"The maid staff is rather lax. I've found dust on the window sash. It has not been open for some time."

"Then, how did the assailant gain entrance?" I asked. My question remained unanswered. Heavy steps sounded outside the door and it opened to admit a man I'd never seen before and hoped never to meet again.

He was short and squat with piggish eyes and a blotchy red face. A bowler sat upon his bald head and his suit appeared rumpled. He grimaced at the sight of Holmes.

"What are you doing here?"

"I came at the request of her Ladyship," Holmes said. "Why are you here?"

"I am a professional."

He pushed passed Holmes and ignoring me, stepped up to the bed.

"Your Ladyship," he said. "I've just heard the unfortunate news and I promise we will find the culprit as soon as possible."

"You'll release the groom then?" Holmes said. "He could not have been in two places at once."

"It is a well-known fact that the groom, Tom Castleberry, was in love with Lady Catherine," Harding said without turning. "He hated her husband and murdered him to have her. When she rebuffed him, he hired a man to kill her."

"On the salary of a groom? This assassin must be inexpensive as well as incompetent."

Harding spun on Holmes and jabbed a gloved finger into his chest.

"I've had enough of your ways, Mr. High-and-Mighty Amateur. I think I'll have you sent back to London with your tail between your legs."

"You'll return with me then? You've spent most of the day there, though it was not on police business. You've been to the theatre in the company of a young woman, one who I doubt is known to your long-suffering wife."

The colour drained from Harding's face. "You've been spying!" he growled.

"No need," Holmes said. "The evidence is quite compelling. The woman lives on Shaftesbury Avenue, does she not?"

"847 Shaftesbury Avenue, sir," Jimmy said, nodding in assent. "Her name is... Bella Brown."

Harding's eyes bulged. He hurried past us and out the door.

Holmes squinted at the boy. "Your powers of observation are astounding. I assume you saw the theatre ticket tucked into his pocket, the mud common to Shaftesbury on his boots, and the greasepaint on the collar of his coat. It escapes me how you knew the address and the young woman's name."

"I saw none of those things, sir," Jimmy replied.

"Then... how did you know? Who told you?"

"He did, sir. He told me."

A soft rapping sounded upon the door at that moment and Mrs. Dornish entered with a bottle of brandy and a glass on a silver tray. Conan Doyle followed at her heels.

"Is the Lady well?" he asked, his face creased with worry. "Mrs. Dornish has revealed all to me."

"Her throat is bruised, and she cannot speak, but she will recover within a few days," I replied as I poured a small amount of brandy into the glass. I handed it to Lady Catherine. When she finished, Conan Doyle approached her and took her hand.

"I am sorry, Catherine."

She squeezed his hand in response.

I looked over to see Holmes pulling young Hampstead aside. The two were deep in conversation. Holmes motioned to the boy's face and he nodded. They both looked toward the Lady and me.

"We will find the one who did this," Conan Doyle vowed. "Your husband will know the truth."

"You intend to continue with the séance?" I asked.

"Yes, John. Will you join us?"

Over Doyle's shoulder, I saw Holmes give a quick nod.

"I should be delighted, old fellow."

"I must bow out, I'm afraid," Holmes answered. "Mrs.

Dornish has prepared rooms for us and, as this promises to be a two-pipe problem, I shall be in mine for the foreseeable future. From there I can also keep an ear open should Lady Catherine be in need."

"I would like to attend, sir," Jimmy said. "If you don't mind."

"Are you a believer, son?" asked Conan Doyle.

"Oh yes, sir. I am."

"Then, I see no reason why you cannot. Madame Herskovaya awaits us in the drawing room."

FIVE

Lamp in hand, Mrs. Dornish led us down the hall, the stairs, and into the drawing room. The lamplight flickered before us and shadows danced in our wake.

When we entered the drawing room, we found a woman seated at a large round table. Her dark and lustrous hair lay fashionably curled upon her head and her strange violet eyes studied us as we took our seats.

I glanced about the room. Dark velvet curtains covered the windows. The same curtains hung above the fireplace mantel. I wondered what they could be hiding.

Mrs. Dornish dimmed the lamps, lit the candle at the centre of the table, and quickly took her leave. Her wide eyes and the way her hands shook, led me to believe she wished no part in the séance.

"Gentleman, I give you the finest medium in all of Europe," Conan Doyle began, as the housekeeper shut the door. "Madame Herskovaya."

I rose to take her hand. Jimmy remained in his seat.

"A spiritual attack has taken place this evening and the time of the spirits is already upon us," Madame Herskovaya said, as the candle's tiny flame flickered before her. "We must not delay another minute. Join hands."

I took the medium's hand and Jimmy's, while he took Conan Doyle's. When Doyle took the medium's right hand, the circle was complete.

The woman leaned forward, swaying back and forth in her chair.

"I invite the spirit of Lord Charles Lightfoot to this table," she said. "Come and join us. Our questions are urgent, and time is short."

The medium's grip on my hand grew tight.

"Your murderer has returned to the house and attacked your wife. Come and reveal his identity."

The candle at the centre of the table suddenly guttered, leaving us in near darkness. I glanced at Jimmy. In the dim light, I found his brows knitted together and a frown upon his lips.

The medium fell forward on the table. Her arms grew slack.

"I am here," a deep voice boomed. It seemed to come from Madame Herskovaya herself.

"Charles?" Conan Doyle said. "Is it you?"

The medium remained face down on the table. "It is I."

Jimmy whispered something under his breath, his voice so low, I could not hear it.

"Do you have an answer for us?" Conan Doyle asked.

The medium shivered and the deep voice grew hollow.

"I am afraid."

"There is nothing more to fear. You are beyond pain."

"No, he will find me."

"I assure you. You are safe."

"No!"

"Please, Charles. For Catherine's sake."

The medium convulsed and shook her dark hair loose. It covered her face. She took a deep breath and blurted out, "It was Castleberry! Tom Castleberry murdered me!"

SIX

Jimmy released my hand and delved into his inner pocket. He put the flask to his lips and drank.

The medium rose and tipped her head back. "Someone has broken the circle. The spirit has fled."

"The spirit was never here to begin with," Jimmy said.

All eyes turned to the boy. Madame Herskovaya glared at him; her hands clenched. "Unbeliever!" she cried.

"Charles Lightfoot has moved on to the next world," Jimmy said, his eyes glowing in the gloom. "He is not in this room, Madame Herskovaya. Why don't you call the true murderer to this place?"

The candle suddenly flared to life and a bone-chilling cold settled over the drawing room. Madame Herskovaya seemed to cower before Jimmy's gaze. Her face grew drawn and pale.

"You have accused an innocent man of a great wrong," Jimmy said. "To cover your own misdeeds."

"I have done nothing," she replied.

"You helped lure the spirit here. You brought misfortune on this house."

Tears glistened in the woman's eyes. She shook her head. "I meant no harm."

"But you have already harmed Lord Charles. You may not have authored his death, but you have aided in it."

"We only wished to confirm the existence of the spectral world. We called the ghost for knowledge; we didn't know it would kill!" she moaned.

"Who aided you?" Jimmy asked.

The medium didn't answer. She covered her mouth with one hand.

"Who!" Jimmy snarled. His expression twisted into one of

pure cruelty and I could've sworn his teeth had grown longer and pointed.

The medium screamed. Sobbing, she rushed from the room. I made to follow her, but Jimmy held me back.

"No, Doctor," Jimmy cried. "I've been a fool!"

"What is it?"

"Lady Catherine and Mr. Holmes—they're both in danger!" He hurried to the fireplace and reaching up, pulled the velvet drape aside. Behind it lay a large, ornate mirror.

Jimmy cast no reflection within the glass.

He must have seen my expression of dread, for he gave me a smile and said, "Fear not, Doctor. I mean you no harm. Meet me in Her Ladyship's bedroom."

With that, he climbed up on the mantelpiece and dived into the mirror.

SEVEN

The house lay in deathly silence as I watched the boy disappear and I realized I was alone in the room. Conan Doyle had also vanished.

My head spun as I rushed from the drawing room, up the stairs, and into the West Wing hall. I had no time to consider the fantastic thing I had just seen, nor wrestle with the reality which now confronted me.

I opened the doors of several rooms, searching for Holmes. I found all of them vacant.

Somewhere, a clock tolled the hour. It ended on twelve.

I pressed on to the Lady's bedchamber. Once there, I threw the door open and found a terrifying sight before my eyes.

It was as if the bedroom had vanished, and a new room had taken its place.

A lamp sat on the table beside a strangely familiar bed. In

fact, I felt as though I'd been in the room before, though my mind could not place it...

"Watson, the door! Do not—"

Too late. Before Holmes could finish, I had shut the door behind me. The lock clicked into place. Holmes hurried to the door and tried it, but it would not open.

"We must find the mirror," Jimmy said. I noticed him for the first time, standing near the window. "It's the source of his power and his means of travel between our worlds. If we destroy it, we destroy this world."

"But... I saw you enter the mirror downstairs. Unless I am mad."

"The one in this room vanished the moment he entered," Holmes said.

"He has hidden it," Jimmy replied.

"Who?" I asked.

"The ghost Madame Herskovaya summoned, the one who was supposed to prove the existence of the spirit world. His name is—"

"Dr. Grimesby Roylott," Holmes said.

Now, I recognized the room. The bed had belonged to Miss Helen Stoner and it had been clamped to the floor. In the wall above, I could see the ventilator between the rooms and the useless bell-rope beside it.

Jimmy appeared stunned by Holmes's revelation. "However did you know?" he asked.

"It was all quite elementary. My investigation of Lady Catherine's room told me many things as did your mentioning the mirror. I found more of that viscous substance upon it and a small crack in the glass. I also found a poker which the Lady had wielded in order to smash the mirror. Unfortunately, Roylott caught the poker before it could finish the job. As you remember, Watson, it was his habit to demonstrate his strength through the bending of pokers. He twisted it into a rather familiar shape before attacking Lady Catherine. You can confirm this, Jimmy, can you not?"

The boy nodded. "She told me in the bedroom when I arrived."

"Told you? But she cannot speak." I said.

"She did not need to. I saw it in her eyes."

I would have questioned the boy's cryptic statement, but a sudden thought struck me. I glanced about the room. "Where is Lady Catherine?"

"Apparently, Roylott has little interest in her, now that she has served her purpose," Holmes said. "She was bait with which to trap us."

"The ghost has been here the whole time," Jimmy said. "He never left the room. He intended to capture Mr. Holmes alone, to kill him, but I chased him away. How long he will stay away is beyond my ken. Even my powers will be no match for his more vengeful nature." The boy's voice grew high once more and he struggled to correct it. "He will, no doubt, return soon."

A low-pitched whistle sounded at that moment. The noise startled both Holmes and myself.

Jimmy looked into my face. His eyes widened and he backed away from the bed.

The whistle sounded again, but before I could lower my eyes to the floor, the lamp went out.

We were plunged into darkness.

I held my breath as several ribbons of light appeared above the bed. They were accompanied by the scent of a strong cigar. Someone had opened the ventilator in the next room.

Something hissed in the dark.

"Beware the Speckled Band!" Holmes whispered.

Green mist seeped in through the ventilator. It descended to the bed and on to the floor, where it coalesced into the form of a tall man clad in a dressing gown. I knew the cruel face. I had seen it in the window when I first arrived.

"Holmes, the busybody," Roylott said, taking a step forward.

A glowing snake suddenly appeared near his slippered feet. It slithered up his leg and body until it reached his head. There, it lay poised as a crown.

"I warned you to stay out of my grip," he sneered. He charged my friend.

Holmes lashed out at Roylott, but his hands went right through him. The ghost grasped him by the throat and pinned him against the wall. I tried to get a grip on Roylott's arm, but my fingers clutched empty air.

"Help me!" I cried in desperation.

Jimmy did not heed my words. His eyes were locked on Roylott's face.

"Jimmy, now!"

The boy turned to me, his expression grave.

"I am sorry, Doctor. I cannot."

The snake slid off Roylott's head, down to his shoulder, and up his arm. "Holmes the meddler," he said. "Meddle no more."

The swamp adder sank its fangs into Holmes's throat and, with a hollow laugh, the ghost dropped him to the ground.

The laughter remained even after he had disappeared.

EIGHT

After the spirit's departure, the air shimmered, and to my astonishment, the room reverted to its original state. Lady Catherine lay upon the bed, as she had before, this time deep in slumber. The mirror stood in the spot we had left it.

I cared for none of these things. A nightmare had unfolded before my eyes.

Holmes still lay upon the carpet, unresponsive to my treatment. The swamp adder's poison seemed as potent in spirit form as in that of a live animal. Holmes was slipping away.

I had not seen my friend die at Reichenbach; I had only imagined his descent into the abyss. To see him die now was more than I could bear.

I scarcely remember Jimmy directing me to lift Holmes's head. But I must've done so, for the next moment, the boy had his flask to my companion's lips.

"That will be of little help," I said.

"It is not what you think, Doctor. There are no spirits in this flask."

"What is it then?"

The boy did not answer. He simply poured the liquid between Holmes's lips. Thick, scarlet drops flowed from the corner of his mouth and down to his chin. They appeared to be... blood.

Horror filled me and I wondered what kind of insanity I had become privy to. I shook my head trying to clear it. I must be wrong. Surely, it could not be blood. My perceptions had been sorely tested by this night. I could not succumb to such strange fancies.

Jimmy pulled the flask away. It left a red stain upon Holmes's lips.

"Again, I must apologize for this, Doctor. It became clear to me that the ghost would not give up his secrets regarding the mirror. The only way to gain release from his world was to allow him to end the thing he hated most. He was unaware of my secret and the fact that this flask grants me certain curative powers. You see, Mr. Holmes is coming around already."

The colour had returned to my friend's cheeks and when his eyes opened, I found them as bright as before. He rose to sitting position with the energy of a much younger man. He focused on the flask in Jimmy's hand.

"I drank from it?"

"And it restored you. I do not know what else it may do.

You were never bitten."

"Bitten?" I asked.

"All in good time, Watson," Holmes said, regaining his feet. "For now, we must find Madame Herskovaya's accomplice, the one who aided her in summoning Roylott's spirit."

"And destroy the means of the summoning," Jimmy added. "I would say, given Roylott's use of them, it's a mirror. Spirits often flee to the looking glass upon the moment of death. That is why most are covered, as they were in this house following the death of Lord Charles. This person uncovered the mirror in Lady Catherine's room, enabling Roylott to attack her."

"I must admit, I'm mystified," I said as we left the bedroom behind us. "Who could have done such a thing?"

Neither Holmes nor Jimmy answered. I wondered whether they had heard me as we descended once more to the drawing room. When they halted outside the room, I knew they had.

"Only one person would unleash such a monster," Holmes said. "He may not have expected Roylott to kill Lord Charles, but he expected him to kill me."

"I believed him innocent," Jimmy said, ruefully, "and did not use my gift as I should have. I will not make that mistake again."

We entered the drawing room. A man stood with his back to us, his eyes on our reflections in the mirror above the fireplace.

"You never cease to amaze me, Holmes," Sir Arthur Conan Doyle said. "You should be dead."

NINE

Conan Doyle continued to gaze into the mirror, a weird grin on his face. I shook my head.

"No, Arthur," I said. "This cannot be."

His expression grew melancholy. "I'm afraid it's true, old man. Oh, it started innocently enough. I came into possession of a mirror from the estate of Stoke Moran, taken after the demise of Dr. Grimesby Roylott. The Romany who sold it to me swore it possessed magical properties, properties which could raise the dead. This was confirmed to me by Madame Herskovaya, who it seems, has fled this house never to return.

"I confided the history of my new prize to Lady Catherine. It was her wish that we raise a spirit using the glass. Both she and Lord Charles hoped it would prove once and for all the existence of the spirit realm.

"I chose Roylott because of his connection to Stoke Moran. I had hoped the transition to the spirit world would have calmed his murderous spirit. I had no idea he would kill Lord Charles. I certainly wished no ill on Lady Catherine. She was but a means to an end."

"You used her... in an attempt to kill Holmes," I said.

Conan Doyle lowered his eyes from the glass.

"A weight was lifted from me when you revealed Sherlock Holmes had fallen to his death at Reichenbach. For the first time in years, I could put my heart behind the work as I truly wished to do. No more sensationalism. No more muck. You were free to write the way you wished, and I was proud to be your agent.

"And, then he returned. He drew you back into that world and it was worse than ever before. You know how insufferably arrogant he is. How he dismisses everything which does not fit in his kingdom of logic. How ironic would his death be if he were killed by the spirit of a man he himself had killed?"

A ripple appeared in the mirror above him.

"I do not know how the spirit failed me, but I know he will not fail again. My only regret is that you and the boy must die with Holmes, John. Where have you left him?"

"Left him? Why he's—"

Holmes laid a hand on my arm. "The boy is not far. In fact, he is closer than you think."

Conan Doyle turned away from the glass and gasped in surprise. Jimmy raised the candlestick he had taken from the table and brought it down across the older man's head.

Conan Doyle fell to the floor, and Jimmy dropped the candlestick beside him. The mirror above the mantelpiece continued to ripple, each ring growing larger as the ghost attempted to enter the room.

The boy crossed to the fireplace and pulled the poker from the rack. He held it out to Holmes.

"From one competitor to another, sir," he said. "Would you do the honours?"

Holmes half-smiled. He accepted the poker and said, "I prefer to be a collaborator." Then, he hefted the poker and with a tremendous swing, struck the mirror.

The glass burst into thousands of glittering shards. They rained down upon the carpet as the ghost's shrieks filled the air.

In a matter of seconds, the ghost of Grimesby Roylott was no more.

TEN

Conan Doyle awoke with no memory of what had transpired that night. Nor did he remember what had taken place in the months since purchasing the mirror. Jimmy suggested that the destruction of the mirror had broken the ghost's hold on him and left him mercifully unaware of the part he had played in Lord Charles's death.

Holmes said we should keep the truth a secret. Not just for Conan Doyle's sake, but because no one would believe us. That Roylott had tapped a genuine resentment in Conan Doyle was undoubted, but that issue was for another time; the man I had known as a friend would surely never have contemplated serious harm to another without such malign urging.

We had no trouble convincing Inspector Harding to join us in complicity. Jimmy's knowledge of his mistress, Bella Brown, persuaded him with appalling ease. With my aid, Holmes created a more routine story concerning Lord Charles' death, stating he had died from natural causes. Harding released it, and Tom Castleberry, with none the wiser.

Lady Catherine had lost her husband, and despite my diagnosis, much of her voice as well. Her interest in exposing the spiritual world waned, though she spent the rest of her life in séances trying to contact Lord Charles.

Madame Irina Herskovaya vanished. She has not been heard from or seen to this day.

Holmes, Jimmy, and I took the afternoon train back to London. It was an extraordinary trip; one which Holmes and I would speak of at length in the coming years. Both of us had gone to Sussex believing in the rational world. We had never expected to return as believers in the supernatural one.

Several questions came to mind as we left the station and I put them to Jimmy as he sat dozing near the window.

"How did you hide your reflection from the mirror?" I inquired. "And, how on earth did you leap into it?

Jimmy smiled and looking into his freckled face, I was struck by how young he truly was.

"You still don't know what I am, Doctor?" he said. "Mr. Holmes deduced my secret following Inspector Harding's first visit."

"I must confess, I do not."

"At the age of three, I was abducted by a woman children called, 'The Bloofer Lady.' She drank my blood and forced me to drink hers.

"A brave band of hunters destroyed her and her hold on me ended. However, unlike other victims, I was far from free.

My physiology developed certain... needs, an addiction if you will." He glanced at Holmes. "Mr Holmes knows what I mean."

"My parents did not understand me nor did the doctors they took me to. For the next five years, I was poked, prodded, taken to sanitariums, and eventually, placed in an asylum. At the age of eight, I was pronounced cured and returned to my family. But I was not cured. My hunger grew and one night, my younger sister...nearly fell to my need. I fled my home and joined Danio Vano and his people to keep her safe.

"The Romany people were good to me." Here he glanced at Holmes, who gave him an almost imperceptible nod. "They helped me with my... addiction by providing another source of sustenance. They also taught me how to mesmerize. I used this talent on Madame Herskovaya and obtained part of her confession. I've even used it on you a time or two."

"Everything you did... it was all a trick?"

The boy smiled and nodded.

"You possess great power. It's a wonder you're not corrupted by it."

"Your stories saved me from such a fate, Doctor. They inspired me to devote my life to fighting injustice. I left the Romany and joined the boys on the streets of London, hoping I would become an Irregular. It has been my fondest wish to meet Mr. Holmes and be like him..." The boy trailed off, his face reddening. He lowered his eyes. "The rest you know."

"You should not live on the streets," Holmes said. "You could work as my page."

"You already have a page, sir, and I believe Billy would be quite put out. No, I have a place where I belong, and I am happy there. However, if you should need me, I am always available for collaboration."

"I shall be glad of your help," Holmes said. He put out his hand and the boy shook it.

ELEVEN

We parted ways with Jimmy at Charing Cross Station, and I found myself torn as he walked away. On the one hand, I found him a courageous and intelligent companion, one who would grow to be a fine man one day. On the other, I hoped I would not meet him again anytime soon. To be near the boy seemed to court danger, the kind I found myself helpless against.

Holmes and I returned to Baker Street. And as I sat upon the settee, I wondered about the events of the weekend past and how the shadows filled me with a new dread. Holmes startled me when he spoke.

"I think, when I retire, I shall buy a little house in the Sussex countryside and take up the keeping of bees."

"Bees? Why bees?"

"They live by ritual and order. Admirable traits in any species. Humans are a cruel lot, whether dead or alive."

"Jimmy spoke of a cruel person in your past."

Holmes breathed smoke. It ringed his head.

"She was one of the most winning women I have ever known, and yet, she found the need to poison her children for their insurance money. She underestimated our intelligence."

I stared at Holmes, speechless. He smiled.

"Jimmy is a good lad," he said. "And, it is a good thing to thirst... for justice."

The Village on the Cliff

by David Marcum

"Watson – wake up. We're nearly there, I think."

I opened my eyes, never having truly been asleep, but rather drifting through one of those dozes into which one sinks while ill. I pulled myself straighter in my seat as I assessed my condition while reaching for my flask.

The soreness at the back of my throat was still present, and there was no denying now that I was coming down with something. It was likely just a typical cold, brought on by fatigue and the recent abrupt change of season. I doubted that it was anything that I'd caught from a patient – like most who are involved in the healing arts, exposure to so many varied illnesses seems to provide an immunity of sorts. It's a phenomenon that seems to be matched only by teachers of small children, who regularly intersect with that veritable stew of childhood diseases that are carried by their students to the common locus of the school to be shared and blended.

My self-diagnosis was of very little comfort, however, as I took the smallest of sips of brandy, realizing that the flask was more empty than full, and that it was unlikely to be replenished anytime soon. I castigated myself for not inquiring as to a refill before we left the station and set off into this barren waste.

We were quite a bit closer to the small range of mountains that had been on the western horizon since we departed – less than an hour before, as I confirmed by checking my watch. Still, the sun was significantly lower in the sky than when I had closed my eyes. I had fitfully dozed almost as soon as Holmes had gigged the horse. Of course he was aware that I wasn't functioning at full muster. Certainly I had slept most of the way down on the interminable train journey, awakening only at various stations of greater or lesser importance when Holmes would leap to the platform with his usual boundless energy to send or receive telegrams. The brisk autumn air would then rush into our compartment, and for a moment my sinuses would ache, radiating down the back of my throat along what seemed to be raw striations. If I had been well, none of this would have caused a second thought.

When possible we had found something to eat, although I had no interest in food, or when we were more hurried Holmes obtained something hot for me to sip, and the heat of the tea or coffee had felt good on my throat. But those stations with a soothing beverage had become few and far between, and I had sipped my brandy instead, its heat offering a comforting but temporary cauterization before I fell back asleep, rattling always westward, ready to assist when needed.

I'd been well the night before, retiring early and expecting Holmes's summons at any moment – although it hadn't arrived until the early morning hours. Two days earlier, Holmes had been alerted by his brother, Mycroft, that Lord -----'s diary had been stolen. The foolish peer had kept the journal against all common sense, as well as in defiance of the security dictates of his department. Explosive details of the behind-the-scenes manoeuvrings that related to the events at Fashoda and threatened to plunge us into war with France were recorded in the little book, an innocent-looking object of blue-dyed leather – and it had been taken by Lord -----'s valet, Edwin Byrnam.

The thief's identity was quickly established by Holmes, although his motivations were still uncertain, and Mycroft had set plans in motion to arrest the man and retrieve the dangerous volume before its contents could be revealed. But the affair was bungled when one of the arresting agents was himself revealed to be a German sympathizer. His own attempt to retrieve the diary spooked Byrnam, who vanished into the warrens of London with his son, Geoffrey. A widower, Byrnam apparently felt that he had nothing else to lose and a fortune to gain.

It took Holmes the better part of a day to get onto the man's trail, and word had arrived late that night that our pursuit must begin immediately. It had been decided that no chances could be taken that someone else might gain the diary – or even have the chance to read it – for after the incident of the German agent, who could be trusted? Therefore, Holmes and I would pursue Byrnam and his son alone, to take him into custody in person so that no one, not even an ignorant provincial policeman, might possibly see the diary's contents. Thus we travelled companionless, our only aid being uninformed watchers along the way who had no idea the identity of our quarry, or the reason for our interest in him. Their job was simply to relay where Byrnam and his offspring left the train back to Mycroft in London, who would then send coded messages ahead for us to collect along the way.

I knew when I awoke and quickly dressed the previous night that all was not right. At Paddington, we were able to catch the very next west-bound train after the one that Byrnam and his son had taken, and I immediately settled into my seat and fell asleep once more, rather than my usual practice of reading the newspaper or a book. There was certainly nothing to see outside as we flew through the night-darkened countryside.

When morning arrived, we were still making our way west, never quite catching up with the elusive valet and his son. As the sun moved across the sky, I began to feel that I had been on the train for days instead of hours. The morning passed in a blur of cold and uneasy dreams, rocking from our passage across the banks and turns of the line and the occasional points, or when passing another train hurrying in the other direction. Byrnam and son seemed to randomly change directions, leaving the train at one station and catching another to a different quarter of the compass, and then doubling back, seeming to sense the pursuit, but always steadily working their way west. Slowly the sun overtook us, and by afternoon we began to chase it. Soon it outpaced us, and as it started to drop toward the far horizon, we reached a bleak and remote halt, somewhere in Wales, where Holmes leapt out to question the station master. In a moment, he beckoned me to join him, where he informed me that Byrnam and his offspring had arrived on the previous train, not more than an hour previous, and had walked out of the station. Somehow, we had managed to stay on his trail.

None of Mycroft's agents, nor any of the uninformed policemen conscripted into this scheme, were waiting at this particular location to verify the Byrnams' passage – for certainly there weren't enough of them available to cover every possible stop. I realized that the pursuit of the fugitives must continue, and that it was up to Holmes and me, on our own.

While I huddled in my coat, Holmes conferred with the station master, who related that the two men – one in his early fifties, the other about half that age – had rented a cart and left by a dirt road headed west out of the village. "But," he added in his awkward English, with something of a cautious tone, "he was anxious, and paying little attention. Do you see in the distance? There, where the road splits? I told him to bear right and head north along the mountain – he wanted to go inland – but he took the wrong path, toward that gap that rises up near the sea."

"And where will that take them?"

The station master mumbled something under his breath, and then said, "We call it *Cig* now. The road ends there."

"Cig?" asked Holmes. He seemed to become sharper then, more especially alert somehow, as if that odd word might mean something – but only someone who had known him for so long would recognize it. "Is that a village?"

"It was once," came the reply. "Not much there now besides a few old houses and a church. It was abandoned years ago, when the fishing couldn't support them any more. But..."

He faded away, and Holmes frowned. "But what?"

"There are some other people there. They arrived back in the summer. They keep to themselves, and we let them. These men that you're after – they shouldn't have gone there. You shouldn't go there either."

"Why?"

The man shook his head and started to turn away, but Holmes stopped him, a hand on his shoulder, and asked about obtaining a cart of our own. The station master scowled but directed us to a stable within sight up the nearby dirt lane that served as the village's main street. Within a few moments, we had made our way there, under the vaguely hostile gazes of a dozen villagers. We entered the ramshackle establishment and transacted with the owner, who seemed rather wary after learning our destination. "Bring the horse back safely," he warned, after demanding extra payment, but without further explanation. Five minutes later we were again following along Byrnam's track. Looking back over my shoulder, I could see the station master watching us, apparently with nothing better to do than see if we also took the left fork toward Cig. We did, and soon both the man and his ramshackle little village were behind us in the spreading darkness.

The sky was clear, with the promise that the night would be cold. The sun was hanging low in front of us, but glancing toward it didn't seem to hurt my eyes, and it didn't appear to lighten the blue metallic tints of the surrounding sky. Rather, something in the atmosphere, far out over the sea, looked to be occluding and muting the star's light to that of a full daytime moon.

I considered whether to take another pull at my flask but refrained, hoping to reserve my supply as long as possible. Again I wished that I had asked the station master about purchasing a fresh bottle before allowing Holmes's urgency to hurry me out of town. I knew now that my sore throat would only get worse as the evening progressed. And did I perhaps feel just the beginnings of a fever?

Beside me, Holmes was congratulating us on the successful pursuit of the Byrnams. He recounted the events of our journey that had occurred while I slept – the running series of messages between him and Mycroft in London, who had coordinated the various officials that had kept watch along the way to determine when Byrnam and his son changed trains, and in which direction. It really sounded like a masterpiece of modern cat-and-mouse. Holmes had confirmed that the two men had been left alone the entire time, and the diary, with its explosive contents, was certainly still in the man's possession. All that remained was to corner them and retrieve it, and if possible take them into custody – although that was of lesser importance. Why flee to this godforsaken corner of the kingdom? Sourly, I pulled my coat tighter.

Thinking of our destination, I glance at Holmes. "You seemed to be interested when the station master mentioned the name of the village. *Cig*. Does that mean something?"

He was silent for a moment, and if he hadn't been holding the reins, I suspect that he would have taken that time to go through the tedious process of lighting his pipe. Finally he spoke. "Do you recall Andrew Bradfield?"

The name was familiar, but at first I couldn't place him, and I was irritated that Holmes would make me guess, rather than simply tell me. Then I remembered the fellow – small, earnest, and possibly a bit too willing to give credence to the impossible.

"He's the one that assisted Alton Peake for a time."

"That's him. Peake brought him up several days ago. He's disappeared."

"Hmm," I replied, non-committally. My throat didn't encourage unnecessary discussion.

"Peake said that Bradford had followed some rumor or another west into Wales. And before he left, he had mentioned the word 'Cig' when he was trying to interest Peake in accompanying him."

"Well, why didn't Peake go, then? He typically chases after any rumor or legend that scurries across his path," I said grumpily, and rather unfairly.

Holmes and I both respected Peake, even though we didn't necessarily agree with his perspective. Whereas Holmes had established himself as a consulting detective from the time he first came down to London in the mid-1870's, Peake had followed a parallel but very dissimilar track as an investigator of the occult. By the time that I met Holmes in early 1881, both he and Peake were already acquainted. I gathered that they had first run across each other in the reading room of the British Library – each of them then with too much time on their collective hands, waiting for clients, and attempting to educate themselves in their chosen professions. Although they have very different philosophies, they've always seemed to enjoy one another's company. Over the years, Peake has been both a casual visitor in our rooms in Baker Street, stopping by to share news and stories before the fire with whisky in hand, and we've also intersected with a few of his investigations during some of our own.

To be fair, he is never gullible, or willing to believe every outrageous tale that he hears, and in each instance that we've seen him in action, he's assisted in debunking a number of supernatural scams. But conversely, he's told us tales of cases that we haven't observed, of doings that are better shared around a dark fire in the woods than a quiet sitting room, relating things that cannot be explained away with logic and reason. Holmes has always been politely interested, and his scepticism has sometimes been a bit more polite than mine, I'm afraid. He has explained to Peake on several occasions that "No ghosts need apply," further adding that if he allowed a supernatural explanation to be a possible option during an investigation, then he ought not even try to find the physical evidence which so consistently proves a more mortal motivation. "If I credit your ghosts and phantoms," he has said, "then I might as well be back in the Dark Ages." Peake usually smiles when Holmes says something along these lines, and then he takes a drink of whisky, but his eyes don't reflect his smile, for they always seem a bit as if he's seen horrors, and that he's still seeing them.

"Peake stopped by last week while you were away in Chelmsford," Holmes continued. "He wanted my advice on conducting a search for a missing person. Apparently waiting for a vibration through the ether wasn't doing very much to locate his former assistant."

I barked a laugh, which devolved into a wheezing cough. Holmes glanced my way and continued. "Peake took Bradfield on as something of an apprentice a few months ago, but he found that the lad was simply too willing to believe every ridiculous story that he heard, without question. It was apparently useful at times – his sincere interest in what he was told encouraged a few mountebanks to become careless, allowing Peake to function quietly and expose them. But Bradfield's trust in one such swindler was noticed by a young widow who took his apparent confidence as an endorsement, and she subsequently gave the man her savings. The scoundrel had absconded before Peake could reveal his methods, disappearing with all that the woman had. Peake was able to track the trickster down and effect arrest, retrieving most of the stolen funds, but he realized then that Bradfield had become a liability, one that couldn't be adequately trained or trusted.

"They parted ways, but a week ago, Bradfield showed up at Peake's Charterhouse Square rooms, wild-eyed and frantic, reporting that he'd come across... something. He wouldn't say what, but he was in obvious distress, and he wished for Peake to drop everything and go with him at once – to Wales. To *Cig*. Peake couldn't get away just then – some bit of business was coming to a crisis – and he begged Bradfield to tell him more, and to wait a few days until he could join him, but the lad was impatient and left without further explanation.

"Peake consulted me about all of this, and I put a few lines in the water, but as you know, I was myself involved in that little matter of the Hucknall coffee poisoning, and I could do no more. I had to report that my sources had failed to identify a location in Wales called 'Cig'. Now I understand that the name is unofficial. How unusual that Byrnam would lead us there after all.

"Perhaps Peake is right, Watson, and there *are* lines and forces all around us, shining like a glowing path or a beam across the sky that our eyes cannot perceive, but yet resonating somewhere in our minds – possibly in that primitive hind-part at the base of our brains where the most basic functions lie. Even as our heart is kept beating, we are sensing what cannot be consciously perceived. What other reason could place the village of Cig in front of me twice in such a short period of time?"

I didn't even bother to comment, as this bit of metaphysical clap-trap was beyond the amount of energy that I currently wished to give it. I closed my eyes and pulled my coat tighter, cold despite the heat of my skin.

As I'd failed to rise to his conversational lure, Holmes fell silent. I reopened my eyes and we both watched the track before us as it led, narrower and rougher but straight as an arrow, to a trio of small mountains standing near the sea. The slopes facing us were already deep in shadow, a dark and featureless blue. But as we pressed inexorably forward, a series of buildings along their base resolved into focus – a half-dozen or so small cottages of the sort often found by the coast, functional and built to withstand harsh weather. In the middle was a church, or what had been once, clearly the centre of the small outpost, slightly bigger than the meagre buildings surrounding it, and topped by a rather squat steeple. Behind this little cluster of weathered and colourless civilization, there was a rather startling gap between two of the mountains showing the line of the sea, lit bright gold by the setting sun, itself now invisible behind the dark rise of the more immediate prominence.

The mountains themselves might better be called hills, for as we approached, it was obvious that they were only a couple of hundred feet high, and no higher. However, in that area, where the rest of the countryside seemed to slope toward the ocean in gradual descents to the shore, or in others to drop abruptly in the form of cliffs formed by geologic collapses in ages past, these freakish anomalies, like jutting upturned fangs, stood out and appeared to be much more dramatically imposing than the dry intellectual measurements that their dimensions would otherwise suggest if only reading about them on paper.

The rises before us were dramatic and tended to focus one's attention to the church steeple, now centring itself before the straight road toward the gap where the sea was visible. And as we moved closer, other details became clear as well – unpleasant stains, dark and damp-looking, on the walls of the dreary buildings; the shingled roofs, and the darkened windows of the houses.

There was a marked lack of trees, as if they had been cut generations ago to burn for heat, and the cool wind rushing from behind us toward the vast empty horizon beyond the looming pinnacles only served to emphasize the loneliness of the place. I think that if there *had* been trees, and the last remaining dead leaves of the season present to brush against one another in that steady breeze, I would have been thoroughly overcome by the desolate emptiness.

I shivered, and it was then that I perceived a solitary figure situated by the door of the church, tall and painfully thin, watching our approach with an unmoving patience, as if he had been carved from the last tree to stand in that godforsaken place and left as a sentinel. Another cart and horse could just be seen in the church's shadow.

I expected Holmes to make some comment, but he, uncharacteristically, appeared to be as daunted as I was by the picture that presented itself – the lonely and abandoned settlement, the dramatic placement before the steep and atypical hills, the mood of the dying day, and the single man who might have been an illusion for all the movement that he had made since coming into sight. The wind didn't seem to touch his garments whatsoever.

I myself had said nothing, due to the strangeness of what I beheld, and also because I was further convinced that I indeed had a fever – which only added to the dream-like feeling of this whole situation. I knew that I would not wake up and be in my chair before the fire in Baker Street – and yet, a part of me convinced myself that none of this fantastic setting could be true, and that any moment my eyes would open to reveal the usual clutter of our sitting room. But they didn't, and as Holmes pulled our horse to a halt, the mysterious man shifted into a smooth forward motion.

"Gentlemen," he said, his feet sliding oddly across the ground underneath a plain brown robe, his only raiment. He was arrayed like a monk of some order that had taken a vow of poverty, but like none that I have ever encountered before. His voice was low, with a curious vibratory quality, as if a bow were being drawn steadily along the lowest string of a *violoncello*, with no effort to change the note or offer any vibrato. "We rarely have visitors. Two others arrived not more than an hour ago–" He gestured to the horse and cart, which were tethered to a railing, "– and now yourselves. Might I conclude that you are following the former?"

I was able to perceive some sort of accent, eastern European perhaps, but nothing more definite than that. As he concluded his question, he stopped walking, having only taken a few steps in that peculiar slipping motion that placed him near Holmes's side of the cart.

It seemed that with his closeness, he intended somehow to prevent Holmes from stepping to the ground, but my friend had propelled himself with so sudden a move that the man had to take a surprised step back, his eyes widening. Now Holmes was facing the man, and I could see the two of them side-by-side, allowing me to realize that Holmes, himself somewhat over six feet in height, looked like a lad near the other man.

He was surely nearly seven feet in height, although he appeared to be even taller due to his excessive leanness. Completely bald, he had a rather knobby head perched on a thin neck. It might have been a trick of the fading light, with the sun now dropping behind the nearby mountains, but he also seemed exceedingly pale – quite grey in fact – except for his thin lips, which had an unusual purplish cast. They were pursed in irritation, apparently at having given ground to the shorter man.

I stepped down more slowly, patting our horse on the nose as I rounded in front of him and came to a stop behind the tall man, who was now forced to take another step back and pivot so as to face the two of us. I could see that his hands, with fingers laced, were long and thin, as might be expected, with ropy veins running along the backs and up under his sleeves. However, they had no colour. On his right hand was a ring supporting a garish stone, as black as night, a large oval running from knuckle to knuckle.

His feet were shod in simple sandals, further emphasizing his superficial resemblance to a monk. I observed that his long nearly prehensile toes were now rather curiously bent at the last joint, a condition known as "mallet toe", where the appendage cannot straighten – a most unusual condition for someone who wore sandals, as it was usually the result of wearing too-tight shoes. The great toe on each foot was much shorter than the rest.

His only other adornment was a small silver crucifix centred on his chest, a couple of inches in length, held in place by a solid-looking chain. It further gave the impression of some sort of obscure religiosity. I glanced past the man and saw that Holmes was looking at the small cross with unusual interest, leaning forward a bit, almost to the point of being rude.

By then we had stood there for most of a minute, and the silence had grown awkward, but that was always a useful tool. When Holmes didn't immediately reply to the man's question, and instead took a moment to glance here and there at the surroundings, the tall man was eventually motivated to the fill the silence.

"I am Brother Adămuș," he said, with a curious lilt to his name, implying that the vowels should be decorated with various and obscure punctuation marks as hints to the foreign pronunciation (and which I have reproduced as best I can, as based on details that I learned much later). He looked from one to the other of us, and then something about Holmes seemed to catch his eye. He squinted a bit before a look of enlightenment crossed his face. "You are Sherlock Holmes," he said, his low voice giving it an odd emphasis. Then inexplicably he frowned.

Holmes raised an eyebrow and he pushed back his fore-and-aft cap to better see the tall man. "I am. Do you know me?"

"Only by way of what I have seen in the press," he said, and then glanced my way. "We do not venture into the greater world, so the others here will not have heard of you – to them you will simply be as other men who arrive here – but as I must sometimes go forth to transact unavoidable business within the nearby village, and it is both my responsibility, and burden, to stay aware of outside events. I recognize you. I have seen mention of you before." Then he turned his head my way. "And thus you would be Dr. Watson."

I acknowledged it and cleared my throat, preparing against the pain there to speak, but he had already looked away, dismissing me in favor of my companion. "I repeat, you must be associated with the two men who arrived earlier, for we rarely have visitors present themselves so easily, and for two groups to appear in a single day..."

"It is true," Holmes confirmed. "The men are fugitives, and we seek their return to answer for crimes committed in London. Can you take us to them?"

"Certainly."

He started to turn, and at that moment, a light suddenly appeared in a window beside the door of the church, apparently a lamp placed there. Somehow its materialization made the rest of the village seem even more lonely, for none of the other windows were lit at all, not in any of the buildings that we could see stretching to either side of us. The cold wind seemed to blow a little more strongly just then.

Seeing the light, Brother Adămuş's lips pulled back into something like a smile, but with no corresponding warmth in his eyes. It was not an improvement. "Ah," he said. "The feast is ready to commence." He raised an eyebrow, and this time he looked directly at me. "Possibly you would care to be a part of it?"

The Village on the Cliff by David Marcum

Perhaps it was a trick of the fast-fading light, but his teeth, as revealed by that curious vulpine smile, had a curiousness to them, a dull greenish cast that gave the sense that the enamel had been polluted somehow. Then his mouth closed, snapped like a silent trap, and he was leading us toward the church. Holmes glanced my way, his look of warning quite obvious. He veered away from our new host, taking hold of our horse's halter.

"You mention 'others'," said Holmes, tying the beast's reins to the church rail – for there was no other place to secure him. The horse already there nickered, and the two stable mates seemed glad to see one another. The stable man's warning to bring back our horse safely crossed my mind. "This spot appears to be quite deserted. Do you live here, or elsewhere, only gathering here at this location for your rites?"

The man paused with one sandalled foot on the single step leading up to the church entrance. Without looking back, he said, "Rites, Mr. Holmes? You assume, then, that we are some religious group?"

Holmes raised an eyebrow. "Forgive me. I'm rather used to make observations and drawing conclusions, and your clothing, as well as the crucifix that you wear, led me to interpret too quickly."

Brother Adămuș turned then, his hand rising even as Holmes spoke, and he stroked his finger up and down the tiny figure of Christ affixed to the long piece of the cross, almost sensuously. Another smile crossed his face as his fingertip continued to trace along the metal, but this time his lips never parted, and his teeth were not revealed. Finally he dropped his hand. I felt that I'd seen something obscene.

"We are not here because of a *religion*," said the man. "We are here to *exist*. We have journeyed to this place to be left alone. And still, here against the edge of the sea, we have...

visitors. You say that you are here because you wish to remove these men that you seek back to London." It was not a question.

"Yes."

"That would be well, then. We prefer that no one intrude – especially any such as you. When we desire contact, we go forth and initiate it for ourselves, on our own terms. Is that so objectionable?"

From another man, the tone would have become strident, but his own voice maintained that curiously low and unnerving vibratory pitch. Apparently his question was rhetorical, for he turned without receiving an answer, and apparently not caring for one. He reached the door and went inside, preceding us without another word.

The building wasn't any warmer inside than out, but that came as no surprise. However, it was more quiet when we were away from the constant wind. I glanced through the door before it closed behind us, and met the eyes of our horse, tied in the creeping darkness. The old fellow seemed to be looking directly toward me, as if attempting to communicate some concern. I realized that I was apparently sicker than I'd believed.

The small anteroom to the old church was plain, with no furniture or decoration, except for a tall, thin, and rickety table underneath the window, where the lamp that we had seen placed from outside was sitting. I wondered who had put it there, and what exactly it signified. The yellowish light barely seemed to illuminate the room, and it effused a strong kerosene odour that I could almost taste, even with my oncoming illness.

The chamber had two doors aside from the one which we had just used – a set of double doors on a wider wall across from the outside door, and a smaller narrow door to the left side on the same wall. It was toward this smaller door that the man walked, before suddenly pausing, as if in thought. As he stood and the pause grew more awkward, the sudden silence, away from the wind, left me nonplussed. I wondered what was to happen next, as Brother Adămuș stood there, his back to us, as if making some sort of decision. Then, I was startled to hear a single rude laugh from deeper in the building beyond the double door – just once, before it ended abruptly.

That in some way seemed to be what was needed to motivate the robed man into motion. He turned away from the small door and looked at Holmes. "But I have been rude," he said. "Night is coming, and you have travelled far. Your friend–" and he tossed an indifferent nod my way, "– is clearly ill. Come – before you meet your prisoner, join us for some refreshment."

And then he turned aside toward the double door, striding with certainty while Holmes glanced to see if I'd heard it. I nodded. *Prisoner* – singular.

We entered a room that was probably twenty feet or more square, not excessively large, but certainly big enough for the sanctuary that it had once been when this had been a village church. The room should have been marginally brighter than the space where we had been. That had been lit by a single lamp, while this room had a half-dozen of them spaced around the perimeter on the same tall thin tables that were by the front window. However, the spacing of the lamps only served to make the centre of the room a dark pool, made more obscure by the contrast with the brighter edges. It had seemingly been converted into something like a banquet hall, with two long tables running from another table placed on a slightly raised dais at the far end of the room, in a configuration resembling something of the symbol Π.

Yet there was nothing unusual about this. What was unnerving was that, as my eyes adjusted to the gloom, I could see that most of the seats at all three tables were filled – by thirty or so individuals who made not a sound, but rather stared ahead, as if gazing into an emptiness that I hoped to never experience. They didn't look up when we came in, and for a moment I feared that they were dead.

But there was one who was not that way. Sitting at the centre of the head table, his motion drawing one's gaze by its contrast to the other corpse-like figures, was a fair-haired man in his mid-twenties. He had a couple of the transfixed men on either side of him, and I could see that they very much resembled our guide, Brother Adămuș. One of the lamps was placed somewhat behind the man who did not belong, serving to highlight him all the more. He was drinking lustily from an awkward and overly large goblet, and I could see that he had what appeared to be wine stains down the front of his shirt. His sloppy movements seemed to indicate that he was already drunk. As I watched, he laughed – that same braying tone that we had heard from the other room.

He tipped up the goblet to a nearly vertical angle to get whatever was left. Then, darting his tongue around his lips like a lizard peeking from a hole, he set it down with a clang that clearly left a dent in the tabletop, before reaching for a short dark bottle placed near his right hand. As he carelessly poured a refill, Brother Adămuș spoke, as loud as he had been outside where the wind was blowing. It seemed thunderous in the otherwise quiet room, and I was reminded of when I had visited hospitals such as Bedlam, where the staff doctors would talk about the patients in their presence as if they weren't there at all.

"Here we meet when we have purpose," he explained. "We feast to celebrate."

"And what is that purpose?" asked Holmes.

"When we have something to feast upon."

A chill ran down my spine, and I somehow became aware then that the gazes of some of the men seated around the tables had shifted from their internal contemplations and had now focused on us instead. It was then that I understood what I must have already seen but not observed: Each of the room's occupants was male. There were no women present. Perhaps I hadn't found that unusual, as I am a member of several clubs in which women are never to be seen, and I've visited countless others while assisting Holmes on his investigations. But here, where we seemed to have found ourselves on the far side of the wall that separates the wild-lands from civilization, it seemed much more sinister.

As I looked around the room, my eyes sharpening in the dim light that reminded me more and more of the back recesses of an opium den, I could tell that each of the seated men was now looking our way without expression. All resembled the tall man beside us, with long bald heads and thin shoulders. Every one appeared to be shaped in the same mould as our chaperone, and from what I could see, they were all clothed in similar robes. Unlike Adămuș, however, none had crucifixes around their necks.

The initial shock of the sight of seeing all these men was wearing off, and I was becoming more aware of my surroundings by the minute. I recognized that I had been smelling a familiar odour since we'd entered – the ketones produced by starving bodies. I had been familiar with this scent for more than twenty years, having first encountered it as a medical student, when working with London's poor. I had found it countless times since then – from the slums of India and Afghanistan to our own shameful Whitechapel, and even in the sitting room in Baker Street, where the occasional visitor would display signs of obvious hunger and neglect. Were these men so thin because they rarely ate? If so, it was no wonder that obtaining food was reason enough for a celebratory feast.

Meanwhile, the young man at the head table continued to drink noisily, with an occasional puffing belch. Those men beside him ignored him, and he in turn made no effort to engage them in conversation.

The scene seemed so static that I was more surprised than I care to admit when one of the men seated near us spoke, apparently addressing Adămuș while never taking his eyes from me.

"More?" he asked simply.

His voice was the same as that of Adămuș, that curious flat-toned buzz as if a thick string were being vibrated. And yet it was different. The curious accent that Adămuș evinced was thicker from this man. Adămuș snapped at him in some language that seemed to slide into one long word, broken occasionally by *sh*'s and *D*-sounds. Apparently we weren't supposed to understand the conversation, and the man had mistakenly spoken in English. In the middle of this flowing drone, I heard the words *Sherlock Holmes*. As he spoke, the man who had asked the initial question frowned, before saying something in reply in the same language. Adămuș gave a short incomprehensible reply, and the conversation seemed to be over.

"I was explaining your reason for being here," said Adămuș.

"Indeed," replied Holmes. "Croatian?"

Adămuș' eyes widened the tiniest fraction. "No, but similar. You speak Croatian, Mr. Holmes?"

"No, but I have been in some of the areas where it is used, and I have heard it before. Your people have migrated from that part of the world?"

"We have. A part of Hungary, southeast of Sibiu, in the Carpathian Mountains. From *Cetatea Poenari*, near the Arges River."

"You are far from home," said Holmes wryly.

"We came to feel rather... unwelcome in that part of the world. We moved west – rather like the Mormons described your book, Doctor."

I cleared my throat, having become rather used to being ignored by the man. "You have read it, then?"

"I have. It was entertaining. I find that as I grow older, my mind needs more diversions, and some of your English writing is quite... distracting."

"I'm surprised," said Holmes, "that you would go in for that sort of thing."

"Again, Mr. Holmes," said Adămuș, "you make the mistake of trying to equate us with a religion. We do not worship anything – at least not in ways that you could understand or tolerate, or that I wish to convey."

"And yet you wear a crucifix."

"Ah, this?" He raised his hand again and touched it, but thankfully he refrained from stroking it as before. "This was simply something that I recently came across and put on for my own amusement."

"You don't strike me as a man who goes in for amusement," countered Holmes. "In addition to being curious about your beliefs and practices, I have a special interest in that particular crucifix. You see, it had previously been described to me – do you see how one of Christ's feet has been broken off? – and the fact that it has appeared here, where its owner had announced an intention to visit just days ago, makes it even more fascinating."

Adămuș frowned. "You expected to find this here? But you said that you were following the two men who arrived earlier today. This trinket has nothing to do with those men."

"True. It's nothing more than coincidence. But I had been told that a man was headed this way, and he has since disappeared. Andrew Bradfield – is the name familiar?"

It was difficult to be certain in that dim light, but Adămuș' lips appeared to tighten. He seemed to catch his lower lip in his teeth for just a moment before replying, "He was here a few days ago. I met him outside, as I did the two of you. We gave him something to drink. Then he was gone."

"As simple as that, then," said Holmes, gesturing toward the seated men. "And now it's time for one of your celebratory feasts."

At that moment, the door on the far side of the room opened with a squeak, and a number of figures began walking into the room, one after another, each carrying platters.

Even as the smell of food wafted my way – boiled pork, apparently – I was shocked to recognize that the bearers of the meat were all women. Each of them wore the same style of drab robes, but otherwise they were much different than the similar-seeming men, a mixture of heights and colourings and weights. While the men all had the same tall thinness and grayish cast to their skins, these women – at least a dozen of them – could have come from anywhere in the British Isles. Blonde, brunette, red-head. Tall and thin, shorter and stouter, they ranged from girls barely out of their teens to more matronly figures nearing mid-life. None, however, appeared to be past their mid-thirties.

What they had in common was that they went about their tasks – setting the platters of meat along the different tables before the collection of curious men – without any expression upon their faces. In fact, each almost had a look in her eyes that resembled someone deep in the throes of mesmerisation.

With the platters on the tables, the men all reached forward, without any urgency or ceremony, and began tearing off chunks of the flesh. Lacking plates or utensils, they used their long slim pale hands to convey the food to their mouths, wolfing great hunks that were barely chewed before being swallowed and replaced by more. Rapidly the feast, such as it was, disappeared. There was nothing else on the table – no vegetables or fruit or bread, no condiments, and nothing to drink. Apparently the only wine to be found was at the head table. I glanced that way and saw the fair young man tentatively chewing on some of the meat apparently taken from a nearby platter. He had an odd look on his face. Then, as if sensing that I was looking his way, his eyes met mine. I looked to find any hint of his thoughts, but I saw nothing but an inebriated greed, as if he were only living in the moment and interested in satisfying his primitive cravings.

The last of the women exited through the door, even as the food was consumed. One by one, the men around the tables lost their inward-turned expressions while they had chewed and swallowed, and refocused in our direction. Tearing my gaze away from their attentions, I looked back to Adămuș when he spoke, his tone now fractionally irritated while his hand grasped the crucifix, his already pale skin whiter across his tight knuckles. "I find your questioning offensive, Mr. Holmes. My brothers feel that you should stay, as we never turn guests away, but I think that it would be best if you depart as planned."

"And Watson too, of course."

Adămuș waited a fraction of a second before replying – a splinter of time that was just long enough to give the sense that the question hadn't been decided yet. Then, "Yes, the doctor as well."

There was danger here. I could feel it now. What I had thought before to be simply bizarre, or something generated by my impending illness, was very real. I had my service revolver with me, having long ago learned never to venture out unless it was in my pocket, and Holmes certainly wasn't defenceless, but there were many of these men around us, and who knew how many more that we hadn't seen?

"I believe," continued Holmes, "that you also indicated that we will be able to take the Byrnams – the men who arrived earlier today – with us."

Adămuș didn't immediately reply, as if he were recalling the conversation from a few minutes earlier, when he had first met us outside the church and recognized Holmes. Clearly he seemed to be weighing how much trouble would be brought upon them by obstructing our purpose. And even though he had already agreed that we depart, I was certain that if he determined that we wouldn't be missed, or if he had any hint that our location was unknown to the greater world, the decision that we could leave would be rescinded.

As if reading my thoughts, Holmes added, "We were careful to leave word about our intentions to visit here, and to speak to several people when we passed through the village and obtained directions to this remote spot."

Adămuş relaxed a bit, as if he had reached some kind of decision. "You may return with the older man. He has confessed his crime to us when he arrived here, and he is being held elsewhere. But his son has chosen to remain." He raised his voice for the first time and looked across the room. "Geoffrey? Do you wish to leave with these men from London?"

The young man – really nothing more than a boy, in spite of his age – looked our way with a spoiled and drunken expression that could barely focus. In the sickly yellow light, the grease from the boiled flesh that he had consumed slicked his fat face. He resolutely shook his head and looked back that the table, finding the wine bottle right where he had last left it.

"So be it," said Adămuş. "He chooses to stay and become a part of us. His celebration will occur in a few days. In the meantime, you may retrieve the father and depart."

He turned toward the door leading back to the small anteroom, and there was a low grumble behind us. For the first time, the men around us showed an emotion – something akin to anger. Two or three of them stood up, one of them not five feet from me. I could see that he was young, about the same age as Geoffrey Byrnam at the front of the room. But where Geoffrey was soft-looking, this thin man was lean and dangerous muscle. He was tense, as if he were about to spring like a dog rarefied by hunger into a hunting machine.

The Village on the Cliff by David Marcum

Adămuș snapped something in his peculiar language, again using Holmes's name and the word *London*. The angry expressions didn't diminish, but no one else stood, and Holmes and I followed Brother Adămuș out. I shut the door behind me, as if doing so would be sufficient to lock away the occupants of that nightmarish chamber.

Without comment, Adămuș took the lamp from the window and then walked to the smaller door. It opened to reveal a set of narrow steps leading into a basement. The steps themselves were of stone, apparently cut out of the very ground upon which the church was built. The walls were stone as well, unevenly shaped, as if the amateur craftsman who had evacuated this chamber had stopped when the required volume was achieved, rather than taking any extra effort to make the area look finished.

There were two doors on the far wall of the basement both with ill-fitting doors. The one on the left seemingly opened into darkness, as revealed by the wide space at the bottom. A cold breeze was forcing its way through the gap, and I could only imagine what lay behind it. The cracks around the other door were lit, and the smell of the boiled meat was stronger there.

As if reading my thoughts, Adămuș said, "That door is to the kitchens, where the women prepare the feasts. There are separate steps leading up to the hall."

I nodded, but Holmes wasn't listening. He was looking over the other side of the room, which was divided from ours by a series of iron bars, placed about eight inches apart, stretching from the wooden ceiling of the old church above and down to fresh-looking holes chiselled out of the raw rock at our feet. A barred door had been hung awkwardly in the centre of it all.

"You have installed a cell," Holmes said, a statement without any surprise.

"We sometimes require it."

"I believe that I understand why you were forced to leave Transylvania," responded Holmes.

"Ah. I shouldn't be surprised that you have perceived so much," responded Adămuș. "You know of that part of the world, then?"

"I read a great deal," said Holmes. "And additionally I happened to pass through there a few years ago, when it was believed that I was dead."

Adămuș now looked puzzled. Without further explanation, Holmes turned back to the cage, peering through the bars at a middle-aged man who was sitting on the floor, watching silently.

"Edwin Byrnam," said Holmes. "Get up. We are returning to London."

The man scrambled to his feet, but didn't approach the door. "Come out," said Adămuș, a stranger quality in his already strange voice. This new tone sounded compelling and commanding, and it seemed to resonate within Byrnam, who complied. "It isn't locked," added Adămuș. Holmes turned his head with interest and, keeping a curious eye upon Byrnam, he reached forward and pulled the door toward him.

I placed myself beside the man, giving him a quick examination, but always ready to reach for my service revolver. He appeared fit, though dishevelled from his irregular dash across the country, as well as his more-recent imprisonment. He took no interest in my examination, and made no protest when I ran across a small book in his jacket pocket, removing it and handing it to Holmes. He flipped through it and nodded, and I knew that we had completed that portion of our mission. Although returning Byrnam to face justice was secondary to securing the diary, I realized now that we had a responsibility to get him away from this place before yet another celebration could occur. Without waiting for any approval from the robed man, I took Byrnam's arm and led him carefully up the steps,

Holmes close behind. I could sense from the awkward way that he ascended that he was placing himself to keep an eye on Adămuș below us while trusting for me to make sure the way before was safe.

I entered the vestibule half-expecting to find it full of the tall robed men, fresh from their feast, yet still hungry. "More," that one grim man had uttered. And yet, the room was empty. In seconds I had the front door open, and we were outside in the cool evening air. I inhaled deeply trying to rid myself of the sickening mixed stew of the stale mildewed building, the scent of starving men, and the terrible steam that had spread from the boiled meat. While I was helping Byrnam into the back of the cart, Holmes paused before Adămuș, whom I saw had followed us outside.

"Andrew Bradfield?" asked Holmes. "The man who arrived a few days ago?"

"As I said, he is no longer here." Adămuș reached up to the crucifix, wrapping his hand around it and giving a sharp tug. The silver chain broke with an audible snap and he tossed it in Holmes's direction. "Give this to his people if you wish."

Holmes caught it and then dropped it into his other hand, allowing the length of chain to coil upon his palm. Then he placed it in a pocket.

The air seemed to have revived Byrnam somewhat by that point. He looked around, as if waking up from a long sleep, confused at where he found himself.

"My son," he said. "Where is my son?"

"He is staying, for now," said Holmes softly. "We will do all that we can to retrieve him, but for now..."

Byrnam attempted to push his way past me, trying awkwardly to climb to the ground. "Geoffrey!" he called pitifully. "Where are you? We must leave!"

"Hold him, Watson," said Holmes quietly, untying Byrnam's horse and roping him to the back of our cart, so that they could pull in tandem. Then, after untying our horse as well, he stepped up and into his seat, picking up the reins. In an even lower voice, he said, "We will return, Mr. Byrnam, but we must be away now. There is danger here."

He had said it quite softly, so low that I was barely able to hear. And yet, from twenty feet or so away, Brother Adămuş spoke. "That is true, Mr. Holmes. There is danger. You are fortunate – more than you know. I would advise that you and your friend do not return. Ever."

Holmes made no response, and in fact did not deign to look in that direction. Rather, he turned the horse and sent us swiftly back the way we had come. But I was in the back with Byrnam, and I did meet Adămuş' gaze as we pulled away. It was as cold and dead as when we first saw him, and in a reversal of our arrival, he gradually disappeared into the surrounding darkness of the church's outline, as did the church as well a few moments later against the now-black mountains. Even the gap between them, where the setting sun had previously shown on the sea, was as nothing.

*****

We reached the village where we knocked up the stable hand, returning both carts and horses. Then we roused what passed for the local innkeeper, obtaining a large upstairs bedroom and sitting room. Throughout our return, Byrnam had been somewhat catatonic. After finding that his son wasn't returning with us, he had sank into that same trance-like state in which we'd found him in the cell. I speculated on some sort of drug, but Holmes was of the opinion that it was something more like hypnotism, although it could be a combination of the two. In any case, it seemed that only time would reveal the truth.

In our room, we put Byrnam to bed, but without discussing it, both Holmes and I tacitly decided to refrain from dropping our guards. Somehow it seemed that the distance between the odd church by the sea and our rooms was not very far at all if Adămuș changed is his mind. With a word of warning, Holmes slipped out to send a telegram to London. He returned, having been gone longer than I would have expected, explaining that he'd found and awakened the station master, only to be told that the telegraph office was closed and nothing could be sent until the morning. With that in mind, Holmes had then gone to the station alone, picked the lock, activated the lines, and sent a message to Mycroft on his own. Knowing that no one would be there to wait for a reply, he'd remained until Mycroft responded, and they had made arrangements.

Upon his return, he enquired after my own condition, and I confessed that I had become worse as the night progressed. He assured me that he had the situation in hand, and encouraged me to sleep. He slipped downstairs and returned in a moment with a bottle of whisky, informing me where the landlord had thought it to be cleverly hidden. With a toddy to sear my throat, I allowed myself to fall asleep, service revolver in hand, in a plush chair that I'd pulled back behind the sitting room's outer door, so that anyone coming in that way might not immediately see me should they gain entry.

*****

I awoke to find the morning light spilling through the east-facing window, and a low conversation taking place across the room. There was nothing threatening in the tone, and more importantly, nothing like the unnerving drone of Adămuș' peculiar voice. I opened my eyes to see two men in chairs before the fireplace – Sherlock Holmes, and his brother Mycroft.

The Village on the Cliff by David Marcum

I believe that I have made mention of Mycroft's proclivity to remain fixed within his orbit when given the choice. However, that is by no means meant to imply that he couldn't move around when necessary. For instance, I had seen him away from his haunts at The Diogenes Club more often than I'd found him there. Seeing Mycroft in Wales was not as surprising as it might have first appeared to those who didn't know better, but I was impressed with the effort that he must have made, certainly arranging for a special train to get him here so quickly.

I glanced at the clock on the mantel, seeing that it was somewhat later than I had expected, nearly ten a.m. I didn't think that I'd given any indication that I was now awake, but I should have known better, for Holmes said, "Watson, Mycroft and the soldiers have already been out to the church. There is no sign of Adămuş or his flock."

I realized that my breathing must have changed, alerting them to the fact that I was awake and listening. Mycroft continued, "Nor was there any indication of Byrnam's son. It seems that they have been spooked, escaping through a set of ancient smuggler's tunnels leading out of the church's basement, and thence to boats they had concealed in caves at the base of the cliffs."

I cleared my throat, but before I could speak, Mycroft continued. "Byrnam mean to sell the diary at Major Everless's estate to the north, but he took a wrong turning. We've had our eye in this direction for quite a while, but it's fortunate that Everless never got a look at Lord -----'s notes."

Mycroft's comments were interesting, but they didn't seem to matter. In fact, at that moment, none of the previous evening seemed real at all. I felt that I was awakening from some kind of vague rolling nightmare, and that in a moment I would roll over and go back to sleep, slipping into another story.

I heard Holmes explaining to Mycroft that I was sicker than he'd thought, and the response about it being obvious, and then I fell back to sleep.

Later that day, Holmes bundled me back to London, on the same train with Mycroft, Byrnam, and a small contingent of soldiers. I slept the entire way, and when we were back at our rooms in Baker Street, I went upstairs and crawled into bed. Mrs. Hudson looked concerned as I passed, but I assured her that things simply had to take their course. And they did – by the next morning, I was a great deal better.

I bathed and shaved, and then came downstairs, pausing to indicate that I was ready for a light breakfast. Then I entered the sitting room to find Holmes smoking his pipe in his chair before the fire, the morning light from the window at his back.

I nodded toward him, and within minutes Mrs. Hudson arrived with fresh provisions, including some much-welcomed hot coffee. Holmes's plate, abandoned on the table from where he'd already eaten, was essentially clean, and as Mrs. Hudson gathered it, I could see that she was pleased. As she departed, I finished the last of my eggs and, taking my coffee cup, moved to sit across from Holmes.

"What have you learned?" I asked. Of course he knew to what I referred.

"Not much," he replied. "Mycroft has traced Adămuş' people back to the location he named in Transylvania – it seems they felt no need to hide their origins when they arrived in England earlier this year. Mycroft's agents are thin on the ground in that part of the world, but he promises to have someone ask some questions at the earliest opportunity – whether their feasts and celebrations were the reason that they had to depart."

I nodded, thinking it likely. I doubted that I could eat boiled pork for a long time to come. "And so they came to England? How curious."

"I suppose so. One would think that they could find better places to hide if they had headed east – although rural Wales does have certain spots where one might be left alone. In any case, one wonders where they will turn up next."

"I hope that Mycroft is keeping an eye out for that as well. These people are a menace to civilized society." I took a sip of coffee. "How is Byrnam?"

"Recovering. Grief-stricken at the loss of his son."

"One must assume that Geoffrey Byrnam *is* lost," I agreed. "Like poor Bradfield."

I pictured the women and their platters and the boiled flesh, and the silent and white-fingered hungry greed of the seated men.

"Indeed." Holmes reached toward the small octagonal table beside his chair, brought with him from when he'd lived in Montague Street, the relic of some long-ago case. Picking up the crucifix and broken chain that rested there, he held them up in the morning light, studying the object as it twirled back and forth. "It was just the merest chance that Adămuş chose to wear this after Bradfield forfeited possession. I saw that the broken piece met the description which I'd been given, and knowing that Cig was Bradfield's destination, it was easy to connect the pieces."

"Cig," I said. "What does that mean?"

"It seems that the original name of the village, before it was abandoned, was *Pen Clogwyn*, roughly 'Cliff-top'. Cig, I've learned, is the name that the locals gave the place after Adămuş' people arrived. I'm told that it means 'meat'."

I found myself suddenly rather queasy, thinking of poor Bradfield, and how he'd somehow stumbled upon knowledge of these people, only to go there and become the focus of their latest celebration. And then Geoffrey Byrnam, who hadn't wanted to leave...

"I wish that Bradfield could have some sort of justice," I said softly. "These... these *cannibals* must be stopped."

"Ah, Watson. Data – we need data. You are making an assumption without full proof."

"But... Adămuş all but confirmed it! He *flaunted* it! I wasn't so ill yet that I imagined that."

"Oh, make no mistake. I agree with you, proof or no proof. And considering where they come from, and the stories that are told in hushed whispers about those from *Cetatea Poenari* in that remote area of the Carpathians, the possibilities are probably very much worse. I truly regret that they have been allowed to slip away–"

"– to set up shop somewhere else," I finished, adding, "and continue with their abominable practices."

"Ah, but perhaps not for long. You see, Alton Peake's interest has now been aroused – that, and his outrage. He has resources that we don't, and pathways that he can explore to find where in the shadows that people such as these hide and scurry. He will be here in–" He glanced at the clock. "– a quarter-hour, and we shall discuss a plan."

And so we did. Peake did indeed have contacts and channels of information that were unique to his own consultancy, and arrangements were quickly made which eventually led to a satisfactory conclusion – although not without cost. But that is another story. Suffice it to say that, on that day, while I recovered and alternately sipped tea or coffee, or brandy or whisky, Holmes and Peake discussed things for which the world is not yet prepared – and possibly one Dr. John H. Watson is not, either...

But I have no choice about it, really, and I suppose that I would have it no other way.

The Tale of the Tantric Detective

by Geoff Dibb

Sherlock Holmes returned to London in spring 1894 following his travels after his escape from the Reichenbach Falls. He became inundated with cases, and my notes for that period fill three enormous manuscript volumes and a despatch box. I was searching through these, some years later, when I came across a file dealing with a most mysterious case from December 1894, and was reminded that I had later added my notes on another curiosity, one from 1887. Now, I can see that this earlier cryptographic enigma was a premonition of sorts of the occult crimes which occurred seven years afterwards...

1887: A Cryptographic Introduction

It was a December morning in Baker Street and, my wife being away for a week, I was back in our familiar rooms. Holmes pulled tobacco from the toe of a Persian slipper, tapped it into his pipe and lit it. "What do you make of this, then, Watson?" he asked as he handed a letter to me. I took it and read the printed heading:

>   Dr. W. W. Wescott MD, MD(Res), DCM
>   Coroner
>   London Coroner's Office

And below this auspicious medical heading, Dr. Wescott had written:

Dear Mr. Holmes,
May I presume on your time? This is an entirely non-criminal matter personal to myself.
Whilst we have not met, I have heard your name mentioned very favourably by officers of Scotland Yard in respect of some difficult cases which have come before me professionally.
In short, I am in possession of some papers - 60 folios - whose origin is a mystery and they bear lengthy inscriptions written in a cipher. I cannot make anything of them but I wonder if you may be able to help me. I do hope so.
I remain Sir, your obedient servant,

William W. Wescott

"How very unusual, Holmes: The London Coroner and mysterious ciphers! Do you intend to help Dr. Wescott?"

"Most certainly, Watson. I have a hiatus in my cases at the moment and the challenge seems to be interesting enough to fill my time. Also, it is useful to build up good relationships with fellow professionals... I think this may be our man now."

Mrs. Hudson showed in a tall, well-built man with an extensive beard and moustachios. He held a small box file in his left hand.

"Pleased to meet you Dr. Wescott," said Holmes as he rose from his favourite armchair.

"And you, Mr. Holmes." They shook hands. "I have heard much of your skills in deduction and I wondered, as I have written, whether you could apply your abilities to a non-criminal matter?"

"Allow me to introduce my friend and colleague, Dr. John Watson."

There followed some rather general medical conversation between the two of us before Holmes asked how he could help.

"Mr. Holmes, I am, in my professional as well as my personal life, a seeker after the truth. Professionally, I am the London Coroner and I hardly have to describe to you two gentlemen the number and variety of cases which come my way and require expert investigation. But this is an entirely personal and private matter." Dr. Wescott paused, clearly gauging his words: "One which I hope you will treat with utmost discretion. I have for many years had a fascination with the Lamaist Buddhism of the Tibetan region."

Holmes nodded. He had travelled extensively in the Tibetan region during the period of his disappearance, and I was certain he would know something of this.

"There are a number of organisations trying to understand the truth of this religion and I have been involved in several: the Rosicrucians, Theosophists led by Madame Blavatsky and, more recently, the Hermetic Order of the Golden Dawn."

These mystical bodies had multiplied and the daily newspapers frequently contained their claims and speculations. How strange it seemed to me to have a man of science and medicine so absorbed in such arcana.

"Mr. Holmes, the folios which I mentioned in my letter have come into my possession. Their origin is obscure — I was given them some time ago by a colleague now dead. I only know that he thought they contained great insights into human development which have been drawn from the most ancient sources."

Dr. Wescott handed over two sheets of paper which I could see were mostly covered with handwriting.

Holmes took the papers and walked over to the window, holding them both up to the light. "Ah, these are identical pieces of paper with the same watermark... I can check it against my watermark index."

He pored over them with great interest.

"There are many types of cipher, Dr. Wescott, and I am the author of a small monograph about the various types. In fact, I am considering writing an extended second edition. This cipher promises to be a fascinating problem for me. I would be delighted to help you."

"Thank you so much," said Dr. Wescott as he rose and crossed to shake Holmes's hand, "I am delighted and obliged. Do you think you would have sufficient data if I left, say, four sheets for your perusal? As these are the only folios I am reluctant to let them all out of my hands."

"Of course, Dr. Wescott, I am certain four would contain sufficient data for me to carry out my analysis."

Dr. Wescott handed over the folios and after a few concluding comments he made his exit and Holmes rubbed his hands together. "How providence supplies us, Watson! At the time of our greatest need, into our laps falls our stimulant for a day or so!" He laughed that quiet, contented laugh I would hear during so many cases as he relished the challenge ahead.

I had much to do on that day and left Holmes and his folios until I returned for our dinner at eight o'clock. Sheets of paper were everywhere in the room and Holmes had a mildly satisfied air about him but we ate with only minor talk between us.

Afterwards, as we arranged our postprandial pipes, I asked him how he had progressed.

"Not at all badly, Watson. The watermark is from 1809 but I am not convinced that the writing is as old as the paper. The layout is interesting: the text is strongly aligned along the right-hand edge of the folios. Therefore, I conclude that our ciphered messages are written from right to left..."

Holmes paused, mentally going over his conclusions.

'We have plenty of data and I looked to see if it was a very simply substitution cipher where the alphabet is shuffled in some way. I carried out a frequency analysis but I could find no letters which predominated, indicating that a far more complex cipher is being used. I looked again at the text and noticed an interesting phrase:

ERPCVT=YLJWPN

"Remember, Watson, we read from the right: the first letters in each word have identical relationships. P is two letters after N and in the second word after the equals sign: V is two letters after T."

"And what does this tell you, Holmes?"

"If these two words are identical, then we have a poly-alphabetic cipher."

I confessed I had never heard of such a thing.

"It just means, Watson, that each letter is enciphered using a different alphabet. I have to find what these alphabets are but I feel I am on the right track!"

The very next morning Holmes announced that he had deciphered the folios and had invited Dr. Wescott to visit us. He arrived and looked astounded.

"Mr. Holmes? You have deciphered the folios in less than one day? This is remarkable!"

"Not really remarkable, Doctor. Let me explain..."

Of course, I had heard much of the explanation before and Dr. Wescott paid great attention.

"This is a poly-alphabetic cipher which relies on a great tabulation – the Tabula Recto."

Holmes brought out his tabulation and put it in front of Dr. Wescott:

The Tale of the Tantric Detective by Geoff Dibb

ABCDEFGHIJKLMNOPQRSTUVWXYZ

1. ABCDEFGHIJKLMNOPQRSTUVWXYZ
2. BCDEFGHIJKLMNOPQRSTUVWXYZA
3. CDEFGHIJKLMNOPQRSTUVWXYZAB
4. DEFGHIJKLMNOPQRSTUVWXYZABC
5. EFGHIJKLMNOPQRSTUVWXYZABCD
6. FGHIJKLMNOPQRSTUVWXYZABCDE
7. GHIJKLMNOPQRSTUVWXYZABCDEF
8. HIJKLMNOPQRSTUVWXYZABCDEFG
9. IJKLMNOPQRSTUVWXYZABCDEFGH
10. JKLMNOPQRSTUVWXYZABCDEFGHI
11. KLMNOPQRSTUVWXYZABCDEFGHIJ
12. LMNOPQRSTUVWXYZABCDEFGHIJK
13. MNOPQRSTUVWXYZABCDEFGHIJKL
14. NOPQRSTUVWXYZABCDEFGHIJKLM
15. OPQRSTUVWXYZABCDEFGHIJKLMN
16. PQRSTUVWXYZABCDEFGHIJKLMNO
17. QRSTUVWXYZABCDEFGHIJKLMNOP
18. RSTUVWXYZABCDEFGHIJKLMNOPQ
19. STUVWXYZABCDEFGHIJKLMNOPQR
20. TUVWXYZABCDEFGHIJKLMNOPQRS
21. UVWXYZABCDEFGHIJKLMNOPQRST
22. VWXYZABCDEFGHIJKLMNOPQRSTU
23. WXYZABCDEFGHIJKLMNOPQRSTUV
24. XYZABCDEFGHIJKLMNOPQRSTUVW
25. YZABCDEFGHIJKLMNOPQRSTUVWX
26. ZABCDEFGHIJKLMNOPQRSTUVWXY

"This Tabula Recto is the tool for encipherment and decipherment. The alphabet along the top is used for the letters in our message. Let's encipher the word 'nought': we look along this top row for our first letter, N, and, as this is the first letter in the message, we look in the first row of the table for the letter below N, which is also N. Remember we are writing from right to left."

Holmes wrote N to the right of a sheet of paper.

"This is where the complexity arises: we look for our second letter O along the top line — it is the second letter so we go down to the second row where we find the letter P." Holmes wrote P to the left of the N on the paper. "And so we carry on — under U on the third line is W, and so on."

Eventually, Holmes had written:

YLJWPN

"This word occurs on this folio." Holmes showed the folio to Dr. Wescott.

"Mr. Holmes! Magnificent!"

"Cryptographically elementary, dear Doctor. But thank you, nevertheless."

Holmes exuded an air of considerable professional pride in his demonstration.

"I have deciphered folios 3 and 4 in their entirety, which you can have. Thereafter it is a trivial matter when armed with the Tabula Recto, which you can have as well." Dr. Wescott eagerly took the proffered Tabula Recto and Holmes's decipherment. "Overall the folios," Holmes continued, "seem to contain rather abstruse rites to be performed by a Master as he questions an Initiate."

"Indeed, Mr. Holmes. Fascinating..." said Dr. Wescott as he started to read Holmes's transcription. "Quite, quite brilliant. I had never heard of a private consulting detective until Inspector Lestrade mentioned the phrase. And then your name occurred whenever a rather unusual piece of evidence had been found and analysed. Your skills are a phenomenon, Mr. Holmes! I am certain we will come across each other again."

Dr. Wescott rose, smiled and shook our hands, "Thank you so much and good day to you, gentlemen."

And with those words Dr. Wescott bowed out of our lives for the next seven years.

December 1894: The Wheathampstead Hall Murder

My papers from 1894 begin in the coldest December in decades. Holmes and I had breakfasted and were staring through our frosted window, out onto snow-white Baker Street. We were warm and preparing our pipes when suddenly Holmes turned his head; his muscles stiffened slightly and his eyes narrowed.

'Watson, listen to that heavy deliberate tread on the stairs... and, oh, behind it a slightly lighter, more nervous arrival. My goodness, Watson, what a morning we are to have! It is Mycroft and Lestrade!"

Mrs Hudson opened the door and, sure enough, she showed in Mycroft Holmes, large, intelligent and indolent, followed by Inspector Lestrade, who looked weary.

"Mycroft, what can bring you here at this hour? And with Inspector Lestrade?"

"Sherlock, this case comes from the very top of Her Majesty's Government..."

"I expected as much when I heard your tread on the stairs."

"It is a murder, Sherlock, the murder of Lord Rothwell Woodlesford at his fortified medieval house, Wheathampstead

Hall in Hertfordshire. For many years Lord Woodlesford was the British Political Officer for the Tibetan region before retiring to his manor house and becoming a noted Tibetologist. Needless to say, the Prime Minister and the Head of the Civil Service have decided that I am the man to co-ordinate this investigation as a matter of urgency. But, as you know, running around the countryside searching for clues is more your type of game than mine..."

"I," Lestrade added, "have been brought in, Mr. Holmes, to lead the police investigation: we cannot have the local force blundering all over this."

Holmes almost laughed, and Mycroft and Lestrade began to brief us.

Lord Woodlesford had been stabbed in the heart in his private room with the door locked on the inside.

"Very queer rooms, Mr. Holmes," said Lestrade, "full of strange statues and picture—"

"Tibetan Buddhist artefacts, Sherlock," interrupted an obviously irritated Mycroft.

"The only way into the room," continued Lestrade, "was through the open French windows which overlook the rear garden. However, Wheathampstead Hall is what remains of the tower of an ancient castle and the bedroom must be thirty feet above the surrounding lawn. There's not a single handhold, drainpipe or window-ledge: it is an impossible climb."

"And the most singular matter, Sherlock," said Mycroft, "is that Lord Woodlesford's butler saw an almost naked man standing on the lawn under Woodlesford's bedroom windows just before he discovered that his master had been murdered. Naked, Sherlock, on the coldest night of the year. What do you make of that?"

"Too early to say, Mycroft... I must not begin to draw conclusions without data, but a most unusual circumstance, certainly. Well Watson, Wheathampstead Hall for us, I think!"

The Tale of the Tantric Detective by Geoff Dibb

*****

Wheathampstead Hall was an intriguing medieval house situated to the east of the village. Holmes and I walked from the railway station and a constable allowed us through the large gates, where we saw the building clearly for the first time. Wheathampstead Hall was broadly square in plan, aligned to face south with the Great Door at the south-east corner. The constable went inside to fetch the butler, who was the only witness to the events of the previous evening.

"Yes, sir, the master retires around 10 o'clock each evening and spends two or maybe three hours carrying out his studies. He likes to leave his windows open: many years in the Himalayas have taught him the benefits of cool, clean air. At about 11:30 I have my final smoke here by the Great Door and I let Red, my setter, have his last run. Well, last night — it was so cold that I decided to just have a cigarette rather than my usual pipe — I was standing right here and I looked over and saw this chap, wearing only a loincloth, right under his Lordship's bedroom. You can see the bedroom windows from here..."

He pointed and we looked up: Lord Woodlesford's rooms were in the south-west corner and his bedroom windows were full length opening onto a more modern, small wrought iron balcony. These looked south, over the lawn which surrounded the Hall.

The walls jutting straight out of the lawns had a smooth rendering and certainly no footholds. About 35 feet above the ground, the attractive half-timbered top story with its slate roof was cantilevered over the lower walls.

"Of course, it was dark; he had dark skin and there was just a slight glow falling from his Lordship's bedroom windows. I was astounded and called out: he looked at me and I tried to set the dog on him but Red just whimpered and slunk back inside. I looked back over and he was like a ghost, the way he moved. Smooth, silent movements and he was over the fence there," he pointed, "where there is a gap in the hedge, and he was gone, he vanished soundlessly into the night."

"And what did you do next?" asked Holmes.

"I ran straight up to his Lordship's rooms. I knocked on the door and shouted. No answer. So I used my duplicate key to open the door. His Lordship was lying in a pool of blood on his back in the middle of the room. I called my wife and the lad, and told the lad to get the doctor and Constable Burton, who arrived in about twenty minutes."

"Thank you very much," said Holmes. "I think we will look outside first then come in to see Lord Woodlesford's apartment.'

We walked towards the spot where the butler had said the man had been standing but before we got within twenty yards of it Holmes stopped. Whilst on the previous night the ground here would have been solid with frost, the thin December sun had thawed the ice a little and, as Holmes commented, "Lestrade's men have turned the entire lawn into a cattle field!" It was true: the lawn was well trodden by many boots. He sighed deeply: "We have little hope of seeing anything in this mud; let us at least look at where our man made his escape."

We walked over to the gap in the hedge through which the mysterious stranger had disappeared. Lestrade's men had not trampled over here. Holmes produced his large magnifying glass and began his meticulous survey in a way I had watched so many times.

"Watson! Look at this." Holmes stood pointing to a patch of soil by the gap in the hedge.

"Is it a footprint, Holmes?"

"It certainly is, Watson... and more: it is a bare footprint! Whoever did it was not wearing boots.... unlike Lestrade's men!"

The Tale of the Tantric Detective by Geoff Dibb

"I am baffled, Holmes, an almost naked man — and barefoot too — on the coldest night of the year?"

"Exactly, Watson. Very singular. This footprint cannot have been made today because the police have been here all the time... but last night when the footprint must have been made, the ground would have been frozen solid..." He drifted off staring at the ground.

With a shake of his head we set off to look at Lord Woodlesford's apartment.

"He was laying there, sir, on the rug, dead, blood everywhere. A terrible sight," said the butler.

'Where was the key?" Holmes was focussed now, this was his element.

"On his desk, sir."

"And the windows were open?"

"Yes, sir, wide open onto the balcony."

Thank you very much, you may leave us my good man, we will call if we need anything further."

The room had evidence on every wall, table and piece of furniture of a life passed in the Himalayas. Over many years Lord Woodlesford had, covertly and overtly, visited every kingdom in the region.

"Remember Watson, Lestrade's men have been here too, carrying out their 'investigations'. We are late." We stood, not moving, but looking. "The fire, Watson, look in the grate."

As Holmes had seen, there were ashes of pieces of paper, all burn or partially burnt. Holmes very carefully lifted some of these onto a sheet of paper: disappointingly, only one looked to have a few markings on the unburned part. We peered at this scrap of paper.

"Very strange." Holmes used a pencil to move it around until it was this way up:

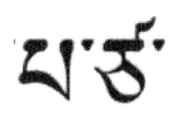

པ་ཙ་

"These are two Tibetan characters: *pa* and *tsa*..." Holmes peered through his magnifying glass, "and there look to be no other characters to the left or the right of them. But I am unsure of their significance from the Tibetan I have learnt."

Holmes placed the piece of paper in his wallet and stared at the room. He shook his head and began a cursory examination of the floor, crawling over it with his large glass. Then he stood up suddenly.

"Look here." He bent to point at a strip of carving on the underside lip of the desk. "It is almost impossible to see — and I suspect our police colleagues have missed it — but in the carving are several round wooden decorations, and I am certain that one of them is a small button."

He pressed a piece of the carving and a shallow drawer shot open, its front carved to match its surroundings and be as invisible as the button which released it. We both looked down to see the secret drawer's contents.

"Aha, Watson! Here is something for us!" There was one small piece of paper bearing three enciphered words in capital letters. "I think we will study this later, there is little time now." And Holmes put it into his wallet with the Tibetan scrap.

Lestrade walked into the room just as Holmes put his wallet into his inside coat pocket.

"Any luck then, Mr. Holmes?"

"You know I don't work with luck, Lestrade."

"Anything at all, then?"

"Yes, come into the garden."

Lestrade patiently followed Holmes who made a sarcastic aside about a 'ploughed field rather then a smooth lawn' until we got to the gap in the hedge: "Look here Lestrade... what do you make of this?"

"It is a bare footmark, Mr. Holmes."

"Indeed it is... and how did it get here?"

"I am sure I do not know, sir. We had not studied it."

"No. Well think about it whilst I see what is on the other side of this fence..." and with that he lightly climbed over into the lane beyond. Holmes cast around, stooping close to the ground, occasionally staring through his glass.

"Anything, Mr. Holmes?" said Lestrade hopefully.

"Very little. This change from frost to soft mud is not helpful. However, I would say that our man went south. But not on a bicycle or a horse or a cart, all of which would have left some evidence of their presence. And the butler particularly mentioned there was no sound. No, the man escaped into the frozen night on foot — and barefoot at that."

Holmes climbed back over the fence. "I suggest you get the local constabulary mobilised, Inspector. We need officers to visit every house and farm to the south of Wheathampstead Hall: our semi-naked man must be a rather obvious addition to the neighbouring population of farm labourers, don't you think?"

"Yes, Mr. Holmes. I agree. I will arrange for a thorough search."

"Meanwhile, Inspector, where is the body? Has it been assumed by the local Police Surgeon? I do need to know about its injuries."

"No, Mr. Holmes, nothing in this case is being dealt with locally. The body of the deceased is now residing in the offices of the Coroner of London, Dr. Wescott."

"Well, Lestrade, I think we will return to London and visit the Coroner. Watson! Onwards..." and as we walked back to the railway station, Holmes looked very content.

"Mr. Holmes, Dr. Watson! Good afternoon." said Dr. Wescott as we were shown into his office, "I must say that I was expecting to see you. I do hope that we are able to help each other in this terrible and important case."

"Quite, Dr. Wescott, it is a most fortunate — if that is the correct word — set of circumstances."

"I will cut to the key facts, Mr. Holmes, as I am certain that is what you would wish. Two salient points arise from the post mortem: firstly, Lord Woodlesford was stabbed in the heart in what I can only describe as a forceful, direct and accurate single thrust. There was nothing amateur here, Mr. Holmes. No defence wounds, nothing, it was as though he was transfixed into immobility. Secondly, and I feel probably most significantly..." Dr. Wescott glanced at us both before he continued: "he was stabbed with what the Tibetans call a *phur ba*: it is a ritual knife with a blade composed of three triangular faces, welded together and meeting at a sharp tip. In this case the distinguishing feature of the fatal wound is that it has this three blade incision, each blade rotated 120° from the other."

"Remarkable, Doctor. I remember seeing *phur bas* when I was in Sikkim and Tibet: they were very much ritual objects, not weapons."

"Quite correct, Mr. Holmes, they are used in religious ceremonies and have great mystical symbolism. It is rare in the Tibetan region for them to be used as knives, but not unknown."

There was a short pause until Dr. Wescott continued: "I had met Lord Woodlesford, Mr. Holmes. His knowledge of Tibet is... was... unrivalled, and my special interest in Tibetan Buddhism did bring us together."

"And how did you meet him?"

"He came forward to join the Golden Dawn and began to work his way through the various rites which I had established from the folios you deciphered. At the time there was considerable effort being put into drawing together ancient Western Magic — the Qabbala, Alchemy, the Tarot — and the teachings of Tibet."

"Had Lord Woodlesford progressed through the orders of the Golden Dawn?"

"Yes indeed. He eventually rose to join a very select group of initiates. Our leader, MacGregor Mathers, began to take the lead in this work and liaised very closely with Lord Woodlesford. I may not have been made aware of the progress being made. But Mathers has been absent in Paris for some time, now."

*****

After we had dined, Holmes returned to his armchair, smoking his pipe.

"Do your travels in Tibet, Holmes, give you any clues as to what this is about?"

"I have been thinking of them a great deal, Watson. To escape Moriarty's men I sailed to Calcutta. Mycroft encouraged me; he sent me my finances and papers for travel. He was very keen to have my first-hand observations of the Great Game being played out in the Himalayan kingdoms. I travelled north to Darjeeling and then to the capital of Sikkim, Gangtok, on the old Silk Road to Lhassa. In Gantok I settled down, awaiting the spring when the mountain pass of *Nathu La* would open. It was there that I met Lama Chogyal Nawang Rinpoche, a great thinker and mystical seer. I had plenty of time and I needed stimulation. There were endless narcotics to relieve the boredom, but Lama Rinpoche knew many of the abbots at the monasteries and he took me to visit the Monastery of *Enchey*

Sangag Rabtenling. This monastery was instituted by Lama Drupthob Karpo where he became a renowned exponent of Buddhist tantric religion and, legend has it, developed flying powers."

I looked at Holmes, curious as to where his thoughts were taking him.

"I have never had much time for religion but I have to say the calm and peace in the Enchey Monastery was wonderful. I was exhausted, Watson; I had spent so long fighting Moriarty and his men, I had almost died at the Reichenbach Falls, I had raced across the globe to escape and needed to recuperate. Here, these monks took themselves away and studied, meditated, perfected yogic exercises in peace and quiet. After my second visit to the monastery, Lama Rinpoche asked if I would like to have a longer stay and I said that I would be delighted to; I stayed for a month or so."

He looked at me and smiled: "You look worried, Watson! No, I have not changed. At heart, I am a man of science: I adopt the scientific practise, established ever since the Enlightenment. But what I saw in Enchey Monastery opened my eyes. I came to understand that these Buddhist practises of meditation, breath control, chanting and yoga were actually a series of lengthy biological experiments taking years for each man. I saw these men could achieve what I would have said were superhuman, even magical powers, but that is a completely superficial view: these are well defined tantric practises called *tum-mo* or inner fire by the Tibetans."

"And," I asked as he fell silent, "has this had any impact on your work?"

"You have written more than once about what I have termed The Science of Deduction and you have outlined some of my methods. Observation, Deduction and Knowledge are the essential elements and my experiences in Sikkim and Tibet have extended my knowledge. It comes down to my precept, that in an investigation, when you have eliminated the impossible, whatever remains, *however improbable*, must be the truth."

"So, for you, Holmes, the 'possible' can include what I would describe as the occult?'

"Yes, but I will not automatically assume that the occult has occurred, Watson! After all, it is very rare. But, back to our case — I have been looking at the enciphered paper I took from Lord Woodlesford's study. I have stared at it long enough and I think I have something.'

"What Holmes?" I said leaning forward to look at the three words on the paper. "First, the cipher is written from right to left and, second, it is a poly-alphabetic substitution cipher. And the last time we came across such a cipher was..."

"Dr. Wescott and his ritual folios!"

"Exactly... seven years ago... but it is not exactly the same cipher..."

"Do you think Dr. Wescott and the Golden Dawn are involved in this murder?"

"By my own precepts, Watson, it is possible that Dr. Wescott is. But I feel his involvement is improbable. He has been very open with us about his membership."

Holmes returned to this piece of paper with renewed effort and I heard him mumble 'Golden Dawn' under his breath.

Ten minutes later Holmes announced that he had it: "The standard Tabula Recto I gave to Dr. Wescott did not work and so I decided to try to add a keyword to it. Simply, you begin the very top line with a keyword and then continue with the rest of the letters of the alphabet which aren't in that word. I was struggling to find a keyword that worked but - thanks to you, Watson - I tried GOLDEN and - *voila!* - it worked!"

"And what does it say?"

"When I write it from left to right it reads:

RETURN
SIKKIM
GOLD"

"Marvellous, Holmes."

"So far so good... but what is this golden Sikkimese artefact which Lord Woodlesford had in his collection? I need to think, Watson..."

*****

The next morning the door opened and Mrs. Hudson showed in what must have been the most resplendently dressed man in London.

"Ah, Lama Rinpoche!" announced Holmes.

Lama Rinpoche might have just stepped out of a monastery high in the snow-clad Himalayas: his overcoat was maroon, wrapped around with a broad belt, and the lining of yellow showed at the lapels; he wore a fur hat and comfortable looking fur lined leather boots which must have kept out the London winter. His brown face had strong Tibetan features, and there was a gleam in his eyes.

They both put their hands together and bowed deeply to each other.

"Watson," said Holmes, "please allow me to introduce Lama Chogyal Nawang Rinpoche."

We approached each other and bowed.

"Dr. Watson, I am delighted to meet you; your tales of Mr. Holmes's criminal investigations have fascinated me over the years."

(I must say that I took great pride in his compliments.)

"I am very pleased to be in London: after Mr. Holmes and I left Tibet we travelled in different directions – I to Christian monasteries in the Egyptian desert, then across North Africa to

Spain, and eventually London." Lama Rinpoche beamed and sat down.

"I have been telling Dr. Watson," said Holmes, "about some of our experiences. But I am delighted, Lama Rinpoche, you are able to join us. Our latest case has many features I am certain you will find of interest."

"Yes, Mr. Holmes, from the telegram you sent me there are many matters which indicate a strong link to my homeland."

"Exactly and I will be pleased to have your views. The very first piece of evidence I noticed was the naked footprint by the gap in the hedge. The fact that it could be made by a bare foot on such a cold night indicated to me the possibility of great heat being generated."

"To me, Mr. Holmes, this footprint, and the evidence that the man was almost naked on such a cold night, indicates a Tibetan Buddhist adept who was practising *tum-mo* meditation. When that footprint was made, the adept was producing so much heat that the ice in the soil was melted and the print was made."

"That is the conclusion that I reached, Lama Rinpoche. But over the fence, in the lane, there was hardly a mark. Certainly no evidence of any vehicle which could give a rapid escape."

Rinpoche nodded. "The description of the way the man moved after the butler had shouted at him – he hardly seemed to run, he was a fluid shadow in the night and silently slipped away – has all the traits which I associate with the *lung-gom-pa* runners of Tibet. A *lung-gom-pa*, Dr. Watson," he said, turning to me, "is someone who has harnessed their spiritual energy to transcend the physical limits of the body. A would-be *lung-gom-pa* lives in a meditation hermitage for years; he is fed but not allowed any human contact. He spends his days meditating, chanting and practising special breathing exercises. Years can pass before he is released from his seclusion and he exists in a netherworld between Being and Non-Being: he is almost a wraith, almost invisible, he can move with the speed of a galloping horse, while hardly touching the ground. A *lung-gom-pa* is a Buddhist adept much more advanced than a *tum-mo* monk. Swiftly and silently, he could be miles away in minutes. He could run for hours."

"So the police's search of the neighbourhood was completely unnecessary?"

"Possibly, Mr. Holmes, a *lung-gom-pa* could have been almost in London in an hour."

"So we will need to throw our net a little wider, Watson!" Holmes peered into the fire, "One major lead is the stab wound: a single, forceful thrust of a *phur ba*."

"This, Mr. Holmes, with the other evidence, indicates to me a breakaway sect of adepts who have undergone the long Buddhist training but have begun to use their powers for other purposes."

"And then we have the scrap of paper we extracted from the fire. It has only two characters on it which I believe are the Tibetan characters: *pa* and *tsa*." Holmes handed him the small scrap of burnt paper.

"You are not mistaken. However, context is all when it comes to meaning: I consider that these two characters – their very form – are an outcome of the ancient Tibetan *Mo* divinatory method which links back thousands of years to the pre-Buddhist *Bon* religion. Dice are used which bear on their faces the syllables of the great Mantra of *Manjusri* which in Tibetan may be separated into the powerful, mystical word *Om* plus the six syllables, *Ah Ra Pa Tsa Na Dhih*."

He wrote out the mantra for us:

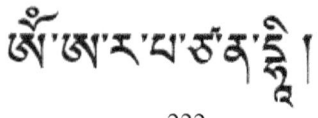

ཨོཾ་ཨ་ར་པ་ཙ་ན་དྷཱི༔ །

"Each of these symbols is written on the face of a die and thrown twice to give the prediction. In *Mo* divination the two symbols are read in the order they appear and *pa tsa* is such an outcome, the worst possible outcome: happiness will be destroyed, the vicious *Yaksha* demon will tear away the earth beneath the agitated water: there is disturbance of mind and great unhappiness."

"Is this, then, a coded message from someone to Lord Woodlesford?"

"Certainly, Mr. Holmes, and the sender, by indicating those syllables, knew that Lord Woodlesford would understand the ancient code. This wasn't just a warning, it was an occult attack upon Lord Woodlesford."

"Just before a physical one," said Holmes.

"So who," I asked, "are these people?"

"I think that Lord Woodlesford is the target because of his activities for the British Government. And the clue to who his enemies are must be found in the cipher message he had hidden in his secret drawer: Return Sikkim Gold."

"Return Sikkim Gold, Mr. Holmes?" asked Rinpoche.

"Yes. That is the enciphered message which we found in Lord Woodlesford's desk."

"I wonder if this is a reference to the British invasion of Sikkim in 1888? I have heard rumours of British troops entering monasteries and some thefts of religious artefacts. Perhaps this is the gold the message refers to?"

"Was Lord Woodlesford involved in this invasion?" I asked.

"I think that Lord Woodlesford had a hand in everything in that region for many years," said Rinpoche, "Your brother, Mr. Holmes, would probably be a better source of information."

"Quite." said Holmes and paused to think. "We are left with knowing very little of the identity of the murderer and, indeed, his or their purpose. We are fairly certain that he is from the Tibetan region, we know he is a Tibetan Buddhist adept, he would be a very visible personage in England today, so can we assume he is being hidden and looked after by someone?"

"I think it extremely likely, Holmes." I suggested.

"I just wonder, Lama Rinpoche, if he is connected in any way with the various occult groups we have learnt about? I am certain that a Tibetan Buddhist adept would be an attractive addition to any occult Lodge carrying out their own studies of Tibetan rituals, practises and meditational systems."

"I am certain that would be the case, Mr. Holmes. But as you have commented, there seem to be an endless number of them."

We discussed the matter further and as Lama Rinpoche left he invited us to his residence the following morning where he would try to help us find the murderer.

*****

After breakfast, Holmes and I made our way to Elm Park Gardens in Chelsea to visit Lama Rinpoche in the house which Mycroft Holmes had provided as thanks for all he had done to assist my friend. It was a beautiful house on the outside and something very different internally. Throughout the house there were many Tibetan sculptures, paintings and *thangkas*. Lama Rinpoche donned his tall, crescent shaped red hat before leading us into a small Buddhist temple. There were large paintings and tapestries on three walls, the floor was covered in oriental carpets and cushions and against the final wall was the altar covered with a Tibetan cloth on which was placed a bronze statue of a seated Buddha. Behind this statue was a large *thangka* of the wheel of life. Incense was burning in three bronze receptacles and Lama Rinpoche asked us to sit down.

"Now, gentlemen, we need to harness the ancient ways of my homeland in order to track down those involved in this crime. And I intend to do it using the very method they have been using: *Mo* divination. They are clearly adepts and may well sense the psychic ritual I am about to perform. But we must persevere..." He looked around and pulled two *sutras* towards him as well as a small drum, finger cymbals and a yak horn with a golden mouthpiece. "This ritual will take time and we all need to concentrate solely on what we are seeking: who is the murderer and where is he? The *Mo* method has been used in Tibet for centuries when any great questions in life arise. When I am fully prepared and ready I will then formulate the question, breathe onto the die, and throw it twice. I will immediately repeat this to generate a second *Mo* divination: how these two results co-ordinate will modify the reading. I may have to undertake this many times to be guided to the divined answer."

Lama Rinpoche turned towards the altar and blew eight strong notes from the yak horn. The smoke of incense swirled around him and a peace descended on the temple as he then beat a steady rhythm on his drum and, within this rhythm, chimed his finger cymbals. This continued for some time before he chanted the mantra of *Manjusri* in a voice so deep it seemed to echo from the heart of the Himalayas:

Om Ah Ra Pa Tsa Na Dhih
Om Ah Ra Pa Tsa Na Dhih
Om Ah Ra Pa Tsa Na Dhih

Eventually, the mantra ceased and I stared at the elaborate designs on the back of Lama Rinpoche's coat as he sat cross legged with his head bowed. Then he faced the Buddha on the altar, whispered into his right fist and threw the die, picked it up and threw it again, wrote the results down and then repeated the actions to conclude the first *Mo* divination. He chimed his finger cymbals and then consulted the long pages of the oracle for several minutes before writing down a conclusion. This was the beginning of over an hour of ritualistic *Mo* divination before the finger cymbals chimed for the final time.

Lama Rinpoche turned towards us: "It is done, gentlemen, I have an answer. It was confusing at times and different threads appeared and intertwined. Eventually my searches began to receive answers which resonated: golden images and impressions became very strong and I felt that these were important symbols. Then came variations of three which I interpreted as *dug gsum* – the three poisons. And I saw the symbol of '*Om*', the primordial sound of the Universe. These three symbols began to conjoin and represent what I saw as a temple: what was becoming disclosed was within the Third Order of the Hermetic Order of the Golden Dawn. It was an extremely secret group, a Lodge within the Order which had assumed its own power and objectives: it was called the Om Lodge. Within it there are possibly two or three of the highest members of the Golden Dawn working with two Tibetan Buddhist adepts. In fact, at the end, through the *Mo* divination, I could detect their presence and I felt them sensing my quest and using their psychic powers to find me..." Lama Rinpoche relaxed into silence from his exertions.

"Have you any impression of where this Om Lodge is?"

"I am afraid not. At that point I felt that to continue risked disclosure. I did sense two adepts alerted by my ritual, still searching for something very important to them."

"If you have divined that they are still searching, I think we can conclude that the Sikkim Gold was not found at Lord Woodlesford's home. It must be somewhere else."

"Yes, these adepts are still searching for their gold — and will kill to get it."

*****

For days we stayed indoors at Baker Street; the freezing London outside became no warmer. Holmes sent a number of telegrams to which replies arrived at all hours. He checked with Lestrade that nothing had been stolen from Wheathampstead Hall and paid another visit to interview the butler and inspect the room again. He was content that nothing had gone missing. Eventually, Holmes became more animated and focussed: he was planning something.

"Have you seen the announcement in today's Society pages, Watson?" he asked after breakfast a week later.

"You know I do not read them, Holmes."

Holmes pushed over the *Morning Post*, folded to show the article of interest. I read:

Sir Stanley Barwick, the Government's adviser in Northern India and the Himalayas, is to return to his home in Holland Park for his Christmas holiday. He will be in London for one night only on Saturday, this weekend, and will then travel to his Irish properties until he returns from there to India in January.

"The trap is set, Watson! Sir Barwick was Lord Woodlesford's next in command and, indeed, the replacement on his retirement. Nothing that happened during Lord Woodlesford's years in the Himalayas could happen without Sir Barwick knowing and taking part."

"Sir Barwick could be at great personal risk, Holmes." I suggested.

The Tale of the Tantric Detective by Geoff Dibb

"He has agreed to our arrangements and remains safely in seclusion in Calcutta. We will hide in his house on Saturday night; you, Lama Rinpoche and I. Bring your trusty service revolver and I will invite Lestrade. This is a life and death matter: these fiends will stop at nothing now."

As darkness descended we three and Lestrade let ourselves into Sir Barwick's large villa in Holland Park and made our way to his study and bedroom high in the building's tower section. His study was elegantly furnished with a large desk, chairs and, just as at Wheathampstead Hall, it had tall windows which opened onto a small wrought iron balcony which overlooked the gardens to the rear. Around the walls were Indian and Tibetan tapestries and a bookcase containing many Buddhist works and some ancient looking *sutras*. Lestrade positioned himself in the next room with the door slightly open onto the landing so he could see anyone coming up the stairs. We opened the French windows and lit two lamps along the wall opposite them. Holmes sat at the heavy desk looking over a Tibetan *sutra*, strongly silhouetted against the lamps. I placed myself behind a tapestry near the door in order to double-check on that means of access, and Lama Rinpoche hid behind another tapestry so that he had a view of the open windows. It was cold and we waited. Somewhere in the house a clock sounded the quarter hours and all was silent except for the sound of Holmes turning the *sutra* pages.

I was keeping a close eye on the study door and so I have to rely on Holmes's and Lama Rinpoche's later recollections for a full description of the sudden action:

"I was looking at the *sutra*, Watson, whilst keeping an eye on the open windows. I was expecting that would be how the murderer would get into the room but I had not decided upon the method he would use; the butler at Wheathampstead Hall had not seen any ropes or other climbing equipment. Eventually I sensed a great silence and, from under my brows, at the very edge of my vision, I thought I saw a moth, a large white moth. I slowly looked up but the moth was flying towards me, getting larger: it was actually a man wearing a loincloth and turban, shining in the full silver moonlight. He came from a dark distance: a smooth, silent, silver, effortlessly floating figure sliding through the solid blackness of the night, through the windows and he landed, slightly bending his knees, on the threshold of the room. He had levitated from the gardens thirty feet below! I was mesmerised."

"This ability," said Rinpoche, "to levitate is a side-effect of the more elevated powers which monks can attain after years of Buddhist mastery."

"It is yet another result of the astonishing experiments these monks carry out," added Holmes.

"I sensed the murderer's arrival before I saw him," added Rinpoche, "and as he landed I knew that Mr. Holmes was in great danger. I had travelled with my only weapons, my ancient *phur-ba* made from meteoritic iron and a double-*vajra dorje*," at this he pulled out the weapon from a voluminous pocket, "which, as you can see, is an iron sphere from which protrude two pairs of pointed iron lotus blooms. It is a powerful Buddhist symbol and a vicious weapon. I leapt out from behind the tapestry and shouted to distract the attacker and to shock Mr. Holmes out of his trance."

As this activity erupted in the room I came from behind my tapestry to see for myself what was happening. Lestrade, too, rushed in. But Lestrade, Holmes and I were powerless to intervene and were engrossed in the high-speed hand-to-hand battle which was whirl-winding its way across the room: skull headed *phur-bas* and double-*vajra dorjes* sparked off each other with great metallic clashes. Arms and feet ripped through the air in a blur, it was hard to tell who was on top. Lama Rinpoche's maroon and gold coat opened and streamed in his hectic wake. Eventually the attacker lunged and his gleaming *phur-ba* pierced Lama Rinpoche's coat, slashing it, and the tri-blade became caught in the fabric: in that split second, Lama Rinpoche crashed down with his *viśvavajra* onto the attacker's skull and he collapsed to the floor, unconscious. We rushed forward and grabbed our man, handcuffing him before he regained consciousness.

At that moment, a figure erupted through the now-ignored open bedroom door and rushed towards the bookcase by the wall. He, too, was half-naked and held a *phur ba* as he spun round to defend his position against all comers, but he had not seen Holmes who, without any of us noticing, had quietly hidden himself in the deep shadow at the end of the bookcase. With a rapid downstroke of his stick, our second half-naked interloper was immobile at his feet.

"You told us there were two of them, Lama Rinpoche, and I knew that our bait was so strong that both would be paying 'Sir Barwick' a visit tonight. It was their last chance to get their hands on the Sikkim Gold. All attention was on our first man and none was on the door or the windows, so I stepped back into the shadows to observe."

Holmes turned to the desk. "I had been in contact with Sir Barwick and he told me that three weeks ago Lord Woodlesford had written to him asking if he could donate a *sutra* to Barwick's collection. The *sutra* was handed to his butler who placed it in the collection in this bookcase. It is the *mdosde gser-od-dampa,* known in the west as The Gold Sutra, and to make sure it was safe I took it to the desk and had been studying it all evening. As you will know, Lama Rinpoche, this is a much revered sutra but this copy is unique: it is the very earliest known to exist in Tibetan. During the 1888 Invasion of Sikkim, Lord Woodlesford joined the British Army and, at some point and by unknown means, The Gold Sutra came into his possession. It was so holy to the monastery that a small number of adepts swore that they would search the earth to find and return it. And here they are.'

Lestrade was very busy handcuffing our invaders and supervising their safe transport to Scotland Yard. Holmes whispered to us: "But, of course, I think we must omit mention of levitating Buddhist adepts to Lestrade... he wouldn't believe us!'

As the criminals were marched away, the inspector turned to Holmes: "When I came in the fight was in full swing: how had our man got into the room?"

"Just like Watson and Lama Rinpoche," said Holmes, "he was hiding behind one of these sumptuous tapestries and emerged from his hiding place when he thought he had his best chance."

Lestrade looked only half satisfied with this explanation but was happy to know that the perpetrators of these crimes were in his custody.

"And what about Lord Woodlesford's murderer? How did he get into that room?'

"I cannot be certain," said Holmes, "but it probably was the same methodology."

"Aha, Mr. Holmes, it shows that even you can be mystified at times."

*****

"Well, Holmes," I said after breakfast the next day, "another successful case for my records."

"Indeed, Watson, but we needed Lama Rinpoche, not just for his ability to handle himself in hand-to-hand combat, but for his vast knowledge of Tibetan Buddhism and his mystic skills. It is certain that the adepts from the monastery knew that the British were involved with taking The Gold Sutra and, at that time, many British seekers were visiting Sikkim and Tibet.

Soon members of The Hermetic Order of the Golden Dawn arrived and these Sikkimese adepts made themselves extremely helpful and travelled back to London with them.

"Their knowledge of Tibetan Buddhist practises was so profound that they soon entered the very highest Order, and within that Order Macgregor Mathers established the secret Om Lodge to study and integrate Tibetan Buddhism with the Qabbalah. The Om Lodge was essentially Mathers, Woodlesford and the two Sikkimese adepts. These adepts were now very well placed to begin their investigations and, of course, they soon discovered that the very man they were working with, Lord Woodlesford, had a role in the invasion of Sikkim and also had a collection of rare *sutras*. I contacted Sir Barwick and learnt of Lord Woodlesford's transferrence of the *mdosde gser-od-dampa*. I knew that this must be the Sikkim Gold they wanted. It was just a question of setting a trap!"

Holmes smoked quietly for a second. "Without Lama Rinpoche, both in Tibet and here, I would be so much poorer in knowledge and experience. Working with him has extended my capabilities as a consulting detective considerably. I am better for it."

Holmes looked pensively out of the window. "Of course, Watson, those two arrested men will use all their powers to escape and I am afraid that Lestrade is just not good enough to keep them in gaol. One day, probably travelling to or from the courtroom, they will use their malign powers and in no time they will be on a boat to India."

Holmes's prediction turned out to be correct and poor Lestrade had a bad time of it in the newspapers. Some weeks later Holmes was delighted to receive a letter from Lama Rinpoche which said that he was sailing to India and that he 'happened' to be on the very same boat as our escapees. The men had, he wrote, "disappeared in mysterious circumstances" when their ship docked in Egypt. Holmes sat in his favourite armchair and laughed in a very satisfied manner.

"*Om tat sat*, Watson!"

The Adventure of the Three Rippers

by Edward M. Erdelac

From the Journal of Professor Abraham Van Helsing (translated from the original Dutch)

5th November 1888

Van Voorhees yet eludes me. My sabbatical from the university draws to a close. I have secured an engagement lecturing The Physiological Society on Friday morning which will extend my stay in London, but it is not enough. God, am I to be foiled in the end by lack of resources? Inspector Swanson has promised to solicit my services should the need arise, yet I know he is dubious of their worth. My room here is fast draining my funds. I am tempted to take up John's kindly offer to stay in Purfleet, but I fear it would take me far from my purpose. Van Voorhees is very near. Three days until the eighth. He must strike again.

I had a peculiar dream last night. I saw his face, tiny in the corner of the eye of the guiltless, wretched janitor, a scheming homunculus leering as he directed the blade toward my dear wife's throat like a man looking out of the glass in a pilot house.

In the manner of dreams, I next saw the honey-coloured Anglican peripteros with its prominent circular spire, which *has been my daily scenery since my arrival here in Marylebone. Majestic between the Corinthian pillars, like the legendary quarry of Wodan's hunt, a great hooved, pitch-black stag stood pawing the stone steps.*

I awoke to the sonorous bell of All Soul's echoing the call to morning mass across the street.

I shall take the air. It is frustrating to know he is somewhere in this city, one among millions and yet, is there any more vile? He is a devil inside a man inside a man. But which man? Or which woman, for that matter?

He watches the women as I watch for him, both of us eager to be about our work. If I could but predict his next act — but I am no medium, and even less a detective.

God grant me aid.

The alacritous ricochet of a violin bounded up Baker Street as I strolled toward our rooms. I noticed more than a few of the passersby touching their ears and grimacing as they directed their collective annoyance up at the open window of 221B, where I discerned the silhouette of Holmes sawing furiously at his instrument.

Paganini's Arpeggio is, of course, not readily to the layman's taste, even when played expertly. I confess to not being fond of it myself. There was something to Holmes's playing this afternoon which added to its discordance. By the time I had ascended the stairs and reached the drawing room, I knew what. He was in his shirt sleeves, and the morocco case sat open on the mantelpiece.

My friend had been in a state of idle melancholy for the better part of a week, due to some matter which he would not confide in me. I perceived it was related to the infamous Ripper case.

Holmes, of course, had been involved in the affair prior to our departure for Dartmoor, back when the fledgling killer's tally yet numbered two. He had been summarily dismissed from the investigation after a row with Sir Charles Warren, the Chief Commissioner. Two years ago, Sir Charles' near-fanatic enforcement of an edict to muzzle dogs had resulted in an overzealous constable clubbing one pitiable cur to death on our very stoop. The incident had soured Holmes on the man. Displeased with Sir Charles's comparatively middling dedication to the Ripper case, Holmes had excoriated him that if he only pursued the murderer with as much zeal as he chased down stray dogs, the women of Whitechapel could breathe easy.

There was assuredly a political element to his dismissal as well. The police simply did not want their most famous case solved by a civilian.

I knew though, that Holmes had in some way defied the injunction, and kept me at arms' length during his private investigations so as to shield me from reprimand should they be discovered.

He had been in constant contact with some person or persons very close to the case. I had seen him scrutinizing the handwriting of the letters reportedly sent by the killer to the Central News Agency, which he received via courier, and a driver I privately questioned admitted to me that Holmes had visited Whitechapel so many nights in the past few weeks he was worried his passenger might actually *be* the Ripper.

Since the end of October, however, Holmes had retreated into indolence, or rather, as much indolence as his vigorous mind was capable of. He pored over his volumes, scraped at his violin, and succumbed to his more unworthy habits.

As I took off my coat, I surreptitiously peered into the morocco case and saw that the last of his tinctures was drained.

He stopped his playing upon perceiving me, and sparing one last look out the window, returned his instrument to its case.

"We shall have a new problem before us soon, Watson," he said without preamble, rolling down his left sleeve and shouldering into his jacket.

"Ah?" I replied, and privately thought that a new conundrum to occupy Holmes's troubled brain could not come fast enough. "How soon?"

Presently there was a knock on the chamber door. Holmes allowed himself a thin smile and bid the client enter as he settled into his chair.

An extraordinary looking gentleman entered. He wore shoulder length hair and a drooping, insistent moustache, and was dressed in a fringed top coat of tanned leather, and knee high gaiters of yellow deerskin, over dungaree trousers and a pair of high heeled boots. His bibbed shirt front was adorned with a number of badges, so many that one had retired to the crown of his wide brimmed hat, which the man wore cocked at a slant. I should say that a colourful kerchief tied about his neck capped off his unique appearance, but that honour surely belonged to the shining, overlarge, ivory-handled revolver thrust brazenly through his wide belt.

The man doffed his hat upon entering. His smile barely poked out from behind his whiskers.

"Which of you gentlemen is Mr. Sherlock Holmes?" he drawled slowly, in the manner of an American.

"I am," Holmes confirmed. "May I present Dr. John Watson?"

The man bobbed his chin at me.

"Watson," Holmes said, "this is Colonel Joe Shelley of Austin, Texas; proprietor of Mexican Joe's Western Wilds of America review, opening in Sheffield tomorrow. Please sit down, Colonel, and tell me about this missing Sioux Indian of

The Adventure of the Three Rippers by Edward M. Erdelac

yours. He's only been with your show five months, so he's not the man who shot you. Why would a Red Indian who doesn't speak a word of English go wandering the streets of London?"

The colonel stood dumbstruck.

"By God you *are* Sherlock Holmes! They told me you'd know who I was and what I was after before I sat down."

"They?" I ventured.

"Mr. Barker and Mr. Levillard," said the colonel.

"Monsieur *le Villard*," Holmes corrected him.

"'At's 'im! They told me if'n I ever found myself in a bind you was the one to go to. But now, sir," he said, dragging the stool from Holmes's workbench and perching on it, "you must tell me how you came by all that."

Holmes nodded and settled back in his chair.

"Firstly, the faint pockmark below your eye. You have obscured it somewhat with stage make-up, but it is perhaps a year old. A birdshot load fired from a .45 revolver much like your own. It is a speciality round intended for displays of marksmanship; blasting clay pigeons and the like. The deliberate location of your wound, rather than on your hand, precludes an accident."

Shelley stroked the white spot I now saw below his eye.

"A salary dispute with my trick shooter," he murmured.

"I see," Holmes continued. "Mexican Joe's handbills are ubiquitous. The local boys have plastered them on every door in Marylebone for tuppence a stack."

"A worthwhile expenditure," said Shelley. "But my likeness ain't on 'em, nor my real name."

"No," said Holmes. "But as Colonel Cody's show departed for America at the end of last April, following the Queen's jubilee, yours is the only troupe of its kind presently touring Europe. Your inner hatband bears the stamp of an Austin haberdashery. As to your name, you were mentioned in the Parisian newspapers three months ago in conjunction with the sixteen year old London girl who followed your employee, an Indian brave named Eagle Eye, across the channel to Neuilly. The family hired a private detective to retrieve her — doubtless our mutual acquaintance Mr. Barker — and an altercation ensued when the lovers were forcibly parted. The Sûreté were involved. An unnamed detective was slightly injured by a tomahawk to the right hand. This is surely Msr. François le Villard, as he apologized to me in a recent letter for the state of his handwriting, citing an injury sustained in the line of duty."

Shelley shifted a bit in his seat.

"I hope you don't mistake my character, Mr. Holmes. That affair was blown way out of proportion by the press. Besides, these young British girls, at the sight of all that buckskin and naked flesh, you know, passions sometimes boil over."

"Indeed?" said Holmes non-committally.

"But, how'd you know my purpose in seeking you out?" Shelley asked hastily, eager to change the subject.

"Your handbills list your performance schedule. You are due in Sheffield in the morning, but are hesitant to proceed. One of your performers has wandered off. An English speaker would give you no concern. That you employ Apache Indians in your show is stated on your fliers. Around April seventh, four Sioux Indians were detained in Whitechapel regarding the murder of a prostitute. The poor woman was in fact slain by a gang of pimps, but they were exonerated with difficulty, owing to the fact that only one of them spoke English.

"The only Sioux in the country were members of Colonel Cody's Wild West Show. No doubt they were stranded when he departed for America. Yours is the most likely place for them to find gainful employment until they can afford passage back. That you command a certain loyalty from your more seasoned performers is evidenced in that you did not dismiss your man Eagle Eye in the face of scandal, nor, I may presume, your quarrelsome trick shooter. Therefore the missing man must be one of the Sioux newcomers."

"That is the damn'dest thing I ever heard, Mr. Holmes," Shelley said, slapping his knee. "Sir, if you are hard up for work, there's always a place for you telling fortunes in my show."

"It's hardly fortune telling," said Holmes, stiffly. "Merely the logical interpretation of observable facts."

"Nevertheless," said Shelley, winking. "Were I you, I'd let the rubes think otherwise and not let onto my tricks. You'll make a better living that way. But how'd you know my man's been missing three days?"

"As for that, if you don't mind, I shall take your advice and keep it to myself, until after I have delivered him, Colonel," Holmes said.

"You'll take the case then?" Shelley asked.

"If you will provide me with his name and description."

"Of course! His name's Black Elk. He's a boy of twenty five, near as I can tell, long haired in the native fashion. He wears his clothes inside out."

"Inside out?" I asked.

"It's some spiritual hokum," Shelley said with a wave of his fingers. "I don't claim to understand it. He's a contrarian and much given to the whims of his peculiar religion. He rides a horse backwards, bathes in dirt, laughs at funerals... During our tour of Pompeii, the damned fool nearly walked into Mount Vesuvius. Personally, I would not care where he ended up as he is damned difficult, but the other Sioux defer to him and are much agitated. They say they will not perform without him."

"Fascinating," Holmes remarked.

"Mr. Holmes, as you know, we depart in the morning. I know it's not a lot of time..."

"Barring unforeseen circumstances, Black Elk will be back safe in your care well before morning," Holmes promised.

"Well thank you!" Shelley said, rising and grasping Holmes's hand in an exuberant handshake. "Ah, there's just one thing, the matter of uh…"

"Remuneration?" Holmes finished for him.

"You see everything," Shelley said, touching the side of his nose. "My funds are tied up at the moment, but after our next performance, once I've tallied expenses…"

"Two complimentary show tickets will be sufficient compensation."

"You got yourself a deal, 'pard. And I'll tune that fiddle of yours to boot. Sounds like it needs it."

I put my hand to my mouth to cover my grin.

"Well, now, Colonel, I would ask that you depart. It seems word of your illustrious presence has spread to the boys of Baker Street, and if we are to track your man, I would rather not have a crowd of children in tow. It will cause undue attention."

I followed Shelley to the window. Down in the darkening street, the urchins of Marylebone had gathered, ruddy faces upturned, talking excitedly among themselves. A few were rowdily indulging in imaginary gun-play with bits of wood carved into the semblance of revolvers.

"Every boy is at heart a cowboy," Shelley said, smiling. He waved his over-sized hat from the casement, to the shrill delight of the children below.

"So it would appear," said Holmes. "There is just one more thing. You were a military man?"

"A Texas Ranger."

"You are familiar with the Indian practice of smoke signalling then?"

"Our scouts employed them on occasion," Shelley said.

"What do three puffs of smoke relay?"

"That is a call for help, Mr. Holmes. Why?"

Holmes only shook his head and smiled.

The Adventure of the Three Rippers by Edward M. Erdelac

Colonel Shelley bid us 'adios' and descended into the street. There was an explosive commotion from the youthful throng, who proceeded to crowd him. Many of the Irregulars were among the admirers.

"Finding one man in London by morning is a tall order, even for you, Holmes," I chided.

Holmes shrugged and put on his coat.

"It's actually a trifle. I confess I could not resist the novelty of tracking an Indian through the London streets."

"You mean you have some idea of where he's at already?"

"You've looked out the window. Our quarry's location is readily discernible."

I strained my eyes, but saw nothing in the street nor on the rooftops that would lead me to believe a fugitive Indian might be hiding in sight of Baker Street. Below, the crowd of children departed on the clinking boot heels of Colonel Shelley.

"Watson, do you have your revolver?"

I had taken to carrying it since the start of the Ripper killings, and acknowledged that I had it now.

"Good. Let's be off, then," said Holmes.

We went down into the cold November air, and were not three steps from the door when a ragged boy, barely ten years old, approached Holmes.

"Mister Holmes, sir?" the boy called.

He was one of the Irregulars, I knew.

"Alfie, isn't it?" Holmes said, looking down on the boy. "Do you not share the other boys' aspirations of riding the range?"

The boy looked as though Holmes had asked him if he wouldn't rather be walking on Mars.

"I dunno know, sir. I just come to say goodbye, as I'm goin' to Camberwell to live with me granddad and I shan't be up on Baker Street much no more."

Holmes raised his eyebrows.

"Ah. Moving up in the world, are we?"

"I just wanted to ask before I left, if you'd had any breakthroughs on the Ripper case."

Here Holmes's expression momentarily darkened, and I saw the return of his previous mood. Inwardly, I cursed the boy for bringing it back.

"The police, in their wisdom, have chosen not to solicit my assistance," Holmes said, tersely.

He turned then, and we resumed our walk down Baker Street.

The boy kept up with us, pestering.

"You think the peelers're close to catchin' 'im?"

"I am sure they're pursuing the matter to the utmost of their ability. You needn't be afraid. The Ripper confines his work to a one mile radius, and young boys are not within his purview. You shall be safe in Camberwell with your grandfather."

"I know sir. Only, I should like to know he is caught and punished. He done me mum in, you see."

Holmes stopped at that.

"What?" he said to the boy, quietly.

"Me mum. Polly Nichols. He done her in last August."

"Good God," I exclaimed.

Holmes looked pale.

"Watson, would you go to the corner and hail a carriage? I shall be along in a moment."

I nodded grimly.

When I had reached the street corner, I looked back, and saw that Holmes was hunkered down, speaking with the child on his level, nodding now and again. I was then somewhat astounded to see him take the boy by the shoulders.

Holmes was not a man given over to sentimental displays. I can count the number of times I have seen him so affected on one hand. Yet, I suppose, with reflection, I should not have been surprised. A man with Holmes's keen talents could apply them to great success in most any endeavour. That he employed them in the service of others surely speaks to the depth of his compassion.

I flagged down a driver.

A moment later Holmes was stalking towards the waiting hansom with purpose as the boy lingered behind for a bit, watching him, before turning and going the opposite way.

"Watson, I regret I must bring The Adventure of the Absent Indian, charming as it is, to a swift conclusion. I have a pressing matter in the East End which I have neglected for too long."

He instructed the driver to proceed to the Langham Hotel with all haste, promising the fellow an additional half-crown, then clambered inside. The carriage went rattling off down Harley Street.

"Holmes," I ventured, "I beg you to remember Sir Charles's warning. If you interfere in their investigation, the consequences could be dire for you."

"And if I do not, Watson," he answered sharply, "how dire the consequences for the poor woman who encounters this fiend? What is the risk of my reputation next to that? No. I intend to dedicate my efforts wholly upon this matter henceforth. They have been most shamefully perfunctory up to this point."

"Then I shall aide you however I am able," I said, resigned to our fate. "Norbury, eh?"

"Yes. Norbury," Holmes affirmed, and turned to the carriage window, staring for some time as though he could pick the Ripper from among the people we passed. He went on this way for the remainder of the ride, and I noticed his bouncing knee, the cocaine's influence translating to a nervous energy.

When we arrived, he fairly leapt from the cab in front of the Langham Hotel.

He gestured expansively to the face of the edifice, as though he were about to expound upon its architecture.

"There, Watson! It is dark now, but do you see it?"

I craned my neck to take in the building, but saw nothing out of the ordinary.

"Three puffs," he prompted.

And then I understood. One of the streaming chimneys which the tenants no doubt kept stoked against the November cold was belching forth a broken issue. Three puffs of smoke at regular intervals.

"I noticed it three days ago," Holmes said. "The Langham staff are too attentive, and its guests generally too particular to overlook a blocked chimney. Besides, the pattern is deliberate. It occurs three times a day for the span of an hour."

"But who is the intended recipient?" I asked.

Holmes had already gone inside. We ascended the stairs to the fifth floor corner room, which we had marked as the parent of the signalling chimney, and soon stood before the door.

Holmes rapped soundly. An oddly familiar voice told us in thickly accented English that the door was unlocked and we were expected.

I took my revolver in hand.

Holmes opened the door.

The apartment was populated by two occupants. One, I presumed, was the wayward Indian, Black Elk. He straightened from the hearth fire, a singed blanket in his hands. He wore a drab English suit. True to Colonel Shelley's description, it was turned inside out.

The other individual I was surprised to find I knew, for he was none other than Professor Abraham Van Helsing of the University of Amsterdam, whom I had met several years ago following a lecture at the University of London Medical School. I had renewed our acquaintance only the day before, when he had spoken before the Physiology Society.

"Why... Dr. Watson?" he ventured, as surprised to see me as I was to see him.

"Professor?" I said, putting away my revolver.

"Black Elk, I presume," said Holmes, addressing the Indian.

"Black *Elk!* Of course!" Van Helsing exclaimed, forgetting us and smiling back at the young Indian. "Like my dream!"

The young man grinned broadly and nodded.

"Your dream?" said Holmes.

"Forgive me, sir. There is much to explain. Three days ago I dreamed of a black stag on the steps of All Saints," Van Helsing said, gesturing to the church spire out his window. "I went for a stroll there and found this young man waiting for me. You say his name is Black Elk?"

Black Elk spoke excitedly in what I assumed to be his native tongue to Van Helsing, gesticulating at Holmes.

"What is he saying?" I asked.

"I have no idea," said Van Helsing. "We have been making do with sketches and pantomime for the past three days. It has been laborious, but from what I gather, he was led to me by vision that came to him as he stood over a volcano."

I looked sharply at Holmes, thinking of Shelley's story that Black Elk had nearly fallen into the crater of Mt. Vesuvius.

"But tell me, why have you come here, Dr. Watson?" Van Helsing asked.

Black Elk went hurriedly to a writing desk in the corner and began tearing through sheets of paper.

"We followed a distress signal," Holmes answered for me, "penned in smoke."

"Ah? But then, it was intended for *you*?" Van Helsing said. "Whoever may you be?"

Black Elk returned with a handful of papers and waved one at Holmes. He tapped the paper soundly with his finger and showed it to Van Helsing, pointing at Holmes.

It was a crude sketch of a long-eared dog with brown spots, neck craned to observe three billowy clouds of grey smoke.

"What a funny coincidence!" I said. "Holmes, doesn't that remind you of...?"

"Toby," said Holmes, recalling the lop-eared hound he sometimes employed. "Yes."

"*Tahca Wakhuwa!*" Black Elk exclaimed, pointing at Holmes.

"Holmes... Holmes." Van Helsing said, screwing up his face. "Ah, but now I see!" he said with a laugh. "You be the Dr. Watson of Holmes and Watson fame! *Gott!* How has this addled brain failed to make the connection? And so you, you are The Great Detective! Mr. Sherlock Holmes!"

Holmes bowed slightly.

"And *you* are Professor Abraham Van Helsing of Amsterdam."

"Dr. Van Helsing gave the lecture to the symposium I attended yesterday," I explained.

"Yes, I know. I saw his name on your invitation. 'A presentation on the forensic applications of optography.' It is why I opted not to attend."

"Ah? You think me a fraud, or do you deny Kuhne's theory?" Van Helsing asked, unperturbed by my friend's barb.

"That the last image a dying man sees may be reproduced from the eyes?" Holmes said, smirking. "Kuhne proved it fraudulent himself eight years ago when he produced a drawing of a guillotine blade supposedly captured from the eyes of an executed criminal in Brucshal; the eyes of a man who died blindfolded."

Holmes put his hands in his pockets and went on.

"As to my estimations of your reputation, that you are an accomplished folklorist and physician, I have no doubt. I wrote a rather hagiographic paper on you in fact, when I was sixteen.

But I think, at the risk of giving insult, that your enthusiasm for your former field of study has at times compromised your reputation in the latter."

"You are not lonesome in your estimation," Van Helsing said, shrugging. "And so we are finding ourselves in an amusing circumstance, yes? A score of years ago, you may have deemed our meeting an honour. Tonight the honour is being mine alone. Providence is not without a sense of irony."

"Providence and I are unacquainted. I was hired to return this young man to his employer," Holmes said briskly. "The hour grows late, and I have another case I must presently attend to."

"The case of Jack The Ripper, no doubt," said Van Helsing. "What other mystery could occupy the mind of London's renowned consulting detective? I am much surprised you have not already identified the killer."

"If you will excuse us..." said Holmes.

"Of course," Van Helsing begged off, removing a cigar from a gold case on table and putting it to his lips. "But I wonder, was your chief suspect in the Ripper killings, until recently, a woman?"

Holmes stopped stone still, as if lightning had struck nearby.

Van Helsing patted down his own pockets, searching, I assumed, for a match. Instead, he produced a photograph from his jacket pocket.

"*This* woman?"

He held it out to us to examine.

The photograph was dim, but quite remarkable. I had never seen such a composition. Rather than the typical staid, stiff studio portrait, the focus was very close on the face, and somehow suggested motion. The usual disconcerting blur fidgeting children typically elicited when entreated to sit still for the exposure was not present. The likeness of the woman was

The Adventure of the Three Rippers by Edward M. Erdelac

crisp and unmistakable. Her arm was swept back, a blade of some sort in her hand. Her expression was ghastly, drawn into a weird leer, the eyes wide and deranged. There was something dark spattered on her face.

"*Wanagi*," said Black Elk, tapping the photograph. "*Wanagi.*"

"What is *wanagi*?" I asked.

Van Helsing shook his head as Black Elk threw up his hands and went over to the hearth. He sat down heavily in the armchair.

Holmes took the photograph from Van Helsing unbidden. He stared at it intently, eyes boring into it.

"How did you obtain this?"

"I extracted it from the eyes of the late Catherine Eddowes, slain the 30th of September."

"Astonishing!" I breathed. "Holmes, Professor Van Helsing spoke of his optographic innovations, displayed some amazing photographs culled from the eyes of animals. I don't claim to fully understand it."

"I introduce a certain chemical into the rhodopsin, an ocular fluid culled from an animal which is alas, quite rare and nearly extinct," Van Helsing explained. "The *rattus nativitatis*."

"But sir," I said, "you didn't mention your process had been put to practical forensic use!"

"I had no proof until Mr. Holmes's expression just now," Van Helsing said, lighting his cigar. "The police dismissed the idea of a female killer."

"I am unsurprised," Holmes said, returning the photograph to Van Helsing. "My own initial suspicions fell on a male perpetrator, and I find their investigation is ever behind my own. But this woman, Alice Sodeaux, a midwife, could pass unnoticed in the Whitechapel streets at all hours due to her sex and profession, even drenched in blood."

"Good lord!" I mumbled, picturing the sight of the woman, a bloody apparition moving unmolested through the night fog. "But why?"

"We may never know," said Holmes. "She hung herself on the 10th of October, near the site of the Chapman killing. Professor Van Helsing, it seems I owe you an apology, and my gratitude. This case has weighed significantly upon me. Perhaps after my business is concluded here, you might entertain me with an encore of the lecture Dr. Watson had the receptiveness to attend."

"I fear the case is not closed, Mr. Holmes," said Van Helsing gravely.

"Is the woman not dead?" I asked.

"As dead as the Ripper's victims," Van Helsing said, "whom she must now be counted amongst. The villain is yet free, and overdue for his next crime, by my calculations."

"I am sorry to say I do not follow you again, Professor," said Holmes.

"You mentioned that you first suspected a male perpetrator."

"Yes. A butcher named Hennell."

"And what removed suspicion, please?"

"He was dead by the time of the killings of September 30th."

"Dead by his own hand?"

"He slit his own throat in his parents' house."

"Not a typical means of self-destruction."

"Hennell was quite disturbed. His parents said he had developed a paranoia that the police were near to arresting him for the slaying of Polly Nichols."

"Killed on the 31st of August," said Van Helsing thoughtfully. "When did this butcher commit suicide?"

"September 17th."

"But he made no mention of the woman killed only days before on the 8th?"

"Annie Chapman," said Holmes. "No. Professor, you have been following this case closely, it seems. Why, may I ask?"

"You were recently in my country, on a delicate matter for poor King William," Van Helsing said.

"In January."

"Were you aware of the three murders in Haarlem?"

"I was not."

"Very similar to your Whitechapel killings," Van Helsing explained. "As though a feral animal were loosed on the women. The matter was not thoroughly investigated due to the victims being patients at Het Dolhuys; a convalescent home for the insane and mostly, the unwanted."

"Mostly, but not all," said Holmes. "You have worried your wedding band for the past few moments. Your wife?"

"My wife. Gone from beauteous Ganymeda to raving Malle Babbe ten years ago now. Yes, she is a resident of Het Dolhuys. It is only thirty minutes to the university by train. Every weekend I am by her side, though she knows me not. I caught the murderer almost in the act of slashing her with a scalpel. Had I been a moment later, I would now be a widower. We struggled, and... Mr. Holmes, it was as though the evil in him fled from his eyes. I imagine I saw it depart, and the man in my grip crumbled to nothing but a half-idiot custodian, docile and confused. I was hailed as a hero, the murders ceased. Yet, I was dissatisfied, and obtained permission to interview my wife's assailant. I found him unthreatening, a man-child. Yet he suffered from terrible, bloody nightmares. Under hypnosis, he divulged a terrible truth.

'There was a certain psychiatrist, Dr. Jacobus Van Voorhees. He departed Het Dolhuys in the night following the attack on my wife, without notice. His personal effects, books, his diary, they were left behind in his office. I perused them.

Among snatches of strange poetry, I learned that he was unsympathetic towards the women under his care. He hated females in fact, as he hated his own mother, a common ah... *lichtekooi*. You understand?"

"A trull," said Holmes, for my benefit. "A woman of the streets."

"In the occult sciences, Van Voorhees was another Averroes," Van Helsing continued. "I found evidence that he had rediscovered an ancient blood ritual which allowed him to shed his physical body; to force his personality into the bodies of others, donning them as you would wear a disguise. But I see by your expression that I am leaving your good graces again."

"It is difficult to accept," Holmes said tactfully.

"Still, a matter of science, Mr. Holmes. Preternatural science. Unknown, as all discoveries must first be. You lent no credence to optography until this very night. How may consciousness be quantified? Can it normally retain cohesiveness once it has departed the biological vehicle? I do not know. But through old and discounted sciences, Van Voorhees found a way. The poor dullard in whose body he committed his murders was unable to cope with the villain's memories. He hung himself in his cell.

"I have followed Van Voorhees for two months now. He leaves a trail of dead women and broken lives behind. I have identified trends in his praxis. He selects the insane, the addicted, or the mentally deficient, often influencing them from afar several nights prior to assuming control, in effect preparing his hosts. The unwilling murderers are left haunted with impressions of his crimes, which more often than not drive them to self-destruction. He must perform his ritual in some secure location, and he must enact a sacrificial killing on or very near the eighth of every month to retain his ability; hence the reason for the double killing on September 30th, to sustain his power through his self-imposed drought of October. He must have known you were close to catching Mrs. Sodeaux and thought it prudent to refrain from activity."

"Why the eighth day?" said Holmes thoughtfully.

"The number has a multitude of numerological significances," said Van Helsing, smoking. "Eight represents a transcendence of the physical. On the eighth day after birth Jewish children may be circumcised, and animals sacrificed, or made divine."

"Do you believe this, Holmes?" I asked quietly.

"That photograph depicts Mrs. Sodeaux," he answered. "I do not say I believe, but I do not believe in dismissing outright anything that could save another woman's life."

"Now you must tell me, Mr. Holmes," said Van Helsing eagerly. "Two of your suspects have died. Have you identified any others since?"

Holmes turned toward the fire, and rested his hand on the mantle. Beside him, Black Elk was snoring gently in the armchair.

"You may be aware of a series of letters received by the police and the newspapers, claiming to be from the Ripper," he said.

"I have read of this," said Van Helsing.

"They are almost all fraudulent, mainly the work of one Mr. Bell to sell copies of The Star."

"What about the one George Lusk received with the human kidney?" I asked. "Wasn't the Eddowes woman missing a kidney?"

"A tasteless practical joke by a group of medical students, I'm afraid."

"You said *almost* all," said Van Helsing.

"October fifth, a letter delivered to Mr. Bulling at the Central New Service. *'Dear Friend. In the name of God hear me I did not kill the female whose body was found at Whitehall.'*"

"Excuse me?" said Van Helsing. "Whitehall?"

The Adventure of the Three Rippers by Edward M. Erdelac

I explained to Van Helsing that the headless and limbless corpse of a woman had been found at the construction site of the new police headquarters. Holmes's brother Mycroft had already solved the case and the police had apprehended the responsible party.

Holmes continued, by rote, closing his eyes.

"'If she was an honest woman I will hunt down and destroy her murderer. If she was a whore, God will bless the hand that slew her, for the women of Moab and Midian shall die and their blood shall mingle with the dust. I never harm any others or the power that protects and helps me in my grand work would quit forever. Do as I do and the light of glory shall shine upon you. I must get to work. Treble event this time. The police reckon my work a practical joke well Jacky's a very practical joker ha ha. Keep this till three are wiped out and you can show the cold meat. Yours truly, Jack The Ripper.'"*

Holmes opened his eyes and turned to us. It had grown dark, and with the fire behind him, only his eyes glittered.

"Ghastly," I remarked.

"This afternoon I received a letter from a Mrs. Meynell, whose husband is editor of the Catholic newspaper Merrie England."

Holmes removed an envelope from his coat pocket, unfolding the letter within.

"This poem was among a batch submitted to her husband. Three stanzas of it have occupied my mind all day:

Swiftly he followed her,
Ha! Ha!
Eagerly followed her,
Ho! Ho!

The Adventure of the Three Rippers by Edward M. Erdelac

*From the rank, the greasy soil,
Red bubbles oozed and stood;
Till it grew a putrid slime,
And where'er his horse has trod,
The ground plash, plashes,
With a wet too like to blood;
And chill terrors like a fungus grow.
Two witch-babies, ho! ho! ho!
There stayed the maiden,
Ha! Ha!
Shed all her beauty;
Ho! Ho!
She shed her flower of beauty,
Grew laidly, old, and dire,
Was the demon-ridden witch,
And the consort of hell-fire:
'Am I lovely noble knight?
See thy hearts own desire!
Now they come, come upon thee, lo.
Two witch-babies, ho! ho! ho!'
Its paunch a-swollen,
Ha! Ha!
Its life a-swollen
Ho! Ho!
Like the days drowned.
Harsh was its hum;
And its paunch was rent
Like a brasten drum;
And the blubbered fat
From its belly doth come
With a sickening ooze - Hell made it so!
Two witch-babies, ho! ho! ho!"*

Holmes folded the horrid thing and put it away.

"God," I said. "A madman's sonnet."

"The subject matter is startling, yes," Holmes admitted. "But it was the use of 'Ha! Ha!' which caught my attention."

"So similar to the newspaper letter," Van Helsing agreed. "And very like the poetry I read in Van Voorhees' diary."

"I know only that the poet is a young opium addict residing in Spitalfields. I intended to interview Mrs. Meynell further tomorrow."

"This poet must be Van Voorhees's current host!" said Van Helsing, excitedly.

"But what you're saying," I said, struggling through it, "that a man may leave his body and control another? It's fantastic! How could you hope to capture such a man?"

It was at that moment that the Indian, Black Elk, gave the most bloodcurdling cry and crashed to the floor.

I rushed to him. The boy was shivering and drenched in sweat.

"What is the matter?" Van Helsing demanded, kneeling by the Indian's side.

Black Elk began to speak, hurriedly, but of course we understood nothing. He gestured impatiently for paper and pencil, and when it was provided, began to hastily sketch. The drawing was crude. A woman lay on a bed in a small room. A dark man bent over her with a knife. Black Elk scribbled across her torso, obscuring her face, her body, the strokes like the slashing of a wild blade. He drew a hearth fire, and a tea kettle upon it, the spout melting.

"God! Where?" Van Helsing demanded, taking Black Elk by the shoulders.

The shaman shook his head and mumbled. He looked exhausted, as though he had undertaken some great exertion. He returned to the drawing, drew an Indian suspended over the grisly scene, and then, another, a rotund, blank-faced form that seemed to overlap the killer's.

"Wanagi," he mumbled, pointing to the ghostly shape.

"He has killed again," Van Helsing said gravely. "I think that Black Elk fought him, but unsuccessfully. You asked how to stop Van Voorhees, Doctor. I believe it is Black Elk's sacred purpose."

I helped the perspiring Indian back into the chair, unsure what to believe.

Black Elk's voice faded to a sleepy whisper.

Holmes stood by the window, his expression inscrutable.

"He promised a triple killing," Van Helsing muttered. "If he succeeds, he will go to ground for three months. We could lose all trace of him. We can only hope Black Elk's exertions left Van Voorhees equally exhausted."

"Only the morning will reveal what is fact and what is fancy," Holmes said.

"You still do not believe, Mr. Holmes?" Van Helsing asked, tiredly.

"We will bring Black Elk back to Baker Street tonight," Holmes declared. "If The Ripper has struck again, we will all know in the morning, and proceed from there. If not, we shall return Black Elk to Colonel Shelley."

Van Helsing nodded slowly.

"That is fair."

Holmes replaced his hat and together we lifted the delirious Indian to his feet between us.

We bid Van Helsing goodnight, and left.

"You can't believe this, Holmes," I reiterated in the carriage as Black Elk slept fitfully between us.

"Belief is irrelevant. Our companion here may be simply suffering from what Hippocrates called 'the Sacred Disease,' and nothing more."

"And if he is not?"

Holmes would not venture to say.

In the morning, the body of Mary J. Kelly was discovered mutilated in her locked room at Miller's Court in Spitalfields.

A man came calling around eleven thirty, an inspector I did not know, who looked more like a bank manager than a policeman. I took him to be Holmes's informant. They spoke lowly in the outside hall, before Holmes re-entered in a passion, and went for his pipe. He looked haggard. I do not recall if he had slept at all that night.

"Shall I wake our aboriginal friend?" I asked sleepily, for Black Elk had occupied my bed while I had dozed on the settee.

"I'm not sure Black Elk slept," Holmes said, glancing up at the ceiling. "I heard him rearranging furniture throughout the night. I expect Mrs. Meynell within the hour. Tell Mrs. Hudson that when Professor Van Helsing arrives, she's to send him straight up."

"What has convinced you, Holmes?" I asked, rising stiffly.

"A melted tea kettle, Watson," he said, lighting his pipe.

From The Journal of Professor Abraham Van Helsing

9th November, 1888

Sgt. Thicke came calling at my room at ten thirty. I was taken by cabriolet to Shoreditch, where the body of Van Voorhees's victim had been removed. It is as Black Elk depicted. Without fear of discovery in the open streets, he glutted his bloodlust to its fullest. Only her green eyes shining from the midst of ruin marked her as human. Those eyes demand much of me. I was permitted to be alone with her remains prior to the arrival of Dr. Bond for the autopsy. It was easy to develop two copies of the optographic imprint.

God, he has used a young man for this butchery; thin, pale, large-eared, near thirty. Can this be the destitute poet Mr. Holmes spoke of?

We shall see. God, may Mary Kelly be the last of Van Voorhees's victims!

A cold, hard rain beat against the broad bow-windows of 221B, casting running shadows across the pale face of Mrs. Alice Meynell, on the settee.

Mrs. Meynell was a conservative Catholic woman, poised, but with anxious eyes, her gloves clenched tightly in her hands.

"I trust my husband's judgement implicitly, you understand, Mr. Holmes," she assured him. "But in this matter, I have reservations."

"Naturally," said Holmes, from the basket chair. "The composition is disconcerting."

"Understand, the poem I sent you is not representative of the greater body of verse Wilfrid intends to publish," Mrs. Meynell said. "Most of this young man's work is deeply spiritual. It shows much promise. But, Wilfrid intends to bring him into our *home*. He assures me he is of good stock; the son of a Lancashire doctor. But whatever his nativity, he is now a transient and an opium addict. I am a charitable woman, Mr. Holmes, but we have six children. Oh, that *horrid* poem! Wilfrid swears he is harmless, but Mr. Holmes, can a mind that concocts such lurid prose be entirely safe?"

"I should be glad to further investigate the poet's character for you, Mrs. Meynell," said Holmes. "If you will but tell me his name and where he may be found."

"His name is Francis Thompson," said Mrs. Meynell. "He gives his residence as The Providence Row Night Refuge."

"In Crispin Street," said Holmes, looking up at me meaningfully.

I knew that it overlooked Miller's Court.

"Have you met Mr. Thompson? Can you describe him?"

There was a commotion on the stair and our door flew open.

Van Helsing swept into the room in a state of disarray, and flung a wide-brimmed Boer hat from his reddish head like a discus. It splattered us all with rainwater and landed squarely on the head of the bearskin rug before the hearth. The Professor took no apparent notice, and plonked his dripping attaché down upon the dining table, snapping it open.

"So sorry. I was delayed at the autopsy." He spared a brief smile for the bewildered Mrs. Meynell. "Madame."

I handed Mrs. Meynell a handkerchief.

Van Helsing whisked a photograph from his case and brandished it.

"The Ripper's latest face!" he declared, somewhat dramatically.

The camera looked up from a low angle. A figure loomed, leering maniacally as Mrs. Sodeaux had in the previous picture. The subject was a man in his late twenties, smooth faced, with dark hair, large eyes, and simian ears. There was a bloody razor in his hand, His shirtfront was darkly stained.

Mrs. Meynell gasped across the back of her hand. She fell over on the settee in a swoon.

"Mr. Francis Thompson, I presume," Holmes said, taking the photograph from Van Helsing as I fanned the delirious lady.

After depositing the editor's wife in a carriage and securing her discretion, I returned to find Holmes and Van Helsing ascending the stair to my room.

The chamber was much disordered. The bed had been pushed to one side. Black Elk sat on the bare floorboards, stripped to a breechclout. He had painted himself red all over, with black and white lightning jags on his joints, a single eagle feather twisted in his hair. The room smelled of some sweet-smelling substance smoking in the ashtray before him. Various unidentifiable native paraphernalia were arranged in some ritualistic order around him.

"What is the matter, my friend?" Van Helsing asked, stooping to Black Elk's level.

The Indian did not respond. He only rocked rhythmically, murmuring some repetitive intonation behind his lips, his eyes glazed over.

"We must proceed to the night refuge in Crispin's Street to apprehend the man in that photograph," said Holmes.

"I will stay with Black Elk," Van Helsing said. "Mr. Holmes, do not forget the dream which brought us together. Remember your poor poet is but a hand. It is the intelligence behind the hand we seek."

Holmes said nothing to that, but descended the stairs.

"Should we inform the police?" I called as we donned our coats and Holmes snatched up his hat and stick.

"How to explain our reasoning?" said Holmes, rapidly descending to the street. "In this instance, the police are predisposed to dismissal of the facts."

"Do *we* know the facts?"

"We soon shall."

*****

The Providence Row Night Refuge towered above the rainy alleys and streets of Spitalfields, a drab, envious counterpart to the white spire of Christchurch that rose to the north. Between the two extremes lay Miller's Court. We could see the police keeping back the morbidly curious. I knew Holmes ached to examine the scene, but we made our way through the downpour to the men's entrance where a half dozen pitiful souls hunkered, awaiting its opening.

The Adventure of the Three Rippers by Edward M. Erdelac

Holmes gained the attention of an elderly black-robed nun, who, taking us to be gentlemen, admitted us.

"Sister, do you shelter a man named Francis Thompson?"

The old nun's perennial scowl deepened.

"He's not in any sort of trouble is he?"

"No," Holmes said, smiling. "Mr. Meynell, the editor of The Merrie England, is considering sponsoring Mr. Thompson. We have been sent to conduct an interview."

The nun looked as though the idea were unseemly.

"Mr. Thompson does keep a bed here, sir, but he is not present."

"Oh?"

"The Sisters of Mercy do not encourage idleness. By day our inmates are required to seek *gainful* employment. He will not return until sunset."

"I see. Is there an administrator I might speak to?"

"The monsignor is inspecting the men's refectory," said the nun.

She led us through the musty, dim halls, past the dormitories, each with a row of ten cots. I spied sisters smoothing the grey sheets and folding over the leather covers.

The banging of pans precluded our entrance into the refectory with its long communal dining table. The nuns busied themselves cooking in the adjoining kitchen. An old priest stood in the light of a rain-washed window speaking congenially to a portly man with a yellow moustache.

The nun excused our interruption, and we introduced ourselves.

"My word!" said the wizened priest, a Father Gilbert. "*The Sherlock Holmes? The detective?"

"*Detective?*" the nun repeated, scandalized.

"That will be all, Sister Joachim," said the priest, raising one knotty finger skyward. "Remember please, where no wood is, there the fire goeth out."

The frowning nun bowed her head and went off. We soon heard her barking orders to the novitiates in the kitchen.

"Father," said the paunchy man, and excused himself.

"I'm sorry, Mr. Holmes," said Father Gilbert. "I am an avid reader of Dr. Watson's accounts, and could not quite contain my surprise. How may I help you?"

"Who was that man you were just speaking to, Father?" Holmes asked.

I looked after the man, surprised at Holmes's interest. He had gone from the room already.

"Oh that is Dr. Von Hoeren," said the priest.

"A medical man?" I asked.

"A psychologist," said Father Gilbert. "He is struggling, as many are. In exchange for giving counsel to some of our more distressed inmates and occasionally entertaining, we let him a room here at the refuge."

"Entertaining? Poetry, I suppose?" Holmes asked.

"Why, yes."

"He is a foreigner? New to London?"

"He came to England only last July. German, I believe."

"Dutch," said Holmes. "May we speak with him, Father?"

"I shall take you to his room."

The priest led us out of the dining area and down the dim corridor.

"Holmes?" I asked, uncertainly.

He whispered rapidly over his shoulder:

"On the third finger of his right hand. The ring bearing a blazon of a pelican feeding its young. The emblem of the Trou Moet Blycken, a rhetorical society based in Haarlem. And his surname. 'Von' is German, yes, and means 'of.' But 'Hoeren' is Dutch for 'whores.'"

Father Gilbert paused at the foot of the tall stair and gestured up.

"If you'll forgive an old man, I don't do well with the stairs these days. His is the first room left of the third floor landing."

Holmes and I ascended, leaving Father Gilbert leaning on the bannister.

"You believe it's Van Voorhees?" I said lowly, feeling for my pistol.

At first, Holmes said nothing. Then, at the top of the stair, he paused, as though he'd gone out of breath, and turned. There was a strange look in his eye, and he grinned, most uncharacteristically.

"Yes, Dr. Watson," he said, in a thick accent. "Joop Van Voorhees. Jack The Ripper. *The man who killed Sherlock Holmes!*"

He struck me soundly on the head with his walking stick, and I stumbled backwards, catching myself on the bannister.

Holmes vaulted over the railing, plunging headfirst down the stairwell, still grinning maniacally.

From The Journal of Professor Abraham Van Helsing

10th *November, 1888*

I do not hope to understand fully the great gifts which God in His wisdom has bestowed upon Black Elk. I was only afforded a glimpse of his powers, but it is not unlike those granted unto the prophet Elijah. I stand in awe.

The city of London owes the Lakota a great debt; for the lives of its poorest women, and surely for that of one of its most favoured sons.

Shortly after Mr. Holmes and Dr. Watson departed for Spitalfields, Black Elk's trance deepened, and I felt compelled to confirm his vital functions. At that time, the herb admixture smoking thickly in the room began to affect my equilibrium.

I lay down on the bed to ease my dizziness, and though I should never have thought that I would drift to sleep, the fumes, compounded by my own exhaustion, compelled me into slumber.

I do not say that what came next was a dream. I know by the later accounts of the participants that it was not.

I found myself above the city, naked and heedless of rain and cold. I saw a bright crimson form moving below me. With the speed of thought, I was suddenly alongside it. It was Black Elk, blazing in his blood red paint. He seemed surprised to see me, though not as taken aback as I was when I heard him speak to me in fluent Dutch.

"Deerstalker is in danger," he said. "The yellow poison in his blood has opened the door for the wanagi. *I couldn't fight it before. Now I'm prepared. You should go back."*

"I cannot!" I answered, marvelling that neither of us were moving our lips. "I have followed Van Voorhees too far."

"Then stay out of the way," Black Elk warned.

We dropped from the sky like diving birds, with no feeling whatsoever of motion. We passed like ghosts through the roof of a tall brown brick building, and down a stairwell, where I saw Holmes and Watson on the top landing.

Holmes said something to Dr. Watson, and then lashed at him with his stick and dove over the railing, cackling like a madman.

I knew that laugh.

Watson, his temple trickling blood, lunged and managed to catch Holmes by the ankle.

While Holmes dangled upside down, I saw it; another shape, like a thing of pipe smoke, superimposed upon the form of the Great Detective. It was the wanagi *— the invasive soul of Van Voorhees, forcing its way into the body of Holmes like a corpulent man trying on a too-small suit.*

"Follow the line back to the source! He must not return to his body!" Black Elk told me, and then he shot toward Holmes.

I perceived that what I had thought was some sort of etheric vapour trailing from the body of Holmes, was in fact a shimmering silver chord that wound further up the landing and down the hall. I rapidly slid along its serpentine length, passing through a door, and there found its anchor. The physical body of Van Voorhees sat in his room, in a similar attitude to that which Black Elk had assumed in the upstairs room of Baker Street. The natural native ritual accoutrements had been replaced by stout black candles and concentric etchings upon the floor, but their purpose was surely identical.

And yet, what could I do? I was as formless as Black Elk and even more helpless in this unfamiliar state. I could not even move closer to his reposing form. Some unseen force, likely the protective circle in which he sat, prevented me.

I returned to find Watson hoisting Holmes back on the stairs.

Black Elk's astral form perched on Holmes's shoulders now. He had a hold of the ears of the ghostly Van Voorhees, and was struggling to extract him. Though he seemed to exert considerable effort, he was bucked free.

Van Voorhees invigorated Holmes's physical body to some preternatural level also, for next he bodily flung Watson off him, and bounded down the stairs.

"A killer, if not a dead man!" he cried through Holmes.

The old priest at the bottom cowered as he passed, running down the hall now.

"Holmes!" cried Watson, and chased after him.

"The room! Van Voorhees is in the room!" I bellowed.

Watson went on, heedless.

I felt a shudder through my form, and saw that Black Elk's finger was touching the centre of my chest. I knew of *things mysterious, and of the young shaman's mission, given him at the mountain of fire by divine Thunder Beings.*

I knew also what I must do.

To my amazement my hand held a kukri *of crackling white lightning, and its purpose was clear. I put it to the silvery tether that ran from Van Voorhees to his body; with one swift chop I parted it. I knew that in his locked room, his body fell dead.*

Black Elk rocketed off downstairs after Holmes. With another thought, I was there too.

Holmes had burst into a kitchen. The nuns working there fell back shrieking at the sight of him, mad-eyed and leering. He took hold of a butcher's knife.

Watson stood in the doorway, his pistol drawn.

"Holmes!" he pleaded. "Holmes!"

Black Elk plunged his red arms deep into Holmes's back. Unmoored from its body, he pulled the invading soul free, his limbs crackling with white lightning. He pushed the swirling, shrieking form of Van Voorhees into a compact ball, which he then swallowed.

Van Voorhees' screams ceased.

Holmes shuddered, dropped the knife with a clatter, and swooned. Dr. Watson was there to catch him.

I next felt a rush of chill air. In the next instant, I was back in the room at Baker Street.

Black Elk stood by the open window.

I sat up groggily, and watched as he coughed something into his hand. It was a ball of yellow hair. He knelt by the ashtray, holding it over the sweet smelling flame, then wrapped the singed hair into a packet of buckskin.

"In a year, I will release it to Maya Owichapaha."

I did not question how it was he suddenly spoke clear English, any more than I thought to wonder how I knew that Old Woman Who Judges would push the soul of Van Voorhees over the bank to the left, rather than allow it to travel south down the good road to reunite with The Great Spirit.

What I asked was:

"What of the mind of Sherlock Holmes?"

*****

"*Kinnikinnik,*" Holmes pronounced, tucking the small leather bag into the Persian slipper nailed to the mantle. "A fine parting gift from our Lakota friend. None of the injurious qualities of modern tobacco. Sumac leaves and the dried inner bark of the red alder. I must revise my monograph."

He went to his case, took out his Stradivarius. Thankfully, he seemed to have set aside Pagannini for the time being, and lost himself in the rustic strains of Muss i Denn. I practically felt the relief of Mrs. Hudson and the rest of Baker Street.

Of the incident at the Night Refuge, Holmes could tell me almost nothing. He gave no credence to Professor Van Helsing's fantastic explanation, only saying later, privately, that he had decided to at last take my advice and curtail his cocaine use. Whether he seemed to think the narcotic had initiated some momentary hysteria in him, he would not say.

There was a lengthy discussion of Holmes's bizarre actions with the Whitechapel police. Van Helsing was permitted to examine Holmes alone. He told me later that he had extracted any residue of Van Voorhees' vile mind via hypnosis, and that Holmes was in no danger. I do not know the truth of this, but Mycroft soon arrived and Holmes was released, the matter officially closed.

Van Voorhees was quietly interred at Leytonstone. Holmes recommended Francis Thompson to the care of the Meynells, with the stipulation that he be remanded to a place of observation instead of their residence. The poet was sent to a priory in Storrington while the Meynells prepared to publish his first book of poetry, wisely omitting the horrific, Ripper-inspired work, 'The Nightmare of The Witch-Babies.'

"That you can play your violin and speak of tobacco, Holmes!" I exclaimed when he had finished and returned his instrument to its case. For my part, I felt as if the world had shifted beneath my feet and I did not know my own address.

"Indeed you are right, Watson," Holmes said airily. "We must depart within the hour if we are to collect our promised seats at Colonel Shelley's next performance. And I have a letter to post to Camberwell on the way."

We dressed in silence. I suppose that my friend saw the bemusement on my face.

"You are wondering what to make of all that has transpired, Watson."

"Well, *yes!*"

"Write it down, old chap," he said, amused, as he wrapped himself in his muffler. "Exorcise your demons with splashes of ink. I would suggest attaining Professor Van Helsing's permission before you seek publication, however."

Then at the door, he smiled and said:

"And perhaps employ a pseudonym."

The Case of the High Pavement Ghosts

by Teika Marija Smits

Isadora Lampblack was in the study, reading a monograph on La Diablesse of Caribbean folklore, when there was a soft knock on the door. It was her butler, Burridge, bringing her the afternoon post. There were three letters on the silver plate that he presented her with, but the one that aroused the most interest was the one addressed in her cousin's hand. What did Sherlock have to communicate?

She studied the cursive. It was, as usual, measured, and as free of tells as possible, but the first two letters – the 'L' and 'a' of Lady – were ever so slightly closer to each other than they should have been. She skimmed her singularly sensitive fingers over the letters and felt the near-negligible grooves in the envelope where the nib had indented the paper. Greater pressure had been exerted on those two letters as well. It would appear that Sherlock had struggled to master himself for a moment and hadn't really wanted to post this. That meant he was asking her for a favour.

The letter confirmed her supposition.

Dear Isadora,
Watson has been contacted by an old friend who requires my help in a matter. As the gentleman resides in Nottingham I

thought it apt that we should meet, particularly as Watson's friend insists that the case requires an investigator with a broad mind. I will expect both you and Fude to dine with us tomorrow evening at our lodgings, the Black Boy Hotel.

Yours etc.

"Apt that we should meet," muttered Isadora. "Rather, 'Isadora, I have been told that this case is of the supernatural yet I can hardly stoop so low as to mention that fact.'"

Isadora sighed and then tucked a stray lock of golden hair that had escaped from her chignon back into place. She turned to Burridge. "Whereabouts is Annabelle?"

"She is in the kitchen, instructing Cook in the art of caramelizing onions."

Isadora smiled wryly. "*This* I would like to see."

*****

Cook, who had worked for the Lampblack family for decades, only tolerated Annabelle Fude's meddling in culinary matters for the sake of her young mistress, whom she had much respect and affection for. But right now, her patience was wearing thin. She was watching the interloper with a grim expression on her face, her arms crossed, her right foot tapping out her irritation. Fude, who was busy jiggling the frying pan over the stove while stirring the onions with a wooden spoon, was blithely unconcerned by Cook's mounting frustration. What added to Cook's annoyance was the fact that Fude, middle-aged and matronly as she was, looked very much at home in her kitchen.

"I've already told you, I know how to do this!" snapped Cook, just as Isadora entered the kitchen. When Cook saw who it was, she uttered an "Oh, Ma'am!" and gave her mistress a hasty curtsey.

Annabelle, unaware of her friend's presence, argued on. "I know you *think* you know how to do it, but you ain't ever done it the way we like. You don't cook them for long enough. They've got to be almost brown, see, not just golden."

Isadora gave a polite cough.

"Oh, Izzy!" said Fude, turning to her friend while continuing to stir the onions. Her round cheeks were red from the heat of the stove, and her dark hair was flying about her face, "I was just showing Cook here–"

"I can see what you're doing. And I hate to interrupt you when you're mid-flow yet–"

"But what's the point of me shooting all these birds," – she waved the spoon at the table piled high with game – "and them not being given the proper garnish?"

"Annabelle! I came to tell you that I have news."

"Well?"

"We will be dining out tomorrow night."

"No, I mean, well what about me killing the birds and not having proper onions to go with 'em?" said Fude.

Isadora sighed. She looked from Cook to Fude and then said, "Now, I suppose, would be a good time to mention that I don't actually like onions. Fried, boiled, pickled or roasted. Pale golden or almost brown."

Fude gawped at Izzy and then turned to Cook who looked equally shocked. "Don't like onions," she said. "But that's imp–"

"No, it is quite possible. And if you'd care to listen, it is Holmes and Watson whom we'll be dining with tomorrow night. Also, you'll have to drag your husband away from his work. I'd like him to accompany us. And I," she said, turning to leave, "have better things to do than argue with you about alliums."

Fude gave the onions one last angry poke and then passed the spoon to Cook. "Here," she said, all enmity now gone, "you take over." She hurried out the kitchen and followed after

Isadora. "Last time I saw that rude cousin of yours he said I'd gained five pounds."

"And?" said Isadora.

"Well, he was wrong. 'Twas only four and a half, I swear."

Isadora suppressed a grin. "Tell him that tomorrow," she replied. "That'll put him in combative mood."

*****

Fude, however, did not mention Holmes's apparent miscalculation at dinner the following evening. Although Watson kept up a steady stream of genial conversation, even managing to coax some words out of the usually quiet and reticent Mr Fude, Holmes offered no pleasantries and his answers were terse, his manner brittle. In short, it was not a good time to rile him.

"Is the case not complex enough for your liking?" asked Isadora over the starter.

Holmes abandoned his pea soup and sat back in his chair, surveying the private dining room they'd been given. He put his hands together and steepled his long fingers. "It is not the lack of complexity that bothers me. It is the small matter of the..."

"Uncanny nature of the case," offered Isadora, her eyes sparkling.

"Indeed," said Holmes.

Holmes's irritation at having to ask for her assistance was clear, but Isadora sensed that his ill temper was more than just about his bruised ego. She noticed him studying the picture of the villainous Charlie Peace that hung on the wall beside them.

"I am still gathering information," Holmes went on, "so will remain open-minded, but it does all seem rather open and closed."

"How so?" said Watson. "The Richardsons are a most loving family – singularly so – and yet their boy is frequently covered in wounds that have appeared as if by magic. And even you, yourself, have been unable to find any evidence of wrongdoing."

"*Yet*," answered Holmes. "Oh, by all appearances they seem virtuous enough, yet what, pray, of their actions behind closed doors?"

"Now, look here, Holmes," said Watson, "are you saying that the man whom I served alongside in the Afghan war – a man I know to be both good and decent – is capable of inflicting injury upon his own son?"

"The very fact of his proximity to violence suggests that it would be only natural for him to view it as a means to disciplining his son."

Before Watson could compose himself enough to reply, Annabelle spoke. "I've never got on with violence as a means of discipline," she said, shaking her head. "Don't sit right with me. And it don't work. Besides, what's the child supposed to have done that is so very wicked that he gets beaten for it?"

"But that's just it!" said Watson, turning to Fude, his face a mixture of relief and gratitude for her support. "The child is an angel! He hasn't done anything wicked at all. And besides," said Watson, addressing Holmes, "why would Richardson want us involved if he were the very one injuring the child!"

"Why indeed," said Holmes, not looking at Watson, but instead, staring at the murky green of his pea soup, lost in reverie.

Isadora gave a polite cough and addressed Watson and Fude. "Sherlock did not accuse your friend of beating his son. He merely stated that a proportion of men involved in war unwittingly recourse to violence in domestic situations since they are not as open – or practised – in alternate forms of disciplinary action."

"Quite," said Holmes, acknowledging the correctness of Isadora's statement with a nod. "There is also the wife – the mother – to consider."

Fude dropped her spoon in the bowl of soup.

"Really, Holmes!" said Watson, outraged, "Farzaneh cannot be the one inflicting such injury."

"Your proof?" said Holmes.

"Richardson himself. He says that Farzaneh is incapable of hurting a fly. And besides, I myself have seen her with the boy when he was but a newborn. She was most attentive to his needs and generous with her affection, even shunning the aid of a nurse."

"He is no longer a babe in arms, Watson," Holmes pointed out. "And people change. Circumstances alter. When I spoke to Richardson in private I noted that he was not as wholehearted in his conviction of his wife's innocence as he was when speaking with you."

Watson opened his mouth to remonstrate with Holmes and then closed it again. A cloud of uncertainty crossed his face.

"And what of the governess?" asked Isadora.

"They have gone through three since the child started receiving these injuries," said Holmes. "The Richardsons, quite reasonably, assumed that they were the source of the maltreatment and decided to dispense with them, leaving the boy in the sole care of his mother. For a short while all was well, and then, apparently, overnight, the cuts and bruises came again. You see, since the father has not always been there – business having called him away – the mother is the one constant. Yet when I interviewed her yesterday, she was in such a state of agitation that I could get nothing sensible out of her."

"Well, what d'you expect?" said Fude. "The poor woman must be beside herself. You know, that's a terrible combination for a mother – knowing that your child's been harmed by God-knows-who or what, and then being accused of that harm."

"My dear lady," began Holmes, all condescension. Fude instantly bristled, so much so that Eric, her usually passive husband, was forced to still her by placing a restraining hand on her forearm. "I did not accuse or judge, I merely sought to listen in order to gather evidence."

"But I know what she must'a seen," said Fude, her voice raised, "a snooty, callous, cold-hearted man who doesn't give two figs about her or her child, and yet who also has the power to have her child taken away from her. Would'a been awful for her."

For a moment there was a tense silence. It was only broken by the arrival of the second course.

"Ah," said Mr Fude, uncharacteristically vocal, "gammon! And how good it smells."

His wife, still looking daggers at Holmes, muttered something under her breath.

"But you know, you have a point. Two, in fact," said Holmes. Though untroubled by what Annabelle had just now said, he was at least sensible of the fact that adding "my dear lady" would not be welcome. "Clearly, we would do better to have the lady speak to someone who, in her opinion, can better empathise with her. This is where you," – Holmes gave a dismissive wave to both Lampblack and Fude – "come in. This case requires a feminine perspective."

Annabelle was just about to give vent to her feelings when Isadora put out a hand, signalling to her to keep her thoughts to herself.

"And the second point, Sherlock," she said, looking into his cold, calculating eyes that were so like her own. "I assume you refer to Fude's 'God-knows-what'? Was it the boy who spoke of ghosts?"

Holmes nodded. "Indeed. Though his mother was quick enough to silence him when he began to elaborate."

"No doubt terrified that you'd cart him off to some madhouse!" cried Fude.

"Awful tasty gammon, don't you think?" exclaimed Eric, desperate to turn the subject if at all possible. Watson, taking his lead, agreed heartily and began to elaborate on the overall deliciousness of the meal.

Annabelle said nothing, and instead took out her annoyance on the gammon, cutting the thick slab of ham with great vigour.

Isadora prodded the heap of string beans with her fork. When there was a lull in Watson's monologue she once again addressed Holmes. "So you require us to talk to both mother and child, and extract a full account of the events from the boy?"

"Yes," said Holmes. "And while you are thus employed I shall be carrying out some... other investigations. A little help from your – what do you call them? – ghostlies would speed things along."

"Annabelle named them my Goose Gate ghosties," replied Isadora. "And I will speak to them tonight."

"Good," said Holmes. "It is all settled then. Though, if, indeed, this is a case of the uncanny, I cannot suppose how you will detect or drive out any supernatural being."

Isadora's eyes glittered. "We have our ways and means. In fact, just last week Mr Fude completed the creation of the Eidolon Glass which I invented many years ago. It is a work of art."

At this point Eric, who never looked anything but astonished or confused, reddened somewhat. "Oh, but the artistry was in the inventing!" he said, proceeding to stuff gammon into his mouth so that he wouldn't be expected to speak further.

"Yes, but what does it do?" asked Holmes of Isadora.

"It uncovers the undetected, the occult."

"Are you saying what I think you're saying?" said Watson, looking from Isadora to Fude's husband, clearly impressed. "You have produced a device through which one can see apparitions?"

Annabelle chuckled. "They're too clever by half, ain't they? I call it the ghost spotter."

"Well, that is—" began Watson.

"Worthy of my inspection," finished Holmes. "So," he said, "that is all decided. You will call on the Richardsons tomorrow morning."

"Their address?" said Isadora.

"94 High Pavement."

Annabelle suddenly froze, her forkful of gammon wavering in mid-air.

"What?" asked Isadora.

Holmes's keen eyes, too, were on the frozen Fude.

Annabelle let out a deep breath. "Oh, nothing."

"You know I respect your intuition," said Isadora. "It has, without fail, proved to be enlightening. Do elaborate."

"A long-ago warning from me mam," she said, the anxious face of her careworn mother flitting across her mind's eye, "to never linger on that street." Suddenly conscious of everyone's eyes on her, she put down her fork and instead took a sip of wine. She gave herself a little shake. "That's better," she said, sounding much more like her usual, jolly self.

Both Holmes and Lampblack visibly relaxed; though for a while their interrogative eyes did not stray from Annabelle.

"Tasty gammon, ain't it?" said Eric, and Watson, once again, took the cue and began to expound on the delights of pork.

*****

The following morning Lampblack and Fude presented themselves at the Richardsons' home, which was a well-kept end-of-terrace at the foot of the Church of St Mary the Virgin. Isadora kept an eye on Fude as they were shown to the sitting room, keen to see if her weathervane intuition would sense anything untoward, but so far Fude seemed untroubled by any presentiments, good or bad.

Both husband and wife were there to greet them as warmly as they could, given the circumstances, though they were unable to successfully conceal their astonishment at the unlikely pairing of their visitors – Isadora, uncommonly beautiful, was tall, blonde and stately; Annabelle was short, plump and dark-haired. The age difference was striking too. Annabelle looked old enough to be Isadora's mother, though by their distinctly contrasting features this would've been a Mendelian impossibility.

"No doubt you are wondering at our incongruous fellowship and the events that led to us working together," said Isadora, quickly raising a gloved hand as the Richardsons began to protest. "It is, indeed, an interesting story, but we will have to forego it for the time being. We are keen to provide you with assistance if we are able to – that is, if the matter involves the supernatural."

At that, Mrs Richardson breathed a sigh of relief and sat down on the sofa. Her husband joined her, and then took hold of her hand, giving it a squeeze.

Lampblack and Fude took their seats in the armchairs closest to them.

"Please, Mrs Richardson–" began Isadora.

"Farzaneh," said the woman. "I do not really look like a Richardson, do I?" she said, with a thick Persian accent. She forced a laugh.

Mr Richardson visibly bristled and then let go of his wife's hand.

"No, you do not look like a Richardson," said Isadora, considering the woman's striking features, her taupe coloured skin. "And yet," she went on, "you are by marriage a Richardson."

Farzaneh's expression was a mixture of defiance and sadness, as though she was wondering *But for how long?*

Mr Richardson suddenly mopped his round, ruddy face with a handkerchief.

"We want to help," said Fude, looking from Mr to Mrs Richardson. "We really do. Just tell us what's been going on."

Farzaneh looked at her husband, who gave her a slight nod, and then took a deep breath. She said that their son, Clement, had always been a sensitive boy. "And for many years he's had a friend from his..." Farzaneh gestured to her forehead.

"An imaginary friend," interjected Mr Richardson.

"He calls him Baxter," Farzaneh said.

"And they're good friends?" asked Fude.

Mr Richardson, rather taken aback by the question, said nothing.

"Oh yes," said Farzaneh. "He talks very happily to Baxter. About his teddies and toys. The books he's read. They plan adventures. Or so he says. It's never been a problem before. But for the past year..." Farzaneh paused.

"Go on," said Isadora.

Mrs Richardson took another deep breath. "Clement says that since we came to live here Baxter has been bullied by two girls who are older than him. They have been trying to shoo Baxter away, saying that this is their house and that he has no right to be here. Clement has been trying to protect his friend, but in doing so, he has been hurt by the girls."

"And these girls are—" said Fude.

"Non-existent," replied Mr Richardson.

"Though the bruises are not," said Isadora.

"I know it doesn't make any sense," went on Mr Richardson.

"On the contrary," said Isadora, "it all makes perfect sense. And if we were to exchange 'non-existent' for 'existent, yet imperceptible' then for those not acquainted with the occult, such as yourself, the matter becomes easier to understand. Now, if we could speak with Clement that would be appreciated."

For a moment, neither Mr or Mrs Richardson said anything or did anything. Then Mrs Richardson rang for the maid, who promptly came with Clement in tow.

The boy, who had inherited his mother's dark eyes and hair and his father's pale skin, as well as the ruddiness, immediately went to his mother. They embraced with much affection.

Farzaneh explained to Clement that Lady Lampblack and Mrs Fude had come to talk to him about Baxter and the naughty girls. They might be able to help.

Clement eyed the two women cautiously. "D'you think you can?" he asked them. "Because they're horrid, the girls. They're nothing but bullies." He glanced at Mr Richardson. "Father says that one must stand up to bullies. That it's the only way to stop them." Clement stood up straighter, looking proud. "And I have. For the sake of Baxter. And because it's the right thing to do. But it isn't working." His face suddenly crumpled and it took him a great effort not to cry. "There's only one of me and two of them. And they're bigger than me. It's not fair."

"No," said Isadora, "it isn't fair."

"It's certainly not," agreed Fude, taking a sweet out of her pocket and pressing it into Clement's clammy hand. "Here you go, me duck, have a pear drop. They always made my George feel better when he got to ruminating about the unfairness of the world. And I must say that even now, old as I am, I enjoy the occasional sweet treat myself."

Isadora suppressed a smile. The adjective 'occasional' was somewhat imprecise.

Clement looked to his mother, who gave him a slight nod, and then put the pear drop in his mouth. As he sucked away, the sour-sweetness bringing him a measure of contentment, Isadora asked him where the girls were to be encountered. "And is Baxter with you now?" she enquired.

Clement shook his head. He glanced anxiously at his mother. "He... he doesn't join me when there are others about." Clement crunched on his sweet. "He's shy. I expect he'll be on the roof. He likes to look at the sky."

"And what of the girls?"

"I've only ever seen them in the nursery. They say it's theirs."

"Do they now?" said Fude. "And I guess they don't want to share?"

Clement shook his head, his eyes round.

"Can we see the nursery?" asked Lampblack.

"Of course," said Mrs Richardson, rising. She urged Clement forward, though he seemed reluctant to move.

"It's all right," said Fude, noting the boy's hesitance. "We'll be with you. And we'll make sure no harm comes to you."

The boy nodded and gave Fude a shy smile.

Farzaneh and Clement then led the way to the nursery, leaving Mr Richardson in the sitting room to mutter about the foolishness of indulging the boy in his crackpot ideas.

*****

The nursery was striking in its chilliness, though it was early summer, the weather warm.

"I apologise for the cold. We haven't lit a fire for a while," said Farzaneh, "Clement's been unwilling to play here."

The Case of the High Pavement Ghosts by Teika Marija Smits

Fude, who had paused on the threshold, was pale, her eyes glazed over.

Isadora, noting Fude's pallid face, her unseeing eyes, asked her what the matter was. "What can you see? What can you sense?"

"The traces of souls in torment. Terrible things were done to them, Izzy. Terrible."

Farzaneh pulled Clement towards her. "What?" she cried, "What happened?"

Fude shook her head. "I don't know. But it was a long time ago. I can feel the pain. The fear." Fude entered the room and then sat down heavily on a tiny chair. She looked ridiculous – her round form precarious on the child's wooden stool, but it was impossible to see the humour in the situation – she was too distressed. "Innocence corrupted."

Farzaneh's hand flew to her mouth and she swayed on the spot.

Isadora, the only one not unsettled by Fude's words, asked Mrs Richardson who the previous tenants had been. She shook her head. "I don't know. But I presume my husband would."

Isadora nodded then pulled out the Eidolon Glass and put it to the middle of her forehead. She then closed her eyes and turned her head left and right. Next, she placed the Eidolon Glass over her right eye and scanned the room. "Residues," she said, speaking more to herself than anyone else. Then she turned abruptly, as though she was following an invisible flying something with her eyes. "Do the girls always enter the room through here?" asked Isadora of Clement, pointing to the gold-framed mirror.

"Yes," he whispered. "How did you know?"

Isadora said nothing and instead inspected the mirror, placing her long, slender fingers at right angles to the surface of the mirror. When she saw that there was no gap between her fingers and their reflection she smiled to herself. She then turned to Clement. "This glass, or lens, that I just now put to my eye and my third eye, allows me to see things that I normally wouldn't see. There are three trails of ghosts around the room. Two of them appear to emanate from the mirror."

"So it's all true," said Farzaneh, astonished, "Baxter, and the girls... And you can prove it?"

"There is very little doubt in the matter," said Isadora. She looked over at Fude, who looked more herself now, though still pale. She helped her off the stool. "Have a pear drop," said Isadora, "it'll do you good."

Annabelle fumbled in her pocket for a sweet and then popped two in her mouth.

"But I would like to know more about these girls," went on Isadora. "So if Clement and Baxter, as well as Fude here, would be willing, I feel sure that we could make further progress."

"What did you have in mind?" said Fude, eyeing Isadora suspiciously. Isadora's plans didn't usually take into account the level of discomfort of those involved in the plan.

Isadora glanced at the mirror. "Let us discuss this in the sitting room. It is far more comfortable there."

*****

Clement agreed to the plan, as did Mr and Mrs Richardson. He said that he thought Baxter would accompany him to the nursery if it helped the ladies to stand up to the bully girls.

"Indeed, it will help," said Isadora. "A lot. I think it highly likely that the girls will be tempted out of their hiding place by Baxter's presence, and when they do venture out Fude will intercede and make light work of them."

Fude rolled her eyes. "Honestly, Izzy, you make it sound as though I'm going to be engaging in fisticuffs or summat like that!"

Isadora, ignoring Fude's comment, crouched down so that she could be at Clement's eye level. "A secret," she said, lowering her voice. "Bullies usually stand down when one asserts oneself. But sometimes they don't. That's when you need to bring in the cavalry. Do you understand?"

Clement nodded and then grinned. "And you and Mrs Fude are like the cavalry?"

"Indeed," said Isadora, standing once more.

"You know," said Clement, in a serious voice. "You're a very pretty lady. I would like to marry you."

Farzaneh suppressed a laugh and Mr Richardson, who had gone bright red, dabbed at his sweaty face with a handkerchief.

Fude grinned, and even dispassionate Isadora couldn't help but smile. "Thank you," she said, "for the proposal. I will give it some thought."

*****

Fude and Clement took themselves off to the nursery while Isadora spoke to Mr and Mrs Richardson about their landlord and the previous tenants. Clement, understandably, was anxious about being in what had become a dreaded room and didn't venture too far from Annabelle. After he'd spent some time showing her all his toys he became silent. He turned to look at the door and then sighed.

"Baxter not here yet?" she asked, as the boy clenched and unclenched a toy soldier.

He shook his head.

"Well, what does he like to do?"

"He likes stories."

Fude went to the bookshelf and picked up a copy of Grimm's Fairy Tales. "Make yourself comfy then," she said, installing herself in the rocking chair.

Clement settled at her feet and looked up at her as she opened the book.

"Got a favourite?" she asked.

"Iron John!" he said.

"Good choice." And she began to read.

After a while, when they were both engrossed in yet another story, Baxter must have slipped in and come to rest next to Clement. Fude, busy reading, didn't see him enter, but as she came to the end of the story, she glanced down at Clement and saw him whispering intently to what looked, to her, like a shimmer in the air. Her heart leapt – it was the boy's companion. But as keen as she was to see Baxter in a more substantial form, she refrained from taking the Eidolon Glass out of her pocket. She didn't want to scare the ghost boy away. She read on as though nothing had happened. After a few more stories Fude feigned tiredness and, yawning loudly, told Clement that she'd be having forty winks. Maybe he could construct something out of his wooden blocks while she had a little doze.

Soon enough, Clement, accompanied by the shimmer that was Baxter, was happily engrossed in building a castle for his toy soldiers. He chattered away while thus absorbed – to himself or Baxter, Fude wasn't sure – and forgot all about his dozing overseer. Unobserved, Fude sneaked a look at Baxter through the glass. What she saw was remarkable – Baxter, unlike other ghosts she'd seen, or sensed, didn't have one set form. He seemed to rapidly cycle through various forms – a mere wisp, then a baby, then a boy the age of Clement. Sometimes it seemed as though he were older than Clement, then he'd become nothing more than a haze of ethereal smoke. Fude hastily put the glass away as there was a lull in Clement's chatter and she became aware of near-invisible motion by the mirror.

The next occurrences happened swiftly and in parallel: two china dolls suddenly levitated upwards and swung at Clement and Baxter, and Fude leaped out of the rocking chair and grabbed the dolls before they made contact with anyone, human or ghost. Clement cried out in shock and then clung to Fude's skirt, Baxter, unnoticed by anyone, vanished from the room.

"Now then!" said Fude, her voice raised, addressing the two shimmers which she could just about make out in the dreary light of the nursery. "We'll have none of that, thank you very much!"

The shimmers swelled and visibly bristled with indignation. They retreated towards the mirror.

"And don't you be going nowhere, young ladies. Otherwise I'll just end up following you. Besides, it's high time we set a few ground rules, eh?"

The shimmers paused and slowly returned to Fude.

"That's it," she said, much more kindly now. But as she took out the Eidolon Glass the shimmers shrunk away from her. "No need to worry 'bout this," she reassured them. "It's just a sort'a magnifying lens that'll let me see you that bit better. You all right with it?"

After a moment there were two whispered yeses.

Fude put the Eidolon Glass to her right eye and then saw who Baxter and Clement's aggressors were. They were two Caucasian girls with shimmering hair, which made Fude think that in life they had been blonde and blue-eyed. One was older than the other, and they were dressed in clothes that had once been fine but had met with ill treatment; their frocks were grubby, ripped and stained with dark spots that Fude took to be blood. There was a pinched expression to their faces and sunken eyes which told Fude of terrible pain.

"Oh, my dears!" said Fude, suddenly unsteady on her feet. The echoes of the awful anguish that she'd sensed earlier came back to her and she sunk to her knees.

The girls drew back in surprise, but didn't leave.

Fude gave herself a mental shake. She had to stay focussed, calm. Just like Izzy.

"Well now," said Fude. "How 'bout some introductions? My name's Annabelle, and this here is Clement." She glanced round at the boy who had retreated behind her, still clutching hold of her skirts. "I'm Clement's new... governess. Friend. How about you two?"

There was a pause then the older girl said, "Elizabeth. And this is–"

"Lucy," said the other.

"Elizabeth and Lucy," Fude repeated. "Lovely names. And I guess you used to live and play here?"

Elizabeth nodded.

Fude considered the mirror. "But you're not always here, are you? You come and go. Through the mirror, don't you?"

Elizabeth's eyes became round. "How do you know?"

"I've got a sense of your movements. And that area by the mirror is awful busy." Fude inhaled deeply, steeling herself for what she had to say next. "I'm guessing that your bodies are somewhere in the house beyond that."

"Yes," whispered Elizabeth.

Lucy stared at Annabelle intently, her eyes glistening.

"So you come across for a bit of respite. But you're none too pleased about the boys being here, eh?"

"It's *our* nursery," said Elizabeth, standing tall. "Why should we have to share it with those nasty, foreign boys?"

"Now, now," said Fude, "there's no need for name-calling." She sighed. "Though I dare say that under normal circumstances you wouldn't lash out like that. I'm guessing you've both been witnesses to the most appalling kinds of human behaviour. It's not exactly going to do you any favours." Again, Fude sighed. Slowly, she got up off her knees, rubbing them as she did so. "What we got here is a situation. But I'm sure we can find some ways of resolving it, that is, if you promise to be honest with me. What do you say, Miss Elizabeth and Miss Lucy?"

The girls looked at each other, came to some unspoken mutual agreement and then nodded at Fude.

"Good," said Fude. "Now, I know that you'd both like to have this nursery all to yourselves. Coming here makes you feel better, don't it?"

The girls said "yes".

"But we got Clement and Baxter to consider. Now, I'm sure the boys would be willing to share," Fude glanced at Clement who quickly nodded his head, "but I'm not convinced that sharing's gonna solve the root problem. Tell me," she said, looking at them intently, "what would make you truly happy?"

"To have the boys gone!" said Elizabeth. She gave Lucy a nudge, but Lucy said nothing.

Fude looked at the younger girl, a kind expression on her motherly face. "Is that true, Lucy?" she asked.

Lucy shook her head and sparkling, lucent tears ran down her face. "I–" she began, "I'd like to see Mama and Papa again. And little Molly. I want..." her bottom lip trembled, "to be whole again."

Fude found herself blinking back tears. "Oh my dear, of course you do. And I ever so much wish I could grant you that. We might be able to find your family and bring them to you, so that you can meet. But, well, you gotta understand that there's no way anyone can make you whole again."

"Why?" said Elizabeth, her voice fierce.

Fude shook her head. There was sorrow in her eyes. "I'm sorry... it's just not the way of things. But as far as I understand there is a place or, rather, a state of being that you can enter. It'll give you peace. Rest."

Lucy, round-eyed, whispered, "Heaven."

Fude nodded and smiled kindly at the little girl.

"What if we don't want to go?" said Elizabeth. "What if we want to stay here?"

Lucy tugged at Elizabeth's sleeve. "I want to go. But you have to come with me."

The older girl considered the younger, then sighed. "I suppose..." She then turned to Fude. "But how do we get there?"

"Leave that to me," said Fude. "Me and my very clever friend, Izzy, will find your parents then put your bones to rest. Then... Heaven'll open up to you. My, what a marvellous sight that'll be!"

The girls looked at Fude, their faces solemn; shining.

"But I'll do this on one condition," went on Fude. "I want the name, if you know it, of the terrible man who hurt and killed you. He needs to be found and justice done."

Elizabeth, the shine suddenly gone, said, "Oh, we know his name. And you can have it. Sherlock Holmes."

*****

Fude lost no time in relaying this information to Isadora once they were back in the privacy of Isadora's town house. "What do you say to that?" said Annabelle, her face still bearing the signs of shock.

"I say it's not true," replied Isadora.

"You mean the girls are lying to me, and that they made all that stuff up?"

"No, I believe we'll find enough evidence to back up the majority of their story. But Sherlock their killer...? Impossible."

Fude was about to protest but Lampblack put a hand out to silence her. "It does, though, help to incriminate the real killer." A wry smile was upon Isadora's face. "He must've thoroughly despised my cousin if he went to the trouble of impersonating him in the hope that the police would see fit to arrest Sherlock. Someone who..." Isadora gave a satisfied sigh. "Of course..."

Fude waited for an explanation but none was forthcoming. "'Course what?" she said, after a moment or two.

"Come!" said Isadora, heading towards the door. "We must meet with Holmes and Watson at once."

"Hold on, Izzy, I haven't had lunch or–"

"Annabelle," said Lampblack, her eyes sparkling, "what does my cousin say when trouble is on the horizon? When things are getting exciting?"

Fude knew what Holmes said. But she didn't like trouble. She liked lunch. "He says," she said with a deep sigh, "that the game is afoot."

*****

It took a while to get a message through to Holmes and Watson, but soon enough the four of them were gathered together in one of the private dining rooms of the Black Boy Hotel, with Fude throwing down some bread and cheese while glancing surreptitiously at Holmes. Lampblack and Holmes weren't inclined to eat – they were fuelled by the fire of the investigation – but Watson was hungry and tucked into a plate of cold meats with gusto.

"All this trudging round makes for an appetite," John commented, in between mouthfuls.

"But what *have* you been doing?" asked Annabelle.

It was then that all four of them began to speak. After a few seconds both Isadora and Holmes slammed their hands onto the table, crying out, "Enough!"

There was silence.

"Ladies first," said Holmes, addressing his cousin.

"Thank you," said Isadora, with a smile. "Though I have a sense that everything we've discovered today will be backed up by your investigations."

She gave a summation of her and Annabelle's findings. Watson goggled at her, open-mouthed, when she came to the part where the ghost girls had named their killer as Holmes. "So, to conclude: the boy was telling the truth. He and his supernatural friend were being bullied out of the nursery by two girls who had been killed approximately twenty-four years ago by a fiend, who, if the rumours are to be believed, is still at large today. A fiend that you, Sherlock, had evidence against, and yet, who had somehow escaped death only to redouble his efforts with the intention of implicating you in his heinous crimes."

Now it was Annabelle's turn to stare at Isadora round-eyed. She dropped the chunk of cheese that she'd been about to eat and took a quick swig of ale.

"It was twenty-three years ago," said Holmes, "A dark affair – and according to information I have recently unearthed, he *is* still at large, though I admit that I wouldn't have thought it possible. I saw him hang." There was a pause as Holmes considered his memory of that gruesome event. "In fact, he's just now returned from the continent where he has spent a goodly amount of his life involved in the trafficking of children. And if he's got wind of my presence, as I intended him to, he will most likely make his move against me soon."

"You got all this from a morning's work?" said Fude.

"Actually," said Holmes, "it's been three days' worth of work. It's amazing what one can glean when disguised as a labourer looking for employment in the Lace Market. But today that labourer brought along his 'daughter' and hinted that he was open to some less-than-savoury ways to earn a better wage."

"Was it Meghan who posed as your daughter?" asked Isadora.

Holmes nodded. "And I must say that she acted her part very well."

"Yes," replied Isadora, "she's a fine actress. And one of my longest-serving ghosties."

"Hold on a mo," said Fude, "back up! I'm getting lost."

"Quite," added Watson, "can you please explain to me what's going on? And were my perambulations around Nottingham, meeting with landlords and agents, of *any* use?"

"Yes of course they were, my dear Watson. Your efforts confirmed my suspicions. Does the name Gunn mean anything to you?" asked Holmes of Fude.

Annabelle gasped. "Oh my! Of course!"

Watson looked at Fude's blanched face and then at Holmes. "Damn it man! Now I'm the only one who doesn't know what the hell you're talking about. Will you please enlighten me?"

"Gunn was a policeman gone bad," Holmes explained. "He was also a friend of the despicable, violin-playing Charlie Peace, whom this wretched town seems to think so well of. I won't bother going into the apparent 'whys' of the matter, but the upshot of his reversal of position with regards to the law was that under the guise of a benevolent landlord, particularly keen to give homes to poor families and abandoned children, he established himself as a mastermind of the most vile aspect of criminality – child trafficking.

"I had to spend a goodly amount of time unravelling his filthy web of influence, particularly as I found a good deal of resistance from those in positions of authority who really did not want Gunn – and, hence, their own peccadilloes – exposed. Oh no, they would far prefer to hide behind their public stature, claiming sinlessness.

"One day, though, he became careless and left a good deal of incriminating evidence at the scene of a brutal murder of a young girl of good breeding who had already been missing for several weeks. And there was a reliable eye witness who testified that he'd seen Gunn and the girl earlier that day. There was no way that Gunn could slither out of my grasp this time. He was sentenced to death."

"I remember it too," said Fude "The papers were full of it. Gunn had been born in Nottingham, so it was the talk of the town. But you said you saw him hang? So how on earth can he still be in play?"

"Why the surprise?" asked Isadora, "When not two hours ago you were conversing with ghosts?"

Fude shrugged. "They were friendly ghosts. A child murderer come back to life don't bear thinking about. Lor' I was that spooked by the tales me mam used to tell about High Pavement and the snatchers who would whisk away children if they did so much as look at the houses on that road. I never forgot her warnings."

"Clever woman," said Holmes. "Watson brought me certain papers from the local house agents – some of the properties on that road were, and still are, owned by Gunn."

"Hence, the two-way mirror and the dead girls," explained Isadora. "A search of the house next door to 94 High Pavement should be illuminating. I have no doubt that the girls' bodies are buried there."

"Quite," said Holmes.

"We should have them interred properly," said Fude. "Bring them the peace they deserve. And give the Richardsons the peace they need. Although, I'd like it if we could find the girls' family before they get buried."

"We will do that," said Isadora, "I should also carry out some investigations into Gunn's apparent immortality. There are several occult methods he may have employed to manage his resurrection. Perhaps a straightforward, though costly, act such as an arcane metamorphosis would—"

"Metamorphosis, what exactly do you mean by that?" asked Holmes.

"It means that he could've given his physical appearance to someone else — and taken on theirs. If this were done at the time of his execution—"

"If it were, you are suggesting that he evaded the hangman's noose and let someone else swing instead." Holmes stared into the middle distance, absorbed in intense cogitation. "And shortly after the execution the eyewitness who testified against him was reported as missing. He was never found, which further suggests the 'resurrected' Gunn removed him.

"It was an insoluble irritation, that aspect, along with many other further irritations — including the sporadic claims I had been in two different places at once, fighting crime at one location and committing crime at another; claims I was, until now, unable to fathom. It seems plain now that Gunn appropriated my name at times, whether from perverse pleasure, or assuming it would muddy the trail."

"We would need to exhume the body," said Isadora, "to see who is in Gunn's grave."

"Indeed," said Holmes, his jittery legs propelling him to stand and act.

They were interrupted by a messenger bringing a letter to Holmes.

Watson, Lampblack and Fude stared at Holmes as he opened the letter and sat back down again.

"Well, well," said Holmes, his eyes alight with excitement. "He has made his move. Listen:

"*Sherlock, how clever of you to find me after all these years. I wondered if you'd ever catch on. The devil knows I left enough clues. But a warning: stay away from my old stamping grounds. I wouldn't want anything bad to happen to my greatest admirer, would I?"*

"Lord Almighty!" cried Fude.

"And this is him?" said Watson. "Gunn?"

"There is no doubt," said Holmes. "It is his handwriting. I recall it from many years ago. And I saw it again the other day, when I made enquiries into the Richardsons' landlord."

"Good heavens!" said Watson. "We must tell the police."

"We will," said Holmes. "But first, a plan. Isadora, am I right in thinking that the Narrow Marsh—"

"Is his old stamping ground, yes."

"Good," said Holmes. "Tonight then, yes?"

Isadora nodded.

"Hold on a mo," said Fude. "You're not telling me that you're going after him, are you? Straight into his trap?"

"Watson and I will have reinforcements of more than one kind." He tipped his head to the two women. "I can no longer discount that Gunn may have certain unnatural tricks up his sleeve, as well as a murderous heart," said Holmes. "But yes. Walking into the trap is the surest way of drawing him out."

Fude took a swig of ale. "How did I know you were gonna say that?"

"Because, my dear," said Holmes, "you are a singularly intuitive lady."

"Yeah, and I knew you were gonna say that too." Fude took another gulp of ale. "Come on, then, let's be hearing your plan."

*****

Nightfall found them in Narrow Marsh, that particularly unpleasant area of Nottingham, south of the city, north of the River Trent. Holmes and Watson were to go on ahead; Lampblack and Fude were the first line of reinforcements, following behind them. Policemen, in pairs, were stationed at the edges of the slum, ready to respond if Gunn's trap was to prove too sticky for the four of them, though both Watson and Fude were carrying revolvers and quite prepared to use them against such a monster.

Holmes had a fairly good idea of where Gunn was to be found, but he also thought it highly probable that he would show himself. *He* would be the bait.

Sure enough, a shadow of a man unpeeled himself from a throng of drunks to slip away and into another filthy alley. But not before showing himself to Holmes and Watson. It was Gunn. They followed him; Lampblack and Fude kept back at a cautious distance.

They hurried along the jumble of cobbled backstreets, the smell of human waste intense, until it was near pitch black and silent. Then they saw an unearthly light. Gunn appeared to be carrying it. Holmes and Watson paused for a moment, wondering at its strangeness, but then hurried on. Lampblack and Fude, too, had seen the light, and stopped.

"What is it?" whispered Annabelle.

"I don't know," said Isadora. "Not an ordinary lantern. It could be a will-o-the-wisp. Or any manner of unearthly creatures or spirits or..." – it was then that the most wonderful music began to play – "...song. Yes," she said, her eyes glazing over. "Siren song, held in a jar..."

Fude heard the music, but it didn't affect her in the way it had affected Isadora.

"You all right, Izzy?" asked Annabelle, the moonlight illuminating her friend's strange expression. She seemed entranced, mesmerized.

Isadora smiled. "We must follow the music."

Holmes and Watson had had the same thought. Isadora went after them, and so Fude had no choice but to follow, puffing and panting as she tried to keep up with the other three.

On and on they went, the light and music leading them through the filthy alleys, until Fude could hear the rhythmic roll of water. They were at the river. And there was the light. This time it was on a boat that was halfway to the other side.

Fude cried out as she realized what was happening – Holmes and Watson were striding into the river, still following the light and eerie music.

"Izzy!" she said, grabbing her arm, "we got to stop them, they're gonna drown themselves!"

But Isadora paid her no intention, pulled herself out of Annabelle's grasp and carried on towards the river.

"Izzy!" she cried, realizing that her friend was under the power of dark magic. Then: "Police!" But although two policemen stepped out of the shadows, they were equally oblivious to her and were themselves rushing headlong into the river.

Annabelle watched with growing panic as Holmes, Watson, Isadora and the two policemen strode heedlessly into the deepening water. They'd be dragged down by the current any moment now.

"Think!" she said, trying to calm herself. "Siren song," she muttered, "siren song." Of course! She couldn't save them all from the might of the river but she *could* break the spell.

She aimed her revolver at the light. It was a way off now and bobbing about, but still, it was as big as a pigeon – an easy target.

Bang! She got it first shot, and the bound magick was shattered along with its container.

There were cries from Holmes, Watson and Isadora, as well as the two policemen, who were now no longer insensitive to the pull of the cold river. Fude waded in to help Isadora who was floundering in the cold, dirty shallows.

"Gunn!" cried Holmes, who'd been the furthest out and was now treading water.

Gunn, furious at this turn of events, pulled out a revolver and fired it at Holmes who, just in time, dived under the water and disappeared from view. Gunn then aimed at Watson who also took cover under the water.

"Come on!" cried Annabelle, dragging her friend out of the river. "We've got to get out of here!"

There was a whoosh as a bullet whistled past the two women and policemen, frighteningly close, and both Isadora and Fude gasped and fell forwards onto the river bank.

Then more shots, though it sounded as though these had been fired upwards, into the night sky. Holmes had emerged from under the water and was rocking the boat, knocking Gunn off-balance. And then Holmes was aboard the boat and grappling with the man who'd almost sent him to his death. There was a splash as Holmes knocked the revolver out of Gunn's hand.

The boat rocked violently as both men wrestled with each other. Then Watson, sopping wet, clambered onto the boat and pointed his revolver at the tussling pair. "I'll shoot sir!" he cried, hoping Gunn wouldn't know he was bluffing – there was a high chance that he'd hit Sherlock instead.

With a tremendous effort, Gunn lunged for the side of the boat, desperate to escape into the river, but Holmes was too quick and pulled him back, just as Watson, seeing his chance to get a clear shot, pulled the trigger. Gunn cried out and collapsed onto Holmes as a blot of dark liquid appeared on the sleeve of his shirt. For a moment, the two men lay still.

"Holmes!" cried Watson, "Good God! Are you hurt?"

"No," said Holmes, "it is only the fiend who is wounded."

Gunn made one last feeble attempt to escape Holmes, who dragged him back roughly.

"Not so confident now, eh?" said Holmes, taking Watson's revolver and keeping it pointed at Gunn's throat. "Take us ashore, Watson."

Watson rowed them back, watching the two men, who were equally formidable, though in opposite ways. Holmes kept his eyes fixed on the silent Gunn, who looked about him, his mind still bent on escape. Watson glanced ahead – there were Isadora and Annabelle sitting on the riverbank, huddled together. Annabelle had placed her dry shawl around Isadora's shoulders and was rubbing some warmth into her friend's arms.

As the boat approached the riverbank and the waiting policemen waded in to help bring the boat ashore, Watson acknowledged the women with a grim nod.

Fude gave him a weak smile and then turned once more to Isadora. "You sure you're all right, Izzy?"

"Just about," Isadora replied, her teeth chattering. "Thanks to you."

"I guess we were just lucky that there was *one* woman about tonight who was immune to the old feminine allure, eh?"

"Indeed," said Isadora, with a mirthless laugh. "Though I'd never have expected Sherlock to fall under the spell of siren song."

"Well, he wasn't exactly immune to Irene Adler, was he? He probably heard *her* in the music."

"True."

Just then a Black Maria rolled up to the riverbank and yet more policemen helped Holmes and Watson escort Gunn from the boat to the carriage. Gunn thrashed around wildly, incensed by the many hands on him, and when he caught sight of Lampblack and Fude he attempted to hurl himself at them. The policemen dragged him back to the carriage, kicking and flailing.

"You!" he cried, addressing Isadora. "I've heard about you. And I know your secrets! You're an abomination!"

Sherlock, on seeing his cousin's shocked face, did not spare Gunn. He punched him in the face, sending him flying into the carriage. "The only abomination here is you! And this time, sir, I'll damn well make sure that you're the one to swing." With that he slammed the door on Gunn.

*****

Together, Holmes and Isadora found the family of the dead sisters. 'Little' Molly was now twenty-five. With the help of the Eidolon Glass, they brought about a reunion that, though desperately sad, was appreciated. In time, the bodies of the girls were buried and they were given the peace they deserved.

The Richardsons, although now free of the cloud of tension that had hovered over them for so long, moved from the house on High Pavement. It held too many bad memories – theirs and others. But before they left, one evening they received one last visit from Isadora, who wanted to talk to Baxter.

"I *think* he's up there," said Clement, indicating to the attic window of his bedroom. "On the roof."

"You think?" said Isadora. "Do you not see him that often nowadays?"

Clement shook his head.

Isadora considered the boy. Although he still had the air of one who had a rich, internal life, he looked less wistful, more content. He had grown an inch or so since that first meeting of theirs.

"I think the connection between you is waning," she said. "Do you mind?"

Clement looked down at his feet before answering. "I both do and I don't. I'm sort of… busy with my own things."

Isadora nodded. "I understand. You don't mind that I talk to him, do you?"

"No."

Isadora hitched up her skirts, and with surprising agility went through the window and leapt lightly up to the apex of the roof, where she could just about make out a shimmer. She sat on the ridge and surveyed all of dusky Nottingham beneath her.

"Evening, Baxter," she said.

The shimmer didn't say anything.

"When my friend, Annabelle, saw you a while back she told me you were a most marvellous ghost. Do you mind if I take a look at you through my glass?"

There was a sigh that sounded like a "no".

"Thank you," she said, as she took out the Eidolon Glass and peered at Baxter through it. Just then he was Clement's age – and the exact image of him. He then became a wisp, and then a baby.

Isadora put the glass away, a sad but kind expression on her face. "You died in your mother's womb, didn't you? Many weeks before your twin brother was born. You cleaved to him, didn't you?"

A whispered "yes".

"Baxter, I think that, soon, it will be time for you to move on. To Heaven. But before you do, make sure to say all your goodbyes. Show yourself to your mother and father. I think they would... like that very much."

There was a pause and then a last "yes".

"Good," said Isadora. "Thank you."

She tilted her head upwards. "The stars are so beautiful, aren't they? I'm not surprised you like to come here."

But when she turned to look at Baxter he had vanished, leaving nothing behind him but starlight and air.

The Adventure of the Abominable Adder

by Will Murray

A most extraordinary medical case came to my attention in the Autumn of 1904.

I was not the consulting physician in the matter. That was another. In fact, before it was all over, there were two, if I do not count myself. However, much of my initial information was secondhand, and here the unfortunate complications commenced.

For a day or two, I dawdled over the account which had been relayed to me by a physician of my acquaintance, a Dr. Selwin. He had a practice in the seaside resort town of Hastings.

Selwin imparted to me the story of a patient of his, a certain widow, whom he called Mrs. Hampstead for reasons of confidentiality, who came to him with a rather curious injury to her ring finger. Selwin could not account for this injury, and the woman's story made absolutely no sense to him. But I get ahead of myself.

Upon hearing the story from Selwin, who was visiting London when I met him, I dismissed it as the complaint of a hysterical woman. Yet the matter appeared to bother poor Selwin, who was of sound mind and good character. Furthermore, he was no fool.

Accordingly, I carried his account in my head for a full day before deciding to unburden myself in the presence of Holmes, who was an aficionado of oddities and queer mysteries of the character I am about to relate.

"I have a rather vexing conundrum for you," I told him as I entered the study where we passed so many hours in conversation during the bygone days when I dwelled at 221B Baker Street.

"Pray sit down, Watson. I am rather bored at the moment. And all things considered, I would rather be vexed than bored."

"I do not wish to waste your time on nonsense," I assured him. "Yet I feel impelled to share the odd account of Dr. Selwin, who recounted it to me."

"He has a medical mystery?"

"I am not so certain that it is medical in nature, but the patient who consulted him did so out of desperation, for she had gone to see a priest and received no satisfaction from him. Conceiving no other recourse, and perhaps wishing a sympathetic ear, she laid the issue before Selwin."

"Is this a confidential matter?" inquired Holmes. "May I have the name of the patient?"

"Medical matters are always confidential," I reminded him. "So I will withhold the woman's name for now — other than to say that she is of good reputation in the community, and is a woman of means, although widowed."

Reaching for his pipe, Holmes remarked, "Her name may not be important. Proceed."

"The woman in question had recently returned from a month in Egypt, where she purchased a curious second-hand gold ring in the form of a coiled viper. For some reason known only to her, she wore it in place of the wedding ring of her late husband."

"Peculiar choice. And quite contrary to custom."

"This woman is a bit of a free thinker. I would not be surprised if she dabbles in the occult. This was her second visit to Egypt. As you know, the country is a magnet for people who believe it to be a fountain of deep mysteries."

"A rather dry fountain," commented Holmes.

I neglected to chuckle, so intent was I on getting the story correct.

"The woman in question had no issues with the ring until the third night of her return from Egypt. As Selwin tells it, she awoke in the middle of the night, feeling a stinging sensation in her ring finger. Lighting a candle, she discovered blood pooling around the coils of the ring. Removing the ring and washing her hands, she discovered two sets of punctures. These punctures were minute, and she could not account for them. She bandaged the digit and returned to bed.

"Intriguing," said Holmes. "My mind already fastens upon possibilities."

"I neglected to tell you, Holmes, that prior to her awakening, she suffered a rather unusual nightmare. In the nightmare, a snake of some magnitude was attempting to sink its fangs into her."

"Dreadful," said Holmes. "But no doubt coincidental."

"I do not know what the woman thought, but she went back to sleep, according to Selwin. When she awoke in the morning, her finger was throbbing; she applied alcohol to the wounds, cleaned them anew, and placed the ring on different finger.

"A week past without incident. And the dream returned. Once more, a sharp stinging sensation awoke her, liberating her from that recurring and distressing image of a vicious viper, but perhaps precipitating the poor woman into a waking nightmare."

"Allow me to skip ahead," murmured Holmes while filling his pipe. "She discovered blood around her repositioned ring and upon removing it there were found puncture wounds, identical as before."

"Precisely. But how did you guess that?"

"As preposterous as the idea might sound, Watson, the trend of your story suggested it, even though, as stated, the story strikes the ear as impossible."

"Do you have any thoughts on the matter?"

"Only preliminary ones. You will recall the infamous poison rings which held reservoirs of poison beneath their bezels. It would not be impossible for a cunning jeweller to include a spring mechanism to inject vile solutions into the veins of unsuspecting victims."

"According to Selwin, the woman suffered no malady beyond the puncture wounds and the emotional distress of the repeated incident. She is otherwise well, and no trace of poison could be found coursing through her system."

"Has the ring been examined?"

"By the priest and by Selwin both. Neither discovered a concealed reservoir or barb, poisoned or otherwise."

"That does not prove that one does not exist," Holmes said dismissively.

"It does not," I agreed. "Yet is it difficult to account for a hidden mechanism that would spring spontaneously so many weeks after purchase."

"Perhaps not so very difficult. One would have to study the ornament carefully, under a microscope if necessary."

"I would agree that a secret yet simple device must be the answer," I allowed. "Obviously, a clockwork mechanism could not be concealed in a ring of such modest size. Therefore, it must be something extraordinarily clever to have escaped professional examination."

"I disagree on that point, Watson. No professional has examined the curious ring. I daresay that neither the priest nor your physician friend possesses the appropriate credentials to examine a murder device with certainty."

"Selwin assured me that the ring was of a piece. And that it was not hollow. It was simply a series of heavy gold loops in the shape of a serpent, with an open mouth and four protruding fangs."

Holmes sat up sharply, and his eyes became glittering. I knew that change in attitude. Prior to this alteration, he had simply been listening as one might to a story of one's visit to an interesting locality. Now something had seized his imagination, taking hold of it firmly.

"What's this?" he said sharply. "You neglected to mention that the serpent ring possessed four exposed fangs."

"Pardon me. I meant to do exactly that. For it did seem salient."

"These marks, how were they spaced on the woman's fingers?"

"I cannot say with certainty, of course. But the woman was convinced that she had been bitten by the very serpent of gold wrapped around her finger."

"Were blood spots observed on the fangs?"

"If they were," I returned, "I do not know about it. Selwin did not say. He, as I, assumed that the marks could not have come from the serpent's delicate golden fangs. They were not positioned in such a way as to inflict puncture marks, for they curved inward, into the yawning maw."

Holmes was now frowning like a gathering thundercloud. His voice grew as sharp and incisive as a knife's edge and his words were slow in coming. He was thinking furiously now.

"One might imagine a single barb embedded in the ring in such a way as to puncture the unsuspecting wearer. But four is out of bounds. No, no, this does not conform with my assumptions."

Holmes had lit his pipe and was now puffing away. He became withdrawn. He shifted in his comfortable chair several times. I noted the way his brow furrowed, and a deep notch appeared between his eyes.

I let him be. I knew my friend well enough to know that to disturb his thoughts would be tantamount to derailing a moving train.

After some time, he looked up and removed the pipe-stem from his thin mouth.

"Watson, I believe that you should arrange for me to meet Dr. Selwin's troubled patient."

"I could make inquiries of Selwin, but this is a delicate matter."

"Say that Sherlock Holmes is offering his services with no thought of a fee. This might intrigue his patient, especially as the lady seems not to have discovered relief through normal channels."

"I will do so tomorrow. Perhaps you are right."

With that, Holmes sank into a profound reverie; he might as well have been a man under the influence of opium. All that mattered now was the problem. And the problem was vexing him, vexing him quite ardently.

With a murmuring goodbye that was not acknowledged, I took my leave.

As I walked home in a light rain, I wondered if I had done the correct thing in bringing up the matter. It was a puzzle to be sure. But it smacked of the occult. My friend Holmes had no use for such matters. In fact, he took delight in dispelling the shadows of the unknown with the torchlight of science.

I had been thinking that the matter had a simple but unusual explanation. If that were true, Holmes would have blurted it out in the first ten minutes of our conversation, as was his wont. Therefore he saw an enigma of considerable impenetrability.

As I passed between the glowing gas lamps, I could only reflect that as mysteries went, this one had its disturbing aspects.

Once I entered my own front door, I returned my dear wife's kiss of greeting, and put the matter out of my head forthwith.

I later came to wish that I had left it there for all time.

*****

The next day, I wrote Dr. Selwin in Hastings. He was good enough to telephone the next day to inform me that he had spoken with his patient, who had consented to see Holmes. There was more to it than that, however, which I had yet to explain to Holmes.

After I shut my practice for the day, I hired a hansom cab, which conveyed me to 221B Baker Street and I lay the entire matter before my friend.

"Well, the news is good," I said, settling into my accustomed chair. "We are invited to Hastings and the residence of Mrs. Arthur Seagrave."

"I am not familiar with the name. No matter. Continue, Watson."

"Mrs. Seagrave is able to receive us this coming Saturday, between the hours of two and four. Apparently she has a quite busy social calendar. However, there is a complication."

Holmes was knocking dottle out of his favourite pipe and looked up with curiosity.

"Mrs. Seagrave had previously made arrangements to consult another person on that day. He is expected at 2 o'clock. Our visits are certain to coincide."

"That is a complication," replied Holmes, "but not necessarily a difficult one. Do you know the name of the person being received at that hour?"

"I do indeed. And when I tell you the name, perhaps you will see the matter as being more involved than at first blush."

"Go on, Watson. Please don't make me struggle for a simple fact."

"The man is a physician, although not of the commonplace type. He is certified, so his bona fides are genuine. But he does not practice in the traditional way. His name is Silence. Dr. John Silence."

Holmes paused one moment and then said, "The so-called psychical doctor?"

"I understand that he abhors the term, but you have it correctly. Dr. Silence does not keep office hours. Nor does he charge his patients — if one could employ that term. Instead, he operates somewhat along your lines. If you are in need, he is open to consultation. But he never charges a fee. Apparently he is independently wealthy and a bit of an altruist."

"I have read about him, but I have never formed a strong opinion regarding his activities. He appears sincere enough. But that is only an impression."

"In the medical field, his sincerity is not questioned, at least so far as I know," I told Holmes. "But his endeavours naturally raise eyebrows. Silence will only treat with patients who are afflicted with maladies that might be called of the spirit or, if you prefer, belonging to the soul."

"A soul doctor, as it were. A novel concept. I imagine the demand in this day and age might be significant."

"Significant, and profitable," I pointed out. "If only the man would charge a proper fee."

"Do I detect a note of professional jealousy?"

"Well, a man who has gone to medical schools and has passed all examinations should at least have the professional courtesy to charge an appropriate fee."

"I see your point," murmured Holmes. "He devalues all other physicians by operating as he does. Tell me, does he lay ghosts?"

I shrugged helplessly. "So many rumours swirl about the man that one hears a great many wild accounts. I do not necessarily credit any of them. But I would be greatly surprised if the suppression of ghosts and spirits were not in his repertoire, as it were."

Sherlock Holmes leaned back thoughtfully, his pipe momentarily forgotten.

"Well, this case seems to be more up his alley than down my lane. But I remain intrigued. And I will confess, Watson, that this man interests me, for the uniqueness of his calling, if for no other reason. I am now doubly interested in the matter of Mrs. Seagrave's peculiar puncture wounds. Even if the cause is mundane, the opportunity to observe Dr. Silence at his work might prove illuminating by itself."

"Illuminating? I don't know, Holmes. I give the man little credit, except that he does not appear to bilk the public as does the average run of charlatans."

"Yet you say that he has the reputation of sincerity. Perhaps this is a case of the delusional assisting the delusional, much like the blind leading the blind."

"Well," I replied with a trace of annoyance, "we will know on Saturday. How you will conduct your investigation with this man gadding about is something I cannot visualize at the moment. Yet Mrs. Seagrave was quite firm in her invitation. We have two hours in which to plumb the depths of this mystery."

"And I have three days beforehand to look into the matter of Dr. John Silence. Perhaps I will learn something of interest before we meet the fellow."

And there we left it. I had begun to regret bringing up the matter. For the question of Silence and his standing in the medical community was a relatively new one, and I found the speculation swirling about him to be annoying. I will confess to the reader that I harboured my own species of hasty judgment, and perhaps that does not reflect well upon me. But I am a traditional physician who came up the hard way in my field. Silence struck me as a gadfly and a dabbler. I had no use for such delvings, or those who undertook them.

*****

I went about my week in the normal fashion. And on Saturday morning, I met Holmes at Baker Street. He had hired a motorcar to take us to Hastings. I looked forward to the drive, for the south coast of England is picturesque.

After we entered the passenger compartment, and the driver left the curb, Holmes stated, "I have made discreet inquiries about Dr. John Silence and his professional activities."

"Yes?" I asked curiously.

"As with your original recounting of the serpentine ring, it is difficult to draw firm and final conclusions about stories received second and third hand. But I have not heard a bad word about the man in terms of his deeds. Insofar as his accomplishments go, since these matters are often delicate, if not embarrassing, very few of his clients are willing to speak to the issues which motivated them to seek his services. I have had several conversations; the only ones that were satisfactory to me involved persons who required aid with seemingly supernatural disturbances, which Silence resolved by pointing out perfectly ordinary solutions. I applaud him for that."

"Intriguing," I admitted.

"However, other persons with whom I spoke seemed to hint at extraordinary events that had to be dealt with by other means. This leads me to conclude that whilst the good doctor may often shine a scientific light on the seemingly inexplicable, this is not always the case."

"A case of the delusional leading the delusional, as you suggested the other day," I pointed out.

"One wonders. Still, the story of the golden ring has its curious aspects. I would like to observe Dr. Silence addressing the matter before I weigh in. Observing his methods may be instructive."

I stared at my friend.

"Surely you are not serious, Holmes? What you are suggesting is akin to my learning how to treat patients by observing the rituals of a Congo witch doctor."

"You jump to conclusions, Watson. Just as I leaped to an erroneous conclusion when I first heard the story of the golden ring with vicious fangs. I prefer to let my observations guide me towards conclusions, this way they are soundly-reasoned and not emotional in nature. For what better ground can we stand upon than that of rationality and objectivity?"

My annoyance subsided. "I take your point, even if it rankles. But I am not remotely open-minded when it comes to the supernatural."

"Still, the only way to confront the apparently inexplicable is with both eyes open, the ears unobstructed and the brain working like a well-oiled thinking machine."

"I do not deny that I have my prejudices," I returned. "But they comfort me. I will hold onto them until I perceive any folly they might harbour."

"On that score, Watson, my prejudices are your prejudices, for the most part. But one must clean the palette in between sips of wine. I am putting my prejudices aside for the moment in order to confront this mystery on its own terms."

With that, Holmes fell silent. He took out his travelling pipe and become busy with it.

The journey was pleasant and occupied the better part of the late morning and early afternoon. Soon enough, the driver pulled up before the address of Mrs. Seagrave.

This house was as one might imagine it would be. Substantial, perhaps less than a century in age, and as well-kept as one would expect of a widow of means.

That we were punctual almost to the minute was not an accident. Holmes had hoped to arrive before the other man. But in that race we were beaten.

A rather tall butler greeted us at the door. Hearing our names, he said crisply, "Of course. You are expected. Dr. Silence has preceded you."

"Not by much, I trust," said Holmes as the doors closed behind us.

"I have just shown him into Madame's sitting room. Follow me, please."

Once we were ushered into the room, Dr. Silence stood up from a chair and smiled graciously. He was a lean fellow of perhaps forty with piercing yet kindly brown eyes and owning a professional beard of the same hue, but was otherwise unremarkable. A quiet intelligence denoted his features, but I perceived none of the odd impressions I expected of a man whose hobby was to engage with the queer and the uncanny.

Introductions were made. Dr. Silence said to Holmes, "Of course I have read of you. What Englishman has not? It is a distinct pleasure to meet you, Mr. Holmes."

"And I, too, have heard of the unusual Dr. Silence. I had not I thought our paths would have crossed, but now that they have..."

"I do not normally suffer outsiders as audience when I treat with my patients," he stated graciously. "But in this instance I am prepared to make an exception without qualm or question."

Holmes replied with equal politeness, "Inasmuch as my understanding is that you were summoned here before I expressed my own interest, I defer to your investigative skills."

"Thank you," said Silence.

Mrs. Seagrave bestowed us all with a welcoming smile and said, "Gentlemen, you may be seated. The time I have set aside for this meeting is not indefinite. We must begin without further ado."

The woman seemed to enjoy the prospect of having two of the most unusual investigators in Great Britain vying for her attention.

After we had found comfortable seats, Dr. Silence asked, "Mrs. Seagrave, let me ask you to begin with how you came by this unusual ring?"

"I was in Cairo, on holiday. I came upon it in what would pass for an antique shop, and although it was unusual in its workmanship, I thought the price surprisingly low for a ring of gold. I know that many detest snakes and serpents, but I find them soothing. I do not know why." She laughed lightly. "Perhaps because I was born under the sign of Scorpio."

I looked to Holmes. His firm expression did not alter in the slightest. But I had no doubt that here was confirmation of his supposition that the woman was a dabbler in the occult — although astrology has taken hold of many feminine imaginations in recent years.

Our hostess continued, "You may now be aware that I happened to wear the ring one night by accident, and awoke to a sharp sensation on my ring finger. Candlelight revealed a quantity of blood, so I removed the ring. There were four puncture wounds. Quite small and exceedingly delicate, three of which matched the fangs of the ring."

I was tempted to step in to question this last when Dr. Silence asked, "Three puncture wounds matched, and not all four?"

Holmes nodded almost imperceptibly.

"One of the lower fangs is deformed," she said. "I was going to take the ring to a jeweller and have it straightened out. I did not connect the ring to the injuries on that first night. I forbore wearing the ring for a week, owing to the soreness of the finger. Then I decided to wear it on the ring finger of the opposite hand, my right hand.

"Nothing happened until the night I forgot to remove the ring again, and the identical experience transpired. A stinging sensation followed by a quantity of blood and the revelation of four pinpricks of exquisite minuteness."

Dr. Silence stood up and approached the woman. "May I examine your fingers?"

"Please do," she said, elevating her hands and placing them palms downward.

As we watched, Dr. Silence took the woman's hands in his own, first the right one and then the left, carefully scrutinizing the puncture wounds. From our vantage point, we could see little of them. Although I had no doubt that Holmes's perceptions were more exacting than my own.

"These are identical, matching perfectly on each finger," pronounced Dr. Silence. "May I take a moment to hold one of your hands?"

"I do not object, doctor."

Dr. Silence took the woman's right hand in both of his, closing his eyes. He stood there in that attitude for several minutes by my watch. I leaned towards Holmes.

"What is this mumbo-jumbo?" I whispered.

Holmes placed a bony finger to his lips, enjoining silence.

When he was finished, Dr. Silence released the woman's hand and stepped back, saying, "No doubt you were wondering the purpose of my procedure. I was making a spiritual connection with you, the better to understand your situation. I do not detect, I am thankful to say, any disturbance in your psychic atmosphere. You seem to be perfectly healthy in that respect."

"That is a relief," said the woman sincerely.

"Now, may I see the ring?"

"It is on the taboret to your left. In the jewel box. You may open it."

Dr. Silence went to the jewel box, lifted the lid and took out a heavy ring of dull gold, which he held in the palm of his hand.

Retreating to his chair, he studied it for some moments in absorbed silence.

Then he once again shut his eyes, closing his fist about the ornament at the same time.

"I am versed in the delicate art of psychometry," he said for the benefit of all of us assembled in the room. "If you would be good enough to remain quiet, I will attempt to absorb the impressions contained within this ring. This may tell me much, or it may impart only a little."

Holmes and I exchanged glances. Here was occultism at its worst.

Holmes paid Dr. Silence no particular heed during the silent operation. His eyes were upon Mrs. Seagrave. He was studying her features, which were composed, as well as her hands, which sat upon her lap, the left placed atop the right. Nothing of her injuries could be seen, of course.

We observed closely the placid expression upon Dr. Silence's grave features. Here and there, I observed a twitch, especially at one corner of his mouth. No expression troubled his bearded face. He might have been a man asleep and dreaming. I could not imagine what was going through the man's mind. But the impression I received overall was one of quiet sincerity.

In due course, Dr. Silence opened his eyes and said, "We have not discussed the dreams or nightmares that have troubled you prior to the two afflictions. But I will attempt to communicate what I perceive of their character."

"Please do," invited Mrs. Seagrave.

"I behold in my mind's eye something in the nature of a void that begins to churn in the manner of a tempest. There is a sensation of clouds, dark and disturbing clouds. Out of this gathering chaos emerges a looming viper possessing darkly gold scales and scarlet eyes. It distends its jaws, and the fangs drip poison. This is a pale gold colour, rather like a fine liquor. With extreme suddenness, the serpent strikes, and the jaws clamp down. When they withdraw, their colour is scarlet."

Mrs. Seagrave gasped audibly at the conclusion of Dr. Silence's recitation.

"That is exactly what I dreamt," she exclaimed in a shocked voice. "Precisely. Even to the colour of the viper's poison. However did you know?"

Opening his palm, Silence revealed the ring to the gas illumination. "This very ring imparted that information to me. I cannot otherwise explain it. Except to say that inanimate objects partake of their surroundings — or should I say, the vibrations of their surroundings. They record them, after a fashion. To one who is sensitive, such as myself, it is possible through mental effort to coax an object to reproduce its sense impressions as one would play a phonograph record."

I looked to Holmes, but his hawk-like features were immobile. He was absorbing everything and offering nothing in return. There was a fixity in his eyes, one that told me that he was oblivious to all inconsequential factors, of which I was lamentably one.

Mrs. Seagrave managed to get sufficient possession of herself to ask a breathless question.

"Dr. Silence, in your professional opinion is my golden ring accursed?"

"I cannot say at the moment. But something dire surrounds, or possibly inhabits, the object. Something that must be confronted and if possible expelled."

"Do you think that the ring itself bit me?"

Here Dr. Silence astonished me by declining to support the superstitious woman's beliefs.

"I think not," he said crisply. "For it is to all outward appearances inert gold. It does not possess any semblance of physical life. Animation does not inform it. It. But it would be interesting to measure the compass of the fangs against your double injury."

Turning to Holmes. Mrs. Seagrave asked, "Mr. Holmes, may I ask your opinion of this rather rare matter?"

"I have none at present."

The woman seemed taken aback by the frankness of my friend's assertion.

"No? Not at all?"

"None at all," replied Holmes quietly. "For I have not yet begun my investigation." Addressing Silence, he asked, "Could I trouble you for that ring?"

The doctor stood up and surrendered the ring in question.

Taking it in his hand, Holmes weighed it in his palm, noting the heaviness of the ornament. "Twenty-four karat, I should judge. Nor is it hollow." Taking the ring in his fingers, he examined it carefully with his naked eye, noting the fine workmanship of the scales. With his thumbnail, he scraped it here and there, attempting to pry up some of these scales, but none surrendered to his probing. There was no bezel to lift, so a reservoir of poison could only be contained in its coils.

Removing a magnifying glass from one pocket of his vest, he began examining it more carefully. I watched both his examination and his facial expression for clues as to his findings. But none were evident to my scrutiny.

"I am confident that this ring does not harbour a reservoir of poison," he announced.

Taking up his watch fob, Holmes used the gold chain to measure the width of the upper fangs. By hooking each one into a separate link in the chain. He did the same for the lower fangs. Their compass was identical. Then he used the chain to measure less precisely the height of the two sets of needle teeth.

Surrendering the ring to me, he walked over to Mrs. Seagrave and asked, "May I examine your hands, Madame?"

These were offered. Holmes employed his watch chain to measure each puncture, both by its relationship to its mate and otherwise.

His face was a frowning mask when he returned to his chair.

Replacing his watch and chain, he stated, "I can agree that the positioning of the fangs precisely match the two pairs of puncture wounds."

Dr. Silence said, "I am not surprised by your statement, Mr. Holmes. But I stand by my judgment that the ring's fangs did not strike the woman in her sleep."

"I did not say that they did. Only that the puncture marks are identical insofar as the theory that they might have done so supposes."

Holmes took the ring back and began speaking as if lecturing.

"I find no indication of a secret spring or barb. And in any event no single barb would account for multiple puncture wounds. Nor is it possible that four barbs could exist where one appears to be impossible. Gold is not malleable, except under hammer or heat, and then there is the fact that the deformed fourth fang of the ring could not inflict a wound. We can safely dispense with the notion that the serpentine ornament somehow achieved animation and bit the poor woman."

"I concur," said Dr. Silence.

"I also note that this ring is fashioned in the form of a serpent of unknown species. If it were Egyptian, one would expect it be an asp. To put it in modern terms, an asp is a cobra. Neither the hood nor the markings of a cobra are evident in the workmanship of this peculiar snake of gold. That it is a viper is without question. We will designate it as an adder, for want of a better term. I cannot assess its age."

"The merchant who sold it to me," inserted Mrs. Seagrave, "swore that it was found in a funerary cave, by a Bedouin tomb robber. This was part of my attraction to it, for I find the lore of Egypt particularly alluring."

Dr. Silence said, "The reputation of the ancient Egyptians for wisdom is well known and equally well founded. There are ceremonies by which problematic objects may be cleansed of evil influences; I propose that we do so with this ring."

Mrs. Seagrave beamed. "I am perfectly willing to permit you to do this. For I am still enamoured of this ring, although I am now less sure of wearing it. Its charm is that of Egypt, which I hold very dear. I have sometimes wondered if I have lived ancient lifetimes in ancient Egypt — a notion that has entered my mind from time to time. When my husband was alive, he did not care to visit modern Egypt. But with his passing, I have toured it twice and expect to visit again."

Abruptly, she turned to Holmes. "We have heard Dr. Silence's opinion on the matter, Mr. Holmes. Now I am keen to know yours."

"Here I must turn to my esteemed colleague, Dr. Watson, in support of a theory forming in my mind. A theory that I will admit has no other foundation than the realization that all other practical explanations appear to have been exhausted."

"Yes, do go on."

"In the annals of medical science, there have been numerous reported cases of psychosomatic injury. While these are rare, they have been collected in sufficient numbers to support a medical theory that certain sensitive persons can manifest physical injuries or symptoms consistent with their beliefs. Is that not so, Watson?"

"Indeed," I said swiftly. "While it is mystifying to the layman, and stretches the credibility of the medical professional, examples abound in the medical literature. I am especially thinking of the stigmata, a bizarre phenomenon whereby persons of deep religious convictions display wounds or symptoms of wounds in the palms of their hands and in their feet, mirroring and mimicking the crucifixion. This cannot be explained in any way other than by some deep trick of the mind affecting the body.

"As scientific men, we cannot invoke the supernatural as an explanation. Nor do we acknowledge it. But strange is the connection between the mind and the body. Healthy persons have sickened without cause and subsequently recovered without explanation. And inexplicable wounds have manifested when there is no instrument to produce them."

"In this instance," advised Holmes, "Mrs. Seagrave is a sensitive soul who is invested in certain beliefs that make her susceptible to this phenomenon. She had a dream — or should I say a nightmare? — in which a serpent was attacking her. Possibly this nightmare was a product of wearing the serpentine ring, and particularly going to bed with such a heavy object constricting her finger. Her subconscious was urging her to remove the serpent. By some trick of the imagination, this manifested in the form of being attacked by an imaginary viper. So strong was her reaction that her body produced pinprick marks in imitation of the effect of fangs."

"But this happened twice," Dr. Silence pointed out — reasonably, I thought.

"Which may prove my point more than if it had transpired once. Having had such a shocking experience, and having mistakenly worn the ring to bed on a second occasion, the nightmare reproduced itself in her sleeping imagination. Having been conditioned by the first experience, her sleeping body responded identically. The mechanism by which such a phenomenon manifests is hardly understood by science. But psychosomatic injuries remains the only conceivable explanation, once all others are dispelled."

"With all due respect, Mr. Holmes," said Dr. Silence patiently, "I cannot agree with you that all the other explanations have been dispelled. But we may test your theory by cleansing the ring."

"Or," countered Holmes, "Mrs. Seagrave may dispense with wearing the ring to bed and the phenomenon will cease to operate."

I looked to Mrs. Seagrave. She said, "I would prefer Dr. Silence's solution to start with. For I am still fascinated by the ring, as I have said." Addressing Dr. Silence she asked, "What will you require to perform this ritual?"

"A suitable vessel in which to submerge the ring, a container of table salt and other things that I carry on my person."

Mrs. Seagrave rang for the butler, and these items were produced forthwith.

The vessel was a simple wash bowl. This was set on the taboret where the ring normally reposed in its jewel box. Water was poured into the bowl, the ring was submerged and salt was applied liberally from a shaker.

Dr. Silence removed from his person a short bundle of some pale vegetable matter I did not immediately recognize.

"This is white sage," he said. "We will burn it in a dish beside the bowl. It produces an incense that will drive away all wayward spirits, should any be dwelling in the vicinity of the frightful ring."

An ashtray was produced by the butler, the sage deposited, with Silence lit with a wooden match. It burned slowly, producing an aroma pleasant to inhale.

While this operation was impending, Holmes addressed Dr. Silence.

"If you don't mind, Silence, could you explain your powers to me?"

"They are the result of a combination of spiritual and scientific training. The details, I am not at liberty to divulge. Nor would they be necessarily completely understood by a man of your mental complexion."

"I see," said Holmes, not taking the observation as personal. "Is it your opinion that any individual could acquire the identical abilities if he subjects himself to the training from which you claim to benefit?"

"I do not," replied the doctor frankly. "One must be sufficiently advanced in mind and spirit to undergo the rigours of training. But one must start from a place of appropriate sensitivity. A man with a sharp intellect such as yours — which I respect greatly — might not be able to achieve the necessary receptivity to begin the training. For all spiritual training must commence with fundamentals.

"Just as personality determines whether a man is fit to be a banker or a priest, and an artist cannot be fashioned from a blacksmith, the raw material must be appropriate for the desired end result. One does not make a mallet out of soft pine. Or a sword out of tin. A dog cannot be a cat or vice versa, a man cannot be a woman or a woman a man. I trust you comprehend my point without taking taking offence. The fundamental nature of things are determined early on, and possibly before birth."

"I see," said Holmes. "You make your meaning plain. I appreciate your frankness, an admirable quality. And tact is sometimes overvalued."

Turning to me, Holmes asked, "Watson, what do you make of all of this?"

"I make nothing sensible."

"Tut-tut, Watson. You and Dr. Silence share the same profession. Have you no sympathy for the man's point of view? No respect for his uncommon training?"

"I possess insufficient knowledge and experience in these arcane matters to formulate an informed opinion," I replied. "I am a medical man. I do not stray from my chosen track any more would a locomotive wander off its rails."

Holmes inquired of Dr. Silence, "I trust you not do not take umbrage at Dr. Watson's dismissal of your talents?"

Dr. Silence smiled with what I thought was polite sympathy. "Not at all. I am accustomed to a certain amount of scepticism, even derision. It is nothing out of the ordinary. But I am confident in my abilities. For I trade upon them just as you gentlemen trade upon your respective talents."

We seemed to be getting nowhere in our exchange, other than to air our differences, however politely. I decided to ask, "How long must the ring be submerged in the salt solution before you are satisfied that it is in your opinion cleansed?"

"Overnight should suffice. For exposure to sunlight followed by moonlight is essential."

"And how will you test your theory?"

"I propose that Mrs. Seagrave wear the ring to bed, if she is agreeable. If nothing untoward happens, I will consider the matter closed and my time well spent."

"I see," murmured Holmes. "I detect a problem with your test."

"What is that?"

"If nothing of the sort transpires, this does not mean that nothing unpleasant will happen again in the future. For your test to be properly considered successful, the ring must be worn more than one additional night."

"I see what you are driving at," admitted Dr. Silence. "I propose, then, something that may satisfy you."

Before Sherlock Holmes could respond, Mrs. Seagrave spoke up, saying quite definitively, "I do not know if I am ready to deliberately wear the ring as yet. Perhaps one of you men may volunteer, if you are brave enough to do so."

Dr. Silence said, "I was just about to suggest that Mr. Holmes wear the ring for a period of time, in order to test my theory. Would a week suffice, Holmes?"

"A week would be sufficient, although not be absolute. But since I am not subject to nightmares, I do not see how this would prove anything."

"Then we are at an impasse."

"I am afraid so."

After some thought, Dr. Silence went over to the ring and removed it from the salt solution. "Then let me suggest another course of action," he said. "Namely, that you wear the ring for a week *before* the cleansing is completed."

"You expect me to be bitten?"

"I expect nothing of the kind. I do not know that a person of your temperament would be subject to psychosomatic or other influences. Only that if this ring is, as I perceive it to be, malevolent in nature, that malevolence would be likely to strike anyone wearing the ring, regardless of their state of mind or attitude toward dark forces."

Holmes did not hesitate. "I accept your challenge. I will wear the ring for a week." He turned his head to Mrs. Seagrave. "Is this agreeable to you, Madame?"

"Eminently so. I will only ask that you guarantee the safety of the ring whilst it is in your possession."

"I will put that guarantee in writing. And I thank you for your trust."

Dr. Silence handed the ring over to Holmes with a solemn expression on his face.

"The rest is up to you, Mr. Holmes. I wish you good luck with your experiment."

With that, we adjourned for tea, the conversation venturing to other matters.

When we departed, Holmes was wearing the ring of dull gold on one finger of his right hand and Mrs. Seagrave was in possession of his written guarantee.

Once we were back in our motor, and were pulling away from the Seagrave domicile, I remarked to Holmes, "This is an unusual turn of events."

"If I am to assert my belief in scientific principles," stated Holmes firmly, "I must be prepared to stand by them when challenged." He lifted the heavy ring to the light. "I do not expect this bauble to trouble me. And a week is only seven days in compass."

"I am sure that this will be nothing more than a minor inconvenience, Holmes," I said with unbridled confidence.

I would soon rue those very words.

*****

That evening, the insistent ringing of the telephone startled me out of a sound sleep. I fumbled for the instrument as my wife sat bolt upright in unwelcome surprise.

"Hello?" I shouted into the receiver. "Who is calling at this hour?"

The familiar voice of Holmes gasped, "Watson! Come quickly! I fear that I have been poisoned."

"Drink milk if you have it!" I told Holmes. I was soon in presentable clothes and carrying my doctor's bag out into the night.

Fortune favored me. Finding a hansom cab not two blocks away from my home, I hired the conveyance. The sleepy driver urged his horse to Baker Street with all due dispatch.

Mrs. Hudson let me into 221B. She was as pale as a spectre.

"It is good that you're come, Dr. Watson. Mr. Holmes is in a bad way."

Rushing upstairs, I found Holmes sprawled upon his bed, the serpentine ring firmly on his finger and blood upon his right hand. There was not a great deal of it, but it had flowed out in ghastly strings.

"Did you drink milk?" I demanded.

"I did. Thankfully, my stomach cramps appear to be subsiding. But some toxin has affected me, I am sure."

Bending down, I touched Holmes's brow. It was clammy. I did not like his colour.

"If I did not know better," he said weakly, "I would think that I was bitten by an Egyptian cobra."

Opening my bag, I took out a stethoscope and listened to his heart. It was pounding. His pulse was not steady. Quickly mixing a bicarbonate of soda, I gave this to my dear friend. He downed the mixture rapidly, then lay back on his pillow, handing me the empty glass.

"I see you have not removed the ring."

"I lacked the strength. It was either remove the ring or summon you. I thought your assistance was more urgent, the damage being done."

Mrs. Hudson brought in a wash bowl and cloth, and I removed the ring, which slid off Holmes's blood-slick finger without resistance. Washing the digits, I was shocked to discover four pinpricks, which bled only slightly.

Applying alcohol, I watched Holmes's reaction. He winced. The alcohol stung. But that was a good sign.

"Describe your symptoms," I invited, as I immobilized the affected arm with bandages and a makeshift splint.

As Holmes did so, I was struck by how similar the sensations were to snakebite, particularly numbness in the bitten hand.

"I would take you to a hospital," I told him, "but I fear too much movement would speed up the transport of whatever courses through your veins. It is best that you lie still whilst I observe you."

I was deep in my professional mode of thinking, and so was concerned with the immediate issue. But in the back of the mind there came a creeping sensation of dread. An hour would tell the tale, possibly less.

Eventually, thank God, all symptoms subsided. Colour returned to his thin features and Holmes sat up at daybreak. Sunlight streaming through the bedroom window seemed to chase away his morbid colouring, or perhaps it was the fact that the sputtering gas lamps had been turned down with the dawn.

In any event, Holmes was soon well enough to have breakfast in bed. As he ate, he told me a story.

"It began with a nightmare, Watson. As dire a nightmare I have ever experienced and I have experienced very few."

"Did you dream of the serpent?"

"A viper as vast as the fabled Midgard serpent of Norse legend. It emerged from an inchoate vortex of clouds and unlike the ring, it had four distinctly intact fangs. When it struck, the sense of being bitten awoke me. I lit a candle, and the light revealed the blood. Before I could make further examination, a grim coldness swept over me and I fell back on the pillow. For perhaps ten minutes I lay there, contemplating death. For I could not muster up the strength to rise again. With an effort of will, I twisted about until I had the telephone in hand. The operator put me in touch with you. The rest you know."

After Holmes finished his breakfast, I made another examination. All appeared well. The creeping numbness had departed. This was mystifying. I myself had considered him close to death only a few short hours ago.

"Tell me how you feel," I invited as I removed the splint.

"Much better. My strength is returning. I am not quite myself, but I feel as if I am approaching a normal state of being."

"You display the same pinpricks on your finger as did Mrs. Seagrave, and you presented symptoms consistent with snakebite."

"If I know my symptoms, they were those of the cobra."

"But did you not yourself point out that the serpent ring is not fashioned in the shape of the cobra?"

"Nevertheless, Watson, the symptoms are identical. I cannot explain it. Except perhaps psychologically."

I studied my dear friend. This was not the Holmes I knew. Or perhaps it was, simply confronted with something out of range of his usual thinking, and dulling his customary sharpness of intellect.

"If you are suggesting that you have experienced psychosomatic snakebite caused by the wearing of this terrible ring," I said sternly, "I would like to point out that you should not have been deluded into thinking you had been bitten by a cobra."

"It does run contrary to my theory," admitted Holmes. "But I must be true to my own experience. Whilst I have never been bitten by a cobra, I have read voluminously on the subject of snakes and the consequences of their bites. No other serpent need apply, Watson."

"I cannot imagine what this means."

Holmes firmed his mouth and his eyes grew thoughtful.

"It means," he said at length, "that a visit to Dr. Silence is in order. I fear that I have no other recourse; I may be out of my league, as it were. Possibly, things are not as they appear to be. But at this stage, I am not even sure what the true meaning of that unadorned assertion might be."

"When you are well enough, I am willing to join you in this consultation."

"I would not have it any other way," smiled Holmes. "For in the present circumstances, your scepticism far exceeds my own. You will be my anchor in reality as I attempt to plumb the depths of the unknown."

*****

That evening, we called upon Dr. Silence at his London townhouse, which also served as his consulting office. A man named Hubbard let us in. We were led to a room furnished and draped in a muted green hue. Reproductions of Arnold Bocklin's moody works decorated the walls. The hearth in the marble-mantled fireplace was crackling.

We selected a pair of armchairs, which Holmes pointed out were bolted to the floor.

"No doubt to calm agitated callers," he remarked. "The soothing colours of the room appear also to be calculated to that effect."

Moments later, Dr. Silence entered and bestowed us with his sympathetic smile. His penetrating brown eyes were warm but curious.

"Have you had an unpleasant experience so soon?" he asked. No mockery troubled in his tone. It was matter-of-fact.

"If you will examine my ring finger," Holmes stated, "you will discover four familiar marks. I had the identical dream that vexed Mrs. Seagrave prior to her attacks, if we may call them that. But I suffered an additional symptom I cannot easily explain."

"What was that?" asked Silence, taking a chair.

"Symptoms consistent with cobra bite overtook me. Fortunately, Dr. Watson came to my aid, and a crisis was averted."

"With all due respect to Dr. Watson, I imagine the symptoms would have subsided on their own. For it is not possible for an inert ring to communicate literal cobra venom into your system, no matter how sympathetic you might be inclined."

"I do not consider myself sympathetic in the least," returned Holmes. "Hence, my bafflement."

"I do not know why the entity inhabiting the ring choose to inflict upon you such a strong lesson of respect," mused Silence. "But you would have survived in any event. Perhaps Dr. Watson's ministrations hastened your psychological recovery, since you have great faith in medical science."

"I have a greater faith in physical reality. And I am unashamed to confess that my own theory of psychosomatic injury still appeals to me as the most likely explanation." Holmes hesitated. "However, after my gruesome experience, I find it sorely lacking."

"I do not blame you. And I applaud you for being as open-minded as you appear to have become curious about what you have so casually dismissed before. I do not entirely reject psychosomatic causes, but permit me to suggest that the psychosis was mentally injected into you by a foul creature having no actual substance, but which had attached itself to the gold ring in a bygone time, most probably because the talisman — for that is what I take it to be — was misused by Egyptian sorcerers."

Holmes considered this. He steepled his fingers, his brow furrowing deeply.

"Are you suggesting that a full explanation requires both psychosomatic and psychic theories?"

Dr. Silence said, "You cannot not be unfamiliar with hypnosis, or mesmerism, to use an older term. People placed under hypnotic trances have been shown to manifest personality traits and physical strength not normally their own."

Holmes nodded.

Silence went on. "The phenomenon of which I speak may be allied with mesmerism, but its origins belong to what men of science commonly deride as the supernatural."

"I reject the supernatural," I snapped, forgetting myself.

"Do you have a superseding theory, Dr. Watson?"

I flushed, feeling suddenly awkward. "I confess that I do not. I am entirely baffled. As much by my good friend's surrender to outré possibilities as I am to the queer phenomenon itself."

That sympathetic smile returned. "Let me propose instead of a theory, a solution. I will soak the ring in an appropriate cleansing solution, and in another day or two when Mr. Holmes is up to the challenge, he may wear the ring again. Or perhaps I should do it."

"I would be very interested in wearing that ring after you have treated it," said Holmes.

"Very good. Return in two days. That should be sufficient. We will say nothing of this to Mrs. Seagrave, except that the experiment is continuing."

With that, we took our leave.

Holmes was thoughtful as we rode back to Baker Street to the clip-clopping of a carriage horse.

I broke the silence by asking a question. "Has it occurred to you, Holmes, that Dr. Silence might be himself a competent hypnotist?"

"You are suggesting that he has hypnotized me into falling for the imaginary spell of the viperous ring?"

"Well, something like that," I admitted.

"It is a subject I have also studied, Watson. Hypnotism requires certain rituals and devices. Silence had no opportunity to hypnotize anyone. Aside from that, his every word and deed has appeared to be sincere and sympathetic. And his demonstration of psychometry was undeniably impressive."

"I will have no truck with the occult," I repeated shortly.

"And I will delve as deeply into this conundrum as I must in order to understand it. For if there are hidden nooks or crannies to reality which are not known to science, I feel it is my bounden duty to shine a light into them."

Owing to pressing matters, I was unable to revisit Dr. Silence the day that Holmes was to reclaim the damnable ring. But that night I slept peacefully.

Holmes telephoned the next morning to report to his slumber had been unbroken as well.

"I shall continue to wear the dread ring until I am satisfied that I am at the very least immune to its malign influence," he stated.

And so a week passed uneventfully.

*****

When next we all convened, we were once again in the sitting room of Mrs. Arthur Seagrave.

Holmes was concluding his report, by saying, "I cannot fully account for my experiences, and I'm forced to fall back upon the theory of psychosomatic illness, all other scientific explanations having no pertinence that I can see."

Dr. Silence smiled as if possessing secret knowledge. I had become accustomed to the man and his ways, with the result that my previous antagonism had been quelled by his unfailing good manners and kindly ways.

"Then how, Mr. Holmes, do you explain the ring having lost its power after a bath of sodium and moonlight?"

"I cannot. I admit it. It would be foolish to do otherwise. Perhaps some phenomenon is operating which I do not perceive, nor understand. I leave it at that. I am content to cling to the psychosomatic theory even though I readily admit that it is incomplete, if not glaringly insufficient."

"Well spoken," said Dr. Silence. "It is a wise man who admits his limitations."

Now Dr. Silence turned to me. "Have you a thought to contribute, Dr. Watson?"

"I confess that I too have failed to come up with a satisfactory answer."

"My dear Watson," inserted Holmes. "I am not admitting failure. I am refusing to be stubborn in the face of what may be the unknowable. As we march through this weary world, invariably we are confronted by things that baffle us. Perhaps a future generation may grapple with this problem, or one like it, and arrive at a satisfactory conclusion. Thus, I consider that I have not failed. I have merely broken off contact with an intractable problem. Perhaps we will contend again in the future, and the outcome will be different. I reserve that right."

"I believe you have the correct attitude for a man of your intellectual skills, Mr. Holmes," observed Dr. Silence quietly. "As one might kill a bee to escape being stung, I am confident that I have killed the pest, so that it does not strike anew."

We turned our attention back to Mrs. Seagrave. She surprised us by her next statement.

"I have changed my mind."

"How so?" asked Dr. Silence.

"After hearing Mr. Holmes account of being, dare I say ectoplasmically envenomed, I fear to keep this fell ring. I am yet a youngish woman, but one day my worldly goods will fall into the hands of my heirs. I do not wish them to contend with this detestable ornament. I intend to have it melted down for its raw gold." She directed her gaze at Dr. Silence. "Would you think that would be the ultimate resolution to the problem, doctor?"

"I am certain of it."

"Very well. I will see that it is done."

Abruptly, Holmes stood up. "Allow me, Madame, to do the honours. Whatever evil this ring harbours, it has done me an ill turn. I wish to return the favour."

"By all means."

The four of us adjourned to a nearby blacksmith, and there, Holmes dropped the golden ring into a crucible, inserting it with great tongs into the furnace. The ring slowly sublimed and became a molten mass.

Withdrawing the tongs carefully, he regarded the smoke curling from the congealing liquid in the bowl.

"If this does not accomplish the job, I cannot imagine what will."

The blacksmith took the crucible and I later learned that the gold had been recast as a thimble. There were no further incidents of any kind.

In parting, we said our farewells to the remarkable Dr. Silence.

"I wonder if we will meet again?" asked the physician.

"Do you not read the future?" inquired Holmes.

Dr. Silence returned a polite laugh. "I am no fortune-teller. As for the future, I prefer to explore it as it comes."

"Well said, well said."

*****

A week later, I was visiting Holmes at Baker Street and chanced to remark, "Reluctant as I am to do so, I am seriously considering writing up your recent adventure."

Holmes did not look up from his newspaper. "I doubt that the general public is ready for such an account. In fact, I would prefer that it not be published until after I have long passed from the present scene."

"I will grant you that courtesy," I told him. "But I am stuck for a title. Shall I call it 'The Adventure of the Vicious Viper,' or would you prefer 'the Angry Asp?'"

"The devilish thing was not shaped like an asp," Holmes snapped back peevishly. "It was an adder. And a particularly abominable adder at that. Let that be your title. We will speak no more of this unpleasant affair."

With those words, I realized that the sceptical Holmes of old had returned. I was glad.

Special Thanks to Our Kickstarter Backers

A sincere thank you goes out to our Kickstarter backers who supported the campaign for Sherlock Holmes and the Occult Detectives. Without their backing, the book you hold in your hands or read on your screen may not have come to fruition.

Thank you to:

"Amazing" Adrian Tallent
Abel Teo
Albion Gould
Alessandro "RumoreBianco" Nosenzo
Alessandro Caffari
Alexander Nirenberg
Allyn Gibson
Amanda Butt
Amara Snively
Analise Salas
Andrea Coletta
Anthony & Suford Lewis
Anthony R. Cardno
Anton Wijs
Ariana Brady
Arron Capone-Langan
Ayle M.
Ben Warner
Beverly D. Heinle
Biba J Reid
Brandon Babcock
Brent Dotson
Brian Dupre
Brian R. Boisvert
Bruce L. Wehrle
Burke Family
Caitlin Jane Hughes
Carl W. Urmer
Carl Wennstam
Caroline Lynch
Cedar Kilcrease
Chad Bowden
Charles Prepolec
CHARLES WARREN
Chris Basler
Chris Brakenbury
Chris Chastain
Chris McCarthy
Christian Dannie Storgaard
Christopher Davis
Christopher J MacDonald

Christopher 'Vulpine' Kalley
Cindy Cripps-Prawak
cneer17
Conor H. Carton
Curtis B. Edmundson
Dale A. Russell
Daniel Baird
David A Wade
David E. Forsythe
David Lars Chamberlain
David Rains
David Schulman
David Tai
Dean S Arashiro
Deb Werth
Deborah Delp
Debra Lovelace
Della-Ann Sewell
DN
Dodson Brown
Douglas Vaughan
Dr. Wolfgang Ditz
DrLight
E.R. Auld
Eldrich Nemo
Elizabeth
Eric Sands
Ethan Otteson
Eugene Doherty
Evadare Volney
Evelina Falk
Ewan Thomson
Fearlessleader
Frank M. Greco
Fred Kiesche

Gary Moring
Gary Phillips
Genevieve Cogman
Geoff Dibb
Geoffrey Kidd
Gilles Bourgeois
Gina Collia
Giovanni Morant
Glarbung
GMarkC
Greg & Meghan Mitchell
Gregory Landegger
Hannah Post
Hannes Winkler
Harry Kay Lesser, Jr.
Helen Luan
Herbert Eder
Howard J. Bampton
Ida Sue Umphers
Ivan Ronald Schablotski
Jacinda Gift
Jamas Enright
James E. Trever
James J. Marshall
Jason Brandt
Jason Epstein
Jason Holtschneider
Javier Cruz
Jeff Sigmund
Jeffrey W Osman
Jenna L Skeen
Jim Jorritsma
Jim Kosmicki
Joe Machin
John A. Freeman

John Bodnar
John Driscoll
John Haines
John N Wood
John Sommerville
Joseph P. Sullivan
JPD
Judy Lynn
Justin Gustainis
K. Patrick Glover
Karen Lytle Sumpter
Kate Perry
Ken Staley
Kevin B. O'Brien
Kevin Hoxsey
L.E. Vellene
Lark Cunningham
Lilly Ibelo
Linda Huang
Linnea Ann Pearson
Lisa Black
Lisa M Gargano
Louisa Mae Bockstedt II
Lucy Jefferies
M.K. Ward
Magenta Griffith
Marc "Coyote" Cayouette
Marcus Henry Yee
Maria-Elisa Biotti
Marjorie Young
Mark Carter
Mark Novak
Mark Robinson
Marsden
Mary Ann Raley

Max Potts
Meaford G
Melissa "Squirrely Murlley" Arnold
Michael Barrett
Michael Krawec
Michael Love
Michael Walker
Mike Brosco
Mike James
Mike Pasqua
Mike Vermilye
Mr. Guy Inagorillasuit
NHB
Niall Gordon
Nicola McBlane
Nina Zumel
Otto Hyvärinen
P Emerson
Patricia Miller
Paul Adams
Paul Hiscock
Paul Leone
Paul Motsuk
Phil Breach
R P Steeves
R.A.Pate
Ray Riethmeier
Renmeleon
Richard Bunting
Richard L. Haas III
Richard Ohnemus
Richard Sands
Rick Siem
Rick Smith

RIJU GANGULY
Robert Barron
Robert Pohle
Rod Mearing
Roger O'Donnell
Ron Bachman
Ronald H. Miller
Roshy
Rusty Waldrup
Sabina
Samuel F.
Sarah Mazul
Sarah Mooring
Scarlett Letter
Scott J. Dahlgren
Shane "Asharon" Sylvia
Shaun Osborne
SHERI COSTA
Sid Sondergard
Simo Muinonen
Som Sengupta
Stephen Press
Steve Smith
Steven Butler

Steven K C Lee
Steven Parry
T. E. Gregory
Tal M. Klein
Tao Wong
Teika and Tom Bellamy
Terry Moore
The Shivers
TheBorg
Thérèse Elaine
Thomas M Colwell
Tim Gambrell
Tim King!
Tina M Noe Good
Tony Ciak
Trevor Prinn
Vicki Hsu
Vivien Limon
Wiley Coyote
Willhameena Power
William Lohman
Yemi
Zachary Williams

For more adventures of Sherlock Holmes and stranger investigators old and new, join us again in Volume Two of 'Sherlock Holmes and the Occult Detectives', out now from Belanger Books.

Belanger Books

Printed in Great Britain
by Amazon